1952

THE ARROW OF GOLD

BOOKS BY JOSEPH CONRAD

ALMAYER'S FOLLY
AN OUTCAST OF THE ISLANDS
THE NIGGER OF THE "NARCISSUS"
TALES OF UNREST
LORD JIM: A ROMANCE
YOUTH: A NARRATIVE
TYPHOON
FALK AND OTHER STORIES
NOSTROMO: A TALE OF THE SEABOARD
THE MIRROR OF THE SEA
THE SECRET AGENT
A SET OF SIX
UNDER WESTERN EYES
A PERSONAL RECORD
'TWIXT LAND AND SEA
CHANCE
WITHIN THE TIDES
VICTORY
THE SHADOWI LINE
THE ARROW OF GOLD
THE RESCUE
NOTES ON LIFE AND LETTERS
THE ROVER
THE SHORTER TALES OF JOSEPH
  CONRAD

WITH FORD M. HUEFFER

ROMANCE: A NOVEL
THE INHERITORS: AN EXTRAVAGANT
  STORY
THE NATURE OF A CRIME

THE ARROW
OF GOLD
A STORY BETWEEN TWO NOTES

BY
JOSEPH CONRAD

Celui qui n'a connu que des hommes
polis et raisonnables, ou ne connait pas
l'homme, ou ne le connait qu'a demi.
—Charactéres

SPECIAL EDITION

PUBLISHED BY
DOUBLEDAY, DORAN & COMPANY, INC.
FOR
P. F. COLLIER & SON COMPANY
NEW YORK
1928

TO
RICHARD CURLE

AUTHOR'S NOTE

HAVING named all the short prefaces written for my books, Author's Notes, this one too must have the same heading for the sake of uniformity if at the risk of some confusion. "The Arrow of Gold," as its sub-title states, is a story between two Notes. But these Notes are embodied in its very frame, belong to its texture, and their mission is to prepare and close the story. They are material to the comprehension of the experience related in the narrative and are meant to determine the time and place together with certain historical circumstances conditioning the existence of the people concerned in the transactions of the twelve months covered by the narrative. It was the shortest way of getting over the preliminaries of a piece of work which could not have been of the nature of a chronicle.

"The Arrow of Gold" is my first after-the-war publication. The writing of it was begun in the autumn of 1917 and finished in the summer of 1918. Its memory is associated with that of the darkest hour of the war, which, in accordance with the well known proverb, preceded the dawn—the dawn of peace.

As I look at them now, these pages, written in the days of stress and dread, wear a look of strange serenity. They were written calmly, yet not in cold blood, and are perhaps the only kind of pages I could have written at that time full of menace, but also full of faith.

The subject of this book I have been carrying about with me for many years, not so much a possession of my memory as an inherent part of myself. It was ever present to my mind and ready to my hand, but I was loth to touch it from a feeling of what I imagined to be mere shyness but which in reality was a very comprehensible mistrust of myself.

In plucking the fruit of memory one runs the risk of spoiling its bloom, especially if it has got to be carried into the market-place. This being the product of my private garden my reluctance can be easily understood; and though some critics have expressed their regret that I had not written this book fifteen years earlier I do not share that opinion. If I took it up so late in life it is because the right moment had not arrived till then. I mean the positive feeling of it, which is a thing that cannot be discussed. Neither will I discuss here the regrets of those critics, which seem to me the most irrelevant thing that could have been said in connection with literary criticism.

I never tried to conceal the origins of the subject matter of this book which I have hesitated so long to write; but some reviewers indulged themselves with a sense of triumph in discovering in it my Dominic of "The Mirror of the Sea" under his own name (a truly wonderful discovery) and in recognising the balancelle *Tremolino* in the unnamed little craft in which Mr. George plied his fantastic trade and sought to allay the pain of his incurable wound. I am not in the least disconcerted by this display of perspicacity. It is the same man and the same balancelle. But for the purposes of a book like "The Mirror of the Sea" all I could make use of was the personal history of the little *Tremolino*. The present work is not in any sense an attempt to develop a subject lightly touched upon in former years and in connection with quite another kind of love. What the story of the *Tremolino* in its anecdotic character has in common with the story of "The Arrow of Gold" is the quality of initiation (through an ordeal which required some resolution to face) into the life of passion. In the few pages at the end of "The Mirror of the Sea" and in the whole volume of "The Arrow of Gold," *that* and no other is the subject offered to the public. The pages and the book form together a complete record; and the only assurance I can give my readers is, that as it stands here with all its imperfections it is given to them complete.

I venture this explicit statement because, amidst much sympathetic appreciation, I have detected here and there a note, as it were, of suspicion. Suspicion of facts concealed, of explanations held back, of inadequate motives. But what is lacking in the facts is simply what I did not know, and what is not explained is what I did not understand myself, and what seems inadequate is the fault of my imperfect insight. And all that I could not help. In the case of this book I was unable to supplement these deficiencies by the exercise of my inventive faculty. It was never very strong; and on this occasion its use would have seemed exceptionally dishonest. It is from that ethical motive and not from timidity that I elected to keep strictly within the limits of unadorned sincerity and to try to enlist the sympathies of my readers without assuming lofty omniscience or descending to the subterfuge of exaggerated emotions.

1920.   J. C.

THE ARROW OF GOLD

FIRST NOTE

THE pages which follow have been extracted from a
pile of manuscript which was apparently meant for the
eye of one woman only. She seems to have been the
writer's childhood's friend. They had parted as children, or very little more than children. Years passed.
Then something recalled to the woman the companion
of her young days and she wrote to him: "I have been
hearing of you lately. I know where life has brought
you. You certainly selected your own road. But to us,
left behind, it always looked as if you had struck out
into a pathless desert. We always regarded you as a
person that must be given up for lost. But you have
turned up again; and though we may never see each
other, my memory welcomes you and I confess to you
I should like to know the incidents on the road which
has led you to where you are now."

And he answers her: "I believe you are the only
one now alive who remembers me as a child. I have
heard of you from time to time, but I wonder what sort
of person you are now. Perhaps if I did know I
wouldn't dare put pen to paper. But I don't know.
I only remember that we were great chums. In fact, I
chummed with you even more than with your brothers.
But I am like the pigeon that went away in the fable
of the Two Pigeons. If I once start to tell you I would
want you to feel that you have been there yourself.
I may overtax your patience with the story of my life
so different from yours, not only in all the facts but
altogether in spirit. You may not understand. You

3

may even be shocked. I say all this to myself; but I know I shall succumb! I have a distinct recollection that in the old days, when you were about fifteen, you always could make me do whatever you liked."

He succumbed. He begins his story for her with the minute narration of this adventure which took about twelve months to develop. In the form in which it is presented here it has been pruned of all allusions to their common past, of all asides, disquisitions, and explanations addressed directly to the friend of his childhood. And even as it is the whole thing is of considerable length. It seems that he had not only a memory but that he also knew how to remember. But as to that opinions may differ.

This, his first great adventure, as he calls it, begins in Marseilles. It ends there, too. Yet it might have happened anywhere. This does not mean that the people concerned could have come together in pure space. The locality had a definite importance. As to the time, it is easily fixed by the events at about the middle years of the seventies, when Don Carlos de Bourbon, encouraged by the general reaction of all Europe against the excesses of communistic Republicanism, made his attempt for the throne of Spain, arms in hand, amongst the hills and gorges of Guipuzcoa. It is perhaps the last instance of a Pretender's adventure for a Crown that History will have to record with the usual grave moral disapproval tinged by a shamefaced regret for the departing romance. Historians are very much like other people.

However, History has nothing to do with this tale. Neither is the moral justification or condemnation of conduct aimed at here. If anything it is perhaps a little sympathy that the writer expects for his buried youth, as he lives it over again at the end of his insignificant course on this earth. Strange person—yet perhaps not so very different from ourselves.

A few words as to certain facts may be added.

It may seem that he was plunged very abruptly into this long adventure. But from certain passages (suppressed here because mixed up with irrelevant matter) it appears clearly that at the time of the meeting in the café, Mills had already gathered, in various quarters, a definite view of the eager youth who had been introduced to him in that ultra-legitimist salon. What Mills had learned represented him as a young gentleman who had arrived furnished with proper credentials and who apparently was doing his best to waste his life in an eccentric fashion, with a bohemian set (one poet, at least, emerged out of it later) on one side, and on the other making friends with the people of the Old Town, pilots, coasters, sailors, workers of all sorts. He pretended rather absurdly to be a seaman himself and was already credited with an ill-defined and vaguely illegal enterprise in the Gulf of Mexico. At once it occurred to Mills that this eccentric youngster was the very person for what the legitimist sympathizers had very much at heart just then: to organize a supply by sea of arms and ammunition to the Carlist detachments in the South. It was precisely to confer on that matter with Doña Rita that Captain Blunt had been despatched from Headquarters.

Mills got in touch with Blunt at once and put the suggestion before him. The Captain thought this the very thing. As a matter of fact, on that evening of Carnival, those two, Mills and Blunt, had been actually looking everywhere for our man. They had decided that he should be drawn into the affair if it could be done. Blunt naturally wanted to see him first. He must have estimated him a promising person. but, from another point of view, not dangerous. Thus lightly was the notorious (and at the same time mysterious) Monsieur George brought into the world; out of the contact of two minds which did not give a single thought to his flesh and blood.

Their purpose explains the intimate tone given to their first conversation and the sudden introduction of Doña Rita's history. Mills, of course, wanted to hear all about it. As to Captain Blunt I suspect that, at the time, he was thinking of nothing else. In addition it was Doña Rita who would have to do the persuading; for, after all, such an enterprise with its ugly and desperate risks was not a trifle to put before a man—however young.

It cannot be denied that Mills seems to have acted somewhat unscrupulously. He himself appears to have had some doubt about it, at a given moment, as they were driving to the Prado. But perhaps Mills, with his penetration, understood very well the nature he was dealing with. He might even have envied it. But it's not my business to excuse Mills. As to him whom we may regard as Mills' victim it is obvious that he has never harboured a single reproachful thought. For him Mills is not to be criticized. A remarkable instance of the great power of mere individuality over the young.

THE ARROW OF GOLD

PART ONE

I

CERTAIN streets have an atmosphere of their own, a sort of universal fame and the particular affection of their citizens. One of such streets is the Cannebiére, and the jest: "If Paris had a Cannebiére it would be a little Marseilles" is the jocular expression of municipal pride. I, too, I have been under the spell. For me it has been a street leading into the unknown.

There was a part of it where one could see as many as five big cafés in a resplendent row. That evening I strolled into one of them. It was by no means full. It looked deserted, in fact, festal and overlighted, but cheerful. The wonderful street was distinctly cold (it was an evening of carnival), I was very idle, and I was feeling a little lonely. So I went in and sat down.

The carnival time was drawing to an end. Everybody, high and low, was anxious to have the last fling. Companies of masks with linked arms and whooping like red Indians swept the streets in crazy rushes while gusts of cold mistral swayed the gas lights as far as the eye could reach. There was a touch of bedlam in all this.

Perhaps it was that which made me feel lonely, since I was neither masked, nor disguised, nor yelling, nor in any other way in harmony with the bedlam element of life. But I was not sad. I was merely in a state of sobriety. I had just returned from my second West Indies voyage. My eyes were still full of tropical splendour, my memory of my experiences, lawful and lawless, which had their charm and their thrill; for they had startled me a little and had amused me considerably. But they had left me untouched Indeed they were other men's adventures, not mine. Except for a little habit of responsibility which I had acquired they had not matured me. I was as young as before. Inconceivably young—still beautifully un-thinking—infinitely receptive.

You may believe that I was not thinking of Don Carlos and his fight for a kingdom. Why should I? You don't want to think of things which you meet every day in the newspapers and in conversation. I had paid some calls since my return and most of my acquaintance were legitimists and intensely interested in the events of the frontier of Spain, for political, religious, or romantic reasons. But I was not inter-ested. Apparently I was not romantic enough. Or was it that I was even more romantic than all those good people? The affair seemed to me commonplace. The man was attending to his business of a Pretender.

On the front page of the illustrated paper I saw lying on a table near me, he looked picturesque enough, seated on a boulder, a big strong man with a square-cut beard, his hands resting on the hilt of a cavalry sabre—and all around him a landscape of savage mountains. He caught my eye on that spiritedly composed woodcut. (There were no inane snapshot-reproductions in those days.) It was the obvious romance for the use of royalists but it arrested my attention.

Just then some masks from outside invaded the

café, dancing hand in hand in a single file led by a burly man with a cardboard nose. He gambolled in wildly and behind him twenty others perhaps, mostly Pierrots and Pierrettes holding each other by the hand and winding in and out between the chairs and tables: eyes shining in the holes of cardboard faces, breasts panting; but all preserving a mysterious silence.

They were people of the poorer sort (white calico with red spots, costumes), but amongst them there was a girl in a black dress sewn over with gold half moons, very high in the neck and very short in the skirt. Most of the ordinary clients of the café didn't even look up from their games or papers. I, being alone and idle, stared abstractedly. The girl costumed as Night wore a small black velvet mask, what is called in French a *"loup."* What made her daintiness join that obviously rough lot I can't imagine. Her uncovered mouth and chin suggested refined prettiness.

They filed past my table; the Night noticed perhaps my fixed gaze and throwing her body forward out of the wriggling chain shot out at me a slender tongue like a pink dart. I was not prepared for this, not even to the extent of an appreciative *"Très joli,"* before she wriggled and hopped away. But having been thus distinguished I could do no less than follow her with my eyes to the door where the chain of hands being broken all the masks were trying to get out at once. Two gentlemen coming in out of the street stood arrested in the crush. The Night (it must have been her idiosyncrasy) put her tongue out at them, too. The taller of the two (he was in evening clothes under a light wide-open overcoat) with great presence of mind chucked her under the chin, giving me the view at the same time of a flash of white teeth in his dark, lean face. The other man was very different; fair, with smooth, ruddy cheeks and burly shoulders. He was wearing a grey suit, obviously bought ready-made, for it seemed too tight for his powerful frame.

That man was not altogether a stranger to me. For the last week or so I had been rather on the look-out for him in all the public places where in a provincial town men may expect to meet each other. I saw him for the first time (wearing that same grey ready-made suit) in a legitimist drawing-room where, clearly, he was an object of interest, especially to the women. I had caught his name as Monsieur Mills. The lady who had introduced me took the earliest opportunity to murmur into my ear: "A relation of Lord X." (*Un proche parent de Lord X.*) And then she added, casting up her eyes: "A good friend of the King." Meaning Don Carlos of course.

I looked at the *proche parent;* not on account of the parentage but marvelling at his air of ease in that cumbrous body and in such tight clothes, too. But presently the same lady informed me further: "He has come here amongst us *un naufragé.*"

I became then really interested. I had never seen a shipwrecked person before. All the boyishness in me was aroused. I considered a shipwreck as an unavoidable event sooner or later in my future.

Meantime the man thus distinguished in my eyes glanced quietly about and never spoke unless addressed directly by one of the ladies present. There were more than a dozen people in that drawing-room, mostly women eating fine pastry and talking passionately. It might have been a Carlist committee meeting of a particularly fatuous character. Even my youth and inexperience were aware of that. And I was by a long way the youngest person in the room. That quiet Monsieur Mills intimidated me a little by his age (I suppose he was thirty-five), his massive tranquillity, his clear, watchful eyes. But the temptation was too great—and I addressed him impulsively on the subject of that shipwreck.

He turned his big fair face towards me with surprise in his keen glance, which (as though he had seen through me in an instant and found nothing objectionable) changed subtly into friendliness. On the matter of the shipwreck he did not say much. He only told me that it had not occurred in the Mediterranean, but on the other side of Southern France—in the Bay of Biscay. "But this is hardly the place to enter on a story of that kind," he observed, looking round at the room with a faint smile as attractive as the rest of his rustic but well-bred personality.

I expressed my regret. I should have liked to hear all about it. To this he said that it was not a secret and that perhaps next time we met. . . .

"But where can we meet?" I cried. "I don't come often to this house, you know."

"Where? Why! on the Cannebière to be sure. Everybody meets everybody else at least once a day on the pavement opposite the *Bourse*."

This was absolutely true. But though I looked for him on each succeeding day he was nowhere to be seen at the usual times. The companions of my idle hours (and all my hours were idle just then) noticed my preoccupation and chaffed me about it in a rather obvious way. They wanted to know whether she, whom I expected to see, was dark or fair; whether that fascination which kept me on tenterhooks of expectation was one of my aristocrats or one of my marine beauties: for they knew I had a footing in both these—shall we say circles? As to themselves they were the bohemian circle, not very wide—half a dozen of us led by a sculptor whom we called Prax for short. My own nick-name was "Young Ulysses." I liked it.

But chaff or no chaff they would have been surprised to see me leave them for the burly and sympathetic Mills. I was ready to drop any easy company of equals to approach that interesting man with every mental deference. It was not precisely because of that shipwreck. He attracted and interested me the more because he was not to be seen. The fear that he might have departed suddenly for England—(or for Spain)—caused me a sort of ridiculous depression as though I had missed a unique opportunity. And it was a joyful reaction which emboldened me to signal to him with a raised arm across that café.

I was abashed immediately afterwards, when I saw him advance towards my table with his friend. The latter was eminently elegant. He was exactly like one of those figures one can see of a fine May evening in the neighbourhood of the Opera-house in Paris. Very Parisian indeed. And yet he struck me as not so perfectly French as he ought to have been, as if one's nationality were an accomplishment with varying degrees of excellence. As to Mills, he was perfectly insular. There could be no doubt about him. They were both smiling faintly at me. The burly Mills attended to the introduction: "Captain Blunt."

We shook hands. The name didn't tell me much. What surprised me was that Mills should have remembered mine so well. I don't want to boast of my modesty but it seemed to me that two or three days was more than enough for a man like Mills to forget my very existence. As to the Captain, I was struck on closer view by the perfect correctness of his personality. Clothes, slight figure, clear-cut, thin, sun-tanned face, pose, all this was so good that it was saved from the danger of banality only by the mobile black eyes of a keenness that one doesn't meet every day in the south of France and still less in Italy. Another thing was that, viewed as an officer in mufti, he did not look sufficiently professional. That imperfection was interesting, too.

You may think that I am subtilizing my impressions on purpose, but you may take it from a man who has lived a rough, a very rough life, that it is the subtleties of personalities, and contacts, and events, that count for interest and memory—and pretty well nothing else. This—you see—is the last evening of that part of my life in which I did not know that woman. These are like the last hours of a previous existence. It isn't my fault that they are associated with nothing better at the decisive moment than the banal splendours of a gilded café and the bedlamite yells of carnival in the street.

We three, however (almost complete strangers to each other), had assumed attitudes of serious amiability round our table. A waiter approached for orders and it was then, in relation to my order for coffee, that the absolutely first thing I learned of Captain Blunt was the fact that he was a sufferer from insomnia. In his immovable way Mills began charging his pipe. I felt extremely embarrassed all at once, but became positively annoyed when I saw our Prax enter the café in a sort of mediæval costume very much like what Faust wears in the third act. I have no doubt it was meant for a purely operatic Faust. A light mantle floated from his shoulders. He strode theatrically up to our table and addressing me as "Young Ulysses" proposed I should go outside on the fields of asphalt and help him gather a few marguerites to decorate a truly infernal supper which was being organized across the road at the Maison Dorée—upstairs. With expostulatory shakes of the head and indignant glances I called his attention to the fact that I was not alone. He stepped back a pace as if astonished by the discovery, took off his plumed velvet toque with a low obeisance so that the feathers swept the floor, and swaggered off the stage with his left hand resting on the hilt of the property dagger at his belt.

Meantime the well-connected but rustic Mills had been busy lighting his briar and the distinguished Captain sat smiling to himself. I was horribly vexed and apologized for that intrusion, saying that the fellow was a future great sculptor and perfectly harmless; but he had been swallowing lots of night air which had got into his head apparently.

Mills peered at me with his friendly but awfully searching blue eyes through the cloud of smoke he had wreathed about his big head. The slim, dark Captain's smile took on an amiable expression. Might he know why I was addressed as "Young Ulysses" by my friend? and immediately he added the remark with urbane playfulness that Ulysses was an astute person. Mills did not give me time for a reply. He struck in: "That old Greek was famed as a wanderer—the first historical seaman." He waved his pipe vaguely at me.

"Ah! *Vraiment!*" The polite Captain seemed incredulous and as if weary. "Are you a seaman? In what sense, pray?" We were talking French and he used the term *homme de mer*.

Again Mills interfered quietly. "In the same sense in which you are a military man." (*Homme de guerre.*)

It was then that I heard Captain Blunt produce one of his striking declarations. He had two of them, and this was the first.

"I live by my sword."

It was said in an extraordinary dandified manner

which in conjunction with the matter made me forget my tongue in my head. I could only stare at him. He added more naturally: "2nd Reg. Castille Cavalry." Then with marked stress in Spanish, "*En las filas legitimas.*"

Mills was heard, unmoved, like Jove in his cloud: "He's on leave here."

"Of course I don't shout that fact on the housetops," the Captain addressed me pointedly, "any more than our friend his shipwreck adventure. We must not strain the toleration of the French authorities too much! It wouldn't be correct—and not very safe either."

I became suddenly extremely delighted with my company. A man who "lived by his sword," before my eyes, close at my elbow! So such people did exist in the world yet! I had not been born too late! And across the table with his air of watchful, unmoved benevolence, enough in itself to arouse one's interest, there was the man with the story of a shipwreck that mustn't be shouted on housetops. Why?

I understood very well why, when he told me that he had joined in the Clyde a small steamer chartered by a relative of his, "a very wealthy man," he observed (probably Lord X, I thought), to carry arms and other supplies to the Carlist army. And it was not a shipwreck in the ordinary sense. Everything went perfectly well to the last moment when suddenly the *Numancia* (a Republican ironclad) had appeared and chased them ashore on the French coast below Bayonne. In a few words, but with evident appreciation of the adventure, Mills described to us how he swam to the beach clad simply in a money belt and a pair of trousers. Shells were falling all round till a tiny French gunboat came out of Bayonne and shooed the *Numancia* away out of territorial waters.

He was very amusing and I was fascinated by the mental picture of that tranquil man rolling in the surf and emerging breathless, in the costume you know, on the fair land of France, in the character of a smuggler of war material. However, they had never arrested or expelled him, since he was there before my eyes. But how and why did he get so far from the scene of his sea adventure was an interesting question. And I put it to him with most naïve indiscretion which did not shock him visibly. He told me that the ship being only stranded, not sunk, the contraband cargo aboard was doubtless in good condition. The French customhouse men were guarding the wreck. If their vigilance could be—h'm—removed by some means, or even merely reduced, a lot of these rifles and cartridges could be taken off quietly at night by certain Spanish fishing boats. In fact, salved for the Carlists, after all. He thought it could be done. . . .

I said with professional gravity that given a few perfectly quiet nights (rare on that coast) it could certainly be done.

Mr. Mills was not afraid of the elements. It was the highly inconvenient zeal of the French custom-house people that had to be dealt with in some way.

"Heavens!" I cried, astonished. "You can't bribe the French Customs. This isn't a South American republic."

"Is it a republic?" he murmured, very absorbed in smoking his wooden pipe.

"Well, isn't it?"

He murmured again, "Oh, so little." At this I laughed, and a faintly humorous expression passed over Mills' face. No. Bribes were out of the question, he admitted. But there were many legitimist sympathies in Paris. A proper person could set them in motion and a mere hint from high quarters to the officials on the spot not to worry over-much about that wreck. . . .

What was most amusing was the cool, reasonable tone of this amazing project. Mr. Blunt sat by very detached, his eyes roamed here and there all over the café; and it was while looking upward at the pink foot of a fleshy and very much foreshortened goddess of some sort depicted on the ceiling in an enormous composition in the Italian style that he let fall casually the words, "She will manage it for you quite easily."

"Every Carlist agent in Bayonne assured me of that," said Mr. Mills. "I would have gone straight to Paris only I was told she had fled here for a rest; tired, discontented. Not a very encouraging report."

"These flights are well known," muttered Mr. Blunt. "You shall see her all right."

"Yes. They told me that you . . ."

I broke in: "You mean to say that you expect a woman to arrange that sort of thing for you?"

"A trifle, for her," Mr. Blunt remarked indifferently. "At that sort of thing women are best. They have less scruples."

"More audacity," interjected Mr. Mills almost in a whisper.

Mr. Blunt kept quiet for a moment, then: "You see," he addressed me in a most refined tone, "a mere man may suddenly find himself being kicked down the stairs."

I don't know why I should have felt shocked by that statement. It could not be because it was untrue. The other did not give me time to offer any remark. He inquired with extreme politeness what did I know of South American republics? I confessed that I knew very little of them. Wandering about the Gulf of Mexico I had a look-in here and there; and amongst others I had a few days in Haiti which was of course unique, being a negro republic. On this Captain Blunt began to talk of negroes at large. He talked of them with knowledge, intelligence, and a sort of contemptuous affection. He generalized, he particularized about the blacks; he told anecdotes. I was interested, a little incredulous, and considerably surprised. What could this man with such a boulevardier exterior that he looked positively like an exile in a provincial town, and with his drawing-room manner—what could he know of negroes?

Mills, sitting silent with his air of watchful intelligence, seemed to read my thoughts, waved his pipe slightly and explained: "The Captain is from South Carolina."

"Oh," I murmured, and then after the slightest of pauses I heard the second of Mr. J. K. Blunt's declarations.

"Yes," he said. "*Je suis Américain, catholique et gentilhomme*," in a tone contrasting so strongly with the smile, which, as it were, underlined the uttered words, that I was at a loss whether to return the smile in kind or acknowledge the words with a grave little bow. Of course I did neither and there fell on us an odd, equivocal silence. It marked our final abandonment of the French language. I was the one to speak first, proposing that my companions should sup with me, not across the way, which would be riotous with more than one "infernal" supper, but in another much more select establishment in a side street away from the Cannebière. It flattered my vanity a little to be able to say that I had a corner table always reserved in the Salon des Palmiers, otherwise Salon Blanc, where the atmosphere was legitimist and extremely decorous besides—even in Carnival time. "Nine tenths of the people there," I said, "would be of your political opinions, if that's an inducement. Come along. Let's be festive," I encouraged them.

I didn't feel particularly festive. What I wanted was to remain in my company and break an inexplicable feeling of constraint of which I was aware. Mills looked at me steadily with a faint, kind smile.

"No," said Blunt. "Why should we go there? They will be only turning us out in the small hours, to go home and face insomnia. Can you imagine anything more disgusting?"

He was smiling all the time, but his deep-set eyes did not lend themselves to the expression of whimsical politeness which he tried to achieve. He had another suggestion to offer. Why shouldn't we adjourn to his rooms? He had there materials for a dish of his own invention for which he was famous all along the line of the Royal Cavalry outpost, and he would cook it for us. There were also a few bottles of some white wine, quite possible, which we could drink out of Venetian cut-glass goblets. A *bivouac* feast, in fact. And he wouldn't turn us out in the small hours. Not he. He couldn't sleep.

Need I say I was fascinated by the idea? Well, yes. But somehow I hesitated and looked towards Mills, so much my senior. He got up without a word. This was decisive; for no obscure premonition, and of something indefinite at that, could stand against the example of his tranquil personality.

THE street in which Mr. Blunt lived presented itself to our eyes, narrow, silent, empty, and dark, but with enough gas-lamps in it to disclose its most striking feature: a quantity of flag-poles sticking out above many of its closed portals. It was the street of Consuls and I remarked to Mr. Blunt that coming out in the morning he could survey the flags of all nations almost —except his own. (The U. S. consulate was on the other side of the town.) He mumbled through his teeth that he took good care to keep clear of his own consulate.

"Are you afraid of the consul's dog?" I asked jocularly. The consul's dog weighed about a pound and a half and was known to the whole town as exhibited on the consular fore-arm in all places, at all hours, but mainly at the hour of the fashionable promenade on the Prado.

But I felt my jest misplaced when Mills growled low in my ear: "They are all Yankees there."

I murmured a confused "Of course."

Books are nothing. I discovered that I had never been aware before that the Civil War in America was not printed matter but a fact only about ten years old. Of course. He was a South Carolinian gentleman. I was a little ashamed of my want of tact. Meantime, looking like the conventional conception of a fashionable reveller, with his opera-hat pushed off his forehead, Captain Blunt was having some slight difficulty with his latch-key; for the house before which we had stopped was not one of those many-storied houses that made up the greater part of the street. It had only one row of windows above the ground floor. Dead walls abutting on to it indicated that it had a garden. Its dark front presented no marked architectural character, and in the flickering light of a street lamp it looked a little as though it had gone down in the world. The greater then was my surprise to enter a hall paved in black and white marble and in its dimness appearing of palatial proportions. Mr. Blunt did not turn up the small solitary gas-jet, but led the way across the black-and-white pavement past the end of the staircase, past a door of gleaming dark wood with a heavy bronze handle. It gave access to his rooms he said; but he took us straight on to the studio at the end of the passage.

It was rather a small place tacked on in the manner of a lean-to to the garden side of the house. A large lamp was burning brightly there. The floor was of mere flag-stones but the few rugs scattered about though extremely worn were very costly. There was also there a beauti-ful sofa upholstered in pink figured silk, an enormous divan with many cushions, some splendid arm-chairs of various shapes (but all very shabby), a round table, and in the midst of these fine things a small common iron stove. Somebody must have been attending it lately, for the fire roared and the warmth of the place was very grateful after the bone-searching cold blasts of mistral outside.

Mills without a word flung himself on the divan and, propped on his arm, gazed thoughtfully at a distant corner where in the shadow of a monumental carved wardrobe an articulated dummy without head or hands but with beautifully shaped limbs composed in a shrink-ing attitude, seemed to be embarrassed by his stare.

As we sat enjoying the *bivouac* hospitality (the dish

was really excellent and our host in a shabby grey jacket still looked the accomplished man-about-town) my eyes kept on straying towards that corner. Blunt noticed this and remarked that I seemed to be attracted by the Empress.

"It's disagreeable," I said. "It seems to lurk there like a shy skeleton at the feast. But why do you give the name of Empress to that dummy?"

"Because it sat for days and days in the robes of a Byzantine Empress to a painter. . . . I wonder where he discovered these priceless stuffs. . . . You knew him, I believe?"

Mills lowered his head slowly, then tossed down his throat some wine out of a Venetian goblet.

"This house is full of costly objects. So are all his other houses, so is his place in Paris—that mysterious Pavilion hidden away in Passy somewhere."

Mills knew the Pavilion. The wine had, I suppose, loosened his tongue. Blunt, too, lost something of his reserve. From their talk I gathered the notion of an eccentric personality, a man of great wealth, not so much solitary as difficult of access, a collector of fine things, a painter known only to very few people and not at all to the public market. But as meantime I had been emptying my Venetian goblet with a certain regularity (the amount of heat given out by that iron stove was amazing; it parched one's throat, and the straw-coloured wine didn't seem much stronger than so much pleasantly flavoured water) the voices and the impressions they conveyed acquired something fantastic to my mind. Suddenly I perceived that Mills was sitting in his shirt-sleeves. I had not noticed him taking off his coat. Blunt had unbuttoned his shabby jacket, exposing a lot of starched shirt-front with the white tie under his dark shaved chin. He had a strange

air or insolence—or so it seemed to me. I addressed
him much louder than I intended really.

"Did you know that extraordinary man?"

"To know him personally one had to be either very
distinguished or very lucky. Mr. Mills here . . ."

"Yes, I have been lucky," Mills struck in. "It was
my cousin who was distinguished. That's how I managed to enter his house in Paris—it was called the
Pavilion—twice."

"And saw Doña Rita twice, too?" asked Blunt with
an indefinite smile and a marked emphasis. Mills was
also emphatic in his reply but with a serious face.

"I am not an easy enthusiast where women are concerned, but she was without doubt the most admirable
find of his amongst all the priceless items he had ac-
cumulated in that house—the most admirable. . . ."

"Ah! But, you see, of all the objects there she was
the only one that was alive," pointed out Blunt with
the slightest possible flavour of sarcasm.

"Immensely so," affirmed Mills. "Not because she
was restless, indeed she hardly ever moved from that
couch between the windows—you know."

"No. I don't know. I've never been in there," announced Blunt with that flash of white teeth so strangely
without any character of its own that it was merely disturbing.

"But she radiated life," continued Mills. "She
had plenty of it, and it had a quality. My cousin and
Henry Allègre had a lot to say to each other and so I
was free to talk to her. At the second visit we were
like old friends, which was absurd considering that all
the chances were that we would never meet again in
this world or in the next. I am not meddling with
theology but it seems to me that in the Elysian fields
she'll have her place in a very special company."

All this in a sympathetic voice and in his unmoved manner. Blunt produced another disturbing white flash and muttered:

"I should say mixed." Then louder: "As for instance . . ."

"As for instance Cleopatra," answered Mills quietly. He added after a pause: "Who was not exactly pretty."

"I should have thought rather a La Vallière," Blunt dropped with an indifference of which one did not know what to make. He may have begun to be bored with the subject. But it may have been put on, for the whole personality was not clearly definable. I, however, was not indifferent. A woman is always an interesting subject and I was thoroughly awake to that interest. Mills pondered for a while with a sort of dispassionate benevolence, at last:

"Yes, Doña Rita as far as I know her is so varied in her simplicity that even that is possible," he said. "Yes. A romantic resigned La Vallière . . . who had a big mouth."

I felt moved to make myself heard.

"Did you know La Vallière, too?" I asked impertinently.

Mills only smiled at me. "No. I am not quite so old as that," he said. "But it's not very difficult to know facts of that kind about a historical personage. There were some ribald verses made at the time, and Louis XIV was congratulated on the possession—I really don't remember how it goes—on the possession of:

> ". . . de ce bec amoureux
>   Qui d'une oreille à l'autre va,
>   Tra la la."

or something of the sort. It needn't be from ear to ear, but it's a fact that a big mouth is often a sign of a certain generosity of mind and feeling. Young man, beware of women with small mouths. Beware of the others, too, of course; but a small mouth is a fatal sign. Well, the royalist sympathizers can't charge Doña Rita with any lack of generosity from what I hear. Why should I judge her? I have known her for, say, six hours altogether. It was enough to feel the seduction of her native intelligence and of her splendid physique. And all that was brought home to me so quickly," he concluded, "because she had what some Frenchman has called the 'terrible gift of familiarity.'"

Blunt had been listening moodily. He nodded assent.

"Yes!" Mills' thoughts were still dwelling in the past. "And when saying good-bye she could put in an instant an immense distance between herself and you. A slight stiffening of that perfect figure, a change of the physiognomy: it was like being dismissed by a person born in the purple. Even if she did offer you her hand—as she did to me—it was as if across a broad river. Trick of manner or a bit of truth peeping out? Perhaps she's really one of those inaccessible beings. What do you think, Blunt?"

It was a direct question which for some reason (as if my range of sensitiveness had been increased already) displeased or rather disturbed me strangely. Blunt seemed not to have heard it. But after a while he turned to me.

"That thick man," he said in a tone of perfect urbanity, "is as fine as a needle. All these statements about the seduction and then this final doubt expressed after only two visits which could not have included more than six hours altogether and this some three years ago! But it is Henry Allègre that you should ask this question. Mr. Mills "

"I haven't the secret of raising the dead," answered Mills good humouredly. "And if I had I would hesitate. It would seem such a liberty to take with a person one had known so slightly in life."

"And yet Henry Allègre is the only person to ask about her, after all this uninterrupted companionship of years, ever since he discovered her; all the time, every breathing moment of it, till, literally, his very last breath. I don't mean to say she nursed him. He had his confidential man for that. He couldn't bear women about his person. But then apparently he couldn't bear this one out of his sight. She's the only woman who ever sat to him, for he would never suffer a model inside his house. That's why the 'Girl in the Hat' and the 'Byzantine Empress' have that family air, though neither of them is really a likeness of Doña Rita. . . . You know my mother?"

Mills inclined his body slightly and a fugitive smile vanished from his lips. Blunt's eyes were fastened on the very centre of his empty plate.

"Then perhaps you know my mother's artistic and literary associations," Blunt went on in a subtly changed tone. "My mother has been writing verse since she was a girl of fifteen. She's still writing verse. She's still fifteen—a spoiled girl of genius. So she requested one of her poet friends—no less than Versoy himself—to arrange for a visit to Henry Allègre's house. At first he thought he hadn't heard aright. You must know that for my mother a man that doesn't jump out of his skin for any woman's caprice is not chivalrous. But perhaps you do know? . . ."

Mills shook his head with an amused air. Blunt, who had raised his eyes from his plate to look at him, started afresh with great deliberation.

"She gives no peace to herself or her friends. My

mother's exquisitely absurd. You understand that all
these painters, poets, art collectors (and dealers in
bric-à-brac, he interjected through his teeth) of my
mother are not in my way; but Versoy lives more like a
man of the world. One day I met him at the fencing
school. He was furious. He asked me to tell my
mother that this was the last effort of his chivalry.
The jobs she gave him to do were too difficult. But I
daresay he had been pleased enough to show the influence he had in that quarter. He knew my mother
would tell the world's wife all about it. He's a spite-
ful, gingery little wretch. The top of his head shines
like a billiard ball. I believe he polishes it every
morning with a cloth. Of course they didn't get further
than the big drawing-room on the first floor, an enormous drawing-room with three pairs of columns in the
middle. The double doors on the top of the staircase
had been thrown wide open, as if for a visit from royalty.
You can picture to yourself my mother, with her white
hair done in some 18th century fashion and her sparkling black eyes, penetrating into those splendours
attended by a sort of bald-headed, vexed squirrel—
and Henry Allègre coming forward to meet them like
a severe prince with the face of a tombstone Crusader,
big white hands, muffled silken voice, half-shut eyes,
as if looking down at them from a balcony. You
remember that trick of his, Mills?"

Mills emitted an enormous cloud of smoke out of his
distended cheeks.

"I daresay he was furious, too," Blunt continued dis-
passionately. "But he was extremely civil. He
showed her all the 'treasures' in the room, ivories,
enamels, miniatures, all sorts of monstrosities from
Japan, from India, from Timbuctoo . . . for all I
know. . . . He pushed his condescension so far as

to have the 'Girl in the Hat' brought down into the drawing-room—half-length, unframed. They put her on a chair for my mother to look at. The 'Byzantine Empress' was already there, hung on the end wall—full length, gold frame weighing half a ton. My mother first overwhelms the 'Master' with thanks, and then absorbs herself in the adoration of the 'Girl in the Hat.' Then she sighs out: 'It should be called Diaphanéité, if there is such a word. Ah! This is the last expression of modernity!' She puts up suddenly her face-à-main and looks towards the end wall. 'And that—Byzantium itself! Who was she, this sullen and beautiful Empress?'

"'The one I had in my mind was Theodosia!' Allègre consented to answer. 'Originally a slave girl—from somewhere.'

"My mother can be marvellously indiscreet when the whim takes her. She finds nothing better to do than to ask the 'Master' why he took his inspiration for those two faces from the same model. No doubt she was proud of her discerning eye. It was really clever of her. Allègre, however, looked on it as a colossal impertinence; but he answered in his silkiest tones:

"'Perhaps it is because I saw in that woman something of the women of all time.'

"My mother might have guessed that she was on thin ice there. She is extremely intelligent. Moreover, she ought to have known. But women can be miraculously dense sometimes. So she exclaims, 'Then she is a wonder!' And with some notion of being complimentary goes on to say that only the eyes of the discoverer of so many wonders of art could have discovered something so marvellous in life. I suppose Allègre lost his temper altogether then; or perhaps he only wanted to pay my mother out, for all these 'Masters' she had been throwing at his head for the last two hours. He insinuates with the utmost politeness:

"'As you are honouring my poor collection with a visit you may like to judge for yourself as to the inspiration of these two pictures. She is upstairs changing her dress after our morning ride. But she wouldn't be very long. She might be a little surprised at first to be called down like this, but with a few words of preparation and purely as a matter of art . . .'

"There were never two people more taken aback. Versoy himself confesses that he dropped his tall hat with a crash. I am a dutiful son, I hope, but I must say I should have liked to have seen the retreat down the great staircase. Ha! Ha! Ha!"

He laughed most undutifully and then his face twitched grimly.

"That implacable brute Allègre followed them down ceremoniously and put my mother into the fiacre at the door with the greatest deference. He didn't open his lips though, and made a great bow as the fiacre drove away. My mother didn't recover from her consternation for three days. I lunch with her almost daily and I couldn't imagine what was the matter. Then one day . . ."

He glanced round the table, jumped up and with a word of excuse left the studio by a small door in a corner. This startled me into the consciousness that I had been as if I had not existed for these two men. With his elbows propped on the table Mills had his hands in front of his face clasping the pipe from which he extracted now and then a puff of smoke, staring stolidly across the room.

I was moved to ask in a whisper:

"Do you know him well?"

"I don't know what he is driving at," he answered

drily. "But as to his mother she is not as volatile as all that. I suspect it was business. It may have been a deep plot to get a picture out of Allègre for somebody. My cousin as likely as not. Or simply to discover what he had. The Blunts lost all their property and in Paris there are various ways of making a little money, without actually breaking anything. Not even the law. And Mrs. Blunt really had a position once—in the days of the Second Empire—and so . . ."

I listened open-mouthed to these things into which my West-Indian experiences could not have given me an insight. But Mills checked himself and ended in a changed tone.

"It's not easy to know what she would be at, either, in any given instance. For the rest, spotlessly honourable. A delightful, aristocratic old lady. Only poor."

A bump at the door silenced him and immediately Mr. John Blunt, Captain of Cavalry in the Army of Legitimity, first-rate cook (as to one dish at least), generous host, entered clutching the necks of four more bottles between the fingers of his hand.

"I stumbled and nearly smashed the lot," he remarked casually. But even I, with all my innocence, never for a moment believed he had stumbled accidentally. During the uncorking and the filling up of glasses a profound silence reigned; but neither of us took it seriously—any more than his stumble.

"One day," he went on again in that curiously flavoured voice of his, "my mother took a heroic decision and made up her mind to get up in the middle of the night. You must understand my mother's phraseology. It meant that she would be up and dressed by nine o'clock. This time it was not Versoy that was commanded for attendance, but I. You may imagine how delighted I was. . . ."

It was very plain to me that Blunt was addressing himself exclusively to Mills: Mills the mind, even more than Mills the man. It was as if Mills represented something initiated and to be reckoned with. I, of course, could have no such pretensions. If I represented anything it was a perfect freshness of sensations and a refreshing ignorance, not so much of what life may give one (as to that I had some ideas at least) but of what it really contains. I knew very well that I was utterly insignificant in these men's eyes. Yet my attention was not checked by that knowledge. It's true they were talking of a woman, but I was yet at the age when this subject by itself is not of overwhelming interest. My imagination would have been more stimulated probably by the adventures and fortunes of a man. What kept my interest from flagging was Mr. Blunt himself. The play of the white gleams of his smile round the suspicion of grimness of his tone fascinated me like a moral incongruity.

So at the age when one sleeps well indeed but does feel sometimes as if the need of sleep were a mere weakness of a distant old age, I kept easily awake; and in my freshness I was kept amused by the contrast of personalities, of the disclosed facts and moral outlook with the rough initiations of my West-Indian experience. And all these things were dominated by a feminine figure which to my imagination had only a floating outline, now invested with the grace of girlhood, now with the prestige of a woman; and indistinct in both these characters. For these two men had *seen* her, while to me she was only being "presented," elusively, in vanishing words, in the shifting tones of an unfamiliar voice.

She was being presented to me now in the Bois de Boulogne at the early hour of the ultra-fashionable world (so I understood), on a light bay "bit of blood"

attended on the off side by that Henry Allègre mounted
on a dark brown powerful weight carrier; and on the
other by one of Allègre's acquaintances (the man had
no real friends), distinguished frequenters of that mysterious Pavilion. And so that side of the frame in
which that woman appeared to one down the perspective of the great Allée was not permanent. That
morning when Mr. Blunt had to escort his mother there
for the gratification of her irresistible curiosity (of
which he highly disapproved) there appeared in succession, at that woman's or girl's bridle-hand, a cavalry
general in red breeches, on whom she was smiling; a
rising politician in a grey suit, who talked to her with
great animation but left her side abruptly to join a
personage in a red fez and mounted on a white horse;
and then, some time afterwards, the vexed Mr. Blunt
and his indiscreet mother (though I really couldn't
see where the harm was) had one more chance of a good
stare. The third party that time was the Royal
Pretender (Allègre had been painting his portrait
lately), whose hearty, sonorous laugh was heard long
before the mounted trio came riding very slowly abreast
of the Blunts. There was colour in the girl's face.
She was not laughing. Her expression was serious
and her eyes thoughtfully downcast. Blunt admitted
that on that occasion the charm, brilliance, and force
of her personality was adequately framed between
those magnificently mounted, paladin-like attendants,
one older than the other but the two composing together admirably in the different stages of their man-
hood. Mr. Blunt had never before seen Henry Allègre
so close. Allègre was riding nearest to the path on
which Blunt was dutifully giving his arm to his mother
(they had got out of their fiacre) and wondering if that
confounded fellow would have the impudence to take

off his hat. But he did not. Perhaps he didn't notice. Allègre was not a man of wandering glances. There were silver hairs in his beard but he looked as solid as a statue. Less than three months afterwards he was gone.

"What was it?" asked Mills, who had not changed his pose for a very long time.

"Oh, an accident. But he lingered. They were on their way to Corsica. A yearly pilgrimage. Sentimental perhaps. It was to Corsica that he carried her off—I mean first of all."

There was the slightest contraction of Mr. Blunt's facial muscles. Very slight; but I, staring at the narrator after the manner of all simple souls, noticed it; the twitch of a pain which surely must have been mental. There was also a suggestion of effort before he went on: "I suppose you know how he got hold of her?" in a tone of ease which was astonishingly ill-assumed for such a worldly, self-controlled, drawing-room person.

Mills changed his attitude to look at him fixedly for a moment. Then he leaned back in his chair and with interest—I don't mean curiosity, I mean interest: "Does anybody know besides the two parties concerned?" he asked, with something as it were renewed (or was it refreshed?) in his unmoved quietness. "I ask because one has never heard any tales. I remember one evening in a restaurant seeing a man come in with a lady—a beautiful lady—very particularly beautiful, as though she had been stolen out of Mahomet's paradise. With Doña Rita it can't be anything as definite as that. But speaking of her in the same strain, I've always felt that she looked as though Allègre had caught her in the precincts of some temple . . . in the mountains."

I was delighted. I had never heard before a woman spoken about in that way, a real live woman that is, not a woman in a book. For this was no poetry and yet it seemed to put her in the category of visions. And I would have lost myself in it if Mr. Blunt had not, most unexpectedly, addressed himself to me.

"I told you that man was as fine as a needle." . . . And then to Mills: "Out of a temple? We know what that means." His dark eyes flashed: "And must it be really in the mountains?" he added.

"Or in a desert," conceded Mills, "if you prefer that. There have been temples in deserts, you know."

Blunt had calmed down suddenly and assumed a nonchalant pose.

"As a matter of fact, Henry Allègre caught her very early one morning in his own old garden full of thrushes and other small birds. She was sitting on a stone, a fragment of some old balustrade, with her feet in the damp grass, and reading a tattered book of some kind. She had on a short, black, two-penny frock (*une petite robe de deux sous*) and there was a hole in one of her stockings. She raised her eyes and saw him looking down at her thoughtfully over that ambrosian beard of his, like Jove at a mortal. They exchanged a good long stare, for at first she was too startled to move; and then he murmured, "*Restez donc.*" She lowered her eyes again on her book and after a while heard him walk away on the path. Her heart thumped while she listened to the little birds filling the air with their noise. She was not frightened. I am telling you this positively because she has told me the tale herself. What better authority can you have . . . ?" Blunt paused.

"That's true. She's not the sort of person to lie about her own sensations," murmured Mills above his clasped hands.

"Nothing can escape his penetration," Blunt remarked to me with that equivocal urbanity which made me always feel uncomfortable on Mills' account. "Positively nothing." He turned to Mills again. "After some minutes of immobility—she told me—she arose from her stone and walked slowly on the track of that apparition. Allègre was nowhere to be seen by that time. Under the gateway of the extremely ugly tenement house, which hides the Pavilion and the garden from the street, the wife of the porter was waiting with her arms akimbo. At once she cried out to Rita: 'You were caught by our gentleman.'

"As a matter of fact, that old woman, being a friend of Rita's aunt, allowed the girl to come into the garden whenever Allègre was away. But Allègre's goings and comings were sudden and unannounced; and that morning, Rita, crossing the narrow, thronged street, had slipped in through the gateway in ignorance of Allègre's return and unseen by the porter's wife.

"The child, she was but little more than that then, expressed her regret of having perhaps got the kind porter's wife into trouble.

"The old woman said with a peculiar smile: 'Your face is not of the sort that gets other people into trouble. My gentleman wasn't angry. He says you may come in any morning you like.'

"Rita, without saying anything to this, crossed the street back again to the warehouse full of oranges where she spent most of her waking hours. Her dreaming, empty, idle, thoughtless, unperturbed hours, she calls them. She crossed the street with a hole in her stocking. She had a hole in her stocking not because her uncle and aunt were poor (they had around them never less than eight thousand oranges, mostly in cases) but because she was then careless and untidy and totally unconscious of her personal appearance. She told me her-self that she was not even conscious then of her personal existence. She was a mere adjunct in the twilight life of her aunt, a Frenchwoman, and her uncle, the orange merchant, a Basque peasant, to whom her other uncle, the great man of the family, the priest of some parish in the hills near Tolosa, had sent her up at the age of thir-teen or thereabouts for safe keeping. She is of peasant stock, you know. This is the true origin of the 'Girl in the Hat' and of the 'Byzantine Empress' which ex-cited my dear mother so much; of the mysterious girl that the privileged personalities great in art, in letters, in politics or simply in the world, could see on the big sofa during the gatherings in Allègre's exclusive Pavil-ion: the Doña Rita of their respectful addresses, mani-fest and mysterious, like an object of art from some unknown period; the Doña Rita of the initiated Paris. Doña Rita and nothing more—unique and indefinable." He stopped with a disagreeable smile.

"And of peasant stock?" I exclaimed in the strangely conscious silence that fell between Mills and Blunt.

"Oh! All these Basques have been ennobled by Don Sanche II," said Captain Blunt moodily. "You see coats of arms carved over the doorways of the most miserable *caserios*. As far as that goes she's Doña Rita right enough whatever else she is or is not in herself or in the eyes of others. In your eyes, for instance, Mills. Eh?"

For a time Mills preserved that conscious silence.

"Why think about it at all?" he murmured coldly at last. "A strange bird is hatched sometimes in a nest in an unaccountable way and then the fate of such a bird is bound to be ill-defined, uncertain, questionable. And so that is how Henry Allègre saw her first? And what happened next?"

"What happened next?" repeated Mr. Blunt, with an affected surprise in his tone. "Is it necessary to ask that question? If you had asked *how* the next happened. . . . But as you may imagine she hasn't told me anything about that. She didn't," he continued with polite sarcasm, "enlarge upon the facts. That confounded Allègre, with his impudent assumption of princely airs, must have (I shouldn't wonder) made the fact of his notice appear as a sort of favour dropped from Olympus. I really can't tell how the minds and the imaginations of such aunts and uncles are affected by such rare visitations. Mythology may give us a hint. There is the story of Danaë, for instance."

"There is," remarked Mills calmly, "but I don't remember any aunt or uncle in that connection."

"And there are also certain stories of the discovery and acquisition of some unique objects of art. The sly approaches, the astute negotiations, the lying and the circumventing . . . for the love of beauty, you know."

With his dark face and with the perpetual smiles playing about his grimness, Mr. Blunt appeared to me positively satanic. Mills' hand was toying absently with an empty glass. Again they had forgotten my existence altogether.

"I don't know how an object of art would feel," went on Blunt, in an unexpectedly grating voice, which, however, recovered its tone immediately. "I don't know. But I do know that Rita herself was not a Danaë, never, not at any time of her life. She didn't mind the holes in her stockings. She wouldn't mind holes in her stockings now. . . . . That is if she manages to keep any stockings at all," he added, with a sort of suppressed fury so funnily unexpected that I would have burst into a laugh if I hadn't been lost in astonishment of the simplest kind.

"No—really!" There was a flash of interest from the quiet Mills.

"Yes, really," Blunt nodded and knitted his brows very devilishly indeed. "She may yet be left without a single pair of stockings."

"The world's a thief," declared Mills, with the utmost composure. "It wouldn't mind robbing a lonely traveller."

"He is so subtle." Blunt remembered my existence for the purpose of that remark and as usual it made me very uncomfortable. "Perfectly true. A lonely traveller. They are all in the scramble from the lowest to the highest. Heavens! What a gang! There was even an Archbishop in it."

"*Vous plaisantez*," said Mills, but without any marked show of incredulity.

"I joke very seldom," Blunt protested earnestly. "That's why I haven't mentioned His Majesty—whom God preserve. That would have been an exaggeration. . . . However, the end is not yet. We were talking about the beginning. I have heard that some dealers in fine objects, quite mercenary people of course (my mother has an experience in that world), show sometimes an astonishing reluctance to part with some specimens, even at a good price. It must be very funny. It's just possible that the uncle and the aunt have been rolling in tears on the floor, amongst their oranges, or beating their heads against the walls from rage and despair. But I doubt it. And in any case Allègre was not the sort of person that gets into any vulgar trouble. And it's just possible that those people stood open-mouthed at all that magnificence. They weren't poor, you know; therefore it wasn't incumbent on them to be honest. They are still there in the old respectable warehouse, I understand. They have kept their position in their *quartier*, I believe. But they didn't keep their niece. It might have been an act of sacrifice! For I seem to remember hearing that after attending for a while some school round the corner the child had been set to keep the books of that orange business. However it might have been, the first fact in Rita's and Allègre's common history is a journey to Italy, and then to Corsica. You know Allègre had a house in Corsica somewhere. She has it now as she has everything he ever had; and that Corsican palace is the portion that will stick the longest to Doña Rita, I imagine. Who would want to buy a place like that? I suppose nobody would take it for a gift. The fellow was having houses built all over the place. This very house where we are sitting belonged to him. Doña Rita has given it to her sister, I understand. Or at any rate the sister runs it. She is my landlady . . ."

"Her sister here!" I exclaimed. "Her sister!"

Blunt turned to me politely, but only for a long mute gaze. His eyes were in deep shadow and it struck me for the first time then that there was something fatal in that man's aspect as soon as he fell silent. I think the effect was purely physical, but in consequence whatever he said seemed inadequate and as if produced by a commonplace, if uneasy, soul.

"Doña Rita brought her down from her mountains on purpose. She is asleep somewhere in this house, in one of the vacant rooms. She lets them, you know, at extortionate prices, that is, if people will pay them, for she is easily intimidated. You see, she has never seen such an enormous town before in her life, nor yet so many strange people. She has been keeping house for the uncle-priest in some mountain gorge for years and years. It's extraordinary he should have let her go. There is something mysterious there, some reason or

other. It's either theology or family. The saintly
uncle in his wild parish would know nothing of any
other reasons. She wears a rosary at her waist.
Directly she had seen some real money she developed
a love of it. If you stay with me long enough, and I
hope you will (I really can't sleep), you will see her
going out to mass at half-past six; but there is nothing
remarkable in her; just a peasant woman of thirty-
four or so. A rustic nun. . . ."

I may as well say at once that we didn't stay as long
as that. It was not that morning that I saw for the
first time Therese of the whispering lips and downcast
eyes slipping out to an early mass from the house of
iniquity into the early winter murk of the city of perdition, in a world steeped in sin. No. It was not on
that morning that I saw Doña Rita's incredible sister
with her brown, dry face, her gliding motion, and her
really nun-like dress, with a black handkerchief enfold-
ing her head tightly, with the two pointed ends hanging
down her back. Yes, nun-like enough. And yet not
altogether. People would have turned round after
her if those dartings out to the half-past six mass hadn't
been the only occasion on which she ventured into the
impious streets. She was frightened of the streets,
but in a particular way, not as if of a danger but as if
of a contamination. Yet she didn't fly back to her
mountains because at bottom she had an indomitable
character, a peasant tenacity of purpose, predatory
instincts. . . .

No, we didn't remain long enough with Mr. Blunt to
see even as much as her back glide out of the house on
her prayerful errand. She was prayerful. She was
terrible. Her one-ideaed peasant mind was as inaccessible as a closed iron safe. She was fatal. . . . It's
perfectly ridiculous to confess that they all seem fatal

to me now; but writing to you like this in all sincerity I don't mind appearing ridiculous. I suppose fatality must be expressed, embodied, like other forces of this earth; and if so why not in such people as well as in other more glorious or more frightful figures?

We remained, however, long enough to let Mr. Blunt's half-hidden acrimony develop itself or prey on itself in further talk about the man Allègre and the girl Rita. Mr. Blunt, still addressing Mills with that story, passed on to what he called the second act, the disclosure, with, what he called, the characteristic Allègre impudence—which surpassed the impudence of kings, millionaries, or tramps, by many degrees— the revelation of Rita's existence to the world at large. It wasn't a very large world, but then it was most choicely composed. How is one to describe it shortly? In a sentence it was the world that rides in the morning in the Bois.

In something less than a year and a half from the time he found her sitting on a broken fragment of stone work buried in the grass of his wild garden, full of thrushes, starlings, and other innocent creatures of the air, he had given her amongst other accomplishments the art of sitting admirably on a horse, and directly they returned to Paris he took her out with him for their first morning ride.

"I leave you to judge of the sensation," continued Mr. Blunt, with a faint grimace, as though the words had an acrid taste in his mouth. "And the consternation," he added venomously. "Many of those men on that great morning had some one of their womenkind with them. But their hats had to go off all the same, especially the hats of the fellows who were under some sort of obligation to Allègre. You would be astonished to hear the names of people, of real personalities in the world, who, not to mince matters, owed money to Allègre. And I don't mean in the world of art only. In the first rout of the surprise some story of an adopted daughter was set abroad hastily, I believe. You know 'adopted' with a peculiar accent on the word— and it was plausible enough. I have been told that at that time she looked extremely youthful by his side, I mean extremely youthful in expression, in the eyes, in the smile. She must have been . . ."

Blunt pulled himself up short, but not so short as not to let the confused murmur of the word "adorable" reach our attentive ears.

The heavy Mills made a slight movement in his chair. The effect on me was more inward, a strange emotion which left me perfectly still; and for the moment of silence Blunt looked more fatal than ever.

"I understand it didn't last very long," he addressed us politely again. "And no wonder! The sort of talk she would have heard during that first springtime in Paris would have put an impress on a much less receptive personality; for of course Allègre didn't close his doors to his friends, and this new apparition was not of the sort to make them keep away. After that first morning she always had somebody to ride at her bridle-hand. Old Doyen, the sculptor, was the first to approach them. At that age a man may venture on anything. He rides a strange animal like a circus horse. Rita had spotted him out of the corner of her eye as he passed them, putting up his enormous paw in a still more enormous glove, airily, you know, like this" (Blunt waved his hand above his head), "to Allègre. He passes on. All at once he wheels his fantastic animal round and comes trotting after them. With the merest casual 'Bonjour, Allègre,' he ranges close to her on the other side and addresses her, hat in hand,

in that booming voice of his like a deferential roar of
the sea very far away. His articulation is not good,
and the first words she really made out were 'I am an
old sculptor. . . . Of course there is that habit.
. . . But I can see you through all that. . . .'

"He put his hat on very much on one side. 'I am
a great sculptor of women,' he declared. 'I gave up
my life to them, poor unfortunate creatures, the most
beautiful, the wealthiest, the most loved. . . . Two
generations of them. . . . Just look at me full in
the eyes, *mon enfant.*'

"They stared at each other. Doña Rita confessed
to me that the old fellow made her heart beat with such
force that she couldn't manage to smile at him. And
she saw his eyes run full of tears. He wiped them
simply with the back of his hand and went on booming
faintly. 'Thought so. You are enough to make one
cry. I thought my artist's life was finished, and here
you come along from devil knows where with this young
friend of mine, who isn't a bad smearer of canvases—
but it's marble and bronze that you want. . . . I
shall finish my artist's life with your face; but I shall
want a bit of those shoulders, too. . . . You hear,
Allègre, I must have a bit of her shoulders, too. I can
see through the cloth that they are divine. If they
aren't divine I will eat my hat. Yes, I will do your
head and then—*nunc dimittis.*'

"These were the first words with which the world
greeted her, or should I say civilization did; already
both her native mountains and the cavern of oranges
belonged to a prehistoric age. 'Why don't you ask
him to come this afternoon?' Allègre's voice suggested
gently. 'He knows the way to the house.'

"The old man said with extraordinary fervour, 'Oh,
yes, I will,' pulled up his horse and they went on. She

told me that she could feel her heart-beats for a long time. The remote power of that voice, those old eyes full of tears, that noble and ruined face, had affected her extraordinarily she said. But perhaps what affected her was the shadow, the still living shadow of a great passion in the man's heart.

"Allègre remarked to her calmly: 'He has been a little mad all his life.'"

III

MILLS lowered the hands holding the extinct and even cold pipe before his big face.

"H'm, shoot an arrow into that old man's heart like this? But was there anything done?"

"A terra-cotta bust, I believe. Good? I don't know. I rather think it's in this house. A lot of things have been sent down from Paris here, when she gave up the Pavilion. When she goes up now she stays in hotels, you know. I imagine it is locked up in one of these things," went on Blunt, pointing towards the end of the studio where amongst the monumental presses of dark oak lurked the shy dummy which had worn the stiff robes of the Byzantine Empress and the amazing hat of the "Girl," rakishly. I wondered whether that dummy had travelled from Paris, too, and whether with or without its head. Perhaps that head had been left behind, having rolled into a corner of some empty room in the dismantled Pavilion. I represented it to myself very lonely, without features, like a turnip, with a mere peg sticking out where the neck should have been. . . . And Mr. Blunt was talking on.

"There are treasures behind these locked doors, brocades, old jewels, unframed pictures, bronzes, chinoiseries. japoneries." . . .

He growled as much as a man of his accomplished manner and voice could growl. "I don't suppose she gave away all that to her sister, but I shouldn't be surprised if that timid rustic didn't lay a claim to the lot

for the love of God and the good of the Church. . . .
And held on with her teeth, too," he added graphically.

Mills' face remained grave. Very grave. I was
amused at those little venomous outbreaks of the fatal
Mr. Blunt. Again I knew myself utterly forgotten.
But I didn't feel dull and I didn't even feel sleepy.
That last strikes me as strange as this distance of time,
in regard of my tender years and of the depressing
hour which precedes the dawn. We had been drinking
that straw-coloured wine, too, I won't say like water
(nobody would have drunk water like that) but, well
. . . and the haze of tobacco smoke was like the
blue mist of great distances seen in dreams.

Yes, that old sculptor was the first who joined them
in the sight of all Paris. It was that old glory that
opened the series of companions of those morning
rides; a series which extended through three successive
Parisian springtimes and comprised a famous physi-
ologist, a fellow who seemed to hint that mankind
could be made immortal or at least everlastingly old;
a fashionable philosopher and psychologist who used
to lecture to enormous audiences of women with his
tongue in his cheek (but never permitted himself anything of the kind when talking to Rita); that surly
dandy Cabanel (but he only once, from mere vanity),
and everybody else at all distinguished including also a
celebrated person who turned out later to be a swindler.
But he was really a genius. . . . All this according
to Mr. Blunt, who gave us all those details with a sort of
languid zest covering a secret irritation.

"Apart from that, you know," went on Mr. Blunt,
"all she knew of the world of men and women (I mean
till Allègre's death) was what she had seen of it from the
saddle two hours every morning during four months
of the year or so. Absolutely all, with Allègre self-

denyingly on her right hand, with that impenetrable air
of guardianship. Don't touch! He didn't like his treasures to be touched unless he actually put some unique
object into your hands with a sort of triumphant murmur, 'Look close at that.' Of course I only have heard
all this. I am much too small a person, you understand, to even . . ."

He flashed his white teeth at us most agreeably,
but the upper part of his face, the shadowed setting of
his eyes, and the slight drawing in of his eyebrows
gave a fatal suggestion. I thought suddenly of the
definition he applied to himself: "*Américain, catholique
et gentilhomme*" completed by that startling "I live
by my sword" uttered in a light drawing-room tone
tinged by a flavour of mockery lighter even than air.

He insisted to us that the first and only time he had
seen Allègre a little close was that morning in the Bois
with his mother. His Majesty (whom God preserve),
then not even an active Pretender, flanked the girl, still
a girl, on the other side, the usual companion for a
month past or so. Allègre had suddenly taken it into
his head to paint his portrait. A sort of intimacy
had sprung up. Mrs. Blunt's remark was that of
the two striking horsemen Allègre looked the more
kingly.

"The son of a confounded millionaire soap-boiler,"
commented Mr. Blunt through his clenched teeth. "A
man absolutely without parentage. Without a single
relation in the world. Just a freak."

"That explains why he could leave all his fortune to
her," said Mills.

"The will, I believe," said Mr. Blunt moodily, "was
written on a half sheet of paper, with his device of an
Assyrian bull at the head. What the devil did he mean
by it? Anyway it was the last time that she surveyed

the world of men and women from the saddle. Less than three months later . . ."

"Allègre died and . . ." murmured Mills in an interested manner.

"And she had to dismount," broke in Mr. Blunt grimly. "Dismount right into the middle of it. Down to the very ground, you understand. I suppose you can guess what that would mean. She didn't know what to do with herself. She had never been on the ground. She . . ."

"Aha!" said Mills.

"Even eh! eh! if you like," retorted Mr. Blunt, in an unrefined tone, that made me open my eyes, which were well opened before, still wider.

He turned to me with that horrible trick of his of commenting upon Mills as though that quiet man whom I admired, whom I trusted, and for whom I had already something resembling affection had been as much of a dummy as that other one lurking in the shadows, pitiful and headless in its attitude of alarmed chastity.

"Nothing escapes his penetration. He can perceive a haystack at an enormous distance when he is interested."

I thought this was going rather too far, even to the borders of vulgarity; but Mills remained untroubled and only reached for his tobacco pouch.

"But that's nothing to my mother's interest. She can never see a haystack, therefore she is always so surprised and excited. Of course Doña Rita was not a woman about whom the newspapers insert little paragraphs. But Allègre was the sort of man. A lot came out in print about him and a lot was talked in the world about her; and at once my dear mother perceived a haystack and naturally became unreasonably absorbed in it. I thought her interest would wear out. But it didn't. She had received a shock and had received an impression by means of that girl. My mother has never been treated with impertinence before, and the æsthetic impression must have been of extraordinary strength. I must suppose that it amounted to a sort of moral revolution, I can't account for her proceedings in any other way. When Rita turned up in Paris a year and a half after Allègre's death some shabby journalist (smart creature) hit upon the notion of alluding to her as the heiress of Mr. Allègre. 'The heiress of Mr. Allègre has taken up her residence again amongst the treasures of art in that Pavilion so well known to the élite of the artistic, scientific, and political world, not to speak of the members of aristocratic and even royal families. . . .' You know the sort of thing. It appeared first in the *Figaro*, I believe. And then at the end a little phrase: 'She is alone.' She was in a fair way of becoming a celebrity of a sort. Daily little allusions and that sort of thing. Heaven only knows who stopped it. There was a rush of 'old friends' into that garden, enough to scare all the little birds away. I suppose one or several of them, having influence with the press, did it. But the gossip didn't stop, and the name stuck, too, since it conveyed a very certain and very significant sort of fact, and of course the Venetian episode was talked about in the houses frequented by my mother. It was talked about from a royalist point of view with a kind of respect. It was even said that the inspiration and the resolution of the war going on now over the Pyrenees had come out from that head. . . . Some of them talked as if she were the guardian angel of Legitimacy. You know what royalist gush is like."

Mr. Blunt's face expressed sarcastic disgust. Mills moved his head the least little bit. Apparently he knew.

"Well, speaking with all possible respect, it seems to have affected my mother's brain. I was already with the royal army and of course there could be no question of regular postal communications with France. My mother hears or overhears somewhere that the heiress of Mr. Allègre is contemplating a secret journey. All the noble Salons were full of chatter about that secret naturally. So she sits down and pens an autograph: 'Madame, informed that you are proceeding to the place on which the hopes of all the right thinking people are fixed, I trust to your womanly sympathy with a mother's anxious feelings, etc., etc.,' and ending with a request to take messages to me and bring news of me. . . . The coolness of my mother!"

Most unexpectedly Mills was heard murmuring a question which seemed to me very odd.

"I wonder how your mother addressed that note?"

A moment of silence ensued.

"Hardly in the newspaper style, I should think," retorted Mr. Blunt, with one of his grins that made me doubt the stability of his feelings and the consistency of his outlook in regard to his whole tale. "My mother's maid took it in a fiacre very late one evening to the Pavilion and brought an answer scrawled on a scrap of paper: 'Write your messages at once' and signed with a big capital R. So my mother sat down again to her charming writing desk and the maid made another journey in a fiacre just before midnight; and ten days later or so I got a letter thrust into my hand at the *avanzadas* just as I was about to start on a night patrol, together with a note asking me to call on the writer so that she might allay my mother's anxieties by telling her how I looked.

"It was signed R only, but I guessed at once and nearly fell off my horse with surprise."

"You mean to say that Doña Rita was actually at the Royal Headquarters lately?" exclaimed Mills, with evident surprise. "Why, we—everybody—thought that all this affair was over and done with."

"Absolutely. Nothing in the world could be more done with than that episode. Of course the rooms in the hotel at Tolosa were retained for her by an order from Royal Headquarters. Two garret-rooms, the place was so full of all sorts of court people; but I can assure you that for the three days she was there she never put her head outside the door. General Mongroviejo called on her officially from the King. A general, not anybody of the household, you see. That's a distinct shade of the present relation. He stayed just five minutes. Some personage from the Foreign department at Headquarters was closeted for about a couple of hours. That was of course business. Then two officers from the staff came together with some explanations or instructions to her. Then Baron H., a fellow with a pretty wife, who had made so many sacrifices for the cause, raised a great to-do about seeing her and she consented to receive him for a moment. They say he was very much frightened by her arrival, but after the interview went away all smiles. Who else? Yes, the Archbishop came. Half an hour. This is more than is necessary to give a blessing, and I can't conceive what else he had to give her. But I am sure he got something out of her. Two peasants from the upper valley were sent for by military authorities and she saw them, too. That friar who hangs about the court had been in and out several times. Well, and lastly, I myself. I got leave from the outposts. That was the first time I talked to her. I would have gone that evening back to the regiment, but the friar met me in the corridor and informed me that I would be ordered to escort that most loyal and noble lady back to the French frontier as a personal mission of the highest honour. I was inclined to laugh at him. He himself is a cheery and jovial person and he laughed with me quite readily—but I got the order before dark all right. It was rather a job, as the Alphonsists were attacking the right flank of our whole front and there was some considerable disorder there. I mounted her on a mule and her maid on another. We spent one night in a ruined old tower occupied by some of our infantry and got away at daybreak under the Alphonsist shells. The maid nearly died of fright and one of the troopers with us was wounded. To smuggle her back across the frontier was another job but it wasn't my job. It wouldn't have done for her to appear in sight of French frontier posts in the company of Carlist uniforms. She seems to have a fearless streak in her nature. At one time as we were climbing a slope absolutely exposed to artillery fire I asked her on purpose, being provoked by the way she looked about at the scenery, 'A little emotion, eh?' And she answered me in a low voice: 'Oh, yes! I am moved. I used to run about these hills when I was little.' And note, just then the trooper close behind us had been wounded by a shell fragment. He was swearing awfully and fighting with his horse. The shells were falling around us about two to the minute.

"Luckily the Alphonsist shells are not much better than our own. But women are funny. I was afraid the maid would jump down and clear out amongst the rocks, in which case we should have had to dismount and catch her. But she didn't do that; she sat perfectly still on her mule and shrieked. Just simply shrieked. Ultimately we came to a curiously shaped rock at the end of a short wooded valley. It was very

still there and the sunshine was brilliant. I said to
Doña Rita: 'We will part in a few minutes. I understand that my mission ends at this rock.' And she
said: 'I know this rock well. This is my country.'

"Then she thanked me for bringing her there and
presently three peasants appeared, waiting for us, two
youths and one shaven old man, with a thin nose like
a sword blade and perfectly round eyes, a character
well known to the whole Carlist army. The two
youths stopped under the trees at a distance, but the
old fellow came quite close up and gazed at her, screw-
ing up his eyes as if looking at the sun. Then he raised
his arm very slowly and took his red *boina* off his bald
head. I watched her smiling at him all the time. I
daresay she knew him as well as she knew the old rock.
Very old rock. The rock of ages—and the aged man—
landmarks of her youth. Then the mules started
walking smartly forward, with the three peasants strid-
ing alongside of them, and vanished between the trees.
These fellows were most likely sent out by her uncle
the Cura.

"It was a peaceful scene, the morning light, the bit
of open country framed in steep stony slopes, a high
peak or two in the distance, the thin smoke of some
invisible *caserios*, rising straight up here and there. Far
away behind us the guns had ceased and the echoes in
the gorges had died out. I never knew what peace
meant before. . . .

"Nor since," muttered Mr. Blunt after a pause and
then went on. "The little stone church of her uncle,
the holy man of the family, might have been round the
corner of the next spur of the nearest hill. I dismounted to bandage the shoulder of my trooper. It
was only a nasty long scratch. While I was busy
about it a bell began to ring in the distance. The sound

fell deliciously on the ear, clear like the morning light. But it stopped all at once. You know how a distant bell stops suddenly. I never knew before what stillness meant. While I was wondering at it the fellow holding our horses was moved to uplift his voice. He was a Spaniard, not a Basque, and he trolled out in Castilian that song you know,

> "'Oh bells of my native village,
> I am going away . . . good-bye!'

He had a good voice. When the last note had floated away I remounted, but there was a charm in the spot, something particular and individual because while we were looking at it before turning our horses' heads away the singer said: 'I wonder what is the name of this place,' and the other man remarked: 'Why, there is no village here,' and the first one insisted: 'No, I mean this spot, this very place.' The wounded trooper decided that it had no name probably. But he was wrong. It had a name. The hill, or the rock, or the wood, or the whole had a name. I heard of it by chance later. It was—Lastaola."

A cloud of tobacco smoke from Mills' pipe drove between my head and the head of Mr. Blunt, who, strange to say, yawned slightly. It seemed to me an obvious affectation on the part of that man of perfect manners, and, moreover, suffering from distressing insomnia.

"This is how we first met and how we first parted," he said in a weary, indifferent tone. "It's quite possible that she did see her uncle on the way. It's perhaps on this occasion that she got her sister to come out of the wilderness. I have no doubt she had a pass from the French Government giving her the completest freedom of action. She must have got it in Paris before leaving."

Mr. Blunt broke out into worldly, slightly cynical smiles.

"She can get anything she likes in Paris. She could get a whole army over the frontier if she liked. She could get herself admitted into the Foreign Office at one o'clock in the morning if it so pleased her. Doors fly open before the heiress of Mr. Allègre. She has inherited the old friends, the old connections. . . . Of course, if she were a toothless old woman . . . But, you see, she isn't. The ushers in all the ministries bow down to the ground therefore, and voices from the innermost sanctums take on an eager tone when they say, '*Faites entrer.*' My mother knows something about it. She has followed her career with the greatest attention. And Rita herself is not even surprised. She accomplishes most extraordinary things, as naturally as buying a pair of gloves. People in the shops are very polite and people in the world are like people in the shops. What did she know of the world? She had seen it only from the saddle. Oh, she will get your cargo released for you all right. How will she do it? . . . Well, when it's done—you follow me, Mills?—when it's done she will hardly know herself."

"It's hardly possible that she shouldn't be aware," Mills pronounced calmly.

"No, she isn't an idiot," admitted Mr. Blunt, in the same matter-of-fact voice. "But she confessed to myself only the other day that she suffered from a sense of unreality. I told her that at any rate she had her own feelings surely. And she said to me: Yes, there was one of them at least about which she had no doubt; and you will never guess what it was. Don't try. I happen to know, because we are pretty good friends."

At that moment we all changed our attitude slightly. Mills' staring eyes moved for a glance towards Blunt, I who was occupying the divan, raised myself on the cushions a little and Mr. Blunt, with half a turn, put his elbow on the table.

"I asked her what it was. I don't see," went on Mr. Blunt, with a perfectly horrible gentleness, "why I should have shown particular consideration to the heiress of Mr. Allègre. I don't mean to that particular mood of hers. It was the mood of weariness. And so she told me. It's fear. I will say it once again: Fear. . . ."

He added after a pause, "There can be not the slightest doubt of her courage. But she distinctly uttered the word fear."

There was under the table the noise of Mills stretching his legs.

"A person of imagination," he began, "a young, virgin intelligence, steeped for nearly five years in the talk of Allègre's studio, where every hard truth had been cracked and every belief had been worried into shreds. They were like a lot of intellectual dogs, you know . . ."

"Yes, yes, of course," Blunt interrupted hastily, "the intellectual personality altogether adrift, a soul without a home . . . but I, who am neither very fine nor very deep, I am convinced that the fear is material."

"Because she confessed to it being that?" insinuated Mills.

"No, because she didn't," contradicted Blunt, with an angry frown and in an extremely suave voice. "In fact, she bit her tongue. And considering what good friends we are (under fire together and all that) I conclude that there is nothing there to boast of. Neither is my friendship, as a matter of fact."

Mills' face was the very perfection of indifference. But I who was looking at him, in my innocence, to discover what it all might mean, I had a notion that it was perhaps a shade too perfect.

"My leave is a farce," Captain Blunt burst out, with a most unexpected exasperation. "As an officer of Don Carlos, I have no more standing than a bandit. I ought to have been interned in those filthy old barracks in Avignon a long time ago. . . . Why am I not? Because Doña Rita exists and for no other reason on earth. Of course it's known that I am about. She has only to whisper over the wires to the Minister of the Interior, 'Put that bird in a cage for me,' and the thing would be done without any more formalities than that. . . . Sad world this," he commented in a changed tone. "Nowadays a gentleman who lives by his sword is exposed to that sort of thing."

It was then for the first time I heard Mr. Mills laugh. It was a deep, pleasant, kindly note, not very loud and altogether free from that quality of derision that spoils so many laughs and gives away the secret hardness of hearts. But neither was it a very joyous laugh.

"But the truth of the matter is that I am *'en mission,'*" continued Captain Blunt. "I have been instructed to settle some things, to set other things going, and, by my instructions, Doña Rita is to be the intermediary for all those objects. And why? Because every bald head in this Republican Government gets pink at the top whenever her dress rustles outside the door. They bow with immense deference when the door opens, but the bow conceals a smirk because of those Venetian days. That confounded Versoy shoved his nose into that business; he says accidentally. He saw them together on the Lido and (those writing fellows are horrible) he wrote what he calls a vignette (I suppose accidentally, too) under that very title. There was in it a Prince and a lady and a big dog.

He described how the Prince on landing from the gondola emptied his purse into the hands of a picturesque old beggar, while the lady, a little way off, stood gazing back at Venice with the dog romantically stretched at her feet. One of Versoy's beautiful prose vignettes in a great daily that has a literary column. But some other papers that didn't care a cent for literature rehashed the mere fact. And that's the sort of fact that impresses your political man, especially if the lady is, well, such as she is . . ."

He paused. His dark eyes flashed fatally, away from us, in the direction of the shy dummy; and then he went on with cultivated cynicism.

"So she rushes down here. Overdone, weary, rest for her nerves. Nonsense. I assure you she has no more nerves than I have."

I don't know how he meant it, but at that moment, slim and elegant, he seemed a mere bundle of nerves himself, with the flitting expressions on his thin, well-bred face, with the restlessness of his meagre brown hands amongst the objects on the table. With some pipe ash amongst a little spilt wine his forefinger traced a capital R. Then he looked into an empty glass profoundly. I have a notion that I sat there staring and listening like a yokel at a play. Mills' pipe was lying quite a foot away in front of him, empty, cold. Perhaps he had no more tobacco. Mr. Blunt assumed his dandified air—nervously.

"Of course her movements are commented on in the most exclusive drawing-rooms and also in other places, also exclusive, but where the gossip takes on another tone. There they are probably saying that she has got a 'coup de cœur' for someone. Whereas I think she is utterly incapable of that sort of thing. That Venetian affair, the beginning of it and the end of it, was nothing

but a *coup de tête*, and all those activities in which I am
involved, as you see (by order of Headquarters, ha, ha,
ha!) are nothing but that, all this connection, all this intimacy into which I have dropped . . . Not to speak
of my mother, who is delightful, but as irresponsible as
one of those crazy princesses that shock their Royal
families. . . ."

He seemed to bite his tongue and I observed that
Mills' eyes seemed to have grown wider than I had ever
seen them before. In that tranquil face it was a great
play of feature. "An intimacy," began Mr. Blunt,
with an extremely refined grimness of tone, "an intimacy with the heiress of Mr. Allègre on the part of
. . . on my part, well, it isn't exactly . . . it's
open . . . well, I leave it to you, what does it
look like?"

"Is there anybody looking on?" Mills let fall, gently,
through his kindly lips.

"Not actually, perhaps, at this moment. But I don't
need to tell a man of the world, like you, that such
things cannot remain unseen. And that they are, well,
compromising, because of the mere fact of the fortune."

Mills got on his feet, looked for his jacket and after
getting into it made himself heard while he looked for
his hat.

"Whereas the woman herself is, so to speak, priceless."

Mr. Blunt muttered the word "Obviously."

By then we were all on our feet. The iron stove
glowed no longer and the lamp, surrounded by empty
bottles and empty glasses, had grown dimmer.

I know that I had a great shiver on getting away from
the cushions of the divan.

"We will meet again in a few hours," said Mr. Blunt.
"Don't forget to come," he said, addressing me. "Oh,

yes, do. Have no scruples. I am authorized to make invitations."

He must have noticed my shyness, my surprise, my embarrassment. And indeed I didn't know what to say.

"I assure you there isn't anything incorrect in your coming," he insisted, with the greatest civility. "You will be introduced by two good friends, Mills and myself. Surely you are not afraid of a very charming woman. . . ."

I was not afraid, but my head swam a little and I only looked at him mutely.

"Lunch precisely at midday. Mills will bring you along. I am sorry you two are going. I shall throw myself on the bed for an hour or two, but I am sure I won't sleep."

He accompanied us along the passage into the black-and-white hall, where the low gas flame glimmered forlornly. When he opened the front door the cold blast of the mistral rushing down the street of the Consuls made me shiver to the very marrow of my bones.

Mills and I exchanged but a few words as we walked down towards the centre of the town. In the chill tempestuous dawn he strolled along musingly, disregarding the discomfort of the cold, the depressing influence of the hour, the desolation of the empty streets in which the dry dust rose in whirls in front of us, behind us, flew upon us from the side streets. The masks had gone home and our footsteps echoed on the flag-stones with unequal sound as of men without purpose, without hope.

"I suppose you will come," said Mills suddenly.

"I really don't know," I said.

"Don't you? Well, remember I am not trying to persuade you; but I am staying at the Hôtel de Louvre and I shall leave there at a quarter to twelve for that lunch. At a quarter to twelve, not a minute later. I suppose you can sleep?"

I laughed.

"Charming age, yours," said Mills, as we came out on the quays. Already dim figures of the workers moved in the biting dawn and the masted forms of ships were coming out dimly, as far as the eye could reach down the old harbour.

"Well," Mills began again, "you may oversleep yourself."

This suggestion was made in a cheerful tone, just as we shook hands at the lower end of the Cannebière. He looked very burly as he walked away from me. I went on towards my lodgings. My head was very full of confused images, but I was really too tired to think.

PART TWO

I

SOMETIMES I wonder yet whether Mills wished me to oversleep myself or not: that is, whether he really took sufficient interest to care. His uniform kindliness of manner made it impossible for me to tell. And I can hardly remember my own feelings. Did I care? The whole recollection of that time of my life has such a peculiar quality that the beginning and the end of it are merged in one sensation of profound emotion, continuous and overpowering, containing the extremes of exultation, full of careless joy and of an invincible sadness—like a day-dream. The sense of all this having been gone through as if in one great rush of imagination is all the stronger in the distance of time, because it had something of that quality even then: of fate unprovoked, of events that didn't cast any shadow before.

Not that those events were in the least extraordinary. They were, in truth, commonplace. What to my backward glance seems startling and a little awful is their punctualness and inevitability. Mills was punctual. Exactly at a quarter to twelve he appeared under the lofty portal of the Hôtel de Louvre, with his fresh face, his ill-fitting grey suit, and enveloped in his own sympathetic atmosphere.

How could I have avoided him? To this day I have a shadowy conviction of his inherent distinction of mind and heart, far beyond any man I have ever met since. He was unavoidable: and of course I never tried to avoid him. The first sight on which his eyes fell was a victoria pulled up before the hotel door, in which I sat with no sentiment I can remember now but that of some slight shyness. He got in without a moment's hesitation, his friendly glance took me in from head to foot and (such was his peculiar gift) gave me a pleasurable sensation.

After we had gone a little way I couldn't help saying to him with a bashful laugh: "You know, it seems very extraordinary that I should be driving out with you like this."

He turned to look at me and in his kind voice:

"You will find everything extremely simple," he said. "So simple that you will be quite able to hold your own. I suppose you know that the world is selfish, I mean the majority of the people in it, often unconsciously I must admit, and especially people with a mission, with a fixed idea, with some fantastic object in view, or even with only some fantastic illusion. That doesn't mean that they have no scruples. And I don't know that at this moment I myself am not one of them."

"That, of course, I can't say," I retorted.

"I haven't seen her for years," he said, "and in comparison with what she was then she must be very grown up by now. From what we heard from Mr. Blunt she had experiences which would have matured her more than they would teach her. There are of course people that are not teachable. I don't know that she is one of them. But as to maturity that's quite another thing. Capacity for suffering is developed in every human being worthy of the name."

"Captain Blunt doesn't seem to be a very happy person," I said. "He seems to have a grudge against everybody. People make him wince. The things they do, the things they say. He must be awfully mature."

Mills gave me a sidelong look. It met mine of the same character and we both smiled without openly looking at each other. At the end of the Rue de Rome the violent chilly breath of the mistral enveloped the victoria in a great widening of brilliant sunshine without heat. We turned to the right, circling at a stately pace about the rather mean obelisk which stands at the entrance to the Prado.

"I don't know whether you are mature or not," said Mills humorously. "But I think you will do. You . . ."

"Tell me," I interrupted, "what is really Captain Blunt's position there?"

And I nodded at the alley of the Prado opening before us between the rows of the perfectly leafless trees.

"Thoroughly false, I should think. It doesn't accord either with his illusions or his pretensions, or even with the real position he has in the world. And so what between his mother and the General Headquarters and the state of his own feelings he . . ."

"He is in love with her," I interrupted again.

"That wouldn't make it any easier. I'm not at all sure of that. But if so it can't be a very idealistic sentiment. All the warmth of his idealism is concentrated upon a certain 'Américain, Catholique et gentilhomme. . . .'"

The smile which for a moment dwelt on his lips was not unkind.

"At the same time he has a very good grip of the material conditions that surround, as it were, the situation."

"What do you mean? That Doña Rita" (the name came strangely familiar to my tongue) "is rich, that she has a fortune of her own?"

"Yes, a fortune," said Mills. "But it was Allègre's

fortune before. . . . And then there is Blunt's fortune: he lives by his sword. And there is the fortune of his mother, I assure you a perfectly charming, clever, and most aristocratic old lady, with the most distinguished connections. I really mean it. She doesn't live by her sword. She . . . she lives by her wits. I have a notion that those two dislike each other heartily at times. . . . Here we are."

The victoria stopped in the side alley, bordered by the low walls of private grounds. We got out before a wrought-iron gateway which stood half open and walked up a circular drive to the door of a large villa of a neglected appearance. The mistral howled in the sunshine, shaking the bare bushes quite furiously. And everything was bright and hard, the air was hard, the light was hard, the ground under our feet was hard.

The door at which Mills rang came open almost at once. The maid who opened it was short, dark, and slightly pockmarked. For the rest, an obvious "*femme-de-chambre*," and very busy. She said quickly, "Madame has just returned from her ride," and went up the stairs leaving us to shut the front door ourselves.

The staircase had a crimson carpet. Mr. Blunt appeared from somewhere in the hall. He was in riding breeches and a black coat with ample square skirts. This get-up suited him but it also changed him extremely by doing away with the effect of flexible slimness he produced in his evening clothes. He looked to me not at all himself but rather like a brother of the man who had been talking to us the night before. He carried about him a delicate perfume of scented soap. He gave us a flash of his white teeth and said:

"It's a perfect nuisance. We have just dismounted. I will have to lunch as I am. A lifelong habit of beginning her day on horseback. She pretends she is unwell unless she does. I daresay, when one thinks there has been hardly a day for five or six years that she didn't begin with a ride. That's the reason she is always rushing away from Paris where she can't go out in the morning alone. Here, of course, it's different. And as I, too, am a stranger here I can go out with her. Not that I particularly care to do it."

These last words were addressed to Mills specially, with the addition of a mumbled remark: "It's a confounded position." Then calmly to me with a swift smile: "We have been talking of you this morning. You are expected with impatience."

"Thank you very much," I said, "but I can't help asking myself what I am doing here."

The upward cast in the eyes of Mills who was facing the staircase made us both, Blunt and I, turn round. The woman of whom I had heard so much, in a sort of way in which I had never heard a woman spoken of before, was coming down the stairs, and my first sensation was that of profound astonishment at this evidence that she did really exist. And even then the visual impression was more of colour in a picture than of the forms of actual life. She was wearing a wrapper, a sort of dressing-gown of pale blue silk embroidered with black and gold designs round the neck and down the front, lapped round her and held together by a broad belt of the same material. Her slippers were of the same colour, with black bows at the instep. The white stairs, the deep crimson of the carpet, and the light blue of the dress made an effective combination of colour to set off the delicate carnation of that face, which, after the first glance given to the whole person, drew irresistibly your gaze to itself by an indefinable quality of charm beyond all analysis and made you think of remote races, of strange generations, of the faces of women sculptured on immemorial monuments and of those lying unsung in their tombs. While she moved downwards from step to step with slightly lowered eyes there flashed upon me suddenly the recollection of words heard at night, of Allègre's words about her, of there being in her "something of the women of all time."

At the last step she raised her eyelids, treated us to an exhibition of teeth as dazzling as Mr. Blunt's and looking even stronger; and indeed, as she approached us she brought home to our hearts (but after all I am speaking only for myself) a vivid sense of her physical perfection in beauty of limb and balance of nerves, and not so much of grace, probably, as of absolute harmony.

She said to us, "I am sorry I kept you waiting." Her voice was low pitched, penetrating, and of the most seductive gentleness. She offered her hand to Mills very frankly as to an old friend. Within the extraordinarily wide sleeve, lined with black silk, I could see the arm, very white, with a pearly gleam in the shadow. But to me she extended her hand with a slight stiffening, as it were a recoil of her person, combined with an extremely straight glance. It was a finely shaped, capable hand. I bowed over it, and we just touched fingers. I did not look then at her face.

Next moment she caught sight of some envelopes lying on the round marble-topped table in the middle of the hall. She seized one of them with a wonderfully quick, almost feline, movement and tore it open, saying to us, "Excuse me, I must . . . Do go into the dining-room. Captain Blunt, show the way."

Her widened eyes stared at the paper. Mr. Blunt threw one of the doors open, but before we passed through it we heard a petulant exclamation accompanied by childlike stamping with both feet and ending in a laugh which had in it a note of contempt.

The door closed behind us; we had been abandoned by Mr. Blunt. He had remained on the other side, possibly to soothe. The room in which we found ourselves was long like a gallery and ended in a rotunda with many windows. It was long enough for two fireplaces of red polished granite. A table laid out for four occupied very little space. The floor inlaid in two kinds of wood in a bizarre pattern was highly waxed, reflecting objects like still water.

Before very long Doña Rita and Blunt rejoined us and we sat down around the table; but before we could begin to talk a dramatically sudden ring at the front door stilled our incipient animation. Doña Rita looked at us all in turn, with surprise and, as it were, with suspicion. "How did he know I was here?" she whispered after looking at the card which was brought to her. She passed it to Blunt, who passed it to Mills, who made a faint grimace, dropped it on the table-cloth, and only whispered to me, "A journalist from Paris."

"He has run me to earth," said Doña Rita. "One would bargain for peace against hard cash if these fellows weren't always ready to snatch at one's very soul with the other hand. It frightens me."

Her voice floated mysterious and penetrating from her lips, which moved very little. Mills was watching her with sympathetic curiosity. Mr. Blunt muttered: "Better not make the brute angry." For a moment Doña Rita's face, with its narrow eyes, its wide brow, and high cheek bones, became very still; then her colour was a little heightened. "Oh," she said softly, "let him come in. He would be really dangerous if he had a mind—you know," she said to Mills.

The person who had provoked all those remarks and as much hesitation as though he had been some sort of wild beast astonished me on being admitted, first by the beauty of his white head of hair and then by his paternal aspect and the innocent simplicity of his manner. They laid a cover for him between Mills and Doña Rita, who quite openly removed the envelopes she had brought with her, to the other side of her plate. As openly the man's round china-blue eyes followed them in an attempt to make out the handwriting of the addresses.

He seemed to know, at least slightly, both Mills and Blunt. To me he gave a stare of stupid surprise. He addressed our hostess.

"Resting? Rest is a very good thing. Upon my word, I thought I would find you alone. But you have too much sense. Neither man nor woman has been created to live alone. . . ." After this opening he had all the talk to himself. It was left to him pointedly, and I verily believe that I was the only one who showed an appearance of interest. I couldn't help it. The others, including Mills, sat like a lot of deaf and dumb people. No. It was even something more detached. They sat rather like a very superior lot of waxworks, with the fixed but indetermined facial expression and with that odd air wax figures have of being aware of their existence being but a sham.

I was the exception; and nothing could have marked better my status of a stranger, the completest possible stranger in the moral region in which those people lived, moved, enjoying or suffering their incomprehensible emotions. I was as much of a stranger as the most hopeless castaway stumbling in the dark upon a hut of natives and finding them in the grip of some situation appertaining to the mentalities, prejudices, and problems of an undiscovered country—of a country of which he had not even had one single clear glimpse before.

It was even worse in a way. It ought to have been

more disconcerting. For, pursuing the image of the castaway blundering upon the complications of an unknown scheme of life, it was I, the castaway, who was the savage, the simple innocent child of nature. Those people were obviously more civilized than I was. They had more rites, more ceremonies, more complexity in their sensations, more knowledge of evil, more varied meanings to the subtle phrases of their language. Naturally! I was still so young! And yet I assure you that just then I lost all sense of inferiority. And why? Of course the carelessness and the ignorance of youth had something to do with that. But there was something else besides. Looking at Doña Rita, her head leaning on her hand, with her dark lashes lowered on the slightly flushed cheek, I felt no longer alone in my youth. That woman of whom I had heard these things I have set down with all the exactness of unfailing memory, that woman was revealed to me young, younger than anybody I had ever seen, as young as myself (and my sensation of my youth was then very acute); revealed with something peculiarly intimate in the conviction, as if she were young exactly in the same way in which I felt myself young; and that therefore no misunderstanding between us was possible and there could be nothing more for us to know about each other. Of course this sensation was momentary, but it was illuminating; it was a light which could not last, but it left no darkness behind. On the contrary it seemed to have kindled magically somewhere within me a glow of assurance, of unaccountable confidence in myself: a warm, steady, and eager sensation of my individual life beginning for good there, on that spot, in that sense of solidarity, in that seduction.

II

FOR this, properly speaking wonderful, reason I was the only one of the company who could listen without constraint to the unbidden guest with that fine head of white hair, so beautifully kept, so magnificently waved, so artistically arranged that respect could not be felt for it any more than for a very expensive wig in the window of a hair-dresser. In fact, I had an inclination to smile at it. This proves how unconstrained I felt. My mind was perfectly at liberty; and so of all the eyes in that room mine was the only pair able to look about in easy freedom. All the other listeners' eyes were cast down, including Mills' eyes, but that I am sure was only because of his perfect and delicate sympathy. He could not have been concerned otherwise.

The intruder devoured the cutlets—if they were cutlets. Notwithstanding my perfect liberty of mind I was not aware of what we were eating. I have a notion that the lunch was a mere show, except of course for the man with the white hair, who was really hungry and who, besides, must have had the pleasant sense of dominating the situation. He stooped over his plate and worked his jaw deliberately while his blue eyes rolled incessantly; but as a matter of fact he never looked openly at any one of us. Whenever he laid down his knife and fork he would throw himself back and start retailing in a light tone some Parisian gossip about prominent people.

He talked first about a certain politician of mark. His "dear Rita" knew him. His costume dated back

71

to '48, he was made of wood and parchment and still
swathed his neck in a white cloth; and even his wife
had never been seen in a low-necked dress. Not once
in her life. She was buttoned up to the chin like her
husband. Well, that man had confessed to him that
when he was engaged in political controversy, not on a
matter of principle but on some special measure in de-
bate, he felt ready to kill everybody.

He interrupted himself for a comment. "I am something like that myself. I believe it's a purely professional feeling. Carry one's point, whatever it is.
Normally I couldn't kill a fly. My sensibility is too
acute for that. My heart is too tender also. Much
too tender. I am a Republican. I am a Red. As to
all our present masters and governors, all those people
you are trying to turn round your little finger, they
are all horrible Royalists in disguise. They are plotting
the ruin of all the institutions to which I am devoted.
But I have never tried to spoil your little game, Rita.
After all, it's but a little game. You know very well
that two or three fearless articles, something in my
style, you know, would soon put a stop to all that underhand backing of your king. I am calling him king
because I want to be polite to you. He is an adventurer, a blood-thirsty, murderous adventurer, for me,
and nothing else. Look here, my dear child, what are
you knocking yourself about for? For the sake of that
bandit? *Allons donc!* A pupil of Henry Allègre can
have no illusions of that sort about any man. And
such a pupil, too! Ah, the good old days in the Pavilion!
Don't think I claim any particular intimacy. It was
just enough to enable me to offer my services to you,
Rita, when our poor friend died. I found myself
handy and so I came. It so happened that I was the
first. You remember, Rita? What made it possible

for everybody to get on with our poor dear Allègre
was his complete, equable, and impartial contempt for
all mankind. There is nothing in that against the
purest democratic principles; but that you, Rita,
should elect to throw so much of your life away for the
sake of a Royal adventurer, it really knocks me over.
For you don't love him. You never loved him, you
know."

He made a snatch at her hand, absolutely pulled it
away from under her head (it was quite startling) and
retaining it in his grasp, proceeded to a paternal patting
of the most impudent kind. She let him go on with
apparent insensibility. Meanwhile his eyes strayed
round the table over our faces. It was very trying.
The stupidity of that wandering stare had a paralyzing
power. He talked at large with husky familiarity.

"Here I come, expecting to find a good sensible girl
who had seen at last the vanity of all those things; half-
light in the rooms; surrounded by the works of her
favourite poets, and all that sort of thing. I say to myself: I must just run in and see the dear wise child, and
encourage her in her good resolutions. . . . And
I fall into the middle of an *intime* lunch-party. For
I suppose it is *intime*. . . . Eh? Very? H'm,
yes . . ."

He was really appalling. Again his wondering stare
went round the table, with an expression incredibly incongruous with the words. It was as though he had
borrowed those eyes from some idiot for the purpose of
that visit. He still held Doña Rita's hand, and, now
and then, patted it.

"It's discouraging," he cooed. "And I believe not
one of you here is a Frenchman. I don't know what
you are all about. It's beyond me. But if we were a
Republic—you know I am an old Jacobin, sans-culotte

and terrorist—if this were a real Republic with the Convention sitting and a Committee of Public Safety attending to national business, you would all get your heads cut off. Ha, ha . . . I am joking, ha, ha! . . . and serve you right, too. Don't mind my little joke."

While he was still laughing he released her hand and she leaned her head on it again without haste. She had never looked at him once.

During the rather humiliating silence that ensued he got a leather cigar case like a small valise out of his pocket, opened it and looked with critical interest at the, six cigars it contained. The tireless *femme-de-chambre* set down a tray with coffee cups on the table. We each (glad, I suppose, of something to do) took one, but he, to begin with, sniffed at his. Doña Rita continued leaning on her elbow, her lips closed in a reposeful expression of peculiar sweetness. There was nothing drooping in her attitude. Her face with the delicate carnation of a rose and downcast eyes was as if veiled in firm immobility and was so appealing that I had an insane impulse to walk round and kiss the forearm on which it was leaning; that strong, well-shaped forearm, gleaming not like marble but with a living and warm splendour. So familiar had I become already with her in my thoughts! Of course I didn't do anything of the sort. It was nothing uncontrollable, it was but a tender longing of a most respectful and purely sentimental kind. I performed the act in my thought quietly, almost solemnly, while the creature with the silver hair leaned back in his chair, puffing at his cigar, and began to speak again.

It was all apparently very innocent talk. He informed his "dear Rita" that he was really on his way to Monte Carlo. A lifelong habit of his at this time of the year; but he was ready to run back to Paris if he could do anything for his "*chère enfant*," run back for a day, for two days, for three days, for any time; miss Monte Carlo this year altogether, if he could be of the slightest use and save her going herself. For instance he could see to it that proper watch was kept over the Pavilion stuffed with all these art treasures. What was going to happen to all those things? . . . Making herself heard for the first time Doña Rita murmured without moving that she had made arrangements with the police to have it properly watched. And I was enchanted by the almost imperceptible play of her lips.

But the anxious creature was not reassured. He pointed out that things had been stolen out of the Louvre, which was, he dared say, even better watched. And there was that marvellous cabinet on the landing, black lacquer with silver herons, which alone would repay a couple of burglars. A wheelbarrow, some old sacking, and they could trundle it off under people's noses.

"Have you thought it all out?" she asked in a cold whisper, while we three sat smoking to give ourselves a countenance (it was certainly no enjoyment) and wondering what we would hear next.

No, he had not. But he confessed that for years and years he had been in love with that cabinet. And anyhow what *was* going to happen to the things? The world was greatly exercised by that problem. He turned slightly his beautifully groomed white head so as to address Mr. Blunt directly.

"I had the pleasure of meeting your mother lately."

Mr. Blunt took his time to raise his eyebrows and flash his teeth at him before he dropped negligently, "I can't imagine where you could have met my mother."

"Why, at Bing's the curio-dealer," said the other

with an air of the heaviest possible stupidity. And yet there was something in these few words which seemed to imply that if Mr. Blunt was looking for trouble he would certainly get it. "Bing was bowing her out of his shop, but he was so angry about something that he was quite rude even to me afterwards. I don't think it's very good for *Madame votre mère* to quarrel with Bing. He is a Parisian personality. He's quite a power in his sphere. All these fellows' nerves are upset from worry as to what will happen to the Allègre collection. And no wonder they are nervous. A big art event hangs on your lips, my dear, great Rita. And by the way, you too ought to remember that it isn't wise to quarrel with people. What have you done to that poor Azzolati? Did you really tell him to get out and never come near you again, or something awful like that? I don't doubt that he was of use to you or to your king. A man who gets invitations to shoot with the President at Rambouillet! I saw him only the other evening; I heard he had been winning immensely at cards; but he looked perfectly wretched, the poor fellow. He complained of your conduct—oh, very much! He told me you had been perfectly brutal with him. He said to me: 'I am no good for anything, *mon cher*. The other day at Rambouillet, whenever I had a hare at the end of my gun I would think of her cruel words and my eyes would run full of tears. I missed every shot' . . . You are not fit for diplomatic work, you know, *ma chère*. You are a mere child at it. When you want a middle-aged gentleman to do anything for you, you don't begin by reducing him to tears. I should have thought any woman would have known that much. A nun would have known that much. What do you say? Shall I run back to Paris and make it up for you with Azzolati?"

He waited for her answer. The compression of his thin lips was full of significance. I was surprised to see our hostess shake her head negatively the least bit, for indeed by her pose, by the thoughtful immobility of her face she seemed to be a thousand miles away from us all, lost in an infinite reverie.

He gave it up. "Well, I must be off. The express for Nice passes at four o'clock. I will be away about three weeks and then you shall see me again. Unless I strike a run of bad luck and get cleaned out, in which case you shall see me before then."

He turned to Mills suddenly.

"Will your cousin come south this year, to that beautiful villa of his at Cannes?"

Mills hardly deigned to answer that he didn't know anything about his cousin's movements.

"A *grand seigneur* combined with a great connoisseur," opined the other heavily. His mouth had gone slack and he looked a perfect and grotesque imbecile under his wiglike crop of white hair. Positively I thought he would begin to slobber. But he attacked Blunt next.

"Are you on your way down, too? A little flutter. . . . It seems to me you haven't been seen in your usual Paris haunts of late. Where have you been all this time?"

"Don't you know where I have been?" said Mr. Blunt with great precision.

"No, I only ferret out things that may be of some use to me," was the unexpected reply, uttered with an air of perfect vacancy and swallowed by Mr. Blunt in blank silence.

At last he made ready to rise from the table. "Think over what I have said, my dear Rita."

"It's all over and done with," was Doña Rita's answer, in a louder tone than I had ever heard her use before. It thrilled me while she continued: "I mean, this thinking." She was back from the remoteness of her meditation, very much so indeed. She rose and moved away from the table, inviting by a sign the other to follow her; which he did at once, yet slowly and as it were warily.

It was a conference in the recess of a window. We three remained seated round the table from which the dark maid was removing the cups and the plates with brusque movements. I gazed frankly at Doña Rita's profile, irregular, animated, and fascinating in an undefinable way, at her well-shaped head with the hair twisted high up and apparently held in its place by a gold arrow with a jewelled shaft. We couldn't hear what she said, but the movement of her lips and the play of her features were full of charm, full of interest, expressing both audacity and gentleness. She spoke with fire without raising her voice. The man listened round-shouldered, but seeming much too stupid to understand. I could see now and then that he was speaking, but he was inaudible. At one moment Doña Rita turned her head to the room and called out to the maid, "Give me my hand-bag off the sofa."

At this the other was heard plainly, "No, no," and then a little lower, "You have no tact, Rita. . . ." Then came her argument in a low, penetrating voice which I caught, "Why not? Between such old friends." However, she waved away the hand-bag, he calmed down, and their voices sank again. Presently I saw him raise her hand to his lips, while with her back to the room she continued to contemplate out of the window the bare and untidy garden. At last he went out of the room, throwing to the table an airy "*Bonjour, bonjour*," which was not acknowledged by any of us three.

III

Mills got up and approached the figure at the window. To my extreme surprise, Mr. Blunt, after a moment of obviously painful hesitation, hastened out after the man with the white hair.

In consequence of these movements I was left to myself and I began to be uncomfortably conscious of it when Doña Rita, near the window, addressed me in a raised voice.

"We have no confidences to exchange, Mr. Mills and I."

I took this for an encouragement to join them. They were both looking at me. Doña Rita added, "Mr. Mills and I are friends from old times, you know."

Bathed in the softened reflection of the sunshine, which did not fall directly into the room, standing very straight with her arms down, before Mills, and with a faint smile directed to me, she looked extremely young, and yet mature. There was even, for a moment, a slight dimple in her cheek.

"How old, I wonder?" I said, with an answering smile.

"Oh, for ages, for ages," she exclaimed hastily, frowning a little, then she went on addressing herself to Mills, apparently in continuation of what she was saying before. . . . "This man's is an extreme case, and yet perhaps it isn't the worst. But that's the sort of thing. I have no account to render to anybody, but I don't want to be dragged along all the gutters where that man picks up his living."

She had thrown her head back a little but there was

no scorn, no angry flash under the dark-lashed eyelids. The words did not ring. I was struck for the first time by the even, mysterious quality of her voice.

"Will you let me suggest," said Mills, with a grave, kindly face, "that being what you are, you have nothing to fear?"

"And perhaps nothing to lose," she went on without bitterness. "No. It isn't fear. It's a sort of dread. You must remember that no nun could have had a more protected life. Henry Allègre had his greatness. When he faced the world he also masked it. He was big enough for that. He filled the whole field of vision for me."

"You found that enough?" asked Mills.

"Why ask now?" she remonstrated. "The truth— the truth is that I never asked myself. Enough or not there was no room for anything else. He was the shadow and the light and the form and the voice. He would have it so. The morning he died they came to call me at four o'clock. I ran into his room bare-footed. He recognized me and whispered, 'You are flawless.' I was very frightened. He seemed to think, and then said very plainly, 'Such is my character. I am like that.' These were the last words he spoke. I hardly noticed them then. I was thinking that he was lying in a very uncomfortable position and I asked him if I should lift him up a little higher on the pillows. You know I am very strong. I could have done it. I had done it before. He raised his hand off the blanket just enough to make a sign that he didn't want to be touched. It was the last gesture he made. I hung over him and then—and then I nearly ran out of the house just as I was, in my nightgown. I think if I had been dressed I would have run out of the garden, into the street—run away altogether. I had never seen

death. I may say I had never heard of it. I wanted
to run from it."

She paused for a long, quiet breath. The harmon-
ized sweetness and daring of her face was made pathetic
by her downcast eyes.

"*Fuir la mort*," she repeated, meditatively in her
mysterious voice.

Mills' big head had a little movement, nothing more.
Her glance glided for a moment towards me like a
friendly recognition of my right to be there, before she
began again.

"My life might have been described as looking at
mankind from a fourth-floor window for years. When
the end came it was like falling out of a balcony into the
street. It was as sudden as that. Once I remember
somebody was telling us in the Pavilion a tale about a
girl who jumped down from a fourth-floor window.
. . . For love, I believe," she interjected very
quickly, "and came to no harm. Her guardian angel
must have slipped his wings under her just in time. He
must have. But as to me, all I know is that I didn't
break anything—not even my heart. Don't be shocked,
Mr. Mills. It's very likely that you don't understand."

"Very likely," Mills assented, unmoved. "But
don't be too sure of that."

"Henry Allègre had the highest opinion of your intelligence," she said unexpectedly and with evident
seriousness. "But all this is only to tell you that when
he was gone I found myself down there unhurt, but
dazed, bewildered, not sufficiently stunned. It so
happened that that creature was somewhere in the
neighbourhood. How he found out. . . . But
it's his business to find out things. And he knows,
too, how to worm his way in anywhere. Indeed,
in the first days he was useful and somehow he made

it look as if Heaven itself had sent him. In my distress I thought I could never sufficiently repay. . . . Well, I have been paying ever since."

"What do you mean?" asked Mills softly. "In hard cash?"

"Oh, it's really so little," she said. "I told you it wasn't the worst case. I stayed on in that house from which I nearly ran away in my nightgown. I stayed on because I didn't know what to do next. He vanished as he had come on the track of something else, I suppose. You know he really has got to get his living some way or other. But don't think I was deserted. On the contrary. People were coming and going, all sorts of people that Henry Allègre used to know—or had refused to know. I had a sensation of plotting and intriguing around me all the time. I was feeling morally bruised, sore all over, when, one day, Don Rafael de Villarel sent in his card. A grandee. I didn't know him, but, as you are aware, there was hardly a personality of mark or position that hasn't been talked about in the Pavilion before me. Of him I had only heard that he was a very austere and pious person, always at Mass, and that sort of thing. I saw a frail little man with a long, yellow face and sunken fanatical eyes, an Inquisitor, an unfrocked monk. One missed a rosary from his thin fingers. He gazed at me terribly and I couldn't imagine what he might want. I waited for him to pull out a crucifix and sentence me to the stake there and then. But no; he dropped his eyes and in a cold, righteous sort of voice informed me that he had called on behalf of the Prince—he called him his Majesty. I was amazed by the change. I wondered now why he didn't slip his hands into the sleeves of his coat, you know, as begging Friars do, when they come for a subscription. He explained that the Prince

asked for permission to call and offer me his condolences
in person. We had seen a lot of him our last two
months in Paris that year. Henry Allègre had taken
a fancy to paint his portrait. He used to ride with us
nearly every morning. Almost without thinking I said
I should be pleased. Don Rafael was shocked at my
want of formality, but bowed to me in silence, very
much as a monk bows, from the waist. If he had only
crossed his hands flat on his chest it would have been
perfect. Then, I don't know why, something moved
me to make him a deep curtsy as he backed out of the
room, leaving me suddenly impressed, not only with
him but with myself too. I had my door closed to
everybody else that afternoon and the Prince came with
a very proper sorrowful face, but five minutes after
he got into the room he was laughing as usual, made
the whole little house ring with it. You know his big,
irresistible laugh. . . ."

"No," said Mills, a little abruptly, "I have never seen
him."

"No," she said, surprised, "and yet you . . ."

"I understand," interrupted Mills. "All this is
purely accidental. You must know that I am a solitary man of books but with a secret taste for adventure
which somehow came out; surprising even me."

She listened with that enigmatic, still, under the eyelids glance, and a friendly turn of the head.

"I know you for a frank and loyal gentleman. . . .
Adventure—and books? Ah, the books! Haven't I
turned stacks of them over! Haven't I? . . ."

"Yes," murmured Mills. "That's what one does."

She put out her hand and laid it lightly on Mills' sleeve.

"Listen, I don't need to justify myself, but if I had
known a single woman in the world, if I had only had the
opportunity to observe a single one of them, I would

have been perhaps on my guard. But you know I
hadn't. The only woman I had anything to do with
was myself, and they say that one can't know oneself.
It never entered my head to be on my guard against his
warmth and his terrible obviousness. You and he were
the only two, infinitely different, people, who didn't
approach me as if I had been a precious object in a
collection, an ivory carving or a piece of Chinese porce-
lain. That's why I have kept you in my memory so
well. Oh! you were not obvious! As to him—I soon
learned to regret I was not some object, some beautiful,
carved object of bone or bronze; a rare piece of porce-
lain, *pâte dure*, not *pâte tendre*. A pretty specimen."

"Rare, yes. Even unique," said Mills, looking at
her steadily with a smile. "But don't try to depreciate
yourself. You were never pretty. You are not pretty.
You are worse."

Her narrow eyes had a mischievous gleam. "Do you
find such sayings in your books?" she asked.

"As a matter of fact I have," said Mills, with a little
laugh, "found this one in a book. It was a woman who
said that of herself. A woman far from common, who
died some few years ago. She was an actress. A great
artist."

"A great! . . . Lucky person! She had that
refuge, that garment, while I stand here with nothing
to protect me from evil fame; a naked temperament
for any wind to blow upon. Yes, greatness in art is a
protection. I wonder if there would have been anything in me if I had tried? But Henry Allègre would
never let me try. He told me that whatever I could
achieve would never be good enough for what I was.
The perfection of flattery! Was it that he thought I
had not talent of any sort? It's possible. He would
know. I've had the idea since that he was jealous.

He wasn't jealous of mankind any more than he was afraid of thieves for his collection; but he may have been jealous of what he could see in me, of some passion that could be aroused. But if so he never repented. I shall never forget his last words. He saw me standing beside his bed, defenceless, symbolic and forlorn, and all he found to say was, 'Well, I am like that.'"

I forgot myself in watching her. I had never seen anybody speak with less play of facial muscles. In the fullness of its life her face preserved a sort of immobility. The words seemed to form themselves, fiery or pathetic, in the air, outside her lips. Their design was hardly disturbed; a design of sweetness, gravity, and force as if born from the inspiration of some artist; for I had never seen anything to come up to it in nature before or since.

All this was part of the enchantment she cast over me; and I seemed to notice that Mills had the aspect of a man under a spell. If he too was a captive then I had no reason to feel ashamed of my surrender.

"And you know," she began again abruptly, "that I have been accustomed to all the forms of respect."

"That's true," murmured Mills, as if involuntarily.

"Well, yes," she reaffirmed. "My instinct may have told me that my only protection was obscurity, but I didn't know how and where to find it. Oh, yes, I had that instinct . . . But there were other instincts and . . . How am I to tell you? I didn't know how to be on guard against myself, either. Not a soul to speak to, or to get a warning from. Some woman soul that would have known, in which perhaps I could have seen my own reflection. I assure you the only woman that ever addressed me directly, and that was in writing, was . . ."

She glanced aside, saw Mr. Blunt returning from the hall and added rapidly in a lowered voice,

"His mother."

The bright, mechanical smile of Mr. Blunt gleamed at us right down the room, but he didn't, as it were, follow it in his body. He swerved to the nearest of the two big fireplaces and finding some cigarettes on the mantelpiece remained leaning on his elbow in the warmth of the bright wood fire. I noticed then a bit of mute play. The heiress of Henry Allègre, who could secure neither obscurity nor any other alleviation to that invidious position, looked as if she would speak to Blunt from a distance; but in a moment the confident eagerness of her face died out as if killed by a sudden thought. I didn't know then her shrinking from all falsehood and evasion; her dread of insincerity and disloyalty of every kind. But even then I felt that at the very last moment her being had recoiled before some shadow of a suspicion. And it occurred to me, too, to wonder what sort of business Mr. Blunt could have had to transact with our odious visitor, of a nature so urgent as to make him run out after him into the hall? Unless to beat him a little with one of the sticks that were to be found there? White hair so much like an expensive wig could not be considered a serious protection. But it couldn't have been that. The transaction, whatever it was, had been much too quiet. I must say that none of us had looked out of the window and that I didn't know when the man did go or if he was gone at all. As a matter of fact he was already far away; and I may just as well say here that I never saw him again in my life. His passage across my field of vision was like that of other figures of that time: not to be forgotten, a little fantastic, infinitely enlightening for my contempt, darkening for my memory which struggles still with the clear lights and the ugly shadows of those unforgotten days.

IV

It was past four o'clock before I left the house, together with Mills. Mr. Blunt, still in his riding costume, escorted us to the very door. He asked us to send him the first fiacre we met on our way to town. "It's impossible to walk in this get-up through the streets," he remarked, with his brilliant smile.

At this point I propose to transcribe some notes I made at the time in little black books which I have hunted up in the litter of the past; very cheap, common little note-books that by the lapse of years have acquired a touching dimness of aspect, the frayed, worn-out dignity of documents.

Expression on paper has never been my forte. My life had been a thing of outward manifestations. I never had been secret or even systematically taciturn about my simple occupations which might have been foolish but had never required either caution or mystery. But in those four hours since midday a complete change had come over me. For good or evil I left that house committed to an enterprise that could not be talked about; which would have appeared to many senseless and perhaps ridiculous, but was certainly full of risks, and, apart from that, commanded discretion on the ground of simple loyalty. It would not only close my lips but it would to a certain extent cut me off from my usual haunts and from the society of my friends; especially of the light-hearted, young, harum-scarum kind. This was unavoidable. It was because I felt myself thrown back upon my own thoughts and forbidden to seek relief amongst other lives—it was perhaps only for that reason at first that I started an irregular, fragmentary record of my days.

I made these notes not so much to preserve the memory (one cared not for any to-morrow then) but to help me to keep a better hold of the actuality. I scribbled them on shore and I scribbled them on the sea; and in both cases they are concerned not only with the nature of the facts but with the intensity of my sensations. It may be, too, that I learned to love the sea for itself only at that time. Woman and the sea revealed themselves to me together, as it were: two mistresses of life's values. The illimitable greatness of the one, the unfathomable seduction of the other working their immemorial spells from generation to generation fell upon my heart at last; a common fortune, an unforgettable memory of the sea's formless might and of the sovereign charm in that woman's form wherein there seemed to beat the pulse of divinity rather than blood.

I begin here with the notes written at the end of that very day.

—Parted with Mills on the quay. We had walked side by side in absolute silence. The fact is he is too old for me to talk to him freely. For all his sympathy and seriousness I don't know what note to strike and I am not at all certain what he thinks of all this. As we shook hands at parting, I asked him how much longer he expected to stay. And he answered me that it depended on R. She was making arrangements for him to cross the frontier. He wanted to see the very ground on which the Principle of Legitimacy was actually asserting itself arms in hand. It sounded to my positive mind the most fantastic thing in the world, this elimination of personalities from what seemed but the merest political, dynastic adventure. So it wasn't Doña Rita, it wasn't Blunt, it wasn't the Pretender with his big infectious laugh, it wasn't all that lot of politicians, archbishops, and generals, of monks, guerrilleros, and smugglers by sea and land, of dubious agents and shady speculators and undoubted swindlers, who were pushing their fortunes at the risk of their precious skins. No. It was the Legitimist Principle asserting itself! Well, I would accept the view but with one reservation. All the others might have been merged into the idea, but I, the latest recruit, I would not be merged in the Legitimist Principle. Mine was an act of independent assertion. Never before had I felt so intensely aware of my personality. But I said nothing of that to Mills. I only told him I thought we had better not be seen very often together in the streets. He agreed. Hearty handshake. Looked affectionately after his broad back. It never occurred to him to turn his head. What was I in comparison with the Principle of Legitimacy?

Late that night I went in search of Dominic. That Mediterranean sailor was just the man I wanted. He had a great experience of all unlawful things that can be done on the seas and he brought to the practice of them much wisdom and audacity. That I didn't know where he lived was nothing since I knew where he loved. The proprietor of a small, quiet café on the quay, a certain Madame Léonore, a woman of thirty-five with an open Roman face and intelligent black eyes, had captivated his heart years ago. In that café with our heads close together over a marble table, Dominic and I held an earnest and endless confabulation while Madame Léonore, rustling a black silk skirt, with gold earrings, with her raven hair elaborately dressed and something nonchalant in her movements, would take occasion, in passing to and fro, to rest her hand for a moment on Dominic's shoulder. Later when the little café had emptied itself of its habitual customers, mostly people connected with the work of ships and cargoes, she came quietly to sit at our table and looking at me very hard with her black, sparkling eyes asked Dominic familiarly what had happened to his Signorino. It was her name for me. I was Dominic's Signorino. She knew me by no other; and our connection has always been somewhat a riddle to her. She said that I was somehow changed since she saw me last. In her rich voice she urged Dominic only to look at my eyes. I must have had some piece of luck come to me either in love or at cards, she bantered. But Dominic answered half in scorn that I was not of the sort that runs after that kind of luck. He stated generally that there were some young gentlemen very clever in inventing new ways of getting rid of their time and their money. However, if they needed a sensible man to help them he had no objection himself to lend a hand. Dominic's general scorn for the beliefs, and activities, and abilities of upper-class people covered the Principle of Legitimacy amply; but he could not resist the opportunity to exercise his special faculties in a field he knew of old. He had been a desperate smuggler in his younger days. We settled the purchase of a fast sailing craft. Agreed that it must be a balancelle and something altogether out of the common. He knew of one suitable but she was in Corsica. Offered to start for Bastia by mail-boat in the morning. All the time the handsome and mature Madame Léonore sat by, smiling faintly, amused at her great man joining like this in a frolic of boys. She said the last words of that evening: "You men never grow up," touching lightly the grey hair above his temple.

A fortnight later.

. . . In the afternoon to the Prado. Beautiful day. At the moment of ringing at the door a strong emotion of an anxious kind. Why? Down the length of the dining-room in the rotunda part full of afternoon light Doña R., sitting cross-legged on the divan in the attitude of a very old idol or a very young child and surrounded by many cushions, waves her hand from afar pleasantly surprised, exclaiming: "What! Back already!" I give her all the details and we talk for two hours across a large brass bowl containing a little water placed between us, lighting cigarettes and dropping them, innumerable, puffed at, yet untasted in the overwhelming interest of the conversation. Found her very quick in taking the points and very intelligent in her suggestions. All formality soon vanished between us and before very long I discovered myself sitting cross-legged, too, while I held forth on the qualities of different Mediterranean sailing craft and on the romantic qualifications of Dominic for the task. I believe I gave her the whole history of the man, mentioning even the existence of Madame Léonore, since the little café would have to be the headquarters of the marine part of the plot.

She murmured, "*Ah! Une belle Romaine,*" thoughtfully. She told me that she liked to hear people of that sort spoken of in terms of our common humanity. She observed also that she wished to see Dominic some day; to set her eyes for once on a man who could be absolutely depended on. She wanted to know whether he had engaged himself in this adventure solely for my sake.

I said that no doubt it was partly that. We had been very close associates in the West Indies from where we had returned together, and he had a notion that I could be depended on, too. But mainly, I suppose, it was

from taste. And there was in him also a fine carelessness as to what he did and a love of venturesome enterprise.

"And you," she said. "Is it carelessness, too?"

"In a measure," I said. "Within limits."

"And very soon you will get tired."

"When I do I will tell you. But I may also get
frightened. I suppose you know there are risks, I mean
apart from the risk of life."

"As for instance," she said.

"For instance, being captured, tried, and sentenced
to what they call 'the galleys,' in Ceuta."

"And all this from that love for . . ."

"Not for Legitimacy," I interrupted the inquiry
lightly. "But what's the use asking such questions?
It's like asking the veiled figure of fate. It doesn't
know its own mind nor its own heart. It has no heart.
But what if I were to start asking you—who have a
heart and are not veiled to my sight?" She dropped
her charming adolescent head, so firm in modelling, so
gentle in expression. Her uncovered neck was round
like the shaft of a column. She wore the same wrapper
of thick blue silk. At that time she seemed to live
either in her riding habit or in that wrapper folded
tightly round her and open low to a point in front.
Because of the absence of all trimming round the neck
and from the deep view of her bare arms in the wide
sleeve this garment seemed to be put directly on her
skin and gave one the impression of one's nearness
to her body which would have been troubling but for
the perfect unconsciousness of her manner. That day
she carried no barbarous arrow in her hair. It was
parted on one side, brushed back severely, and tied with
a black ribbon, without any bronze mist about her
forehead or temple. This smoothness added to the

many varieties of her expression also that of child-like
innocence.

Great progress in our intimacy brought about unconsciously by our enthusiastic interest in the matter of our
discourse and, in the moments of silence, by the sympathetic current of our thoughts. And this rapidly
growing familiarity (truly, she had a terrible gift for it)
had all the varieties of earnestness; serious, excited,
ardent, and even gay. She laughed in contralto; but
her laugh was never very long; and when it had ceased,
the silence of the room with the light dying in all its
many windows seemed to lie about me warmed by its
vibration.

As I was preparing to take my leave after a longish
pause into which we had fallen as into a vague dream,
she came out of it with a start and a quiet sigh. She
said, "I had forgotten myself." I took her hand and
was raising it naturally, without premeditation, when
I felt suddenly the arm to which it belonged become
insensible, passive, like a stuffed limb, and the whole
woman go inanimate all over! Brusquely I dropped
the hand before it reached my lips; and it was so lifeless
that it fell heavily on to the divan.

I remained standing before her. She raised to me not
her eyes but her whole face, inquisitively—perhaps in
appeal.

"No! This isn't good enough for me," I said.

The last of the light gleamed in her long enigmatic
eyes as if they were precious enamel in that shadowy
head which in its immobility suggested a creation of
a distant past: immortal art, not transient life. Her
voice had a profound quietness. She excused herself.

"It's only habit—or instinct—or what you like. I
have had to practice that in self-defence lest I should be
tempted sometimes to cut the arm off."

I remembered the way she had abandoned this very arm and hand to the white-haired ruffian. It rendered me gloomy and idiotically obstinate.

"Very ingenious. But this sort of thing is of no use to me," I declared.

"Make it up," suggested her mysterious voice, while her shadowy figure remained unmoved, indifferent amongst the cushions.

I didn't stir either. I refused in the same low tone.

"No. Not before you give it to me yourself, some day."

"Yes—some day," she repeated in a breath in which there was no irony but rather hesitation, reluctance— what did I know?

I walked away from the house in a curious state of gloomy satisfaction with myself.

And this is the last extract. A month afterwards.

—This afternoon going up to the Villa I was for the first time accompanied in my way by some misgivings. To-morrow I sail.

First trip and therefore in the nature of a trial trip; and I can't overcome a certain gnawing emotion, for it is a trip that *mustn't* fail. In that sort of enterprise there is no room for mistakes. Of all the individuals engaged in it will every one be intelligent enough, faithful enough, bold enough? Looking upon them as a whole it seems impossible; but as each has got only a limited part to play they may be found sufficient each for his particular trust. And will they be all punctual, I wonder? An enterprise that hangs on the punctuality of many people, no matter how well disposed and even heroic, hangs on a thread. This I have perceived to be also the greatest of Dominic's concerns. He, too, wonders. And when he breathes his doubts the smile lurking under the dark curl of his moustaches is not reassuring.

But there is also something exciting in such speculations and the road to the Villa seemed to me shorter than ever before.

Let in by the silent, ever-active, dark lady's maid, who is always on the spot and always on the way somewhere else, opening the door with one hand, while she passes on, turning on one for a moment her quick, black eyes, which just miss being lustrous, as if someone had breathed on them lightly.

On entering the long room I perceive Mills established in an armchair which he had dragged in front of the divan. I do the same to another and there we sit side by side facing R., tenderly amiable yet somehow distant among her cushions, with an immemorial seriousness in her long, shaded eyes and her fugitive smile hovering about but never settling on her lips. Mills, who is just back from over the frontier, must have been asking R. whether she had been worried again by her devoted friend with the white hair. At least I concluded so because I found them talking of the heart-broken Azzolati. And after having answered their greetings I sit and listen to Rita addressing Mills earnestly.

"No, I assure you Azzolati had done nothing to me. I knew him. He was a frequent visitor at the Pavilion, though I, personally, never talked with him very much in Henry Allègre's lifetime. Other men were more interesting, and he himself was rather reserved in his manner to me. He was an international politician and financier—a nobody. He, like many others, was admitted only to feed and amuse Henry Allègre's scorn of the world, which was insatiable—I tell you."

"Yes," said Mills. "I can imagine."

"But I know. Often when we were alone Henry

Allègre used to pour it into my ears. If ever anybody saw mankind stripped of its clothes as the child sees the king in the German fairy tale, it's I! Into my ears! A child's! Too young to die of fright. Certainly not old enough to understand—or even to believe. But then his arm was about me. I used to laugh, sometimes. Laugh! At this destruction—at these ruins!"

"Yes," said Mills, very steady before her fire. "But you have at your service the everlasting charm of life; you are a part of the indestructible."

"Am I? . . . But there is no arm about me now. The laugh! Where is my laugh? Give me back my laugh. . . ."

And she laughed a little on a low note. I don't know about Mills, but the subdued shadowy vibration of it echoed in my breast which felt empty for a moment and like a large space that makes one giddy.

"The laugh is gone out of my heart, which at any rate used to feel protected. That feeling's gone, too. And I myself will have to die some day."

"Certainly," said Mills in an unaltered voice. "As to this body you. . . ."

"Oh, yes! Thanks. It's a very poor jest. Change from body to body as travellers used to change horses at post houses. I've heard of this before. . . ."

"I've no doubt you have," Mills put on a submissive air. "But are we to hear any more about Azzolati?"

"You shall. Listen. I had heard that he was invited to shoot at Rambouillet—a quiet party, not one of these great shoots. I hear a lot of things. I wanted to have a certain information, also certain hints conveyed to a diplomatic personage who was to be there, too. A personage that would never let me get in touch with him though I had tried many times."

"Incredible!" mocked Mills solemnly.

"The personage mistrusts his own susceptibility.
Born cautious," explained Doña Rita crisply with the
slightest possible quiver of her lips. "Suddenly I
had the inspiration to make use of Azzolati, who had
been reminding me by a constant stream of messages
that he was an old friend. I never took any notice
of those pathetic appeals before. But in this emer-
gency I sat down and wrote a note asking him to come
and dine with me in my hotel. I suppose you know
I don't live in the Pavilion. I can't bear the Pavilion
now. When I have to go there I begin to feel after an
hour or so that it is haunted. I seem to catch sight of
somebody I know behind columns, passing through
doorways, vanishing here and there. I hear light
footsteps behind closed doors. . . . My own!"

Her eyes, her half-parted lips, remained fixed till
Mills suggested softly, "Yes, but Azzolati."

Her rigidity vanished like a flake of snow in the sunshine. "Oh! Azzolati. It was a most solemn affair.
It had occurred to me to make a very elaborate toilet.
It was most successful. Azzolati looked positively
scared for a moment as though he had got into the
wrong suite of rooms. He had never before seen me
en toilette, you understand. In the old days once out
of my riding habit I would never dress. I draped myself, you remember, Monsieur Mills. To go about
like that suited my indolence, my longing to feel free
in my body, as at that time when I used to herd goats.
. . . But never mind. My aim was to impress
Azzolati. I wanted to talk to him seriously."

There was something whimsical in the quick beat of
her eyelids and in the subtle quiver of her lips. "And
behold! the same notion had occurred to Azzolati.
Imagine that for this tête-à-tête dinner the creature
had got himself up as if for a reception at court. He

displayed a brochette of all sorts of decorations on the lapel of his *frac* and had a broad ribbon of some order across his shirt front. An orange ribbon. Bavarian, I should say. Great Roman Catholic, Azzolati. It was always his ambition to be the banker of all the Bourbons in the world. The last remnants of his hair were dyed jet black and the ends of his moustache were like knitting needles. He was disposed to be as soft as wax in my hands. Unfortunately I had had some irritating interviews during the day. I was keeping down sudden impulses to smash a glass, throw a plate on the floor, do something violent to relieve my feelings. His submissive attitude made me still more nervous. He was ready to do anything in the world for me providing that I would promise him that he would never find my door shut against him as long as he lived. You understand the impudence of it, don't you? And his tone was positively abject, too. I snapped back at him that I had no door, that I was a nomad. He bowed ironically till his nose nearly touched his plate but begged me to remember that to his personal knowledge I had four houses of my own about the world. And you know this made me feel a homeless outcast more than ever—like a little dog lost in the street—not knowing where to go. I was ready to cry and there the creature sat in front of me with an imbecile smile as much as to say 'here is a poser for you. . . .' I gnashed my teeth at him. Quietly, you know . . . I suppose you two think that I am stupid."

She paused as if expecting an answer but we made no sound and she continued with a remark.

"I have days like that. Often one must listen to false protestations, empty words, strings of lies all day long, so that in the evening one is not fit for anything, not even for truth if it comes in one's way. That idiot

treated me to a piece of brazen sincerity which I
couldn't stand. First of all he began to take me into
his confidence; he boasted of his great affairs, then
started groaning about his overstrained life which left
him no time for the amenities of existence, for beauty,
or sentiment, or any sort of ease of heart. His heart!
He wanted me to sympathize with his sorrows. Of
course I ought to have listened. One must pay for
service. Only I was nervous and tired. He bored me.
I told him at last that I was surprised that a man of such
immense wealth should still keep on going like this
reaching for more and more. I suppose he must have
been sipping a good deal of wine while we talked and
all at once he let out an atrocity which was too much
for me. He had been moaning and sentimentalizing
but then suddenly he showed me his fangs. 'No,'
he cries, 'you can't imagine what a satisfaction it is to
feel all that penniless, beggarly lot of the dear, honest,
meritorious poor wriggling and slobbering under one's
boots.' You may tell me that he is a contemptible
animal anyhow, but you should have heard the tone!
I felt my bare arms go cold like ice. A moment before
I had been hot and faint with sheer boredom. I
jumped up from the table, rang for Rose, and told her
to bring me my fur cloak. He remained in his chair
leering at me curiously. When I had the fur on my
shoulders and the girl had gone out of the room I gave
him the surprise of his life. 'Take yourself off instantly,' I said. 'Go trample on the poor if you like
but never dare speak to me again.' At this he leaned
his head on his arm and sat so long at the table shading
his eyes with his hand that I had to ask, calmly—you
know—whether he wanted me to have him turned out
into the corridor. He fetched an enormous sigh. 'I
have only tried to be honest with you, Rita.' But by

the time he got to the door he had regained some of his impudence. 'You know how to trample on a poor fellow, too,' he said. 'But I don't mind being made to wriggle under your pretty shoes, Rita. I forgive you. I thought you were free from all vulgar sentimentalism and that you had a more independent mind. I was mistaken in you, that's all.' With that he pretends to dash a tear from his eye—crocodile!—and goes out, leaving me in my fur by the blazing fire, my teeth going like castanets. . . . Did you ever hear of anything so stupid as this affair?" she concluded in a tone of extreme candour and a profound unreadable stare that went far beyond us both. And the stillness of her lips was so perfect directly she ceased speaking that I wondered whether all this had come through them or only had formed itself in my mind.

Presently she continued as if speaking for herself only.

"It's like taking the lids off boxes and seeing ugly toads staring at you. In every one. Every one. That's what it is having to do with men more than mere—Good morning—Good evening. And if you try to avoid meddling with their lids, some of them will take them off themselves. And they don't even know, they don't even suspect what they are showing you. Certain confidences—they don't see it—are the bitterest kind of insult. I suppose Azzolati imagines himself a noble beast of prey. Just as some others imagine themselves to be most delicate, noble, and refined gentlemen. And as likely as not they would trade on a woman's troubles—and in the end make nothing of that either. Idiots!"

The utter absence of all anger in this spoken meditation gave it a character of touching simplicity. And as if it had been truly only a meditation we conducted ourselves as though we had not heard it. Mills began to speak of his experiences during his visit to the army of the Legitimist King. And I discovered in his speeches that this man of books could be graphic and picturesque. His admiration for the devotion and bravery of the army was combined with the greatest distaste for what he had seen of the way its great qualities were misused. In the conduct of this great enterprise he had seen a deplorable levity of outlook, a fatal lack of decision, an absence of any reasoned plan.

He shook his head.

"I feel that you of all people, Doña Rita, ought to be told the truth. I don't know exactly what you have at stake."

She was rosy like some impassive statue in a desert in the flush of the dawn.

"Not my heart," she said quietly. "You must believe that."

"I do. Perhaps it would have been better if you . . ."

"No, *Monsieur le Philosophe*. It would not have been better. Don't make that serious face at me," she went on with tenderness in a playful note, as if tenderness had been her inheritance of all time and playfulness the very fibre of her being. "I suppose you think that a woman who has acted as I did and has not staked her heart on it is . . . How do you know to what the heart responds as it beats from day to day?"

"I wouldn't judge you. What am I before the knowledge you were born to? You are as old as the world."

She accepted this with a smile. I who was innocently watching them was amazed to discover how much a fleeting thing like that could hold of seduction without the help of any other feature and with that unchanging glance.

"With me it is *pun d'onor*. To my first independent friend."

"You were soon parted," ventured Mills, while I sat still under a sense of oppression.

"Don't think for a moment that I have been scared off," she said. "It is they who are frightened. I suppose you heard a lot of Headquarters gossip?"

"Oh, yes," Mills said meaningly. "The fair and the dark are succeeding each other like leaves blown in the wind dancing in and out. I suppose you have noticed that leaves blown in the wind have a look of happiness."

"Yes," she said, "that sort of leaf is dead. Then why shouldn't it look happy? And so I suppose there is no uneasiness, no occasion for fears amongst the 're-sponsibles.'"

"Upon the whole not. Now and then a leaf seems as if it would stick. There is for instance Madame . . ."

"Oh, I don't want to know, I understand it all, I am as old as the world."

"Yes," said Mills thoughtfully, "you are not a leaf, you might have been a tornado yourself."

"Upon my word," she said, "there was a time that they thought I could carry him off, away from them all —beyond them all. Verily, I am not very proud of their fears. There was nothing reckless there worthy of a great passion. There was nothing sad there worthy of a great tenderness."

"And is *this* the word of the Venetian riddle?" asked Mills, fixing her with his keen eyes.

"If it pleases you to think so, Señor," she said indifferently. The movement of her eyes, their veiled gleam became mischievous when she asked, "And Don Juan Blunt, have you seen him over there?"

"I fancy he avoided me. Moreover, he is always with his regiment at the outposts. He is a most valorous captain. I heard some people describe him as foolhardy."

"Oh, he needn't seek death," she said in an indefinable tone. "I mean as a refuge. There will be nothing in his life great enough for that."

"You are angry. You miss him, I believe, Doña Rita."

"Angry? No! Weary. But of course it's very inconvenient. I can't very well ride out alone. A solitary amazon swallowing the dust and the salt spray of the Corniche promenade would attract too much attention. And then I don't mind you two knowing that I am afraid of going out alone."

"Afraid?" we both exclaimed together.

"You men are extraordinary. Why do you want me to be courageous? Why shouldn't I be afraid? Is it because there is no one in the world to care what would happen to me?"

There was a deep-down vibration in her tone for the first time. We had not a word to say. And she added after a long silence:

"There is a very good reason. There is a danger."

With wonderful insight Mills affirmed at once:

"Something ugly."

She nodded slightly several times. Then Mills said with conviction:

"Ah! Then it can't be anything in yourself. And if so . . ."

I was moved to extravagant advice.

"You should come out with me to sea then. There may be some danger there but there's nothing ugly to fear."

She gave me a startled glance quite unusual with her, more than wonderful to me; and suddenly as though she had seen me for the first time she exclaimed in a tone of compunction:

"Oh! And there is this one, too! Oh, why should

he run his head into danger for those things that will all crumble into dust before long?"

I said: "*You* won't crumble into dust."

And Mills chimed in:

"That young enthusiast will always have his sea."

We were all standing up now. She kept her eyes on me, and repeated with a sort of whimsical enviousness:

"The sea! The violet sea—and he is longing to rejoin it! . . . At night! Under the stars! . . . A lover's meeting," she went on, thrilling me from head to foot with those two words, accompanied by a wistful smile pointed by a suspicion of mockery. She turned away. "And you, Monsieur Mills?" she asked.

"I am going back to my books," he declared with a very serious face. "My adventure is over."

"Each one to his love," she bantered us gently. "Didn't I love books, too, at one time! They seemed to contain all wisdom and hold a magic power, too. Tell me, Monsieur Mills, have you found amongst them in some black-letter volume the power of foretelling a poor mortal's destiny, the power to look into the future? Anybody's future . . ." Mills shook his head. . . . "What, not even mine?" she coaxed as if she really believed in a magic power to be found in books.

Mills shook his head again. "No, I have not the power," he said. "I am no more a great magician, than you are a poor mortal. You have your ancient spells. You are as old as the world. Of us two it's you that are more fit to foretell the future of the poor mortals on whom you happen to cast your eyes."

At these words she cast her eyes down and in the moment of deep silence I watched the slight rising and falling of her breast. Then Mills pronounced distinctly:

"Good-bye, old Enchantress."

They shook hands cordially. "Good-bye, poor Magician," she said.

Mills made as if to speak but seemed to think better of it. Doña Rita returned my distant bow with a slight, charmingly ceremonious inclination of her body.

"*Bon voyage* and a happy return," she said formally.

I was following Mills through the door when I heard her voice behind us raised in recall:

"Oh, a moment . . . I forgot . . ."

I turned round. The call was for me, and I walked slowly back wondering what she could have forgotten. She waited in the middle of the room with lowered head, with a mute gleam in her deep blue eyes. When I was near enough she extended to me without a word her bare white arm and suddenly pressed the back of her hand against my lips. I was too startled to seize it with rapture. It detached itself from my lips and fell slowly by her side. We had made it up and there was nothing to say. She turned away to the window and I hurried out of the room.

PART THREE

I

It was on our return from that first trip that I took Dominic up to the Villa to be presented to Doña Rita. If she wanted to look on the embodiment of fidelity, resource, and courage, she could behold it all in that man. Apparently she was not disappointed. Neither was Dominic disappointed. During the half-hour's interview they got into touch with each other in a wonderful way as if they had some common and secret standpoint in life. Maybe it was their common lawlessness, and their knowledge of things as old as the world. Her seduction, his recklessness, were both simple, masterful and, in a sense, worthy of each other.

Dominic was, I won't say awed by this interview. No woman could awe Dominic. But he was, as it were, rendered thoughtful by it, like a man who had not so much an experience as a sort of revelation vouchsafed to him. Later, at sea, he used to refer to La Señora in a particular tone and I knew that henceforth his devotion was not for me alone. And I understood the inevitability of it extremely well. As to Doña Rita she, after Dominic left the room, had turned to me with animation and said: "But he is perfect, this man." Afterwards she often asked after him and used to refer to him in conversation. More than once she said to me: "One would like to put the care of one's personal safety into the hands of that man. He looks as if he simply couldn't fail one." I admitted that this was

very true, especially at sea. Dominic couldn't fail.
But at the same time I rather chaffed Rita on her preoccupation as to personal safety that so often cropped
up in her talk.

"One would think you were a crowned head in a
revolutionary world," I used to tell her.

"That would be different. One would be standing
then for something, either worth or not worth dying for.
One could even run away then and be done with it. But
I can't run away unless I got out of my skin and left
that behind. Don't you understand? You are very
stupid . . ." But she had the grace to add, "On
purpose."

I don't know about the on purpose. I am not certain
about the stupidity. Her words bewildered one often
and bewilderment is a sort of stupidity. I remedied it
by simply disregarding the sense of what she said. The
sound was there and also her poignant heart-gripping
presence giving occupation enough to one's faculties.
In the power of those things over one there was mystery
enough. It was more absorbing than the mere obscurity of her speeches. But I daresay she couldn't understand that.

Hence, at times, the amusing outbreaks of temper in
word and gesture that only strengthened the natural,
the invincible force of the spell. Sometimes the brass
bowl would get upset or the cigarette box would fly
up, dropping a shower of cigarettes on the floor.
We would pick them up, re-establish everything, and
fall into a long silence, so close that the sound of the
first word would come with all the pain of a separation.

It was at that time, too, that she suggested I should
take up my quarters in her house in the street of the
Consuls. There were certain advantages in that move.
In my present abode my sudden absences might have

been in the long run subject to comment. On the other hand, the house in the street of the Consuls was a known outpost of Legitimacy. But then it was covered by the occult influence of her who was referred to in confidential talks, secret communications, and discreet whispers of Royalist salons as: "Madame de Lastaola."

That was the name which the heiress of Henry Allègre had decided to adopt when, according to her own expression, she had found herself precipitated at a moment's notice into the crowd of mankind. It is strange how the death of Henry Allègre, which certainly the poor man had not planned, acquired in my view the character of a heartless desertion. It gave one a glimpse of amazing egoism in a sentiment to which one could hardly give a name, a mysterious appropriation of one human being by another as if in defiance of unexpressed things and for an unheard-of satisfaction of an inconceivable pride. If he had hated her he could not have flung that enormous fortune more brutally at her head And his unrepentant death seemed to lift for a moment the curtain on something lofty and sinister like an Olympian's caprice.

Doña Rita said to me once with humorous resignation: "You know, it appears that one must have a name. That's what Henry Allègre's man of business told me. He was quite impatient with me about it. But my name, *amigo*, Henry Allègre had taken from me like all the rest of what I had been once. All that is buried with him in his grave. It wouldn't have been true. That is how I felt about it. So I took that one." She whispered to herself: "Lastaola," not as if to test the sound but as if in a dream.

To this day I am not quite certain whether it was the name of any human habitation, a lonely *caserio* with a half-effaced carving of a coat of arms over its door, or of some hamlet at the dead end of a ravine with a stony slope at the back. It might have been a hill for all I know or perhaps a stream. A wood, or perhaps a combination of all these: just a bit of the earth's surface. Once I asked her where exactly it was situated and she answered, waving her hand cavalierly at the dead wall of the room: "Oh, over there." I thought that this was all that I was going to hear but she added moodily, "I used to take my goats there, a dozen or so of them, for the day. From after my uncle had said his Mass till the ringing of the evening bell."

I saw suddenly the lonely spot, sketched for me some time ago by a few words from Mr. Blunt, populated by the agile, bearded beasts with cynical heads, and a little misty figure dark in the sunlight with a halo of dishevelled rust-coloured hair about its head.

The epithet of rust-coloured comes from her. It was really tawny. Once or twice in my hearing she had referred to "my rust-coloured hair" with laughing vexation. Even then it was unruly, abhorring the restraints of civilization, and often in the heat of a dispute getting into the eyes of Madame de Lastaola, the possessor of coveted art treasures, the heiress of Henry Allègre. She proceeded in a reminiscent mood, with a faint flash of gaiety all over her face, except her dark blue eyes that moved so seldom out of their fixed scrutiny of things invisible to other human beings.

"The goats were very good. We clambered amongst the stones together. They beat me at that game. I used to catch my hair in the bushes."

"Your rust-coloured hair," I whispered.

"Yes, it was always this colour. And I used to leave bits of my frock on thorns here and there. It was pretty thin, I can tell you. There wasn't much at that time between my skin and the blue of the sky. My legs were as sunburnt as my face; but really I didn't tan very much. I had plenty of freckles though. There were no looking-glasses in the Presbytery but uncle had a piece not bigger than my two hands for his shaving. One Sunday I crept into his room and had a peep at myself. And wasn't I startled to see my own eyes looking at me! But it was fascinating, too. I was about eleven years old then, and I was very friendly with the goats, and I was as shrill as a cicada and as slender as a match. Heavens! When I overhear myself speaking sometimes, or look at my limbs, it doesn't seem to be possible. And yet it is the same one. I do remember every single goat. They were very clever. Goats are no trouble really: they don't scatter much. Mine never did even if I had to hide myself out of their sight for ever so long."

It was but natural to ask her why she wanted to hide, and she uttered vaguely what was rather a comment on my question:

"It was like fate." But I chose to take it otherwise, teasingly, because we were often like a pair of children.

"Oh, really," I said, "you talk like a pagan. What could you know of fate at that time? What was it like? Did it come down from Heaven?"

"Don't be stupid. It used to come along a cart-track that was there and it looked like a boy. Wasn't he a little devil though. You understand, I couldn't know that. He was a wealthy cousin of mine. Round there we are all related, all cousins—as in Brittany. He wasn't much bigger than myself but he was older, just a boy in blue breeches and with good shoes on his feet, which of course interested and impressed me. He yelled to me from below, I screamed to him from above, he came up and sat down near me on a stone, never said a word, let me look at him for half an hour before he condescended to ask me who I was. And the airs he gave himself! He quite intimidated me sitting there perfectly dumb. I remember trying to hide my bare feet under the edge of my skirt as I sat below him on the ground.

"*C'est comique, eh!*" she interrupted herself to comment in a melancholy tone. I looked at her sympathetically and she went on:

"He was the only son from a rich farmhouse two miles down the slope. In winter they used to send him to school at Tolosa. He had an enormous opinion of himself; he was going to keep a shop in a town by and by and he was about the most dissatisfied creature I have ever seen. He had an unhappy mouth and unhappy eyes and he was always wretched about something: about the treatment he received, about being kept in the country and chained to work. He was moaning and complaining and threatening all the world, including his father and mother. He used to curse God, yes, that boy, sitting there on a piece of rock like a wretched little Prometheus with a sparrow pecking at his miserable little liver. And the grand scenery of mountains all round, ha, ha, ha!"

She laughed in contralto: a penetrating sound with something generous in it; not infectious, but in others provoking a smile.

"Of course I, poor little animal, I didn't know what to make of it, and I was even a little frightened. But at first because of his miserable eyes I was sorry for him, almost as much as if he had been a sick goat. But, frightened or sorry, I don't know how it is, I always wanted to laugh at him, too, I mean from the very first day when he let me admire him for half an hour. Yes, even then I had to put my hand over my mouth more than once for the sake of good manners, you understand. And yet, you know, I was never a laughing child.

"One day he came up and sat down very dignified a little bit away from me and told me he had been thrashed for wandering in the hills.

"'To be with me?' I asked. And he said: 'To be with you! No. My people don't know what I do.' I can't tell why, but I was annoyed. So instead of raising a clamour of pity over him, which I suppose he expected me to do, I asked him if the thrashing hurt very much. He got up, he had a switch in his hand, and walked up to me, saying, 'I will soon show you.' I went stiff with fright; but instead of slashing at me he dropped down by my side and kissed me on the cheek. Then he did it again, and by that time I was gone dead, all over and he could have done what he liked with the corpse but he left off suddenly and then I came to life again and I bolted away. Not very far. I couldn't leave the goats altogether. He chased me round and about the rocks, but of course I was too quick for him in his nice town boots. When he got tired of that game he started throwing stones. After that he made my life very lively for me. Sometimes he used to come on me unawares and then I had to sit still and listen to his miserable ravings, because he would catch me round the waist and hold me very tight. And yet I often felt inclined to laugh. But if I caught sight of him at a distance and tried to dodge out of the way he would start stoning me into a shelter I knew of and then sit outside with a heap of stones at hand so that I daren't show the end of my nose for hours. He would sit there and rave and abuse me till I would burst into a crazy laugh in my hole; and then I could see him through the leaves rolling on the ground and biting his fists with rage. Didn't he hate me! At the same time

I was often terrified. I am convinced now that if I
had started crying he would have rushed in and perhaps strangled me there. Then as the sun was about
to set he would make me swear that I would marry
him when I was grown up. 'Swear, you little wretched
beggar,' he would yell to me. And I would swear.
I was hungry, and I didn't want to be made black and
blue all over with stones. Oh, I swore ever so many
times to be his wife. Thirty times a month for two
months. I couldn't help myself. It was no use complaining to my sister Therese. When I showed her
my bruises and tried to tell her a little about my trouble
she was quite scandalized. She called me a sinful girl,
a shameless creature. I assure you it puzzled my head
so that, between Therese my sister and José the boy,
I lived in a state of idiocy almost. But luckily at the
end of the two months they sent him away from home
for good. Curious story to happen to a goatherd
living all her days out under God's eye, as my uncle the
Cura might have said. My sister Therese was keeping
house in the Presbytery. She's a terrible person."

"I have heard of your sister Therese," I said.

"Oh, you have! Of my big sister Therese, six, ten
years older than myself perhaps? She just comes a
little above my shoulder, but then I was always a long
thing. I never knew my mother. I don't even know
how she looked. There are no paintings or photo-
graphs in our farmhouses amongst the hills. I haven't
even heard her described to me. I believe I was never
good enough to be told these things. Therese decided that I was a lump of wickedness, and now she
believes that I will lose my soul altogether unless I take
some steps to save it. Well, I have no particular
taste that way. I suppose it is annoying to have a
sister going fast to eternal perdition, but there are

compensations.   The funniest thing is that it's Therese,
I believe, who managed to keep me out of the Presbytery when I went out of my way to look in on them on
my return from my visit to the *Quartel Real* last year.
I couldn't have stayed much more than half an hour
with them anyway, but still I would have liked to get
over the old doorstep.   I am certain that Therese per-
suaded my uncle to go out and meet me at the bottom
of the hill.   I saw the old man a long way off and I
understood how it was.   I dismounted at once and
met him on foot.   We had half an hour together walking up and down the road.   He is a peasant priest, he
didn't know how to treat me.   And of course I was
uncomfortable, too.   There wasn't a single goat about
to keep me in countenance.   I ought to have embraced
him.   I was always fond of the stern, simple old man.
But he drew himself up when I approached him and
actually took off his hat to me.   So simple as that!
I bowed my head and asked for his blessing.   And he
said: 'I would never refuse a blessing to a good Legitimist.'   So stern as that!   And when I think that I was
perhaps the only girl of the family or in the whole
world that he ever in his priest's life patted on the
head!   When I think of that! . . . I believe
at that moment I was as wretched as he was himself.
I handed him an envelope with a big red seal which
quite startled him.   I had asked the Marquis de Villarel
to give me a few words for him, because my uncle has
a great influence in his district; and the Marquis
penned with his own hand some compliments and
an inquiry about the spirit of the population.   My
uncle read the letter, looked up at me with an air of
mournful awe, and begged me to tell his excellency that
the people were all for God, their lawful King and their
old privileges.   I said to him then, after he had asked

me about the health of His Majesty in an awfully
gloomy tone—I said then: 'There is only one thing that
remains for me to do, uncle, and that is to give you
two pounds of the very best snuff I have brought here
for you.' What else could I have got for the poor old
man? I had no trunks with me. I had to leave behind
a spare pair of shoes in the hotel to make room in my
little bag for that snuff. And fancy! That old priest
absolutely pushed the parcel away. I could have
thrown it at his head; but I thought suddenly of that
hard, prayerful life, knowing nothing of any ease or
pleasure in the world, absolutely nothing but a pinch
of snuff now and then. I remembered how wretched
he used to be when he lacked a copper or two to get
some snuff with. My face was hot with indignation,
but before I could fly out at him I remembered how
simple he was. So I said with great dignity that as
the present came from the King and as he wouldn't
receive it from my hand there was nothing else for me
to do but to throw it into the brook; and I made as if
I were going to do it, too. He shouted: 'Stay, unhappy
girl! Is it really from His Majesty, whom God preserve?' I said contemptuously, 'Of course.' He
looked at me with great pity in his eyes, sighed deeply,
and took the little tin from my hand. I suppose he
imagined me in my abandoned way wheedling the
necessary cash out of the King for the purchase of
that snuff. You can't imagine how simple he is.
Nothing was easier than to deceive him; but don't
imagine I deceived him from the vainglory of a mere
sinner. I lied to the dear man, simply because I
couldn't bear the idea of him being deprived of the only
gratification his big, ascetic, gaunt body ever knew on
earth. As I mounted my mule to go away he murmured coldly: 'God guard you, Señora!' Señora!

What sternness! We were off a little way already when his heart softened and he shouted after me in a terrible voice: 'The road to Heaven is repentance!' And then after a silence, again the great shout 'Repentance!' thundered after me. Was that sternness or simplicity, I wonder? Or a mere unmeaning superstition, a mechanical thing? If there lives anybody completely honest in this world, surely it must be my uncle. And yet—who knows?

"Would you guess what was the next thing I did? Directly I got over the frontier I wrote from Bayonne asking the old man to send me out my sister here. I said it was for the service of the King. You see, I had thought suddenly of that house of mine in which you once spent the night talking with Mr. Mills and Don Juan Blunt. I thought it would do extremely well for Carlist officers coming this way on leave or on a mission. In hotels they might have been molested, but I knew that I could get protection for my house. Just a word from the ministry in Paris to the Prefect. But I wanted a woman to manage it for me. And where was I to find a trustworthy woman? How was I to know one when I saw her? I don't know how to talk to women. Of course my Rose would have done for me that or anything else; but what could I have done myself without her? She has looked after me from the first. It was Henry Allègre who got her for me eight years ago. I don't know whether he meant it for a kindness but she's the only human being on whom I can lean. She knows . . . What doesn't she know about me! She has never failed to do the right thing for me unasked. I couldn't part with her. And I couldn't think of anybody else but my sister.

"After all it was somebody belonging to me. But it seemed the wildest idea. Yet she came at once. Of

course I took care to send her some money. She likes
money. As to my uncle there is nothing that he
wouldn't have given up for the service of the King.
Rose went to meet her at the railway station. She told
me afterwards that there had been no need for me to
be anxious about her recognizing MademoiselleTherese.
There was nobody else in the train that could be mistaken for her. I should think not! She had made for
herself a dress of some brown stuff like a nun's habit
and had a crooked stick and carried all her belongings
tied up in a handkerchief. She looked like a pilgrim
to a saint's shrine. Rose took her to the house. She
asked when she saw it: 'And does this big place really
belong to our Rita?' My maid of course said that it
was mine. 'And how long did our Rita live here?'—
Madame has never seen it unless perhaps the outside,
as far as I know. I believe Mr. Allègre lived here for
some time when he was a young man.'—'The sinner
that's dead?'—'Just so,' says Rose. You know nothing ever startles Rose. 'Well, his sins are gone with
him,' said my sister, and began to make herself at
home.

"Rose was going to stop with her for a week but on
the third day she was back with me with the remark
that Mlle. Therese knew her way about very well already and preferred to be left to herself. Some little
time afterwards I went to see that sister of mine. The
first thing she said to me, 'I wouldn't have recognized
you, Rita,' and I said, 'What a funny dress you have,
Therese, more fit for the portress of a convent than for
this house.'—'Yes,' she said, 'and unless you give this
house to me, Rita, I will go back to our country. I
will have nothing to do with your life, Rita. Your
life is no secret for me.'

"I was going from room to room and Therese was

following me. 'I don't know that my life is a secret to anybody,' I said to her, 'but how do you know anything about it?' And then she told me that it was through a cousin of ours, that horrid wretch of a boy, you know. He had finished his schooling and was a clerk in a Spanish commercial house of some kind, in Paris, and apparently had made it his business to write home whatever he could hear about me or ferret out from those relations of mine with whom I lived as a girl. I got suddenly very furious. I raged up and down the room (we were alone upstairs), and Therese scuttled away from me as far as the door. I heard her say to herself, 'It's the evil spirit in her that makes her like this.' She was absolutely convinced of that. She made the sign of the cross in the air to protect herself. I was quite astounded. And then I really couldn't help myself. I burst into a laugh. I laughed and laughed; I really couldn't stop till Therese ran away. I went downstairs still laughing and found her in the hall with her face to the wall and her fingers in her ears kneeling in a corner. I had to pull her out by the shoulders from there. I don't think she was frightened; she was only shocked. But I don't suppose her heart is desperately bad, because when I dropped into a chair feeling very tired she came and knelt in front of me and put her arms round my waist and entreated me to cast off from me my evil ways with the help of saints and priests. Quite a little programme for a reformed sinner. I got away at last. I left her sunk on her heels before the empty chair looking after me. 'I pray for you every night and morning, Rita,' she said.— 'Oh, yes. I know you are a good sister,' I said to her. I was letting myself out when she called after me, 'And what about this house, Rita?' I said to her, 'Oh, you may keep it till the day I reform and enter a convent.'

The last I saw of her she was still on her knees looking after me with her mouth open. I have seen her since several times, but our intercourse is, at any rate on her side, as of a frozen nun with some great lady. But I believe she really knows how to make men comfortable. Upon my word I think she likes to look after men. They don't seem to be such great sinners as women are. I think you could do worse than take up your quarters at number 10. She will no doubt develop a saintly sort of affection for you, too."

I don't know that the prospect of becoming a favourite of Doña Rita's peasant sister was very fascinating to me. If I went to live very willingly at No. 10 it was because everything connected with Doña Rita had for me a peculiar fascination. She had only passed through the house once as far as I knew; but it was enough. She was one of those beings that leave a trace. I am not unreasonable—I mean for those that knew her. That is, I suppose, because she was so unforgettable. Let us remember the tragedy of Azzolati the ruthless, the ridiculous financier with a criminal soul (or shall we say heart) and facile tears. No wonder, then, that for me, who may flatter myself without undue vanity with being much finer than that grotesque international intriguer, the mere knowledge that Doña Rita had passed through the very rooms in which I was going to live between the strenuous times of the sea-expeditions, was enough to fill my inner being with a great content. Her glance, her darkly brilliant blue glance, had run over the walls of that room which most likely would be mine to slumber in. Behind me, somewhere near the door, Therese, the peasant sister, said in a funnily compassionate tone and in an amazingly landlady-of-a-boarding-house spirit of false persuasiveness:

"You will be very comfortable here, Señor. It is so

peaceful here in the street. Sometimes one may think oneself in a village. It's only a hundred and twenty-five francs for the friends of the King. And I shall take such good care of you that your very heart will be able to rest."

II

Doña Rita was curious to know how I got on with her peasant sister and all I could say in return for that inquiry was that the peasant sister was in her own way amiable. At this she clicked her tongue amusingly and repeated a remark she had made before: "She likes young men. The younger the better." The mere thought of those two women being sisters aroused one's wonder. Physically they were altogether of different design. It was also the difference between living tissue of glowing loveliness with a divine breath, and a hard hollow figure of baked clay.

Indeed Therese did somehow resemble an achievement, wonderful enough in its way, in unglazed earthenware. The only gleam perhaps that one could find on her was that of her teeth, which one used to get between her dull lips unexpectedly, startlingly, and a little inexplicably, because it was never associated with a smile. She smiled with compressed mouth. It was indeed difficult to conceive of those two birds coming from the same nest. And yet . . . Contrary to what generally happens, it was when one saw those two women together that one lost all belief in the possibility of their relationship near or far. It extended even to their common humanity. One, as it were, doubted it. If one of the two was representative, then the other was either something more or less than human. One wondered whether these two women belonged to the same scheme of creation. One was secretly amazed to see them standing together, speaking

121

to each other, having words in common, understanding each other. And yet! . . . Our psychological sense is the crudest of all; we don't know, we don't perceive how superficial we are. The simplest shades escape us, the secret of changes, of relations. No, upon the whole, the only feature (and yet with enormous differences) which Therese had in common with her sister, as I told Doña Rita, was amiability.

"For, you know, you are a most amiable person yourself," I went on. "It's one of your characteristics, of course much more precious than in other people. You transmute the commonest traits into gold of your own; but after all there are no new names. You are amiable. You were most amiable to me when I first saw you."

"Really. I was not aware. Not specially. . . ."

"I had never the presumption to think that it was special. Moreover, my head was in a whirl. I was lost in astonishment first of all at what I had been listening to all night. Your history, you know, a wonderful tale with a flavour of wine in it and wreathed in clouds, with that amazing, decapitated, mutilated dummy of a woman lurking in a corner, and with Blunt's smile gleaming through a fog, the fog in my eyes, from Mills' pipe, you know. I was feeling quite inanimate as to body and frightfully stimulated as to mind all the time. I had never heard anything like that talk about you before. Of course I wasn't sleepy, but still I am not used to do altogether without sleep like Blunt . . ."

"Kept awake all night listening to my story!" She marvelled.

"Yes. You don't think I am complaining, do you? I wouldn't have missed it for the world. Blunt in a ragged old jacket and a white tie and that incisive polite voice of his seemed strange and weird. It seemed as though he were inventing it all rather angrily. I had doubts as to your existence."

"Mr. Blunt is very much interested in my story."

"Anybody would be," I said. "I was. I didn't sleep a wink. I was expecting to see you soon—and even then I had my doubts."

"As to my existence?"

"It wasn't exactly that, though of course I couldn't tell that you weren't a product of Captain Blunt's sleeplessness. He seemed to dread exceedingly to be left alone and your story might have been a device to detain us . . ."

"He hasn't enough imagination for that," she said.

"It didn't occur to me. But there was Mills, who apparently believed in your existence. I could trust Mills. My doubts were about the propriety. I couldn't see any good reason for being taken to see you. Strange that it should be my connection with the sea which brought me here to the Villa."

"Unexpected perhaps."

"No. I mean particularly strange and significant."

"Why?"

"Because my friends are in the habit of telling me (and each other) that the sea is my only love. They were always chaffing me because they couldn't see or guess in my life at any woman, open or secret . . ."

"And is that really so?" she inquired negligently.

"Why, yes. I don't mean to say that I am like an innocent shepherd in one of those interminable stories of the eighteenth century. But I don't throw the word love about indiscriminately. It may be all true about the sea; but some people would say that they love sausages."

"You are horrible."

"I am surprised."

"I mean your choice of words."

"And you have never uttered a word yet that didn't change into a pearl as it dropped from your lips. At least not before me."

She glanced down deliberately and said, "This is better. But I don't see any of them on the floor."

"It's you who are horrible in the implications of your language. Don't see any on the floor! Haven't I caught up and treasured them all in my heart? I am not the animal from which sausages are made."

She looked at me suavely and then with the sweetest possible smile breathed out the word: "No."

And we both laughed very loud. O! days of innocence! On this occasion we parted from each other on a light-hearted note. But already I had acquired the conviction that there was nothing more lovable in the world than that woman; nothing more life-giving, inspiring, and illuminating than the emanation of her charm. I meant it absolutely—not excepting the light of the sun.

From this there was only one step further to take. The step into a conscious surrender; the open perception that this charm, warming like a flame, was also all-revealing like a great light; giving new depth to shades, new brilliance to colours, an amazing vividness to all sensations and vitality to all thoughts: so that all that had been lived before seemed to have been lived in a drab world and with a languid pulse.

A great revelation this. I don't mean to say it was soul-shaking. The soul was already a captive before doubt, anguish, or dismay could touch its surrender and its exaltation. But all the same the revelation turned many things into dust; and, amongst others, the sense of the careless freedom of my life. If that life ever had any purpose or any aim outside itself I would have said that it threw a shadow across its path.

But it hadn't. There had been no path. But there was a shadow, the inseparable companion of all light. No illumination can sweep all mystery out of the world. After the departed darkness the shadows remain, more mysterious because as if more enduring; and one feels a dread of them of which one was free before. What if they were to be victorious at the last? They, or what perhaps lurks in them: fear, deception, desire, disillusion—all silent at first before the song of triumphant love vibrating in the light. Yes. Silent. Even desire itself! All silent. But not for long!

This was, I think, before the third expedition. Yes, it must have been the third, for I remember that it was boldly planned and that it was carried out without a hitch. The tentative period was over; all our arrangements had been perfected. There was, so to speak, always an unfailing smoke on the hill and an unfailing lantern on the shore. Our friends, mostly bought for hard cash and therefore valuable, had acquired confidence in us. This, they seemed to say, is no unfathomable roguery of penniless adventures. This is but the reckless enterprise of men of wealth and sense and needn't be inquired into. The young *caballero* has got real gold pieces in the belt he wears next his skin; and the man with the heavy moustaches and unbelieving eyes is indeed very much of a man. They gave to Dominic all their respect and to me a great show of deference; for I had all the money, while they thought that Dominic had all the sense. That judgment was not exactly correct. I had my share of judgment and audacity which surprises me now that the years have chilled the blood without dimming the memory. I remember going about the business with a lighthearted, clear-headed recklessness which, according as its decisions were sudden or considered, made Dominic draw his breath through his clenched teeth, or look hard at me before he gave me either a slight nod of assent or a sarcastic "Oh, certainly"—just as the humour of the moment prompted him.

One night as we were lying on a bit of dry sand under the lee of a rock, side by side, watching the light of our little vessel dancing away at sea in the windy distance, Dominic spoke suddenly to me.

"I suppose Alphonso and Carlos, Carlos and Alphonso, they are nothing to you, together or separately?"

I said: "Dominic, if they were both to vanish from the earth together or separately it would make no difference to my feelings."

He remarked: "Just so. A man mourns only for his friends. I suppose they are no more friends to you than they are to me. Those Carlists make a great consumption of cartridges. That is well. But why should we do all those mad things that you will insist on us doing till my hair," he pursued with grave, mocking exaggeration, "till my hair tries to stand up on my head? and all for that Carlos, let God and the devil each guard his own, for that Majesty as they call him, but after all a man like another and—no friend."

"Yes, why?" I murmured, feeling my body nestled at ease in the sand.

It was very dark under the overhanging rock on that night of clouds and of wind that died and rose and died again. Dominic's voice was heard speaking low between the short gusts.

"Friend of the Señora, eh?"

"That's what the world says, Dominic."

"Half of what the world says are lies," he pronounced dogmatically. "For all his majesty he may be a good enough man. Yet he is only a king in the mountains and to-morrow he may be no more than you. Still a woman like that—one, somehow, would grudge her to a better king. She ought to be set up on a high pillar for people that walk on the ground to raise their eyes up to. But you are otherwise, you gentlemen. You, for instance, Monsieur, you wouldn't want to see her set up on a pillar."

"That sort of thing, Dominic," I said, "that sort of thing, you understand me, ought to be done early."

He was silent for a time. And then his manly voice was heard in the shadow of the rock.

"I see well enough what you mean. I spoke of the multitude, that only raise their eyes. But for kings and suchlike that is not enough. Well, no heart need despair; for there is not a woman that wouldn't at some time or other get down from her pillar for no bigger bribe perhaps than just a flower which is fresh to-day and withered to-morrow. And then, what's the good of asking how long any woman has been up there? There is a true saying that lips that have been kissed do not lose their freshness."

I don't know what answer I could have made. I imagine Dominic thought himself unanswerable. As a matter of fact, before I could speak, a voice came to us down the face of the rock crying secretly, "Olà, down there! All is safe ashore."

It was the boy who used to hang about the stable of a muleteer's inn in a little shallow valley with a shallow little stream in it, and where we had been hiding most of the day before coming down to the shore. We both started to our feet and Dominic said, "A good boy that. You didn't hear him either come or go above our heads. Don't reward him with more than one peseta, Señor, whatever he does. If you were to give him two he would go mad at the sight of so much wealth and throw up his job at the Fonda, where he is so useful to run errands, in that way he has of skimming along the paths without displacing a stone."

Meantime he was busying himself with striking a fire to set alight a small heap of dry sticks he had made ready beforehand on that spot which in all the circuit of the Bay was perfectly screened from observation from the land side.

The clear flame shooting up revealed him in the black cloak with a hood of a Mediterranean sailor. His eyes watched the dancing dim light to seaward. And he talked the while.

"The only fault you have, Señor, is being too generous with your money. In this world you must give sparingly. The only things you may deal out without counting, in this life of ours which is but a little fight and a little love, is blows to your enemy and kisses to a woman. . . . Ah! here they are coming in."

I noticed the dancing light in the dark west much closer to the shore now. Its motion had altered. It swayed slowly as it ran towards us, and, suddenly, the darker shadow as of a great pointed wing appeared gliding in the night. Under it a human voice shouted something confidently.

"*Bueno*," muttered Dominic. From some receptacle I didn't see he poured a lot of water on the blaze, like a magician at the end of a successful incantation that had called out a shadow and a voice from the immense space of the sea. And his hooded figure vanished from my sight in a great hiss and the warm feel of ascending steam.

"That's all over," he said, "and now we go back for more work, more toil, more trouble, more exertion with hands and feet, for hours and hours. And all the time the head turned over the shoulder, too."

We were climbing a precipitous path sufficiently dangerous in the dark, Dominic, more familiar with it, going first and I scrambling close behind in order that I might grab at his cloak if I chanced to slip or miss my footing. I remonstrated against this arrangement as we stopped to rest. I had no doubt I would grab at his cloak if I felt myself falling. I couldn't help doing that. But I would probably only drag him down with me.

With one hand grasping a shadowy bush above his head he growled that all this was possible, but that it was all in the bargain, and urged me onwards.

When we got on to the level that man whose even breathing no exertion, no danger, no fear or anger could disturb, remarked as we strode side by side:

"I will say this for us, that we are carrying out all this deadly foolishness as conscientiously as though the eyes of the Señora were on us all the time. And as to risk, I suppose we take more than she would approve of, I fancy, if she ever gave a moment's thought to us out here. Now, for instance, in the next half hour, we may come any moment on three carabineers who would let off their pieces without asking questions. Even your way of flinging money about cannot make safety for men set on defying a whole big country for the sake of—what is it exactly?—the blue eyes, or the white arms of the Señora."

He kept his voice equably low. It was a lonely spot and but for a vague shape of a dwarf tree here and there we had only the flying clouds for company. Very far off a tiny light twinkled a little way up the seaward shoulder of an invisible mountain. Dominic moved on.

"Fancy yourself lying here, on this wild spot, with a leg smashed by a shot or perhaps with a bullet in your side. It might happen. A star might fall. I have watched stars falling in scores on clear nights in the Atlantic. And it was nothing. The flash of a pinch of gunpowder in your face may be a bigger matter. Yet somehow it's pleasant as we stumble in the dark to think of our Señora in that long room with a shiny floor and all that lot of glass at the end, sitting on that divan, you call it, covered with carpets as if expecting a king indeed. And very still . . ."

He remembered her—whose image could not be dismissed.

I laid my hand on his shoulder.

"That light on the mountain side flickers exceedingly, Dominic. Are we in the path?"

He addressed me then in French, which was between us the language of more formal moments.

"*Prenez mon bras, Monsieur.* Take a firm hold, or I will have you stumbling again and falling into one of those beastly holes, with a good chance to crack your head. And there is no need to take offence. For, speaking with all respect, why should you, and I with you, be here on this lonely spot, barking our shins in the dark on the way to a confounded flickering light where there will be no other supper but a piece of a stale sausage and a draught of leathery wine out of a stinking skin? Pah!"

I had good hold of his arm. Suddenly he dropped the formal French and pronounced in his inflexible voice:

"For a pair of white arms, Señor. *Bueno.*"

He could understand.

III

ON OUR return from that expedition we came gliding into the old harbour so late that Dominic and I, making for the café kept by Madame Léonore, found it empty of customers, except for two rather sinister fellows playing cards together at a corner table near the door. The first thing done by Madame Léonore was to put her hands on Dominic's shoulders and look at arm's length into the eyes of that man of audacious deeds and wild stratagems who smiled straight at her from under his heavy and, at that time, uncurled moustaches.

Indeed we didn't present a neat appearance, our faces unshaven, with the traces of dried salt sprays on our smarting skins and the sleeplessness of full forty hours filming our eyes. At least it was so with me who saw as through a mist Madame Léonore moving with her mature nonchalant grace, setting before us wine and glasses with a faint swish of her ample black skirt. Under the elaborate structure of black hair her jet-black eyes sparkled like good-humoured stars and even I could see that she was tremendously excited at having this lawless wanderer Dominic within her reach and as it were in her power. Presently she sat down by us, touched lightly Dominic's curly head silvered on the temples (she couldn't really help it), gazed at me for a while with a quizzical smile, observed that I looked very tired, and asked Dominic whether for all that I was likely to sleep soundly to-night.

"I don't know," said Dominic. "He's young. And there is always the chance of dreams."

"What do you men dream of in those little barques of yours tossing for months on the water?"

"Mostly of nothing," said Dominic. "But it has happened to me to dream of furious fights."

"And of furious loves, too, no doubt," she caught him up in a mocking voice.

"No, that's for the waking hours," Dominic drawled, basking sleepily with his head between his hands in her ardent gaze. "The waking hours are longer."

"They must be, at sea," she said, never taking her eyes off him. "But I suppose you do talk of your loves sometimes."

"You may be sure, Madame Léonore," I interjected, noticing the hoarseness of my voice, "that you at any rate are talked about a lot at sea."

"I am not so sure of that now.   There is that strange lady from the Prado that you took him to see, Signorino. She went to his head like a glass of wine into a tender youngster's.   He is such a child, and I suppose that I am another.   Shame to confess it, the other morning I got a friend to look after the café for a couple of hours, wrapped up my head, and walked out there to the other end of the town.   .   .   .   Look at these two sitting up! And I thought they were so sleepy and tired, the poor fellows!"

She kept our curiosity in suspense for a moment.

"Well, I have seen your marvel, Dominic," she continued in a calm voice. "She came flying out of the gate on horseback and it would have been all I would have seen of her if—and this is for you, Signorino— if she hadn't pulled up in the main alley to wait for a very good-looking cavalier. He had his moustaches so, and his teeth were very white when he smiled at her. But his eyes are too deep in his head for my taste. I didn't like it. It reminded me of a certain very severe priest who used to come to our village when I was young; younger even than your marvel, Dominic."

"It was no priest in disguise, Madame Léonore," I said, amused by her expression of disgust. "That's an American."

"Ah! *Un Americano!* Well, never mind him. It was her that I went to see."

"What! Walked to the other end of the town to see Doña Rita!" Dominic addressed her in a low bantering tone. "Why, you were always telling me you couldn't walk further than the end of the quay to save your life—or even mine, you said."

"Well, I did; and I walked back again and between the two walks I had a good look. And you may be sure—that will surprise you both—that on the way back—oh, Santa Madre, wasn't it a long way, too—I wasn't thinking of any man at sea or on shore in that connection."

"No. And you were not thinking of yourself, either, I suppose," I said. Speaking was a matter of great effort for me, whether I was too tired or too sleepy, I can't tell. "No, you were not thinking of yourself. You were thinking of a woman, though."

"*Si.* As much a woman as any of us that ever breathed in the world. Yes, of her! Of that very one! You see, we women are not like you men, indifferent to each other unless by some exception. Men say we are always against one another but that's only men's conceit. What can she be to me? I am not afraid of the big child here," and she tapped Dominic's forearm on which he rested his head with a fascinated stare. "With us two it is for life and death, and I am rather pleased that there is something yet in him that can catch fire on occasion. I would have thought less of him if he hadn't been able to get out of hand a little.

for something really fine.   As for you, Signorino," she
turned on me with an unexpected and sarcastic sally,
"I am not in love with you yet."   She changed her
tone from sarcasm to a soft and even dreamy note.
"A head like a gem," went on that woman born in some
by-street of Rome, and a plaything for years of God
knows what obscure fates.   "Yes, Dominic!   *Antica.*
I haven't been haunted by a face since—since I was
sixteen years old.   It was the face of a young cavalier
in the street.   He was on horseback, too.   He never
looked at me, I never saw him again, and I loved him
for—for days and days and days.   That was the sort
of face he had.   And her face is of the same sort.
She had a man's hat, too, on her head.   So high!"

"A man's hat on her head," remarked with profound
displeasure Dominic, to whom this wonder, at least,
of all the wonders of the earth, was apparently unknown.

"*Si.*   And her face has haunted me.   Not so long as
that other but more touchingly because I am no longer
sixteen and this is a woman.   Yes, I did think of her.
I myself was once that age and I, too, had a face of my
own to show to the world, though not so superb.   And
I, too, didn't know why I had come into the world any
more than she does."

"And now you know," Dominic growled softly, with
his head still between his hands.

She looked at him for a long time, opened her lips
but in the end only sighed lightly.

"And what do you know of her, you who have seen
her so well as to be haunted by her face?" I asked.

I wouldn't have been surprised if she had answered
me with another sigh.   For she seemed only to be
thinking of herself and looked not in my direction.   But
suddenly she roused up.

"Of her?" she repeated in a louder voice. "Why should I talk of another woman? And then she is a great lady."

At this I could not repress a smile which she detected at once.

"Isn't she? Well, no, perhaps she isn't; but you may be sure of one thing, that she is both flesh and shadow more than any one that I have seen. Keep that well in your mind: She is for no man! She would be vanishing out of their hands like water that cannot be held."

I caught my breath. "Inconstant," I whispered.

"I don't say that. Maybe too proud, too wilful, too full of pity. Signorino, you don't know much about women. And you may learn something yet or you may not; but what you learn from her you will never forget."

"Not to be held," I murmured; and she whom the quayside called Madame Léonore closed her outstretched hand before my face and opened it at once to show its emptiness in illustration of her expressed opinion. Dominic never moved.

I wished good-night to these two and left the café for the fresh air and the dark spaciousness of the quays augmented by all the width of the old Port where between the trails of light the shadows of heavy hulls appeared very black, merging their outlines in a great confusion. I left behind me the end of the Cannebiére, a wide vista of tall houses and much-lighted pavements losing itself in the distance with an extinction of both shapes and lights. I slunk past it with only a side glance and sought the dimness of quiet streets away from the centre of the usual night gaieties of the town. The dress I wore was just that of a sailor come ashore from some coaster, a thick blue woollen shirt or rather a sort of jumper, with a knitted cap like a tam-o'-shanter worn very much on one side and with a red

tuft of wool in the centre. This was even the reason
why I had lingered so long in the café. I didn't want
to be recognized in the streets in that costume and still
less to be seen entering the house in the street of the
Consuls. At that hour when the performances were
over and all the sensible citizens in their beds I didn't
hesitate to cross the Place of the Opera. It was dark,
the audience had already dispersed. The rare passers-
by I met hurrying on their last affairs of the day paid no
attention to me at all. The street of the Consuls I
expected to find empty, as usual at that time of the
night. But as I turned a corner into it I overtook
three people who must have belonged to the locality.
To me, somehow, they appeared strange. Two girls
in dark cloaks walked ahead of a tall man in a top hat.
I slowed down, not wishing to pass them by, the more
so that the door of the house was only a few yards distant. But to my intense surprise those people stopped
at it and the man in the top hat, producing a latchkey,
let his two companions through, followed them, and
with a heavy slam cut himself off from my astonished
self and the rest of mankind.

In the stupid way people have I stood and meditated
on the sight, before it occurred to me that this was
the most useless thing to do. After waiting a little
longer to let the others get away from the hall I entered
in my turn. The small gas-jet seemed not to have
been touched ever since that distant night when Mills
and I trod the black-and-white marble hall for the
first time on the heels of Captain Blunt—who lived by
his sword. And in the dimness and solitude which kept
no more trace of the three strangers than if they had
been the merest ghosts I seemed to hear the ghostly
murmur, "*Américain,   catholique   et   gentilhomme.
Amér . . .*" Unseen by human eye I ran up the

flight of steps swiftly and on the first floor stepped into my sitting-room of which the door was open . . . *"et gentilhomme."* I tugged at the bell pull and somewhere down below a bell rang as unexpected for Therese as a call from a ghost.

I had no notion whether Therese could hear me. I seemed to remember that she slept in any bed that happened to be vacant. For all I knew she might have been asleep in mine. As I had no matches on me I waited for a while in the dark. The house was perfectly still. Suddenly without the slightest preliminary sound light fell into the room and Therese stood in the open door with a candlestick in her hand.

She had on her peasant brown skirt. The rest of her was concealed in a black shawl which covered her head, her shoulders, arms, and elbows completely, down to her waist. The hand holding the candle protruded from that envelope which the other invisible hand clasped together under her very chin. And her face looked like a face in a painting. She said at once:

"You startled me, my young Monsieur."

She addressed me most frequently in that way as though she liked the very word "young." Her manner was certainly peasant-like with a sort of plaint in the voice, while the face was that of a serving Sister in some small and rustic convent.

"I meant to do it," I said. "I am a very bad person."

"The young are always full of fun," she said as if she were gloating over the idea. "It is very pleasant."

"But you are very brave," I chaffed her, "for you didn't expect a ring, and after all it might have been the devil who pulled the bell."

"It might have been. But a poor girl like me is not afraid of the devil. I have a pure heart. I have been

to confession last evening. No. But it might have
been an assassin that pulled the bell ready to kill a
poor harmless woman. This is a very lonely street.
What could prevent you from killing me now and then
walking out again free as air?"

While she was talking like this she had lighted the
gas and with the last words she glided through the
bedroom door leaving me thunderstruck at the unexpected character of her thoughts.

I couldn't know that there had been during my absence a case of atrocious murder which had affected the
imagination of the whole town; and though Therese did
not read the papers (which she imagined to be full of im-
pieties and immoralities invented by godless men) yet if
she spoke at all with her kind, which she must have done
at least in shops, she could not have helped hearing of it.
It seems that for some days people could talk of nothing
else. She returned gliding from the bedroom hermeti-
cally sealed in her black shawl just as she had gone in,
with the protruding hand holding the lighted candle and
relieved my perplexity as to her morbid turn of mind by
telling me something of the murder story in a strange
tone of indifference even while referring to its most
horrible features. "That's what carnal sin (*péché de
chair*) leads to," she commented severely and passed
her tongue over her thin lips. "And then the devil
furnishes the occasion."

"I can't imagine the devil inciting me to murder you,
Therese," I said, "and I didn't like that ready way you
took me for an example, as it were. I suppose pretty
near every lodger might be a potential murderer, but
I expected to be made an exception."

With the candle held a little below her face, with that
face of one tone and without relief she looked more than
ever as though she had come out of an old, cracked,

smoky painting, the subject of which was altogether beyond human conception. And she only compressed her lips.

"All right," I said, making myself comfortable on a sofa after pulling off my boots. "I suppose any one is liable to commit murder all of a sudden. Well, have you got many murderers in the house?"

"Yes," she said, "it's pretty good. Upstairs and downstairs," she sighed. "God sees to it."

"And bye-the-bye, who is that grey-headed murderer in a tall hat whom I saw shepherding two girls into this house?"

She put on a candid air in which one could detect a little of her peasant cunning.

"Oh, yes. They are two dancing girls at the Opera, sisters, as different from each other as I and our poor Rita. But they are both virtuous and that gentleman, their father, is very severe with them. Very severe indeed, poor motherless things. And it seems to be such a sinful occupation."

"I bet you make them pay a big rent, Therese. With an occupation like that . . ."

She looked at me with eyes of invincible innocence and began to glide towards the door, so smoothly that the flame of the candle hardly swayed. "Good-night," she murmured.

"Good-night, Mademoiselle."

Then in the very doorway she turned right round as a marionette would turn.

"Oh, you ought to know, my dear young Monsieur, that Mr. Blunt, the dear handsome man, has arrived from Navarre three days ago or more. Oh," she added with a priceless air of compunction, "he is such a charming gentleman."

And the door shut after her.

IV

THAT night I passed in a state, mostly open-eyed, I believe, but always on the border between dreams and waking. The only thing absolutely absent from it was the feeling of rest. The usual sufferings of a youth in love had nothing to do with it. I could leave her, go away from her, remain away from her, without an added pang or any augmented consciousness of that torturing sentiment of distance so acute that often it ends by wearing itself out in a few days. Far or near was all one to me, as if one could not get ever any further but also never any nearer to her secret: the state like that of some strange wild faiths that get hold of mankind with the cruel mystic grip of unattainable perfection, robbing them of both liberty and felicity on earth. A faith presents one with some hope, though. But I had no hope, and not even desire as a thing outside myself, that would come and go, exhaust or excite. It was in me just like life was in me; that life of which a popular saying affirms that "it is sweet." For the general wisdom of mankind will always stop short on the limit of the formidable.

What is best in a state of brimful, equable suffering is that it does away with the gnawings of petty sensations. Too far gone to be sensible to hope and desire I was spared the inferior pangs of elation and impatience. Hours with her or hours without her were all alike, all in her possession! But still there are shades and I will admit that the hours of that morning were perhaps a little more difficult to get through than the others.

I had sent word of my arrival of course. I had written a note. I had rung the bell. Therese had appeared herself in her brown garb and as monachal as ever. I had said to her:

"Have this sent off at once."

She had gazed at the addressed envelope, smiled (I was looking up at her from my desk), and at last took it up with an effort of sanctimonious repugnance. But she remained with it in her hand looking at me as though she were piously gloating over something she could read in my face.

"Oh, that Rita, that Rita," she murmured. "And you, too! Why are you trying, you, too, like the others, to stand between her and the mercy of God? What's the good of all this to you? And you such a nice, dear, young gentleman. For no earthly good, only making all the kind saints in heaven angry, and our mother ashamed in her place amongst the blessed."

"Mademoiselle Therese," I said, "*vous êtes folle.*"

I believed she was crazy. She was cunning, too. I added an imperious: "*Allez,*" and with a strange docility she glided out without another word. All I had to do then was to get dressed and wait till eleven o'clock.

The hour struck at last. If I could have plunged into a light wave and been transported instantaneously to Doña Rita's door it would no doubt have saved me an infinity of pangs too complex for analysis; but as this was impossible I elected to walk from end to end of that long way. My emotions and sensations were childlike and chaotic inasmuch that they were very intense and primitive, and that I lay very helpless in their unrelaxing grasp. If one could have kept a record of one's physical sensations it would have been a fine collection of absurdities and contradictions. Hardly touching the ground and yet leaden-footed; with a sinking heart and an excited brain; hot and trembling with a secret faintness, and yet as firm as a rock and with a sort of indifference to it all, I did reach the door which was frightfully like any other commonplace door, but at the same time had a fateful character: a few planks put together—and an awful symbol; not to be approached without awe—and yet coming open in the ordinary way to the ring of the bell.

It came open. Oh, yes, very much as usual. But in the ordinary course of events the first sight in the hall should have been the back of the ubiquitous, busy, silent maid hurrying off and already distant. But not at all! She actually waited for me to enter. I was extremely taken aback and I believe spoke to her for the first time in my life.

"*Bonjour*, Rose."

She dropped her dark eyelids over those eyes that ought to have been lustrous but were not, as if somebody had breathed on them the first thing in the morning. She was a girl without smiles. She shut the door after me, and not only did that but in the incredible idleness of that morning she, who had never a moment to spare, started helping me off with my overcoat. It was positively embarrassing from its novelty. While busying herself with those trifles she murmured without any marked intention:

"Captain Blunt is with Madame."

This didn't exactly surprise me. I knew he had come up to town; I only happened to have forgotten his existence for the moment. I looked at the girl also without any particular intention. But she arrested my movement towards the dining-room door by a low, hurried, if perfectly unemotional appeal:

"Monsieur George!"

That of course was not my name. It served me then as it will serve for this story. In all sorts of strange places I was alluded to as "that young gentleman they call Monsieur George." Orders came from "Monsieur George" to men who nodded knowingly. Events pivoted about "Monsieur George." I haven't the slightest doubt that in the dark and tortuous streets of the old Town there were fingers pointed at my back: "There goes Monsieur George." I had been introduced discreetly to several considerable persons as "Monsieur George." I had learned to answer to the name quite naturally; and to simplify matters I was also "Monsieur George" in the street of the Consuls and in the Villa on the Prado. I verily believe that at that time I had the feeling that the name of George really belonged to me. I waited for what the girl had to say. I had to wait some time, though during that silence she gave no sign of distress or agitation. It was for her obviously a moment of reflection. Her lips were compressed a little in a characteristic, capable manner. I looked at her with a friendliness I really felt towards her slight, unattractive, and dependable person.

"Well," I said at last, rather amused by this mental hesitation. I never took it for anything else. I was sure it was not distrust. She appreciated men and things and events solely in relation to Doña Rita's welfare and safety. And as to that I believed myself above suspicion. At last she spoke.

"Madame is not happy." This information was given to me not emotionally but as it were officially. It hadn't even a tone of warning. A mere statement. Without waiting to see the effect she opened the dining-room door, not to announce my name in the usual way but to go in and shut it behind her. In that short moment I heard no voices inside. Not a sound reached me

while the door remained shut; but in a few seconds
it came open again and Rose stood aside to let me
pass.

Then I heard something: Doña Rita's voice raised a
little on an impatient note (a very, very rare thing)
finishing some phrase of protest with the words:

". . . Of no consequence."

I heard them as I would have heard any other words,
for she had that kind of voice which carries a long distance. But the maid's statement occupied all my
mind. "Madame *n'est pas heureuse.*" It had a dreadful precision . . . "Not happy . . ." This
unhappiness had almost a concrete form—something
resembling a horrid bat. I was tired, excited, and
generally overwrought. My head felt empty. What
were the appearances of unhappiness? I was still
naïve enough to associate them with tears, lamentations,
extraordinary attitudes of the body and some sort of
facial distortion, all very dreadful to behold. I didn't
know what I should see; but in what I did see there was
nothing startling, at any rate from that nursery point
of view which apparently I had not yet outgrown.

With immense relief the apprehensive child within
me beheld Captain Blunt warming his back at the more
distant of the two fireplaces; and as to Doña Rita there
was nothing extraordinary in her attitude either, except
perhaps that her hair was all loose about her shoulders.
I hadn't the slightest doubt they had been riding together that morning, but she, with her impatience of all
costume (and yet she could dress herself admirably and
wore her dresses triumphantly), had divested herself of
her riding habit and sat cross-legged enfolded in that
ample blue robe like a young savage chieftain in a
blanket. It covered her very feet. And before the
normal fixity of her enigmatical eyes the smoke of the

cigarette ascended ceremonially, straight up, in a slender spiral.

"How are you," was the greeting of Captain Blunt with the usual smile which would have been more amiable if his teeth hadn't been, just then, clenched quite so tight. How he managed to force his voice through that shining barrier I could never understand. Doña Rita tapped the couch engagingly by her side but I sat down instead in the armchair nearly opposite her, which, I imagine, must have been just vacated by Blunt. She inquired with that particular gleam of the eyes in which there was something immemorial and gay:

"Well?"

"Perfect success."

"I could hug you."

At any time her lips moved very little but in this instance the intense whisper of these words seemed to form itself right in my very heart; not as a conveyed sound but as an imparted emotion vibrating there with an awful intimacy of delight. And yet it left my heart heavy.

"Oh, yes, for joy," I said bitterly but very low; "for your Royalist, Legitimist, joy." Then with that trick of very precise politeness which I must have caught from Mr. Blunt I added:

"I don't want to be embraced—for the King."

And I might have stopped there. But I didn't. With a perversity which should be forgiven to those who suffer night and day and are as if drunk with an exalted unhappiness, I went on: "For the sake of an old cast-off glove; for I suppose a disdained love is not much more than a soiled, flabby thing that finds itself on a private rubbish heap because it has missed the fire."

She listened to me, unreadable, unmoved, narrowed

eyes, closed lips, slightly flushed face, as if carved six
thousand years ago in order to fix for ever that something secret and obscure which is in all women. Not
the gross immobility of a Sphinx proposing roadside
riddles but the finer immobility, almost sacred, of a
fateful figure seated at the very source of the passions
that have moved men from the dawn of ages.

Captain Blunt, with his elbow on the high mantelpiece, had turned away a little from us and his attitude
expressed excellently the detachment of a man who does
not want to hear. As a matter of fact, I don't suppose
he could have heard. He was too far away, our voices
were too contained. Moreover, he didn't want to hear.
There could be no doubt about it; but she addressed him
unexpectedly.

"As I was saying to you, Don Juan, I have the greatest difficulty in getting myself, I won't say, understood,
but simply believed."

No pose of detachment could avail against the warm
waves of that voice. He had to hear. After a moment
he altered his position as it were reluctantly, to answer
her.

"That's a difficulty that women generally have."

"Yet I have always spoken the truth."

"All women speak the truth," said Blunt imperturb-
ably. And this annoyed her.

"Where are the men I have deceived?" she cried.

"Yes, where?" said Blunt in a tone of alacrity as
though he had been ready to go out and look for them
outside.

"No! But show me one. I say—where is he?"

He threw his affectation of detachment to the winds,
moved his shoulders slightly, very slightly, made a step
nearer to the couch, and looked down on her with an
expression of amused courtesy.

"Oh, I don't know. Probably nowhere. But if such a man could be found I am certain he would turn out a very stupid person. You can't be expected to furnish every one who approaches you with a mind. To expect that would be too much, even from you who know how to work wonders at such little cost to yourself."

"To myself?" she repeated in a loud tone.

"Why this indignation? I am simply taking your word for it."

"Such little cost!" she exclaimed under her breath.

"I mean to your person."

"Oh, yes," she murmured, glanced down, as it were upon herself, then added very low: "This body."

"Well, it is you," said Blunt with visibly contained irritation. "You don't pretend it's somebody else's. It can't be. You haven't borrowed it. . . . It fits you too well," he ended between his teeth.

"You take pleasure in tormenting yourself," she remonstrated, suddenly placated; "and I would be sorry for you if I didn't think it's the mere revolt of your pride. And you know you are indulging your pride at my expense. As to the rest of it, as to my living, acting, working wonders at a little cost . . . it has all but killed me morally. Do you hear? Killed."

"Oh, you are not dead yet," he muttered.

"No," she said with gentle patience. "There is still some feeling left in me; and if it is any satisfaction to you to know it, you may be certain that I shall be conscious of the last stab."

He remained silent for a while and then with a polite smile and a movement of the head in my direction he warned her.

"Our audience will get bored."

"I am perfectly aware that Monsieur George is here

and that he has been breathing a very different atmosphere from what he gets in this room. Don't you find this room extremely confined?" she asked me.

The room was very large but it is a fact that I felt oppressed at that moment. This mysterious quarrel between those two people, revealing something more close in their intercourse than I had ever before suspected, made me so profoundly unhappy that I didn't even attempt to answer. And she continued:

"More space. More air. Give me air, air." She seized the embroidered edges of her blue robe under her white throat and made as if to tear them apart, to fling it open on her breast, recklessly, before our eyes. We both remained perfectly still. Her hands dropped nervelessly by her side. "I envy you, Monsieur George. If I am to go under I should prefer to be drowned in the sea with the wind on my face. What luck, to feel nothing less than all the world closing over one's head!"

A short silence ensued before Mr. Blunt's drawing-room voice was heard with playful familiarity.

"I have often asked myself whether you weren't really a very ambitious person, Doña Rita."

"And I ask myself whether you have any heart." She was looking straight at him and he gratified her with the usual cold white flash of his even teeth before he answered.

"Asking yourself? That means that you are really asking me. But why do it so publicly? I mean it. One single, detached presence is enough to make a public. One alone. Why not wait till he returns to those regions of space and air—from which he came."

His particular trick of speaking of any third person as of a lay figure was exasperating. Yet at the moment I did not know how to resent it, but, in any case, Doña

Rita would not have given me time. Without a moment's hesitation she cried out:

"I only wish he could take me out there with him."

For a moment Mr. Blunt's face became as still as a mask and then instead of an angry it assumed an indulgent expression. As to me I had a rapid vision of Dominic's astonishment, awe, and sarcasm which was always as tolerant as it is possible for sarcasm to be. But what a charming, gentle, gay, and fearless companion she would have made! I believed in her fearlessness in any adventure that would interest her. It would be a new occasion for me, a new viewpoint for that faculty of admiration she had awakened in me at sight—at first sight—before she opened her lips—before she ever turned her eyes on me. She would have to wear some sort of sailor costume, a blue woollen shirt open at the throat. . . . Dominic's hooded cloak would envelop her amply, and her face under the black hood would have a luminous quality, adolescent charm, and an enigmatic expression. The confined space of the little vessel's quarterdeck would lend itself to her cross-legged attitudes, and the blue sea would balance gently her characteristic immobility that seemed to hide thoughts as old and profound as itself. As restless, too—perhaps.

But the picture I had in my eye, coloured and simple like an illustration to a nursery-book tale of two venturesome children's escapade, was what fascinated me most. Indeed I felt that we two were like children under the gaze of a man of the world—who lived by his sword. And I said recklessly:

"Yes, you ought to come along with us for a trip. You would see a lot of things for yourself."

Mr. Blunt's expression had grown even more indulgent if that were possible. Yet there was something ineradicably ambiguous about that man. I did not like the indefinable tone in which he observed:

"You are perfectly reckless in what you say, Doña Rita. It has become a habit with you of late."

"While with you reserve is a second nature, Don Juan."

This was uttered with the gentlest, almost tender, irony. Mr. Blunt waited a while before he said:

"Certainly . . . Would you have liked me to be otherwise?"

She extended her hand to him on a sudden impulse.

"Forgive me! I may have been unjust, and you may only have been loyal. The falseness is not in us. The fault is in life itself, I suppose. I have been always frank with you."

"And I obedient," he said, bowing low over her hand. He turned away, paused to look at me for some time and finally gave me the correct sort of nod. But he said nothing and went out, or rather lounged out with his worldly manner of perfect ease under all conceivable circumstances. With her head lowered Doña Rita watched him till he actually shut the door behind him. I was facing her and only heard the door close.

"Don't stare at me," were the first words she said.

It was difficult to obey that request. I didn't know exactly where to look, while I sat facing her. So I got up, vaguely full of goodwill, prepared even to move off as far as the window, when she commanded:

"Don't turn your back on me."

I chose to understand it symbolically.

"You know very well I could never do that. I couldn't. Not even if I wanted to." And I added: "It's too late now."

"Well, then, sit down. Sit down on this couch."

I sat down on the couch. Unwillingly? Yes. I was at that stage when all her words, all her gestures, all her silences were a heavy trial to me, put a stress on my resolution, on that fidelity to myself and to her which lay like a leaden weight on my untried heart. But I didn't sit down very far away from her, though that soft and billowy couch was big enough, God knows! No, not very far from her. Self-control, dignity, hopelessness itself, have their limits. The halo of her tawny hair stirred as I let myself drop by her side. Whereupon she flung one arm round my neck, leaned her temple against my shoulder and began to sob; but that I could not guess from her slight, convulsive movements because in our relative positions I could only see the mass of her tawny hair brushed back, yet with a halo of escaped hair which as I bent my head over her tickled my lips, my cheek, in a maddening manner.

We sat like two venturesome children in an illustration to a tale, scared by their adventure. But not for long. As I instinctively, yet timidly, sought for her other hand I felt a tear strike the back of mine, big and heavy as if fallen from a great height. It was too much for me. I must have given a nervous start. At once I heard a murmur: "You had better go away now."

I withdrew myself gently from under the light weight of her head, from this unspeakable bliss and inconceivable misery, and had the absurd impression of leaving her suspended in the air. And I moved away on tiptoe.

Like an inspired blind man led by Providence I found my way out of the room, but really I saw nothing till in the hall the maid appeared by enchantment before me holding up my overcoat. I let her help me into it. And then (again as if by enchantment) she had my hat in her hand.

"No. Madame isn't happy," I whispered to her distractedly.

She let me take my hat out of her hand and while I was putting it on my head I heard an austere whisper:

"Madame should listen to her heart."

Austere is not the word; it was almost freezing, this unexpected, dispassionate rustle of words. I had to repress a shudder, and as coldly as herself I murmured:

"She has done that once too often."

Rose was standing very close to me and I caught distinctly the note of scorn in her indulgent compassion.

"Oh, that! . . . Madame is like a child."

It was impossible to get the bearing of that utterance from that girl who, as Doña Rita herself had told me, was the most taciturn of human beings; and yet of all human beings the one nearest to herself. I seized her head in my hands and turning up her face I looked straight down into her black eyes which should have been lustrous. Like a piece of glass breathed upon they reflected no light, revealed no depths, and under my ardent gaze remained tarnished, misty, unconscious.

"Will Monsieur kindly let me go. Monsieur shouldn't play the child, either." (I let her go.) "Madame could have the world at her feet. Indeed she has it there; only she doesn't care for it."

How talkative she was, this maid with unsealed lips! For some reason or other this last statement of hers brought me immense comfort.

"Yes?" I whispered breathlessly.

"Yes! But in that case what's the use of living in fear and torment?" she went on, revealing a little more of herself to my astonishment. She opened the door for me and added:

"Those that don't care to stoop ought at least make themselves happy."

I turned in the very doorway: "There is something which prevents that?" I suggested.

"To be sure there is. *Bonjour*, Monsieur."

PART FOUR

I

"Such a charming lady in a grey silk dress and a hand as white as snow. She looked at me through such funny glasses on the end of a long handle. A very great lady but her voice was as kind as the voice of a saint. I have never seen anything like that. She made me feel so timid."

The voice uttering these words was the voice of Therese and I looked at her from a bed draped heavily in brown silk curtains fantastically looped up from ceiling to floor. The glow of a sunshiny day was toned down by closed jalousies to a mere transparency of darkness. In this thin medium Therese's form appeared flat without detail, as if cut out of black paper. It glided towards the window and with a click and a scrape let in the full flood of light which smote my aching eyeballs painfully.

In truth all that night had been the abomination of desolation to me. After wrestling with my thoughts, if the acute consciousness of a woman's existence may be called a thought, I had apparently dropped off to sleep only to go on wrestling with a nightmare, a senseless and terrifying dream of being in bonds which, even after waking, made me feel powerless in all my limbs. I lay still, suffering acutely from a renewed sense of existence, unable to lift an arm, and wondering why I was not at sea, how long I had slept, how long Therese had been talking before her voice had reached me in that purgatory of hopeless longing and unanswerable questions to which I was condemned.

It was Therese's habit to begin talking directly she entered the room with the tray of morning coffee. This was her method for waking me up. I generally regained the consciousness of the external world on some pious phrase asserting the spiritual comfort of early mass, or on angry lamentations about the unconscionable rapacity of the dealers in fish and vegetables; for after mass it was Therese's practice to do the marketing for the house. As a matter of fact the necessity of having to pay, to actually give money to people, infuriated the pious Therese. But the matter of this morning's speech was so extraordinary that it might have been the prolongation of a nightmare: a man in bonds having to listen to weird and unaccountable speeches against which, he doesn't know why, his very soul revolts.

In sober truth my soul remained in revolt though I was convinced that I was no longer dreaming. I watched Therese coming away from the window with that helpless dread a man bound hand and foot may be excused to feel. For in such a situation even the absurd may appear ominous. She came up close to the bed and folding her hands meekly in front of her turned her eyes up to the ceiling.

"If I had been her daughter she couldn't have spoken more softly to me," she said sentimentally.

I made a great effort to speak.

"Mademoiselle Therese, you are raving."

"She addressed me as Mademoiselle, too, so nicely. I was struck with veneration for her white hair but her face, believe me, my dear young Monsieur, has not so many wrinkles as mine."

She compressed her lips with an angry glance at me as if I could help her wrinkles, then she sighed.

"God sends wrinkles, but what is our face?" she digressed in a tone of great humility. "We shall have glorious faces in Paradise. But meantime God has permitted me to preserve a smooth heart."

"Are you going to keep on like this much longer?" I fairly shouted at her. "What are you talking about?"

"I am talking about the sweet old lady who came in a carriage. Not a fiacre. I can tell a fiacre. In a little carriage shut in with glass all in front. I suppose she is very rich. The carriage was very shiny outside and all beautiful grey stuff inside. I opened the door to her myself. She got out slowly like a queen. I was struck all of a heap. Such a shiny beautiful little carriage. There were blue silk tassels inside, beautiful silk tassels."

Obviously Therese had been very much impressed by a brougham, though she didn't know the name for it. Of all the town she knew nothing but the streets which led to a neighbouring church frequented only by the poorer classes and the humble quarter around, where she did her marketing. Besides, she was accustomed to glide along the walls with her eyes cast down; for her natural boldness would never show itself through that nun-like mien except when bargaining, if only on a matter of threepence. Such a turn-out had never been presented to her notice before. The traffic in the street of the Consuls was mostly pedestrian and far from fashionable. And anyhow Therese never looked out of the window. She lurked in the depths of the house like some kind of spider that shuns attention. She used to dart at one from some dark recesses which I never explored.

Yet it seemed to me that she exaggerated her raptures for some reason or other. With her it was very difficult to distinguish between craft and innocence.

"Do you mean to say," I asked suspiciously, "that an old lady wants to hire an apartment here? I hope you told her there was no room, because, you know, this house is not exactly the thing for venerable old ladies."

"Don't make me angry, my dear young Monsieur. I have been to confession this morning. Aren't you comfortable? Isn't the house appointed richly enough for anybody?"

That girl with a peasant-nun's face had never seen the inside of a house other than some half-ruined *caserio* in her native hills.

I pointed out to her that this was not a matter of splendour or comfort but of "convenances." She pricked up her ears at that word which probably she had never heard before; but with woman's uncanny intuition I believe she understood perfectly what I meant. Her air of saintly patience became so pronounced that with my own poor intuition I perceived that she was raging at me inwardly. Her weather-tanned complexion, already affected by her confined life, took on an extraordinary clayey aspect which reminded me of a strange head painted by El Greco which my friend Prax had hung on one of his walls and used to rail at; yet not without a certain respect.

Therese, with her hands still meekly folded about her waist, had mastered the feelings of anger so unbecoming to a person whose sins had been absolved only about three hours before, and asked me with an insinuating softness whether she wasn't an honest girl enough to look after any old lady belonging to a world which after all was sinful. She reminded me that she had kept house ever since she was "so high" for her uncle the priest: a man well-known for his saintliness in a large district extending even beyond Pampeluna. The character of a house depended upon the person who

ruled it. She didn't know what impenitent wretches
had been breathing within these walls in the time of
that godless and wicked man who had planted every
seed of perdition in "our Rita's" ill-disposed heart.
But he was dead and she, Therese, knew for certain
that wickedness perished utterly, because of God's
anger (*la colère du bon Dieu*). She would have no hesitation in receiving a bishop, if need be, since "our
Rita," with her poor, wretched, unbelieving heart, had
nothing more to do with the house.

All this came out of her like an unctuous trickle of
some acrid oil. The low, voluble delivery was enough
by itself to compel my attention.

"You think you know your sister's heart?" I asked.

She made small eyes at me to discover if I was angry.
She seemed to have an invincible faith in the virtuous
dispositions of young men. And as I had spoken in
measured tones and hadn't got red in the face she let
herself go.

"Black, my dear young Monsieur, Black. I always knew it. Uncle, poor saintly man, was too holy
to take notice of anything. He was too busy with his
thoughts to listen to anything I had to say to him. For
instance, as to her shamelessness. She was always ready
to run half naked about the hills . . ."

"Yes. After your goats. All day long. Why
didn't you mend her frocks?"

"Oh, you know about the goats. My dear young
Monsieur, I could never tell when she would fling over
her pretended sweetness and put her tongue out at me.
Did she tell you about a boy, the son of pious and rich
parents, whom she tried to lead astray into the wildness
of thoughts like her own, till the poor dear child drove
her off because she outraged his modesty? I saw him
often with his parents at Sunday mass. The grace of

God preserved him and made him quite a gentleman in Paris. Perhaps it will touch Rita's heart, too, some day. But she was awful then. When I wouldn't listen to her complaints she would say: 'All right, sister, I would just as soon go clothed in rain and wind.' And such a bag of bones, too, like the picture of a devil's imp. Ah, my dear young Monsieur, you don't know how wicked her heart is. You aren't bad enough for that yourself. I don't believe you are evil at all in your innocent little heart. I never heard you jeer at holy things. You are only thoughtless. For instance, I have never seen you make the sign of the cross in the morning. Why don't you make a practice of crossing yourself directly you open your eyes? It's a very good thing. It keeps Satan off for the day."

She proffered that advice in a most matter-of-fact tone as if it were a precaution against a cold, compressed her lips, then returning to her fixed idea, "but the house is mine," she insisted very quietly with an accent which made me feel that Satan himself would never manage to tear it out of her hands.

"And so I told the great lady in grey. I told her that my sister had given it to me and that surely God would not let her take it away again."

"You told that grey-headed lady, an utter stranger! You are getting more crazy every day. You have neither good sense nor good feeling, Mademoiselle Therese, let me tell you. Do you talk about your sister to the butcher and the greengrocer, too? A downright savage would have more restraint. What's your object? What do you expect from it? What pleasure do you get from it? Do you think you please God by abusing your sister? What do you think you are?"

"A poor lone girl amongst a lot of wicked people. Do

you think I want to go forth amongst those abomina-
tions? It's that poor sinful Rita that wouldn't let me
be where I was, serving a holy man, next door to a
church, and sure of my share of Paradise. I simply
obeyed my uncle. It's he who told me to go forth and
attempt to save her soul, bring her back to us, to a
virtuous life. But what would be the good of that?
She is given over to worldly, carnal thoughts. Of
course we are a good family and my uncle is a great man
in the country, but where is the reputable farmer or
God-fearing man of that kind that would dare to bring
such a girl into his house to his mother and sisters?
No, let her give her ill-gotten wealth up to the deserving
and devote the rest of her life to repentance."

She uttered these righteous reflections and presented
this programme for the salvation of her sister's soul in a
reasonable convinced tone which was enough to give
goose flesh to one all over.

"Mademoiselle Therese," I said, "you are nothing
less than a monster."

She received that true expression of my opinion as
though I had given her a sweet of a particularly delicious kind. She liked to be abused. It pleased her to be
called names. I did let her have that satisfaction to her
heart's content. At last I stopped because I could do
no more, unless I got out of bed to beat her. I have a
vague notion that she would have liked that, too, but
I didn't try. After I had stopped she waited a little
before she raised her downcast eyes.

"You are a dear, ignorant, flighty young gentleman,"
she said. "Nobody can tell what a cross my sister is to
me except the good priest in the church where I go every
day."

"And the mysterious lady in grey," I suggested sar-
castically.

"Such a person might have guessed it," answered Therese, seriously, "but I told her nothing except that this house had been given me in full property by our Rita. And I wouldn't have done that if she hadn't spoken to me of my sister first. I can't tell too many people about that. One can't trust Rita. I know she doesn't fear God but perhaps human respect may keep her from taking this house back from me. If she doesn't want me to talk about her to people why doesn't she give me a properly stamped piece of paper for it?"

She said all this rapidly in one breath and at the end had a sort of anxious gasp which gave me the opportunity to voice my surprise. It was immense.

"That lady, the strange lady, spoke to you of your sister first!" I cried.

"The lady asked me, after she had been in a little time, whether really this house belonged to Madame de Lastaola. She had been so sweet and kind and condescending that I did not mind humiliating my spirit before such a good Christian. I told her that I didn't know how the poor sinner in her mad blindness called herself, but that this house had been given to me truly enough by my sister. She raised her eyebrows at that but she looked at me at the same time so kindly, as much as to say, 'Don't trust much to that, my dear girl,' that I couldn't help taking up her hand, soft as down, and kissing it. She took it away pretty quick but she was not offended. But she only said, 'That's very generous on your sister's part,' in a way that made me run cold all over. I suppose all the world knows our Rita for a shameless girl. It was then that the lady took up those glasses on a long gold handle and looked at me through them till I felt very much abashed. She said to me, 'There is nothing to be unhappy about. Madame de Lastaola is a very remarkable person who has done many surprising things. She is not to be judged like other people and as far as I know she has never wronged a single human being. . . .' That put heart into me, I can tell you; and the lady told me then not to disturb her son. She would wait till he woke up. She knew he was a bad sleeper. I said to her: 'Why, I can hear the dear sweet gentleman this moment having his bath in the fencing-room,' and I took her into the studio. They are there now and they are going to have their lunch together at twelve o'clock."

"Why on earth didn't you tell me at first that the lady was Mrs. Blunt?"

"Didn't I? I thought I did," she said innocently. I felt a sudden desire to get out of that house, to fly from the reinforced Blunt element which was to me so oppressive.

"I want to get up and dress, Mademoiselle Therese," I said.

She gave a slight start and without looking at me again glided out of the room, the many folds of her brown skirt remaining undisturbed as she moved.

I looked at my watch; it was ten o'clock. Therese had been late with my coffee. The delay was clearly caused by the unexpected arrival of Mr. Blunt's mother, which might or might not have been expected by her son. The existence of those Blunts made me feel uncomfortable in a peculiar way as though they had been the denizens of another planet with a subtly different point of view and something in the intelligence which was bound to remain unknown to me. It caused in me a feeling of inferiority which I intensely disliked. This did not arise from the actual fact that those people originated in another continent. I had met Americans before. And the Blunts were Americans. But so little! That was the trouble. Captain Blunt might have been a Frenchman as far as languages, tones, and manners went. But you could not have mistaken him for one. . . . Why? You couldn't tell. It was something indefinite. It occurred to me while I was towelling hard my hair, face, and the back of my neck, that I could not meet J. K. Blunt on equal terms in any relation of life except perhaps arms in hand, and in preference with pistols, which are less intimate, acting at a distance—but arms of some sort. For physically his life, which could be taken away from him, was exactly like mine, held on the same terms and of the same vanishing quality.

I would have smiled at my absurdity if all, even the most intimate, vestige of gaiety had not been crushed out of my heart by the intolerable weight of my love for Rita. It crushed, it overshadowed, too, it was immense. If there were any smiles in the world (which I didn't believe) I could not have seen them. Love for Rita . . . if it was love, I asked myself despairingly, while I brushed my hair before a glass. It did not seem to have any sort of beginning as far as I could remember. A thing the origin of which you cannot trace cannot be seriously considered. It is an illusion. Or perhaps mine was a physical state, some sort of disease akin to melancholia which is a form of insanity? The only moments of relief I could remember were when she and I would start squabbling like two passionate infants in a nursery, over anything under heaven, over a phrase, a word sometimes, in the great light of the glass rotunda, disregarding the quiet entrances and exits of the ever-active Rose, in great bursts of voices and peals of laughter. . . .

I felt tears come into my eyes at the memory of her laughter, the true memory of the senses almost more penetrating than the reality itself. It haunted me. All

that appertained to her haunted me with the same awful
intimacy, her whole form in the familiar pose, her very
substance in its colour and texture, her eyes, her lips,
the gleam of her teeth, the tawny mist of her hair, the
smoothness of her forehead, the faint scent that she
used, the very shape, feel, and warmth of her high-
heeled slipper that would sometimes in the heat of the
discussion drop on the floor with a crash, and which I
would (always in the heat of the discussion) pick up
and toss back on the couch without ceasing to argue.
And besides being haunted by what was Rita on earth
I was haunted also by her waywardness, her gentleness
and her flame, by that which the high gods called Rita
when speaking of her amongst themselves. Oh, yes,
certainly I was haunted by her but so was her sister
Therese—who was crazy. It proved nothing. As
to her tears, since I had not caused them, they only
aroused my indignation. To put her head on my shoulder, to weep these strange tears, was nothing short of an
outrageous liberty. It was a mere emotional trick.
She would have just as soon leaned her head against
the over-mantel of one of those tall, red granite chimney-
pieces in order to weep comfortably. And then when
she had no longer any need of support she dispensed
with it by simply telling me to go away. How convenient! The request had sounded pathetic, almost
sacredly so, but then it might have been the exhibition
of the coolest possible impudence. With her one could
not tell. Sorrow, indifference, tears, smiles, all with
her seemed to have a hidden meaning. Nothing could
be trusted. . . . "Heavens! Am I as crazy as
Therese?" I asked myself with a passing chill of fear,
while occupied in equalizing the ends of my neck-tie.

I felt suddenly that "this sort of thing" would kill me.
The definition of the cause was vague, but the thought

itself was no mere morbid artificiality of sentiment but a
genuine conviction. "That sort of thing" was what I
would have to die from. It wouldn't be from the innumerable doubts. Any sort of certitude would be also
deadly. It wouldn't be from a stab—a kiss would kill
me as surely. It would not be from a frown or from any
particular word or any particular act—but from having
to bear them all, together and in succession—from
having to live with "that sort of thing." About the
time I finished with my neck-tie I had done with life
too. I absolutely did not care because I couldn't tell
whether, mentally and physically, from the roots of my
hair to the soles of my feet—whether I was more weary
or unhappy.

And now my toilet was finished, my occupation was
gone. An immense distress descended upon me. It
has been observed that the routine of daily life, that
arbitrary system of trifles, is a great moral support.
But my toilet was finished, I had nothing more to do
of those things consecrated by usage and which leave
you no option. The exercise of any kind of volition
by a man whose consciousness is reduced to the sensation that he is being killed by "that sort of thing"
cannot be anything but mere trifling with death, an
insincere pose before himself. I wasn't capable of it.
It was then that I discovered that being killed by
"that sort of thing," I mean the absolute conviction
of it, was, so to speak, nothing in itself. The horrible
part was the waiting. That was the cruelty, the tragedy, the bitterness of it. "Why the devil don't I drop
dead now?" I asked myself peevishly, taking a clean
handkerchief out of the drawer and stuffing it in my
pocket.

This was absolutely the last thing, the last ceremony
of an imperative rite. I was abandoned to myself now

and it was terrible.   Generally I used to go out, walk
down to the port, take a look at the craft I loved with a
sentiment that was extremely complex, being mixed up
with the image of a woman; perhaps go on board, not
because there was anything for me to do there but just
for nothing, for happiness, simply as a man will sit con-
tented in the companionship of the beloved object. For
lunch I had the choice of two places, one Bohemian,
the other select, even aristocratic, where I had still my
reserved table in the *petit salon*, up the white staircase.
In both places I had friends who treated my erratic
appearances with discretion, in one case tinged with
respect, in the other with a certain amused tolerance. I
owed this tolerance to the most careless, the most confirmed of those Bohemians (his beard had streaks of grey
amongst its many other tints) who, once bringing his
heavy hand down on my shoulder, took my defence
against the charge of being disloyal and even foreign to
that milieu of earnest visions taking beautiful and revolutionary shapes in the smoke of pipes, in the jingle of
glasses.

"That fellow (*ce garçon*) is a primitive nature, but he
may be an artist in a sense.   He has broken away from
his conventions.   He is trying to put a special vibration
and his own notion of colour into his life; and perhaps
even to give it a modelling according to his own ideas.
And for all you know he may be on the track of a
masterpiece; but observe: if it happens to be one nobody
will see it.   It can be only for himself.   And even he
won't be able to see it in its completeness except on his
death-bed.   There is something fine in that."

I had blushed with pleasure; such fine ideas had
never entered my head.   But there was something fine.
. . .   How far all this seemed!   How mute and how
still!   What a phantom he was, that man with a beard

of at least seven tones of brown. And those shades
of the other kind such as Baptiste with the shaven
diplomatic face, the *maître d'hotel* in charge of the *petit
salon*, taking my hat and stick from me with a deferential remark: "Monsieur is not very often seen
nowadays." And those other well-groomed heads
raised and nodding at my passage—"*Bonjour.*" "*Bonjour*"—following me with interested eyes; these young
X's and Z's, low-toned, markedly discreet, lounging
up to my table on their way out with murmurs: "Are
you well?"—"Will one see you anywhere this evening?"—not from curiosity, God forbid, but just from
friendliness; and passing on almost without waiting
for an answer. What had I to do with them, this elegant dust, these moulds of provincial fashion?

I also often lunched with Doña Rita without invitation. But that was now unthinkable. What had I to
do with a woman who allowed somebody else to make
her cry and then with an amazing lack of good feeling
did her offensive weeping on my shoulder? Obviously I
could have nothing to do with her. My five minutes'
meditation in the middle of the bedroom came to an
end without even a sigh. The dead don't sigh, and
for all practical purposes I was that, except for the
final consummation, the growing cold, the *rigor mortis*
—that blessed state! With measured steps I crossed
the landing to my sitting-room.

II

THE windows of that room gave out on the street of the Consuls which as usual was silent. And the house itself below me and above me was soundless, perfectly still. In general the house was quiet, dumbly quiet, without resonances of any sort, something like what one would imagine the interior of a convent would be. I suppose it was very solidly built. Yet that morning I missed in the stillness that feeling of security and peace which ought to have been associated with it. It is, I believe, generally admitted that the dead are glad to be at rest. But I wasn't at rest. What was wrong with that silence? There was something incongruous in that peace. What was it that had got into that stillness? Suddenly I remembered: the mother of Captain Blunt.

Why had she come all the way from Paris? And why should I bother my head about it? H'm—the Blunt atmosphere, the reinforced Blunt vibration stealing through the walls, through the thick walls and the almost more solid stillness. Nothing to me, of course—the movements of Mme. Blunt, *mère*. It was maternal affection which had brought her south by either the evening or morning Rapide, to take anxious stock of the ravages of that insomnia. Very good thing, insomnia, for a cavalry officer perpetually on outpost duty, a real godsend, so to speak; but on leave a truly devilish condition to be in.

The above sequence of thoughts was entirely unsympathetic and it was followed by a feeling of satisfaction that I, at any rate, was not suffering from insomnia. I could always sleep in the end. In the end. Escape into a nightmare. Wouldn't he revel in that if he could! But that wasn't for him. He had to toss about open-eyed all night and get up weary, weary. But oh, wasn't I weary, too, waiting for a sleep without dreams.

I heard the door behind me open. I had been standing with my face to the window and, I declare, not knowing what I was looking at across the road—the Desert of Sahara or a wall of bricks, a landscape of rivers and forests or only the Consulate of Paraguay. But I had been thinking, apparently, of Mr. Blunt with such intensity that when I saw him enter the room it didn't really make much difference. When I turned about, the door behind him was already shut. He advanced towards me, correct, supple, hollow-eyed, and smiling; and as to his costume ready to go out except for the old shooting jacket which he must have affectioned particularly, for he never lost any time in getting into it at every opportunity. Its material was some tweed mixture; it had gone inconceivably shabby, it was shrunk from old age, it was ragged at the elbows; but any one could see at a glance that it had been made in London by a celebrated tailor, by a distinguished specialist. Blunt came towards me in all the elegance of his slimness and affirming in every line of his face and body, in the correct set of his shoulders and the careless freedom of his movements, the superiority, the inexpressible superiority, the unconscious, the unmarked, the not-to-be-described, and even not-to-be-caught, superiority of the naturally born and the perfectly finished man of the world, over the simple young man. He was smiling, easy, correct, perfectly delightful, fit to kill.

He had come to ask me, if I had no other engagement,
to lunch with him and his mother in about an hour's
time. He did it in a most *dégagé* tone. His mother
had given him a surprise. The completest . . .
The foundation of his mother's psychology was her
delightful unexpectedness. She could never let things
be (this in a peculiar tone which he checked at once)
and he really would take it very kindly of me if I
came to break the tête-à-tête for a while (that is if
I had no other engagement. Flash of teeth). His
mother was exquisitely and tenderly absurd. She had
taken it into her head that his health was endangered
in some way. And when she took anything into her
head . . . Perhaps I might find something to
say which would reassure her. His mother had two
long conversations with Mills on his passage through
Paris and had heard of me (I knew how that thick man
could speak of people, he interjected ambiguously) and
his mother, with an insatiable curiosity for anything
that was rare (filially humorous accent here and a softer
flash of teeth), was very anxious to have me presented
to her (courteous intonation, but no teeth). He hoped
I wouldn't mind if she treated me a little as an "interesting young man." His mother had never got
over her seventeenth year, and the manner of the spoilt
beauty of at least three counties at the back of the
Carolinas. That again got overlaid by the *sans-façon*
of a *grande dame* of the Second Empire.

I accepted the invitation with a worldly grin and a
perfectly just intonation, because I really didn't care
what I did. I only wondered vaguely why that fellow
required all the air in the room for himself. There did
not seem enough left to go down my throat. I didn't
say that I would come with pleasure or that I would be
delighted, but I said that I would come. He seemed

to forget his tongue in his head, put his hands in his pockets and moved about vaguely. "I am a little nervous this morning," he said in French, stopping short and looking me straight in the eyes. His own were deep sunk, dark, fatal. I asked with some malice, that no one could have detected in my intonation, "How's that sleeplessness?"

He muttered through his teeth, "*Mal. Je ne dors plus.*" He moved off to stand at the window with his back to the room. I sat down on a sofa that was there and put my feet up, and silence took possession of the room.

"Isn't this street ridiculous?" said Blunt suddenly, and, crossing the room rapidly, waved his hand to me, "*À bientôt donc,*" and was gone. He had seared himself into my mind. I did not understand him nor his mother then; which made them more impressive; but I have discovered since that those two figures required no mystery to make them memorable. Of course, it isn't every day that one meets a mother that lives by her wits and a son that lives by his sword, but there was a perfect finish about their ambiguous personalities which is not to be met twice in a life-time. I shall never forget that grey dress with ample skirts and long corsage yet with infinite style, the ancient as if ghostly beauty of outlines, the black lace, the silver hair, the harmonious, restrained movements of those white, soft hands like the hands of a queen—or an abbess; and in the general fresh effect of her person the brilliant eyes like two stars with the calm reposeful way they had of moving on and off one, as if nothing in the world had the right to veil itself before their once sovereign beauty. Captain Blunt with smiling formality introduced me by name, adding with a certain relaxation of the formal tone the comment: "The 'Monsieur

George' whose fame you tell me has reached even Paris." Mrs. Blunt's reception of me, glance, tones, even to the attitude of the admirably corseted figure, was most friendly, approaching the limit of half-familiarity. I had the feeling that I was beholding in her a captured ideal. No common experience! But I didn't care. It was very lucky perhaps for me that in a way I was like a very sick man who has yet preserved all his lucidity. I was not even wondering to myself at what on earth I was doing there. She breathed out: "*Comme c'est romantique*," at large to the dusty studio as it were; then pointing to a chair at her right hand, and bending slightly towards me she said:

"I have heard this name murmured by pretty lips in more than one royalist salon."

I didn't say anything to that ingratiating speech. I had only an odd thought that she could not have had such a figure, nothing like it, when she was seventeen and wore snowy muslin dresses on the family plantation in South Carolina, in pre-abolition days.

"You won't mind, I am sure, if an old woman whose heart is still young elects to call you by it," she declared.

"Certainly, Madame. It will be more romantic," I assented with a respectful bow.

She dropped a calm, "Yes—there is nothing like romance while one is young. So I will call you Monsieur George." She paused and then added, "I could never got old," in a matter-of-fact final tone as one would remark, "I could never learn to swim," and I had the presence of mind to say in a tone to match, "*C'est évident*, Madame." It was evident. She couldn't get old; and across the table her thirty-year-old son who couldn't get sleep sat listening with courteous detachment and the narrowest possible line of white underlining his silky black moustache.

"Your services are immensely appreciated," she said with an amusing touch of importance as of a great official lady. "Immensely appreciated by people in a position to understand the great significance of the Carlist movement in the South. There it has to combat anarchism, too. I who have lived through the Commune . . ."

Therese came in with a dish, and for the rest of the lunch the conversation so well begun drifted amongst the most appalling inanities of the religious-royalist-legitimist order. The ears of all the Bourbons in the world must have been burning. Mrs. Blunt seemed to have come into personal contact with a good many of them and the marvellous insipidity of her recollections was astonishing to my inexperience. I looked at her from time to time thinking: She has seen slavery, she has seen the Commune, she knows two continents, she has seen a civil war, the glory of the Second Empire, the horrors of two sieges; she has been in contact with marked personalities, with great events, she has lived on her wealth, on her personality, and there she is, with her plumage unruffled, as glossy as ever, unable to get old:—a sort of Phœnix free from the slightest signs of ashes and dust, all complacent amongst those inanities as if there had been nothing else in the world. In my youthful haste I asked myself what sort of airy soul she had.

At last Therese put a dish of fruit on the table, a small collection of oranges, raisins, and nuts. No doubt she had bought that lot very cheap and it did not look at all inviting. Captain Blunt jumped up. "My mother can't stand tobacco smoke. Will you keep her company, *mon cher*, while I take a turn with a cigar in that ridiculous garden? The brougham from the hotel will be here very soon."

He left us in the white flash of an apologetic grin. Almost directly he reappeared, visible from head to foot through the glass side of the studio, pacing up and down the central path of that "ridiculous" garden: for its elegance and its air of good breeding the most remarkable figure that I have ever seen before or since. He had changed his coat. Madame Blunt *mère* lowered the long-handled glasses through which she had been contemplating him with an appraising, absorbed expression which had nothing maternal in it. But what she said to me was:

"You understand my anxieties while he is campaigning with the King."

She had spoken in French and she had used the expression "*mes transes*" but for all the rest, intonation, bearing, solemnity, she might have been referring to one of the Bourbons. I am sure that not a single one of them looked half as aristocratic as her son.

"I understand perfectly, Madame. But then that life is so romantic."

"Hundreds of young men belonging to a certain sphere are doing that," she said very distinctly, "only their case is different. They have their positions, their families to go back to; but we are different. We are exiles, except of course for the ideals, the kindred spirit, the friendships of old standing we have in France. Should my son come out unscathed he has no one but me and I have no one but him. I have to think of his life. Mr. Mills (what a distinguished mind that is!) has reassured me as to my son's health. But he sleeps very badly, doesn't he?"

I murmured something affirmative in a doubtful tone and she remarked quaintly, with a certain curtness,

"It's so unnecessary, this worry! The unfortunate position of an exile has its advantages. At a certain height of social position (wealth has got nothing to do with it, we have been ruined in a most righteous cause), at a certain established height one can disregard narrow prejudices. You see examples in the aristocracies of all the countries. A chivalrous young American may offer his life for a remote ideal which yet may belong to his familial tradition. We, in our great country, have every sort of tradition. But a young man of good connections and distinguished relations must settle down some day, dispose of his life."

"No doubt, Madame," I said, raising my eyes to the figure outside—"*Américain, Catholique et gentil-homme*"—walking up and down the path with a cigar which he was not smoking. "For myself, I don't know anything about those necessities. I have broken away for ever from those things."

"Yes, Mr. Mills talked to me about you. What a golden heart that is. His sympathies are infinite."

I thought suddenly of Mills pronouncing on Mme. Blunt, whatever his text on me might have been: "She lives by her wits." Was she exercising her wits on me for some purpose of her own? And I observed coldly:

"I really know your son so very little."

"Oh, *voyons*," she protested. "I am aware that you are very much younger, but the similitudes of opinions, origins and perhaps at bottom, faintly, of character, of chivalrous devotion—no, you must be able to understand him in a measure. He is infinitely scrupulous and recklessly brave."

I listened deferentially to the end yet with every nerve in my body tingling in hostile response to the Blunt vibration, which seemed to have got into my very hair.

"I am convinced of it, Madame. I have even heard of your son's bravery. It's extremely natural in a man who, in his own words, 'lives by his sword.'"

She suddenly departed from her almost inhuman perfection, betrayed "nerves" like a common mortal, of course very slightly, but in her it meant more than a blaze of fury from a vessel of inferior clay. Her admirable little foot, marvellously shod in a black shoe, tapped the floor irritably. But even in that display there was something exquisitely delicate. The very anger in her voice was silvery, as it were, and more like the petulance of a seventeen-year-old beauty.

"What nonsense! A Blunt doesn't hire himself."

"Some princely families," I said, "were founded by men who have done that very thing. The great Condottieri, you know."

It was in an almost tempestuous tone that she made me observe that we were not living in the fifteenth century. She gave me also to understand with some spirit that there was no question here of founding a family. Her son was very far from being the first of the name. His importance lay rather in being the last of a race which had totally perished, she added in a completely drawing-room tone, "in our Civil War."

She had mastered her irritation and through the glass side of the room sent a wistful smile to his address, but I noticed the yet unextinguished anger in her eyes full of fire under her beautiful white eyebrows. For she was growing old! Oh, yes, she was growing old, and secretly weary, and perhaps desperate.

III

WITHOUT caring much about it I was conscious of sudden illumination. I said to myself confidently that these two people had been quarrelling all the morning. I had discovered the secret of my invitation to that lunch. They did not care to face the strain of some obstinate, inconclusive discussion for fear, maybe, of it ending in a serious quarrel. And so they had agreed that I should be fetched downstairs to create a diversion. I cannot say I felt annoyed. I didn't care. My perspicacity did not please me either. I wished they had left me alone—but nothing mattered. They must have been in their superiority accustomed to make use of people, without compunction. From necessity, too. She especially. She lived by her wits. The silence had grown so marked that I had at last to raise my eyes; and the first thing I observed was that Captain Blunt was no longer to be seen in the garden. Must have gone indoors. Would rejoin us in a moment. Then I would leave mother and son to themselves.

The next thing I noticed was that a great mellowness had descended upon the mother of the last of his race. But these terms, irritation, mellowness, appeared gross when applied to her. It is impossible to give an idea of the refinement and subtlety of all her transformations. She smiled faintly at me.

"But all this is beside the point. The real point is that my son, like all fine natures, is a being of strange contradictions which the trials of life have not yet rec-

onciled in him. With me it is a little different. The
trials fell mainly to my share—and of course I have
lived longer. And then men are much more complex
than women, much more difficult, too. And you,
Monsieur George? Are you complex, with unexpected
resistances and difficulties in your *être intime*—your
inner self? I wonder now . . ."

The Blunt atmosphere seemed to vibrate all over my
skin. I disregarded the symptom. "Madame," I said,
"I have never tried to find out what sort of being I
am."

"Ah, that's very wrong. We ought to reflect on
what manner of beings we are. Of course we are all
sinners. My John is a sinner like the others," she
declared further, with a sort of proud tenderness as
though our common lot must have felt honoured and
to a certain extent purified by this condescending
recognition.

"You are too young perhaps as yet . . . But
as to my John," she broke off, leaning her elbow on the
table and supporting her head on her old, impeccably
shaped, white forearm emerging from a lot of precious,
still older, lace trimming the short sleeve. "The
trouble is that he suffers from a profound discord between the necessary reactions to life and even the impulses of nature and the lofty idealism of his feelings;
I may say, of his principles. I assure you that he won't
even let his heart speak uncontradicted."

I am sure I don't know what particular devil looks
after the associations of memory, and I can't even imagine the shock which it would have been for Mrs.
Blunt to learn that the words issuing from her lips had
awakened in me the visual perception of a dark-skinned,
hard-driven lady's maid with tarnished eyes; even of the
tireless Rose handing me my hat while breathing out

the enigmatic words: "Madame should listen to her heart." A wave from the atmosphere of another house rolled in, overwhelming and fiery, seductive and cruel, through the Blunt vibration, bursting through it as through tissue paper and filling my heart with sweet murmurs and distracting images, till it seemed to break, leaving an empty stillness in my breast.

After that for a long time I heard Mme. Blunt *mère* talking with extreme fluency and I even caught the individual words, but I could not in the revulsion of my feelings get hold of the sense. She talked apparently of life in general, of its difficulties, moral and physical, of its surprising turns, of its unexpected contacts, of the choice and rare personalities that drift on it as if on the sea; of the distinction that letters and art gave to it, the nobility and consolations there are in æsthetics, of the privileges they confer on individuals and (this was the first connected statement I caught) that Mills agreed with her in the general point of view as to the inner worth of individualities and in the particular instance of it on which she had opened to him her innermost heart. Mills had a universal mind. His sympathy was universal, too. He had that large comprehension—oh, not cynical, not at all cynical, in fact rather tender—which was found in its perfection only in some rare, very rare Englishmen. The dear creature was romantic, too. Of course he was reserved in his speech but she understood Mills perfectly. Mills apparently liked me very much.

It was time for me to say something. There was a challenge in the reposeful black eyes resting upon my face. I murmured that I was very glad to hear it. She waited a little, then uttered meaningly, "Mr. Mills is a little bit uneasy about you."

"It's very good of him," I said. And indeed I

thought that it was very good of him, though I did ask myself vaguely in my dulled brain why he should be uneasy. Somehow it didn't occur to me to ask Mrs. Blunt. Whether she had expected me to do so or not I don't know, but after a while she changed the pose she had kept so long and folded her wonderfully preserved white arms. She looked a perfect picture in silver and grey, with touches of black here and there. Still I said nothing more in my dull misery. She waited a little longer, then she woke me up with a crash. It was as if the house had fallen, and yet she had only asked me:

"I believe you are received on very friendly terms by Madame de Lastaola on account of your common exertions for the cause. Very good friends, are you not?"

"You mean Rita," I said stupidly, but I felt stupid, like a man who wakes up only to be hit on the head.

"Oh, Rita," she repeated with unexpected acidity, which somehow made me feel guilty of an incredible breach of good manners. "H'm, Rita. . . . Oh, well, let it be Rita—for the present. Though why she should be deprived of her name in conversation about her, really I don't understand. Unless a very special intimacy . . ."

She was distinctly annoyed. I said sulkily, "It isn't her name."

"It is her choice, I understand, which seems almost a better title to recognition on the part of the world. It didn't strike you so before? Well, it seems to me that choice has got more right to be respected than heredity or law. Moreover, Mme de Lastaola," she continued in an insinuating voice, "that most rare and fascinating young woman is, as a friend like you cannot deny, outside legality altogether. Even in that she is an exceptional creature. For she is exceptional—you agree?"

I had gone dumb, I could only stare at her.

"Oh, I see, you agree. No friend of hers could deny."

"Madame," I burst out, "I don't know where a question of friendship comes in here with a person whom you yourself call so exceptional. I really don't know how she looks upon me. Our intercourse is of course very close and confidential. Is that also talked about in Paris?"

"Not at all, not in the least," said Mrs. Blunt, easy, equable, but with her calm, sparkling eyes holding me in angry subjection. "Nothing of the sort is being talked about. The references to Mme. de Lastaola are in a very different tone, I can assure you, thanks to her discretion in remaining here. And, I must say, thanks to the discreet efforts of her friends. I am also a friend of Mme. de Lastaola, you must know. Oh, no, I have never spoken to her in my life and have seen her only twice, I believe. I wrote to her though, that I admit. She or rather the image of her has come into my life, into that part of it where art and letters reign undisputed like a sort of religion of beauty to which I have been faithful through all the vicissitudes of my existence. Yes, I did write to her and I have been preoccupied with her for a long time. It arose from a picture, from two pictures and also from a phrase pronounced by a man, who in the science of life and in the perception of æsthetic truth had no equal in the world of culture. He said that there was something in her of the women of all time. I suppose he meant the inheritance of all the gifts that make up an irresistible fascination—a great personality. Such women are not born often. Most of them lack opportunities. They never develop. They end obscurely. Here and there one survives to make her mark—even in history. . . . And even that is not a very enviable fate. They are at another pole from the so-called dangerous women who are merely coquettes. A coquette has got to work for her success. The others have nothing to do but simply exist. You perceive the view I take of the difference?"

I perceived the view. I said to myself that nothing in the world could be more aristocratic. This was the slave-owning woman who had never worked, even if she had been reduced to live by her wits. She was a wonderful old woman. She made me dumb. She held me fascinated by the well-bred attitude, something sublimely aloof in her air of wisdom.

I just simply let myself go admiring her as though I had been a mere slave of æsthetics: the perfect grace, the amazing poise of that venerable head, the assured as if royal—yes, royal—even flow of the voice. . . . But what was it she was talking about now? These were no longer considerations about fatal women. She was talking about her son again. My interest turned into mere bitterness of contemptuous attention. For I couldn't withhold it though I tried to let the stuff go by. Educated in the most aristocratic college in Paris . . . at eighteen . . . call of duty . . . with General Lee to the very last cruel minute . . . after that catastrophe—end of the world —return to France—to old friendships, infinite kindness—but a life hollow, without occupation. . . Then 1870—and chivalrous response to adopted country's call and again emptiness, the chafing of a proud spirit without aim and handicapped not exactly by poverty but by lack of fortune. And she, the mother, having to look on at this wasting of a most accomplished man, of a most chivalrous nature that practically had no future before it

"You understand me well, Monsieur George. A nature like this! It is the most refined cruelty of fate to look at. I don't know whether I suffered more in times of war or in times of peace. You understand?"

I bowed my head in silence. What I couldn't understand was why he delayed so long in joining us again. Unless he had had enough of his mother? I thought without any great resentment that I was being victimized; but then it occurred to me that the cause of his absence was quite simple. I was familiar enough with his habits by this time to know that he often managed to snatch an hour's sleep or so during the day. He had gone and thrown himself on his bed.

"I admire him exceedingly," Mrs. Blunt was saying in a tone which was not at all maternal. "His distinction, his fastidiousness, the earnest warmth of his heart. I know him well. I assure you that I would never have dared to suggest," she continued with an extraordinary haughtiness of attitude and tone that aroused my attention, "I would never have dared to put before him my views of the extraordinary merits and the uncertain fate of the exquisite woman of whom we speak, if I had not been certain that, partly by my fault, I admit, his attention has been attracted to her and his—his heart engaged."

It was as if someone had poured a bucket of cold water over my head. I woke up with a great shudder to the acute perception of my own feelings and of that aristocrat's incredible purpose. How it could have germinated, grown and matured in that exclusive soil was inconceivable. She had been inciting her son all the time to undertake wonderful salvage work by annexing the heiress of Henry Allègre—the woman and the fortune.

There must have been an amazed incredulity in my eyes, to which her own responded by an unflinching black brilliance which suddenly seemed to develop a scorching quality even to the point of making me feel extremely thirsty all of a sudden. For a time my tongue literally clove to the roof of my mouth. I don't know whether it was an illusion but it seemed to me that Mrs. Blunt had nodded at me twice as if to say: "You are right, that's so." I made an effort to speak but it was very poor. If she did hear me it was because she must have been on the watch for the faintest sound.

"His heart engaged. Like two hundred others, or two thousand, all around," I mumbled.

"Altogether different. And it's no disparagement to a woman surely. Of course her great fortune protects her in a certain measure."

"Does it?" I faltered out and that time I really doubt whether she heard me. Her aspect in my eyes had changed. Her purpose being disclosed, her well-bred ease appeared sinister, her aristocratic repose a treacherous device, her venerable graciousness a mask of unbounded contempt for all human beings whatever. She was a terrible old woman with those straight, white wolfish eyebrows. How blind I had been! Those eyebrows alone ought to have been enough to give her away. Yet they were as beautifully smooth as her voice when she admitted: "That protection naturally is only partial. There is the danger of her own self, poor girl. She requires guidance."

I marvelled at the villainy of my tone as I spoke, but it was only assumed.

"I don't think she has done badly for herself, so far," I forced myself to say. "I suppose you know that she began life by herding the village goats."

In the course of that phrase I noticed her wince just the least bit. Oh, yes, she winced; but at the end of it she smiled easily.

"No, I didn't know. So she told you her story! Oh, well, I suppose you are very good friends. A goatherd—really? In the fairy tale I believe the girl that marries the prince is—what is it?—a *gardeuse d'oies*. And what a thing to drag out against a woman. One might just as soon reproach any of them for coming unclothed into the world. They all do, you know. And then they become—what you will discover when you have lived longer, Monsieur George—for the most part futile creatures, without any sense of truth and beauty, drudges of all sorts, or else dolls to dress. In a word—ordinary."

The implication of scorn in her tranquil manner was immense. It seemed to condemn all those that were not born in the Blunt connection. It was the perfect pride of Republican aristocracy, which has no gradations and knows no limit, and, as if created by the grace of God, thinks it ennobles everything it touches: people, ideas, even passing tastes!

"How many of them," pursued Mrs. Blunt, "have had the good fortune, the leisure to develop their intelligence and their beauty in æsthetic conditions as this charming woman had? Not one in a million. Perhaps not one in an age."

"The heiress of Henry Allègre," I murmured.

"Precisely. But John wouldn't be marrying the heiress of Henry Allègre."

It was the first time that the frank word, the clear idea, came into the conversation and it made me feel ill with a sort of enraged faintness.

"No," I said. "It would be Mme. de Lastaola then."

"Mme. la Comtesse de Lastaola as soon as she likes after the success of this war."

"And you believe in its success?"

"Do you?"

"Not for a moment," I declared, and was surprised to see her look pleased.

She was an aristocrat to the tips of her fingers; she really didn't care for anybody. She had passed through the Empire, she had lived through a siege, had rubbed shoulders with the Commune, had seen everything, no doubt, of what men are capable in the pursuit of their desires or in the extremity of their distress, for love, for money, and even for honour; and in her precarious connection with the very highest spheres she had kept her own honourability unscathed while she had lost all her prejudices. She was above all that. Perhaps "the world" was the only thing that could have the slightest checking influence; but when I ventured to say something about the view it might take of such an alliance she looked at me for a moment with visible surprise.

"My dear Monsieur George, I have lived in the great world all my life. It's the best that there is, but that's only because there is nothing merely decent anywhere. It will accept anything, forgive anything, forget anything in a few days. And after all whom will he be marrying? A charming, clever, rich, and altogether uncommon woman. What did the world hear of her? Nothing. The little it saw of her was in the Bois for a few hours every year, riding by the side of a man of unique distinction and of exclusive tastes, devoted to the cult of æsthetic impressions; a man of whom as far as aspect, manner, and behaviour goes, she might have been the daughter. I have seen her myself. I went on purpose. I was immensely struck. I was even moved. Yes. She might have been—except for that something radiant in her that marked her apart from all the other daughters of men. The few remarkable personalities

that count in society and who were admitted into Henry
Allègre's Pavilion treated her with punctilious reserve.
I know that, I have made enquiries. I know she sat
there amongst them like a marvellous child, and for
the rest what can they say about her? That when
abandoned to herself by the death of Allègre she has
made a mistake? I think that any woman ought to
be allowed one mistake in her life. The worst they
can say of her is that she discovered it, that she had
sent away a man in love directly she found out that
his love was not worth having; that she had told him to
go and look for his crown, and that, after dismissing
him, she had remained generously faithful to his cause,
in her person and fortune. And this, you will allow, is
rather uncommon upon the whole."

"You make her out very magnificent," I murmured,
looking down upon the floor.

"Isn't she?" exclaimed the aristocratic Mrs. Blunt,
with an almost youthful ingenuousness, and in those
black eyes which looked at me so calmly there was a
flash of the Southern beauty, still naïve and romantic,
as if altogether untouched by experience. "I don't
think there is a single grain of vulgarity in all her enchanting person. Neither is there in my son. I suppose you won't deny that he is uncommon." She
paused.

"Absolutely," I said in a perfectly conventional
tone. I was now on my mettle that she should not discover what there was humanly common in my nature.
She took my answer at her own valuation and was
satisfied.

"They can't fail to understand each other on the very
highest level of idealistic perceptions. Can you imagine my John thrown away on some enamoured white
goose out of a stuffy old salon? Why, she couldn't

even begin to understand what he feels or what he needs."

"Yes," I said impenetrably, "he is not easy to understand."

"I have reason to think," she said with a suppressed smile, "that he has a certain power over women. Of course I don't know anything about his intimate life but a whisper or two have reached me, like that, floating in the air, and I could hardly suppose that he would find an exceptional resistance in that quarter of all others. But I should like to know the exact degree."

I disregarded an annoying tendency to feel dizzy that came over me and was very careful in managing my voice.

"May I ask, Madame, why you are telling me all this?"

"For two reasons," she condescended graciously.

"First of all because Mr. Mills told me that you were much more mature than one would expect. In fact you look much younger than I was prepared for."

"Madame," I interrupted her, "I may have a certain capacity for action and for responsibility, but as to the regions into which this very unexpected conversation has taken me I am a great novice. They are outside my interest. I have had no experience."

"Don't make yourself out so hopeless," she said in a spoilt-beauty tone. "You have your intuitions. At any rate you have a pair of eyes. You are everlastingly over there, so I understand. Surely you have seen how far they are . . ."

I interrupted again and this time bitterly, but always in a tone of polite enquiry:

"You think her facile, Madame?"

She looked offended. "I think her most fastidious. It is my son who is in question here."

And I understood then that she looked on her son as irresistible. For my part I was just beginning to think that it would be impossible for me to wait for his return. I figured him to myself lying dressed on his bed sleeping like a stone. But there was no denying that the mother was holding me with an awful, tortured interest. Twice Therese had opened the door, had put her small head in and drawn it back like a tortoise. But for some time I had lost the sense of us two being quite alone in the studio. I had perceived the familiar dummy in its corner but it lay now on the floor as if Therese had knocked it down angrily with a broom for a heathen idol. It lay there prostrate, handless, without its head, pathetic, like the mangled victim of a crime.

"John is fastidious, too," began Mrs. Blunt again. "Of course you wouldn't suppose anything vulgar in his resistances to a very real sentiment. One has got to understand his psychology. He can't leave himself in peace. He is exquisitely absurd."

I recognized the phrase. Mother and son talked of each other in identical terms. But perhaps "exquisitely absurd" was the Blunt family saying? There are such sayings in families and generally there is some truth in them. Perhaps this old woman was simply absurd. She continued:

"We had a most painful discussion all this morning. He is angry with me for suggesting the very thing his whole being desires. I don't feel guilty. It's he who is tormenting himself with his infinite scrupulosity."

"Ah," I said, looking at the mangled dummy like the model of some atrocious murder. "Ah, the fortune. But that can be left alone."

"What nonsense! How is it possible? It isn't contained in a bag, you can't throw it into the sea. **And** moreover, it isn't her fault. I am astonished that you should have thought of that vulgar hypocrisy. No, it isn't her fortune that checks my son; it's something much more subtle. Not so much her history as her position. He is absurd. It isn't what has happened in her life. It's her very freedom that makes him torment himself and her, too—as far as I can understand."

I suppressed a groan and said to myself that I must really get away from there.

Mrs. Blunt was fairly launched now.

"For all his superiority he is a man of the world and shares to a certain extent its current opinions. He has no power over her. She intimidates him. He wishes he had never set eyes on her. Once or twice this morning he looked at me as if he could find it in his heart to hate his old mother. There is no doubt about it—he loves her, Monsieur George. He loves her, this poor, luckless, perfect *homme du monde*."

The silence lasted for some time and then I heard a murmur: "It's a matter of the utmost delicacy between two beings so sensitive, so proud. It has to be managed."

I found myself suddenly on my feet and saying with the utmost politeness that I had to beg her permission to leave her alone as I had an engagement: but she motioned me simply to sit down—and I sat down again.

"I told you I had a request to make," she said. "I have understood from Mr. Mills that you have been to the West Indies, that you have some interests there."

I was astounded. "Interests! I certainly have been there," I said, "but   . . ."

She caught me up. "Then why not go there again? I am speaking to you frankly because   . . ."

"But, Madame, I am engaged in this affair with Doña Rita, even if I had any interests elsewhere. I won't tell you about the importance of my work. I didn't suspect it but you brought the news of it to me, and so I needn't point it out to you."

And now we were frankly arguing with each other.

"But where will it lead you in the end? You have all your life before you, all your plans, prospects, perhaps dreams, at any rate your own tastes and all your life-time before you. And would you sacrifice all this to—the Pretender? A mere figure for the front page of illustrated papers."

"I never think of him," I said curtly, "but I suppose Doña Rita's feelings, instincts, call it what you like—or only her chivalrous fidelity to her mistakes——"

"Doña Rita's presence here in this town, her withdrawal from the possible complications of her life in Paris has produced an excellent effect on my son. It simplifies infinite difficulties, I mean moral as well as material. It's extremely to the advantage of her dignity, of her future, and of her peace of mind. But I am thinking, of course, mainly of my son. He is most exacting."

I felt extremely sick at heart. "And so I am to drop everything and vanish," I said, rising from my chair again. And this time Mrs. Blunt got up, too, with a lofty and inflexible manner but she didn't dismiss me yet.

"Yes," she said distinctly. "All this, my dear Monsieur George, is such an accident. What have you got to do here? You look to me like somebody who would find adventures wherever he went as interesting and perhaps less dangerous than this one."

She slurred over the word "dangerous" but I picked it up.

"What do you know of its dangers, Madame, may I ask?" But she did not condescend to hear.

"And then you, too, have your chivalrous feelings," she went on, unswerving, distinct, and tranquil. "You are not absurd. But my son is. He would shut her up in a convent for a time if he could."

"He isn't the only one," I muttered.

"Indeed!" she was startled, then lower, "Yes. That woman must be the centre of all sorts of passions," she mused audibly. "But what have you got to do with all this? It's nothing to you."

She waited for me to speak.

"Exactly, Madame," I said, "and therefore I don't see why I should concern myself in all this one way or another."

"No," she assented with a weary air, "except that you might ask yourself what is the good of tormenting a man of noble feelings, however absurd. His Southern blood makes him very violent sometimes. I fear——" And then for the first time during this conversation, for the first time since I left Doña Rita the day before, for the first time I laughed.

"Do you mean to hint, Madame, that Southern gentlemen are dead shots? I am aware of that—from novels."

I spoke looking her straight in the face and I made that exquisite, aristocratic old woman positively blink by my directness. There was a faint flush on her delicate old cheeks but she didn't move a muscle of her face. I made her a most respectful bow and went out of the studio.

IV

THROUGH the great arched window of the hall I saw the hotel brougham waiting at the door. On passing the door of the front room (it was originally meant for a drawing-room but a bed for Blunt was put in there) I banged with my fist on the panel and shouted: "I am obliged to go out. Your mother's carriage is at the door." I didn't think he was asleep. My view now was that he was aware beforehand of the subject of the conversation, and if so I did not wish to appear as if I had slunk away from him after the interview. But I didn't stop—I didn't want to see him—and before he could answer I was already halfway up the stairs running noiselessly up the thick carpet which also covered the floor of the landing. Therefore opening the door of my sitting-room quickly I caught by surprise the person who was in there watching the street, half concealed by the window curtain. It was a woman. A totally unexpected woman. A perfect stranger. She came away quickly to meet me. Her face was veiled and she was dressed in a dark walking costume and a very simple form of hat. She murmured: "I had an idea that Monsieur was in the house," raising a gloved hand to lift her veil. It was Rose and she gave me a shock. I had never seen her before but with her little black silk apron and a white cap with ribbons on her head. This outdoor dress was like a disguise. I asked anxiously:

"What has happened to Madame?"

"Nothing. I have a letter," she murmured, and I

saw it appear between the fingers of her extended hand, in a very white envelope which I tore open impatiently. It consisted of a few lines only. It began abruptly:

"If you are gone to sea then I can't forgive you for not sending the usual word at the last moment. If you are not gone why don't you come? Why did you leave me yesterday? You leave me crying—I who haven't cried for years and years, and you haven't the sense to come back within the hour, within twenty hours! This conduct is idiotic"—and a sprawling signature of the four magic letters at the bottom.

While I was putting the letter in my pocket the girl said in an earnest undertone: "I don't like to leave Madame by herself for any length of time."

"How long have you been in my room?" I asked.

"The time seemed long. I hope Monsieur won't mind the liberty. I sat for a little in the hall but then it struck me I might be seen. In fact, Madame told me not to be seen if I could help it."

"Why did she tell you that?"

"I permitted myself to suggest that to Madame. It might have given a false impression. Madame is frank and open like the day but it won't do with everybody. There are people who would put a wrong construction on anything. Madame's sister told me Monsieur was out."

"And you didn't believe her?"

"*Non*, Monsieur. I have lived with Madame's sister for nearly a week when she first came into this house. She wanted me to leave the message, but I said I would wait a little. Then I sat down in the big porter's chair in the hall and after a while, everything being very quiet, I stole up here. I know the disposition of the apartments. I reckoned Madame's sister would think that I got tired of waiting and let myself out."

"And you have been amusing yourself watching the street ever since?"

"The time seemed long," she answered evasively. "An empty *coupé* came to the door about an hour ago and it's still waiting," she added, looking at me inquisitively. "It seems strange."

"There are some dancing girls staying in the house," I said negligently. "Did you leave Madame alone?"

"There's the gardener and his wife in the house."

"Those people keep at the back. Is Madame alone? That's what I want to know."

"Monsieur forgets that I have been three hours away; but I assure Monsieur that here in this town it's perfectly safe for Madame to be alone."

"And wouldn't it be anywhere else? It's the first I hear of it."

"In Paris, in our apartments in the hotel, it's all right, too; but in the Pavilion, for instance, I wouldn't leave Madame by herself, not for half an hour."

"What is there in the Pavilion?" I asked.

"It's a sort of feeling I have," she murmured reluctantly. . . . "Oh! There's that *coupé* going away."

She made a movement towards the window but checked herself. I hadn't moved. The rattle of wheels on the cobble-stones died out almost at once.

"Will Monsieur write an answer?" Rose suggested after a short silence.

"Hardly worth while," I said. "I will be there very soon after you. Meantime, please tell Madame from me that I am not anxious to see any more tears. Tell her this just like that, you understand. I will take the risk of not being received."

She dropped her eyes, said: "*Oui*, Monsieur," and at

my suggestion waited, holding the door of the room
half open, till I went downstairs to see the road clear.

It was a kind of deaf-and-dumb house. The black-
and-white hall was empty and everything was perfectly still. Blunt himself had no doubt gone away
with his mother in the brougham, but as to the others,
the dancing girls, Therese, or anybody else that its
walls may have contained, they might have been all
murdering each other in perfect assurance that the
house would not betray them by indulging in any
unseemly murmurs. I emitted a low whistle which
didn't seem to travel in that peculiar atmosphere
more than two feet away from my lips, but all the
same Rose came tripping down the stairs at once.
With just a nod to my whisper: "Take a fiacre," she
glided out and I shut the door noiselessly behind her.

The next time I saw her she was opening the door
of the house on the Prado to me, with her cap and the
little black silk apron on, and with that marked personality of her own, which had been concealed so perfectly in the dowdy walking dress, very much to the
fore.

"I have given Madame the message," she said in her
contained voice, swinging the door wide open. Then
after relieving me of my hat and coat she announced
me with the simple words: "*Voilà* Monsieur," and
hurried away. Directly I appeared Doña Rita, away
there on the couch, passed the tips of her fingers over
her eyes and holding her hands up palms outwards
on each side of her head, shouted to me down the
whole length of the room, "The dry season has set
in." I glanced at the pink tips of her fingers perfunc-
torily and then drew back. She let her hands fall negligently as if she had no use for them any more and
put on a serious expression.

"So it seems," I said, sitting down opposite her. "For how long, I wonder."

"For years and years. One gets so little encouragement. First you bolt away from my tears, then you send an impertinent message, and then when you come at last you pretend to behave respectfully, though you don't know how to do it. You should sit much nearer the edge of the chair and hold yourself very stiff, and make it quite clear that you don't know what to do with your hands."

All this in a fascinating voice with a ripple of badinage that seemed to play upon the sober surface of her thoughts. Then seeing that I did not answer she altered the note a bit.

"*Amigo* George," she said, "I take the trouble to send for you and here I am before you, talking to you, and you say nothing."

"What am I to say?"

"How can I tell? You might say a thousand things. You might, for instance, tell me that you were sorry for my tears."

"I might also tell you a thousand lies. What do I know about your tears? I am not a susceptible idiot. It all depends upon the cause. There are tears of quiet happiness. Peeling onions will also bring tears."

"Oh, you are not susceptible," she flew out at me. "But you are an idiot all the same."

"Is it to tell me this that you have written to me to come?" I asked with a certain animation.

"Yes. And if you had as much sense as the talking parrot I owned once you would have read between the lines that all I wanted you here for was to tell you what I think of you."

"Well, tell me what you think of me."

"I would in a moment if I could be half as impertinent as you are."

"What unexpected modesty," I said.

"These, I suppose, are your sea manners."

"I wouldn't put up with half that nonsense from anybody at sea. Don't you remember you told me yourself to go away? What was I to do?"

"How stupid you are. I don't mean that you pretend. You really are. Do you understand what I say? I will spell it for you. S-t-u-p-i-d. Ah, now I feel better. Oh, *amigo* George, my dear fellow-conspirator for the King—the King. Such a king! *Vive le Roi!* Come, why don't you shout *Vive le Roi*, too?"

"I am not your parrot," I said.

"No, he never sulked. He was a charming, good-mannered bird, accustomed to the best society, whereas you, I suppose, are nothing but a heartless vagabond like myself."

"I daresay you are, but I suppose nobody had the insolence to tell you that to your face."

"Well, very nearly. It was what it amounted to. I am not stupid. There is no need to spell out simple words for me. It just came out. Don Juan struggled desperately to keep the truth in. It was most pathetic. And yet he couldn't help himself. He talked very much like a parrot."

"Of the best society," I suggested.

"Yes, the most honourable of parrots. I don't like parrot-talk. It sounds so uncanny. Had I lived in the Middle Ages I am certain I would have believed that a talking bird must be possessed by the devil. I am sure Therese would believe that now. My own sister! She would cross herself many times and simply quake with terror."

"But you were not terrified," I said. "May I ask when that interesting communication took place?"

"Yesterday, just before you blundered in here of all days in the year. I was sorry for him."

"Why tell me this? I couldn't help noticing it. I regretted I hadn't my umbrella with me."

"Those unforgiven tears! Oh, you simple soul! Don't you know that people never cry for anybody but themselves? . . . *Amigo* George, tell me—what are we doing in this world?"

"Do you mean all the people, everybody?"

"No, only people like you and me. Simple people, in this world which is eaten up with charlatanism of all sorts so that even we, the simple, don't know any longer how to trust each other."

"Don't we? Then why don't you trust him? You are dying to do so, don't you know?"

She dropped her chin on her breast and from under her straight eyebrows the deep blue eyes remained fixed on me, impersonally, as if without thought.

"What have you been doing since you left me yesterday?" she asked.

"The first thing I remember I abused your sister horribly this morning."

"And how did she take it?"

"Like a warm shower in spring. She drank it all in and unfolded her petals."

"What poetical expressions he uses! That girl is more perverted than one would think possible, considering what she is and whence she came. It's true that I, too, come from the same spot."

"She is slightly crazy. I am a great favourite with her. I don't say this to boast."

"It must be very comforting."

"Yes, it has cheered me immensely. Then after a

morning of delightful musing on one thing and another I went to lunch with a charming lady and spent most of the afternoon talking with her."

Doña Rita raised her head.

"A lady! Women seem such mysterious creatures to me. I don't know them. Did you abuse her? Did she —how did you say that?—unfold her petals, too? Was she really and truly . . . ?"

"She is simply perfection in her way and the conversation was by no means banal. I fancy that if your late parrot had heard it, he would have fallen off his perch. For after all, in that Allègre Pavilion, my dear Rita, you were but a crowd of glorified *bourgeois.*"

She was beautifully animated now. In her motionless blue eyes like melted sapphires, around those red lips that almost without moving could breathe enchanting sounds into the world, there was a play of light, that mysterious ripple of gaiety that seemed always to run and faintly quiver under her skin even in her gravest moods; just as in her rare moments of gaiety its warmth and radiance seemed to come to one through infinite sadness, like the sunlight of our life hiding the invincible darkness in which the universe must work out its impenetrable destiny.

"Now I think of it! . . . Perhaps that's the reason I never could feel perfectly serious while they were demolishing the world about my ears. I fancy now that I could tell beforehand what each of them was going to say. They were repeating the same words over and over again, those great clever men, very much like parrots who also seem to know what they say. That doesn't apply to the master of the house, who never talked much. He sat there mostly silent and looming up three sizes bigger than any of them."

"The ruler of the aviary," I muttered viciously.

"It annoys you that I should talk of that time?" she asked in a tender voice. "Well, I won't, except for once to say that you must not make a mistake: in that aviary he was the man. I know because he used to talk to me afterwards sometimes. Strange! For six years he seemed to carry all the world and me with it in his hand. . . ."

"He dominates you yet," I shouted.

She shook her head innocently as a child would do. "No, no. You brought him into the conversation yourself. You think of him much more than I do." Her voice dropped sadly to a hopeless note. "I hardly ever do. He is not the sort of person to merely flit through one's mind and so I have no time. Look. I had eleven letters this morning and there were also five telegrams before midday, which have tangled up everything. I am quite frightened."

And she explained to me that one of them—the long one on the top of the pile, on the table over there— seemed to contain ugly inferences directed at herself in a menacing way. She begged me to read it and see what I could make of it.

I knew enough of the general situation to see at a glance that she had misunderstood it thoroughly and even amazingly. I proved it to her very quickly. But her mistake was so ingenious in its wrongheaded- ness and arose so obviously from the distraction of an acute mind, that I couldn't help looking at her ad- miringly.

"Rita," I said, "you are a marvellous idiot."

"Am I? Imbecile," she retorted with an enchanting smile of relief. "But perhaps it only seems so to you in contrast with the lady so perfect in her way. What is her way?"

"Her way I should say, lies somewhere between her

sixtieth and seventieth years and I have walked tête-à-
tête with her for some little distance this afternoon."

"Heavens," she whispered, thunderstruck. "And
meantime I had the son here. He arrived about five
minutes after Rose left with that note for you," she
went on in a tone of awe. "As a matter of fact, Rose
saw him across the street but she thought she had better
go on to you."

"I am furious with myself for not having guessed that
much," I said bitterly. "I suppose you got him out
of the house about five minutes after you heard I was
coming here. Rose ought to have turned back when
she saw him on his way to cheer your solitude. That
girl is stupid after all, though she has got a certain
amount of low cunning which no doubt is very useful at
times."

"I forbid you to talk like this about Rose. I won't
have it. Rose is not to be abused before me."

"I only mean to say that she failed in this instance to
read your mind, that's all."

"This is, without exception, the most unintelligent
thing you have said ever since I have known you. You
may understand a lot about running contraband and
about the minds of a certain class of people, but as to
Rose's mind let me tell you that in comparison with hers
yours is absolutely infantile, my adventurous friend.
It would be contemptible if it weren't so—what shall I
call it?—babyish. You ought to be slapped and put
to bed." There was an extraordinary earnestness in
her tone and when she ceased I listened yet to the
seductive inflexions of her voice, that no matter in what
mood she spoke seemed only fit for tenderness and love.
And I thought suddenly of Azzolati being ordered to
take himself off from her presence for ever, in that voice
the very anger of which seemed to twine itself gently

round one's heart. No wonder the poor wretch could
not forget the scene and couldn't restrain his tears on
the plain of Rambouillet. My moods of resentment
against Rita, hot as they were, had no more duration
than a blaze of straw. So I only said:

"Much *you* know about the management of children."

The corners of her lips stirred quaintly; her animosity,
especially when provoked by a personal attack upon
herself, was always tinged by a sort of wistful humour
of the most disarming kind.

"Come, *amigo* George, let us leave poor Rose alone.
You had better tell me what you heard from the lips of
the charming old lady. Perfection, isn't she? I have
never seen her in my life, though she says she has seen
me several times. But she has written to me on three
separate occasions and every time I answered her as if I
were writing to a queen. *Amigo* George, how does
one write to a queen? How should a goatherd that
could have been mistress of a king, how should she
write to an old queen from very far away: from over
the sea?"

"I will ask you as I have asked the old queen: why do
you tell me all this, Doña Rita?"

"To discover what's in your mind," she said, a little
impatiently.

"If you don't know that yet!" I exclaimed under
my breath.

"No, not in your mind. Can any one ever tell what
is in a man's mind? But I see you won't tell."

"What's the good? You have written to her before,
I understand. Do you think of continuing the corres-
pondence?"

"Who knows?" she said in a profound tone. "She
is the only woman that ever wrote to me. I returned

her three letters to her with my last answer, explaining humbly that I preferred her to burn them herself. And I thought that would be the end of it. But an occasion may still arise."

"Oh, if an occasion arises," I said, trying to control my rage, "you may be able to begin your letter by the words *'Chère Maman.'*"

The cigarette box, which she had taken up without removing her eyes from me, flew out of her hand and opening in mid-air scattered cigarettes for quite a surprising distance all over the room. I got up at once and wandered off picking them up industriously. Doña Rita's voice behind me said indifferently:

"Don't trouble, I will ring for Rose."

"No need," I growled, without turning my head, "I can find my hat in the hall by myself, after I've finished picking up . . ."

"Bear!"

I returned with the box and placed it on the divan near her. She sat cross-legged, leaning back on her arms, in the blue shimmer of her embroidered robe and with the tawny halo of her unruly hair about her face which she raised to mine with an air of resignation.

"George, my friend," she said, "we have no manners."

"You would never have made a career at court, Doña Rita," I observed. "You are too impulsive."

"This is not bad manners, that's sheer insolence. This has happened to you before. If it happens again, as I can't be expected to wrestle with a savage and desperate smuggler single-handed, I will go upstairs and lock myself in my room till you leave the house. Why did you say this to me?"

"Oh, just for nothing, out of a full heart."

"If your heart is full of things like that, then my dear

friend, you had better take it out and give to it the
crows. No! you said that for the pleasure of appearing terrible. And you see you are not terrible at all,
you are rather amusing. Go on, continue to be amusing. Tell me something of what you heard from the
lips of that aristocratic old lady who thinks that all
men are equal and entitled to the pursuit of happiness."

"I hardly remember now. I heard something about
the unworthiness of certain white geese out of stuffy
drawing-rooms. It sounds mad, but the lady knows
exactly what she wants. I also heard your praises sung.
I sat there like a fool not knowing what to say."

"Why? You might have joined in the singing."

"I didn't feel in the humour, because, don't you see,
I had been incidentally given to understand that I was
an insignificant and superfluous person who had better
get out of the way of serious people."

"Ah, *par exemple!*"

"In a sense, you know, it was flattering; but for the
moment it made me feel as if I had been offered a pot
of mustard to sniff."

She nodded with an amused air of understanding
and I could see that she was interested. "Anything
more?" she asked, with a flash of radiant eagerness in
all her person and bending slightly forward towards me.

"Oh, it's hardly worth mentioning. It was a sort
of threat wrapped up, I believe, in genuine anxiety
as to what might happen to my youthful insignificance.
If I hadn't been rather on the alert just then I wouldn't
even have perceived the meaning. But really an allusion to 'hot Southern blood' could have only one meaning. Of course I laughed at it, but only '*pour l'honneur*'
and to show I understood perfectly. In reality it left
me completely indifferent."

Doña Rita looked very serious for a minute.

"Indifferent to the whole conversation?"

I looked at her angrily.

"To the whole . . . You see I got up rather out of sorts this morning. Unrefreshed, you know. As if tired of life."

The liquid blue in her eyes remained directed at me without any expression except that of its usual mysterious immobility, but all her face took on a sad and thoughtful cast. Then as if she had made up her mind under the pressure of necessity:

"Listen, *amigo*," she said, "I have suffered domination and it didn't crush me because I have been strong enough to live with it; I have known caprice, you may call it folly if you like, and it left me unharmed because I was great enough not to be captured by anything that wasn't really worthy of me. My dear, it went down like a house of cards before my breath. There is something in me that will not be dazzled by any sort of prestige in this world, worthy or unworthy. I am telling you this because you are younger than myself."

"If you want me to say that there is nothing petty or mean about you, Doña Rita, then I do say it."

She nodded at me with an air of accepting the rendered justice and went on with the utmost simplicity.

"And what is it that is coming to me now with all the airs of virtue? All the lawful conventions are coming to me, all the glamours of respectability! And nobody can say that I have made as much as the slightest little sign to them. Not so much as lifting my little finger. I suppose you know that?"

"I don't know. I do not doubt your sincerity in anything you say. I am ready to believe. You are not one of those who have to work."

"Have to work—what do you mean?"

"It's a phrase I have heard. What I meant was that it isn't necessary for you to make any signs."

She seemed to meditate over this for a while.

"Don't be so sure of that," she said, with a flash of mischief, which made her voice sound more melancholy than before. "I am not so sure myself," she continued with a curious, vanishing, intonation of despair. "I don't know the truth about myself because I never had an opportunity to compare myself to anything in the world. I have been offered mock adulation, treated with mock reserve or with mock devotion, I have been fawned upon with an appalling earnestness of purpose, I can tell you; but these later honours, my dear, came to me in the shape of a very loyal and very scrupulous gentleman. For he is all that. And as a matter of fact I was touched."

"I know. Even to tears," I said provokingly. But she wasn't provoked, she only shook her head in negation (which was absurd) and pursued the trend of her spoken thoughts.

"That was yesterday," she said. "And yesterday he was extremely correct and very full of extreme self-esteem which expressed itself in the exaggerated delicacy with which he talked. But I know him in all his moods. I have known him even playful. I didn't listen to him. I was thinking of something else. Of things that were neither correct nor playful and that had to be looked at steadily with all the best that was in me. And that was why, in the end—I cried—yesterday."

"I saw it yesterday and I had the weakness of being moved by those tears for a time."

"If you want to make me cry again I warn you you won't succeed."

"No, I know. He has been here to-day and the dry season has set in."

"Yes, he has been here. I assure you it was perfectly unexpected. Yesterday he was railing at the world at large, at me who certainly have not made it, at himself and even at his mother. All this rather in parrot language, in the words of tradition and morality as understood by the members of that exclusive club to which he belongs. And yet when I thought that all this, those poor hackneyed words, expressed a sincere passion I could have found in my heart to be sorry for him. But he ended by telling me that one couldn't believe a single word I said, or something like that. You were here then, you heard it yourself."

"And it cut you to the quick," I said. "It made you depart from your dignity to the point of weeping on any shoulder that happened to be there. And considering that it was some more parrot-talk after all (men have been saying that sort of thing to women from the beginning of the world) this sensibility seems to me childish."

"What perspicacity," she observed, with an indulgent, mocking smile, then changed her tone. "Therefore he wasn't expected to-day when he turned up, whereas you, who were expected, remained subject to the charms of conversation in that studio. It never occurred to you . . . did it? No! What had become of your perspicacity?"

"I tell you I was weary of life," I said in a passion.

She had another faint smile of a fugitive and unrelated kind as if she had been thinking of far-off things, then roused herself to grave animation.

"He came in full of smiling playfulness. How well I know that mood! Such self-command has its beauty; but it's no great help for a man with such fateful eyes. I could see he was moved in his correct, restrained way, and in his own way, too, he tried to move me with something that would be very simple. He told me that ever since we became friends, we two, he had not an hour of continuous sleep, unless perhaps when coming back dead-tired from outpost duty, and that he longed to get back to it and yet hadn't the courage to tear himself away from here. He was as simple as that. He's a *très galant homme* of absolute probity, even with himself. I said to him: The trouble is, Don Juan, that it isn't love but mistrust that keeps you in torment. I might have said jealousy, but I didn't like to use that word. A parrot would have added that I had given him no right to be jealous. But I am no parrot. I recognized the rights of his passion which I could very well see. He is jealous. He is not jealous of my past or of the future; but he is jealously mistrustful of *me*, of what I am, of my very soul. He believes in a soul in the same way Therese does, as something that can be touched with grace or go to perdition; and he doesn't want to be damned with me before his own judgment seat. He is a most noble and loyal gentleman, but I have my own Basque peasant soul and don't want to think that every time he goes away from my feet—yes, *mon cher*, on this carpet, look for the marks of scorching—that he goes away feeling tempted to brush the dust off his moral sleeve. That! Never!"

With brusque movements she took a cigarette out of the box, held it in her fingers for a moment, then dropped it unconsciously.

"And then, I don't love him," she uttered slowly as if speaking to herself and at the same time watching the very quality of that thought. "I never did. At first he fascinated me with his fatal aspect and his cold society smiles. But I have looked into those eyes too often. There are too many disdains in this aristocratic republican without a home. His fate may be cruel, but it will always be commonplace. While he sat there trying in a worldly tone to explain to me the problems, the scruples, of his suffering honour, I could see right into his heart and I was sorry for him. I was sorry enough for him to feel that if he had suddenly taken me by the throat and strangled me slowly, *avec délices,* I could forgive him while I choked. How correct he was! But bitterness against me peeped out of every second phrase. At last I raised my hand and said to him, 'Enough.' I believe he was shocked by my plebeian abruptness but he was too polite to show it. His conventions will always stand in the way of his nature. I told him that everything that had been said and done during the last seven or eight months was inexplicable unless on the assumption that he was in love with me,—and yet in everything there was an implication that he couldn't forgive me my very existence. I did ask him whether he didn't think that it was absurd on his part . . ."

"Didn't you say that it was exquisitely absurd?" I asked.

"Exquisitely! . . ." Doña Rita was surprised at my question. "No. Why should I say that?"

"It would have reconciled him to your abruptness. It's their family expression. It would have come with a familiar sound and would have been less offensive."

"Offensive," Doña Rita repeated earnestly. "I don't think he was offended; he suffered in another way, but I didn't care for that. It was I that had become offended in the end, without spite, you understand, but past bearing. I didn't spare him. I told him plainly that to want a woman formed in mind and body, mistress of herself, free in her choice, independent in her thoughts; to love her apparently for what she is and at the same time to demand from her the candour and the innocence that could be only a shocking pretence; to know her such as life had made her and at the same time to despise her secretly for every touch with which her life had fashioned her—that was neither generous nor high minded; it was positively frantic. He got up and went away to lean against the mantelpiece, there, on his elbow and with his head in his hand. You have no idea of the charm and the distinction of his pose. I couldn't help admiring him: the expression, the grace, the fatal suggestion of his immobility. Oh, yes, I am sensible to æsthetic impressions, I have been educated to believe that there is a soul in them."

With that enigmatic, under the eyebrows glance fixed on me she laughed her deep contralto laugh without mirth but also without irony, and profoundly moving by the mere purity of the sound.

"I suspect he was never so disgusted and appalled in his life. His self-command is the most admirable worldly thing I have ever seen. What made it beautiful was that one could feel in it a tragic suggestion as in a great work of art."

She paused with an inscrutable smile that a painter might have put on the face of some symbolic figure for the speculation and wonder of many generations. I said:

"I always thought that love for you could work great wonders. And now I am certain."

"Are you trying to be ironic?" she said sadly and very much as a child might have spoken.

"I don't know," I answered in a tone of the same simplicity. "I find it very difficult to be generous."

"I, too," she said with a sort of funny eagerness. "I didn't treat him very generously. Only I didn't say much more. I found I didn't care what I said—and it would have been like throwing insults at a beautiful composition. He was well inspired not to move. It has spared him some disagreeable truths and perhaps I would even have said more than the truth. I am not fair. I am no more fair than other people. I would have been harsh. My very admiration was making me more angry. It's ridiculous to say of a man got up in correct tailor clothes, but there was a funereal grace in his attitude so that he might have been reproduced in marble on a monument to some woman in one of those atrocious Campo Santos: the bourgeois conception of an aristocratic mourning lover. When I came to that conclusion I became glad that I was angry or else I would have laughed right out before him."

"I have heard a woman say once, a woman of the people—do you hear me, Doña Rita?—therefore deserving your attention, that one should never laugh at love."

"My dear," she said gently, "I have been taught to laugh at most things by a man who never laughed himself; but it's true that he never spoke of love to me, love as a subject that is. So perhaps . . . But why?"

"Because (but maybe that old woman was crazy), because, she said, there was death in the mockery of love."

Doña Rita moved slightly her beautiful shoulders and went on:

"I am glad, then, I didn't laugh. And I am also glad I said nothing more. I was feeling so little generous that if I had known something then of his mother's allusion to 'white geese' I would have advised him to get one of them and lead it away on a beautiful blue ribbon. Mrs. Blunt was wrong, you know, to be so scornful. A white goose is exactly what her son wants. But look how badly the world is arranged.

Such white birds cannot be got for nothing and he has not enough money even to buy a ribbon. Who knows! Maybe it was this which gave that tragic quality to his pose by the mantelpiece over there. Yes, that was it. Though no doubt I didn't see it then. As he didn't offer to move after I had done speaking I became quite unaffectedly sorry and advised him very gently to dismiss me from his mind definitely. He moved forward then and said to me in his usual voice and with his usual smile that it would have been excellent advice but unfortunately I was one of those women who can't be dismissed at will. And as I shook my head he insisted rather darkly: 'Oh, yes, Doña Rita, it is so. Cherish no illusions about that fact.' It sounded so threatening that in my surprise I didn't even acknowledge his parting bow. He went out of that false situation like a wounded man retreating after a fight. No, I have nothing to reproach myself with. I did nothing. I led him into nothing. Whatever illusions have passed through my head I kept my distance, and he was so loyal to what he seemed to think the redeeming proprieties of the situation that he has gone from me for good without so much as kissing the tips of my fingers. He must have felt like a man who had betrayed himself for nothing. It's horrible. It's the fault of that enormous fortune of mine, and I wish with all my heart that I could give it to him; for he couldn't help his hatred of the thing that is: and as to his love, which is just as real, well—could I have rushed away from him to shut myself up in a convent? Could I? After all I have a right to my share of daylight."

V

I took my eyes from her face and became aware that dusk was beginning to steal into the room. How strange it seemed. Except for the glazed rotunda part its long walls, divided into narrow panels separated by an order of flat pilasters, presented, depicted on a black background and in vivid colours, slender women with butterfly wings and lean youths with narrow birds' wings. The effect was supposed to be Pompeiian and Rita and I had often laughed at the delirious fancy of some enriched shopkeeper. But still it was a display of fancy, a sign of grace; but at that moment these figures appeared to me weird and intrusive and strangely alive in their attenuated grace of unearthly beings concealing a power to see and hear.

Without words, without gestures, Doña Rita was heard again. "It may have been as near coming to pass as this." She showed me the breadth of her little finger nail. "Yes, as near as that. Why? How? Just like that, for nothing. Because it had come up. Because a wild notion had entered a practical old woman's head. Yes. And the best of it is that I have nothing to complain of. Had I surrendered I would have been perfectly safe with these two. It is they or rather he who couldn't trust me, or rather that something which I express, which I stand for. Mills would never tell me what it was. Perhaps he didn't know exactly himself. He said it was something like genius. My genius! Oh, I am not conscious of it, believe me, I am not conscious of it. But if I were I wouldn't pluck it out and cast it away. I am ashamed of nothing, of nothing! Don't be stupid enough to think that I have the slightest regret. There is no regret. First of all because I am I—and then because . . . My dear, believe me, I have had a horrible time of it myself lately."

This seemed to be the last word. Outwardly quiet, all the time, it was only then that she became composed enough to light an enormous cigarette of the same pattern as those made specially for the King—*por el Rey!* After a time, tipping the ash into the bowl on her left hand, she asked me in a friendly, almost tender, tone:

"What are you thinking of, *amigo?*"

"I was thinking of your immense generosity. You want to give a crown to one man, a fortune to another. That is very fine. But I suppose there is a limit to your generosity somewhere."

"I don't see why there should be any limit—to fine intentions! Yes, one would like to pay ransom and be done with it all."

"That's the feeling of a captive; and yet somehow I can't think of you as ever having been anybody's captive."

"You do display some wonderful insight sometimes. My dear, I begin to suspect that men are rather conceited about their powers. They think they dominate us. Even exceptional men will think that; men too great for mere vanity, men like Henry Allègre for instance, who by his consistent and serene detachment was certainly fit to dominate all sorts of people. Yet for the most part they can only do it because women choose more or less consciously to let them do so. Henry Allègre, if any man, might have been certain of his own power; and yet, look: I was a chit of a girl,

I was sitting with a book where I had no business to be, in his own garden, when he suddenly came upon me, an ignorant girl of seventeen, a most uninviting creature with a tousled head, in an old black frock and shabby boots. I could have run away. I was perfectly capable of it. But I stayed looking up at him and—in the end it was HE who went away and it was I who stayed."

"Consciously?" I murmured.

"Consciously? You may just as well ask my shadow that lay so still by me on the young grass in that morning sunshine. I never knew before how still I could keep. It wasn't the stillness of terror. I remained, knowing perfectly well that if I ran he was not the man to run after me. I remember perfectly his deep-toned, politely indifferent '*Restez donc.*' He was mistaken. Already then I hadn't the slightest intention to move. And if you ask me again how far conscious all this was the nearest answer I can make you is this: that I remained on purpose, but I didn't know for what purpose I remained. Really, that couldn't be expected. . . . Why do you sigh like this? Would you have preferred me to be idiotically innocent or abominably wise?"

"These are not the questions that trouble me," I said. "If I sighed it is because I am weary."

"And getting stiff, too, I should say, in this Pompeiian armchair. You had better get out of it and sit on this couch as you always used to do. That, at any rate, is not Pompeiian. You have been growing of late extremely formal, I don't know why. If it is a pose then for goodness' sake drop it. Are you going to model yourself on Captain Blunt? You couldn't, you know. You are too young."

"I don't want to model myself on anybody," I said. "And anyway Blunt is too romantic; and, moreover, he has been and is yet in love with you—a thing that requires some style, an attitude, something of which I am altogether incapable."

"You know it isn't so stupid, what you have just said. Yes, there is something in this."

"I am not stupid," I protested, without much heat.

"Oh, yes, you are. You don't know the world enough to judge. You don't know how wise men can be. Owls are nothing to them. Why do you try to look like an owl? There are thousands and thousands of them waiting for me outside the door: the staring, hissing beasts. You don't know what a relief of mental ease and intimacy you have been to me in the frankness of gestures and speeches and thoughts, sane or insane, that we have been throwing at each other. I have known nothing of this in my life but with you. There had always been some fear, some constraint, lurking in the background behind everybody, everybody—except you, my friend."

"An unmannerly, Arcadian state of affairs. I am glad you like it. Perhaps it's because you were intelligent enough to perceive that I was not in love with you in any sort of style."

"No, you were always your own self, unwise and reckless and with something in it kindred to mine, if I may say so without offence."

"You may say anything without offence. But has it never occurred to your sagacity that I just, simply, loved you?"

"Just—simply," she repeated in a wistful tone.

"You didn't want to trouble your head about it, is that it?"

"My poor head. From your tone one might think you yearned to cut it off. No, my dear, I have made up my mind not to lose my head."

"You would be astonished to know how little I care for your mind."

"Would I? Come and sit on the couch all the same," she said after a moment of hesitation. Then, as I did not move at once, she added with indifference: "You may sit as far away as you like, it's big enough, goodness knows."

The light was ebbing slowly out of the rotunda and to my bodily eyes she was beginning to grow shadowy. I sat down on the couch and for a long time no word passed between us. We made no movement. We did not even turn towards each other. All I was conscious of was the softness of the seat which seemed somehow to cause a relaxation of my stern mood, I won't say against my will but without any will on my part. Another thing I was conscious of, strangely enough, was the enormous brass bowl for cigarette ends. Quietly, with the least possible action, Doña Rita moved it to the other side of her motionless person. Slowly, the fantastic women with butterflies' wings and the slender-limbed youths with the gorgeous pinions on their shoulders were vanishing into their black backgrounds with an effect of silent discretion, leaving us to ourselves.

I felt suddenly extremely exhausted, absolutely overcome with fatigue since I had moved; as if to sit on that Pompeiian chair had been a task almost beyond human strength, a sort of labour that must end in collapse. I fought against it for a moment and then my resistance gave way. Not all at once but as if yielding to an irresistible pressure (for I was not conscious of any irresistible attraction) I found myself with my head resting, with a weight I felt must be crushing, on Doña Rita's shoulder which yet did not give way, did not flinch at all. A faint scent of violets filled the tragic emptiness of my head and it seemed impossible to me that I should not cry from sheer weakness. But I remained dry-eyed. I only felt myself slipping lower and lower and I caught her round the waist, clinging to her not from any intention but purely by instinct. All that time she hadn't stirred. There was only the slight movement of her breathing that showed her to be alive; and with closed eyes I imagined her to be lost in thought, removed, by an incredible meditation while I clung to her, to an immense distance from the earth. The distance must have been immense because the silence was so perfect, the feeling as if of eternal stillness. I had a distinct impression of being in contact with an infinity that had the slightest possible rise and fall, was pervaded by a warm, delicate scent of violets and through which came a hand from somewhere to rest lightly on my head. Presently my ear caught the faint and regular pulsation of her heart, firm and quick, infinitely touching in its persistent mystery, disclosing itself into my very ear—and my felicity became complete.

It was a dreamlike state combined with a dreamlike sense of insecurity. Then in that warm and scented infinity, or eternity, in which I rested lost in bliss but ready for any catastrophe, I heard the distant, hardly audible, and fit to strike terror into the heart, ringing of a bell. At this sound the greatness of spaces departed. I felt the world close about me; the world of darkened walls, of very deep grey dusk against the panes, and I asked in a pained voice:

"Why did you ring, Rita?"

There was a bell rope within reach of her hand. I had not felt her move, but she said very low:

"I rang for the lights."

"You didn't want the lights."

"It was time," she whispered secretly.

Somewhere within the house a door slammed. I got away from her, feeling small and weak as if the best part of me had been torn away and irretrievably lost. Rose must have been somewhere near the door.

"It's abominable," I murmured to the still, idol-like shadow on the couch.

The answer was a hurried, nervous whisper: "I tell you it was time. I rang because I had no strength to push you away."

I suffered a moment of giddiness before the door opened, light streamed in, and Rose entered, preceding a man in a green baize apron whom I had never seen, carrying on an enormous tray three Argand lamps fitted into vases of Pompeiian form. Rose distributed them over the room. In the flood of soft light the winged youths and the butterfly women reappeared on the panels, affected, gorgeous, callously unconscious of anything having happened during their absence. Rose attended to the lamp on the nearest mantelpiece, then turned about and asked in a confident undertone:

"*Monsieur dîne ?*"

I had lost myself with my elbows on my knees and my head in my hands, but I heard the words distinctly. I heard also the silence which ensued. I sat up and took the responsibility of the answer on myself.

"Impossible. I am going to sea this evening."

This was perfectly true, only I had totally forgotten it till then. For the last two days my being was no longer composed of memories but exclusively of sensations of the most absorbing, disturbing, exhausting nature. I was like a man who has been buffeted by the sea or by a mob till he loses all hold on the world in the misery of his helplessness. But now I was recovering. And naturally the first thing I remembered was the fact that I was going to sea.

"You have heard, Rose," Doña Rita said at last with some impatience.

The girl waited a moment longer before she said:

"Oh, yes! There is a man waiting for Monsieur in the hall. A seaman."

It could be no one but Dominic. It dawned upon me that since the evening of our return I had not been near him or the ship, which was completely unusual, unheard of, and well calculated to startle Dominic.

"I have seen him before," continued Rose, "and as he told me he has been pursuing Monsieur all the afternoon and didn't like to go away without seeing Monsieur for a moment, I proposed to him to wait in the hall till Monsieur was at liberty."

I said: "Very well," and with a sudden resumption of her extremely busy, not-a-moment-to-lose manner Rose departed from the room. I lingered in an imaginary world full of tender light, of unheard-of colours, with a mad riot of flowers and an inconceivable happiness under the sky arched above its yawning precipices, while a feeling of awe enveloped me like its own proper atmosphere. But everything vanished at the sound of Doña Rita's loud whisper full of boundless dismay, such as to make one's hair stir on one's head.

"*Mon Dieu!* And what is going to happen now?"

She got down from the couch and walked to a window. When the lights had been brought into the room all the panes had turned inky black; for the night had come and the garden was full of tall bushes and trees screening off the gas lamps of the main alley of the Prado. Whatever the question meant she was not likely to see an answer to it outside. But her whisper had offended me, had hurt something infinitely deep, infinitely subtle and infinitely clear-eyed in my nature. I said after her from the couch on which I had remained, "Don't lose your composure. You will always have some sort of bell at hand."

I saw her shrug her uncovered shoulders impatiently. Her forehead was against the very blackness of the panes; pulled upward from the beautiful, strong nape of her neck, the twisted mass of her tawny hair was held high upon her head by the arrow of gold.

"You set up for being unforgiving," she said without anger.

I sprang to my feet while she turned about and came towards me bravely, with a wistful smile on her bold, adolescent face.

"It seems to me," she went on in a voice like a wave of love itself, "that one should try to understand before one sets up for being unforgiving. Forgiveness is a very fine word. It is a fine invocation."

"There are other fine words in the language such as fascination, fidelity, also frivolity; and as for invocations there are plenty of them, too; for instance: alas, heaven help me."

We stood very close together, her narrow eyes were as enigmatic as ever, but that face, which, like some ideal conception of art, was incapable of anything like untruth and grimace, expressed by some mysterious means such a depth of infinite patience that I felt profoundly ashamed of myself.

"This thing is beyond words, altogether," I said: "Beyond forgiveness, beyond forgetting, beyond anger or jealousy. . . . There is nothing between us two that could make us act together."

"Then we must fall back perhaps on something within us, that—you admit it?—we have in common."

"Don't be childish," I said. "You give one, with a perpetual and intense freshness, feelings and sensations that are as old as the world itself, and you imagine that your enchantment can be broken off anywhere, at any time! But it can't be broken. And forgetfulness, like everything else, can only come from you. It's an impossible situation to stand up against."

She listened with slightly parted lips as if to catch some further resonances.

"There is a sort of generous ardour about you," she said, "which I don't really understand. No, I don't know it. Believe me, it is not of myself I am thinking. And you—you are going out to-night to make another landing."

"Yes, it is a fact that before many hours I will be sailing away from you to try my luck once more."

"Your wonderful luck," she breathed out.

"Oh, yes, I am wonderfully lucky. Unless the luck really is yours—in having found somebody like me, who cares at the same time so much and so little for what you have at heart."

"What time will you be leaving the harbour?" she asked.

"Some time between midnight and daybreak. Our men may be a little late in joining, but certainly we will be gone before the first streak of light."

"What freedom!" she murmured enviously. "It's something I shall never know. . . ."

"Freedom!" I protested. "I am a slave to my word. There will be a string of carts and mules on a certain part of the coast, and a most ruffianly lot of men, men you understand, men with wives and children and sweethearts, who from the very moment they start on a trip risk a bullet in the head at any moment, but who have a perfect conviction that I will never fail them. That's

my freedom. I wonder what they would think if they
knew of your existence."

"I don't exist," she said.

"That's easy to say. But I will go as if you didn't
exist—yet only because you do exist. You exist in
me. I don't know where I end and you begin. You
have got into my heart and into my veins and into my
brain."

"Take this fancy out and trample it down in the
dust," she said in a tone of timid entreaty.

"Heroically," I suggested with the sarcasm of
despair.

"Well, yes, heroically," she said; and there passed between us dim smiles, I have no doubt of the most touching imbecility on earth. We were standing by then
in the middle of the room with its vivid colours on a
black background, with its multitude of winged figures
with pale limbs, with hair like halos or flames, all
strangely tense in their strained, decorative attitudes.
Doña Rita made a step towards me, and as I attempted
to seize her hand she flung her arms round my neck. I
felt their strength drawing me towards her and by a
sort of blind and desperate effort I resisted. And all
the time she was repeating with nervous insistence:

"But it is true that you will go. You will surely.
Not because of those people but because of me. You
will go away because you feel you must."

With every word urging me to get away, her clasp
tightened, she hugged my head closer to her breast. I
submitted, knowing well that I could free myself by one
more effort which it was in my power to make. But
before I made it, in a sort of desperation, I pressed a
long kiss into the hollow of her throat. And lo—there
was no need for any effort. With a stifled cry of surprise her arms fell off me as if she had been shot. I

must have been giddy, and perhaps we both were giddy, but the next thing I knew there was a good foot of space between us in the peaceful glow of the ground-glass globes, in the everlasting stillness of the winged figures. Something in the quality of her exclamation, something utterly unexpected, something I had never heard before, and also the way she was looking at me with a sort of incredulous, concentrated attention, disconcerted me exceedingly. I knew perfectly well what I had done and yet I felt that I didn't understand what had happened. I became suddenly abashed and I muttered that I had better go and dismiss that poor Dominic. She made no answer, gave no sign. She stood there lost in a vision—or was it a sensation?—of the most absorbing kind. I hurried out into the hall, shamefaced, as if I were making my escape while she wasn't looking. And yet I felt her looking fixedly at me, with a sort, of stupefaction on her features—in her whole attitude— as though she had never even heard of such a thing as a kiss in her life.

A dim lamp (of Pompeiian form) hanging on a long chain left the hall practically dark. Dominic, advancing towards me from a distant corner, was but a little more opaque shadow than the others. He had expected me on board every moment till about three o'clock, but as I didn't turn up and gave no sign of life in any other way he started on his hunt. He sought news of me from the *garçons* at the various cafés, from the *cochers de fiacre* in front of the Exchange, from the tobacconist lady at the counter of the fashionable *debit de tabac*, from the old man who sold papers outside the *cercle*, from the flower-girl at the door of the fashionable restaurant where I had my table. That young woman, whose business name was Irma, had come on duty about midday. She said to Dominic:

"I think I've seen all his friends this morning but I haven't seen him for a week. What has become of him?"

"That's exactly what I want to know," Dominic replied in a fury and then went back to the harbour on the chance that I might have called either on board or at Madame Léonore's café.

I expressed to him my surprise that he should fuss about me like an old hen over a chick. It wasn't like him at all. And he said that "*en effet*" it was Madame Léonore who wouldn't give him any peace. He hoped I wouldn't mind, it was best to humour women in little things; and so he started off again, made straight for the street of the Consuls, was told there that I wasn't at home, but the woman of the house looked so funny that he didn't know what to make of it. Therefore, after some hesitation, he took the liberty to inquire at this house, too, and being told that I couldn't be disturbed, had made up his mind not to go on board without actually setting his eyes on me and hearing from my own lips that nothing was changed as to sailing orders.

"There is nothing changed, Dominic," I said.

"No change of any sort?" he insisted, looking very sombre and speaking gloomily from under his black moustaches in the dim glow of the alabaster lamp hanging above his head. He peered at me in an extraordinary manner as if he wanted to make sure that I had all my limbs about me. I asked him to call for my bag at the other house, on his way to the harbour, and he departed reassured, not, however, without remarking ironically that ever since she saw that American cavalier Madame Léonore was not easy in her mind about me.

As I stood alone in the hall, without a sound of any sort, Rose appeared before me.

"Monsieur will dine after all," she whispered calmly.

"My good girl, I am going to sea to-night."

"What am I going to do with Madame?" she murmured to herself. "She will insist on returning to Paris."

"Oh, have you heard of it?"

"I never get more than two hours' notice," she said. "But I know how it will be," her voice lost its calmness. "I can look after Madame up to a certain point but I cannot be altogether responsible. There is a dangerous person who is everlastingly trying to see Madame alone. I have managed to keep him off several times but there is a beastly old journalist who is encouraging him in his attempts, and I daren't even speak to Madame about it."

"What sort of person do you mean?"

"Why, a man," she said scornfully.

I snatched up my coat and hat.

"Aren't there dozens of them?"

"Oh! But this one is dangerous. Madame must have given him a hold on her in some way. I ought not to talk like this about Madame and I wouldn't to anybody but Monsieur. I am always on the watch, but what is a poor girl to do? . . . Isn't Monsieur going back to Madame?"

"No, I am not going back. Not this time." A mist seemed to fall before my eyes. I could hardly see the girl standing by the closed door of the Pompeiian room with extended hand, as if turned to stone. But my voice was firm enough. "Not this time," I repeated, and became aware of the great noise of the wind amongst the trees, with the lashing of a rain squall against the door. "Perhaps some other time," I added.

I heard her say twice to herself: "*Mon Dieu! Mon Dieu!*" and then a dismayed: "What can Monsieur expect me to do?" But I had to appear insensible to her distress and that not altogether because, in fact, I had no option but to go away. I remember also a distinct wilfulness in my attitude and something half-contemptuous in my words as I laid my hand on the knob of the front door.

"You will tell Madame that I am gone. It will please her. Tell her that I am gone—heroically."

Rose had come up close to me. She met my words by a despairing outward movement of her hands as though she were giving everything up.

"I see it clearly now that Madame has no friends," she declared with such a force of restrained bitterness that it nearly made me pause. But the very obscurity of actuating motives drove me on and I stepped out through the doorway muttering: "Everything is as Madame wishes it."

She shot at me a swift: "You should resist," of an extraordinary intensity, but I strode on down the path. Then Rose's schooled temper gave way at last and I heard her angry voice screaming after me furiously through the wind and rain: "No! Madame has no friends. Not one!"

PART FIVE

I

THAT night I didn't get on board till just before midnight and Dominic could not conceal his relief at having me safely there. Why he should have been so uneasy it was impossible to say but at the time I had a sort of impression that my inner destruction (it was nothing less) had affected my appearance, that my doom was as it were written on my face. I was a mere receptacle for dust and ashes, a living testimony to the vanity of all things. My very thoughts were like a ghostly rustle of dead leaves. But we had an extremely successful trip, and for most of the time Dominic displayed an unwonted jocularity of a dry and biting kind with which, he maintained, he had been infected by no other person than myself. As, with all his force of character, he was very responsive to the moods of those he liked, I have no doubt he spoke the truth. But I know nothing about it. The observer, more or less alert, whom each of us carries in his own consciousness, failed me altogether, had turned away his face in sheer horror, or else had fainted from the strain. And thus I had to live alone, unobserved even by myself.

But the trip had been successful. We re-entered the harbour very quietly as usual and when our craft had been moored unostentatiously amongst the plebeian stone-carriers, Dominic, whose grim joviality had subsided in the last twenty-four hours of our homeward run, abandoned me to myself as though indeed

I had been a doomed man. He only stuck his head for a moment into our little cuddy where I was changing my clothes and being told in answer to his question that I had no special orders to give, went ashore without waiting for me.

Generally we used to step on the quay together and I never failed to enter for a moment Madame Léonore's café. But this time when I got on the quay Dominic was nowhere to be seen. What was it? Abandonment—discretion—or had he quarrelled with his Léonore before leaving on the trip?

My way led me past the café and through the glass panes I saw that he was already there. On the other side of the little marble table Madame Léonore, leaning with mature grace on her elbow, was listening to him absorbed. Then I passed on and—what would you have!—I ended by making my way into the street of the Consuls. I had nowhere else to go. There were my things in the apartment on the first floor. I couldn't bear the thought of meeting anybody I knew.

The feeble gas flame in the hall was still there, on duty, as though it had never been turned off since I last crossed the hall at half-past eleven in the evening to go to the harbour. The small flame had watched me letting myself out; and now, exactly of the same size, the poor little tongue of light (there was something wrong with that burner) watched me letting myself in as indeed it had done many times before. Generally the impression was that of entering an untenanted house, but this time before I could reach the foot of the stairs Therese glided out of the passage leading into the studio After the usual exclamations she assured me that everything was ready for me upstairs, had been for days, and offered to get me something to eat at once. I accepted and said I would be down in the studio in half an hour. I found her there by the side of the laid table ready for conversation. She began by telling me—the dear, poor young Monsieur—in a sort of plaintive chant, that there were no letters for me, no letters of any kind, no letters from anybody. Glances of absolutely terrifying tenderness mingled with flashes of cunning swept over me from head to foot while I tried to eat.

"Are you giving me Captain Blunt's wine to drink?" I asked, noting the straw-coloured liquid in my glass.

She screwed up her mouth as if she had a twinge of toothache and assured me that the wine belonged to the house. I would have to pay her for it. As far as personal feelings go, Blunt, who addressed her always with polite seriousness, was not a favourite with her. The "charming, brave Monsieur" was now fighting for the King and religion against the impious Liberals. He went away the very morning after I had left and, oh! she remembered, he had asked her before going away whether I was still in the house. Wanted probably to say good-bye to me, shake my hand, the dear, polite Monsieur.

I let her run on in dread expectation of what she would say next, but she stuck to the subject of Blunt for some time longer. He had written to her once about some of his things which he wanted her to send to Paris to his mother's address; but she was going to do nothing of the kind. She announced this with a pious smile; and in answer to my questions I discovered that it was a stratagem to make Captain Blunt return to the house.

"You will get yourself into trouble with the police, Mademoiselle Therese, if you go on like that," I said. But she was as obstinate as a mule and assured me with the utmost confidence that many people would be ready to defend a poor honest girl. There was something behind this attitude which I could not fathom. Suddenly she fetched a deep sigh.

"Our Rita, too, will end by coming to her sister."

The name for which I had been waiting deprived me of speech for the moment. The poor mad sinner had rushed off to some of her wickednesses in Paris. Did I know? No? How could she tell whether I did know or not? Well! I had hardly left the house, so to speak, when Rita was down with her maid, behaving as if the house did really still belong to her. . . .

"What time was it?" I managed to ask. And with the words my life itself was being forced out through my lips. But Therese, not noticing anything strange about me, said it was something like half-past seven in the morning. The "poor sinner" was all in black as if she were going to church (except for her expression, which was enough to shock any honest person), and after ordering her with frightful menaces not to let anybody know she was in the house she rushed upstairs and locked herself up in my bedroom, while "that French creature" (whom she seemed to love more than her own sister) went into my salon and hid herself behind the window curtain.

I had recovered sufficiently to ask in a quiet natural voice whether Doña Rita and Captain Blunt had seen each other. Apparently they had not seen each other. The polite captain had looked so stern while packing up his kit that Therese dared not speak to him at all. And he was in a hurry, too. He had to see his dear mother off to Paris before his own departure. Very stern. But he shook her hand with a very nice bow.

Therese elevated her right hand for me to see. It was broad and short with blunt fingers, as usual. The pressure of Captain Blunt's handshake had not altered its unlovely shape.

"What was the good of telling him that our Rita was here?" went on Therese. "I would have been ashamed of her coming here and behaving as if the house be-longed to her! I had already said some prayers at his intention at the half-past six mass, the brave gentleman. That maid of my sister Rita was upstairs watching him drive away with her evil eyes, but I made a sign of the cross after the fiacre, and then I went upstairs and banged at your door, my dear kind young Monsieur, and shouted to Rita that she had no right to lock herself in any of my *locataires'* rooms. At last she opened it—and what do you think? All her hair was loose over her shoulders. I suppose it all came down when she flung her hat on your bed. I noticed when she arrived that her hair wasn't done properly. She used your brushes to do it up again in front of your glass."

"Wait a moment," I said, and jumped up, upsetting my wine to run upstairs as fast as I could. I lighted the gas, all the three jets in the middle of the room, the jet by the bedside and two others flanking the dressing-table. I had been struck by the wild hope of finding a trace of Rita's passage, a sign or something. I pulled out all the drawers violently, thinking that perhaps she had hidden there a scrap of paper, a note. It was perfectly mad. Of course there was no chance of that. Therese would have seen to it. I picked up one after another all the various objects on the dressing-table. On laying my hands on the brushes I had a profound emotion, and with misty eyes I examined them meticulously with the new hope of finding one of Rita's tawny hairs entangled amongst the bristles by a miraculous chance. But Therese would have done away with that chance, too. There was nothing to be seen, though I held them up to the light with a beating heart. It was written that not even *that* trace of her passage on the earth should remain with me; not to help but, as it were, to soothe the memory. Then I lighted a cigarette and came downstairs slowly. My unhappiness became dulled, as the grief of those who mourn for the dead gets dulled in the overwhelming sensation that everything is over, that a part of themselves is lost beyond recall, taking with it all the savour of life.

I discovered Therese still on the very same spot of the floor, her hands folded over each other and facing my empty chair before which the spilled wine had soaked a large portion of the table-cloth. She hadn't moved at all. She hadn't even picked up the overturned glass. But directly I appeared she began to speak in an ingratiating voice.

"If you have missed anything of yours upstairs, my dear young Monsieur, you mustn't say it's me. You don't know what our Rita is."

"I wish to goodness," I said, "that she had taken something."

And again I became inordinately agitated as though it were my absolute fate to be everlastingly dying and reviving to the tormenting fact of her existence. Perhaps she had taken something? Anything. Some small object. I thought suddenly of a Rhenish-stone match-box. Perhaps it was that. I didn't remember having seen it when upstairs. I wanted to make sure at once. At once. But I commanded myself to sit still.

"And she so wealthy," Therese went on. "Even you with your dear generous little heart can do nothing for our Rita. No man can do anything for her— except perhaps one, but she is so evilly disposed towards him that she wouldn't even see him, if in the goodness of his forgiving heart he were to offer his hand to her

It's her bad conscience that frightens her. He loves her more than his life, the dear, charitable man."

"You mean some rascal in Paris that I believe persecutes Doña Rita. Listen, Mademoiselle Therese, if you know where he hangs out you had better let him have word to be careful. I believe he, too, is mixed up in the Carlist intrigue. Don't you know that your sister can get him shut up any day or get him expelled by the police?"

Therese sighed deeply and put on a look of pained virtue.

"Oh, the hardness of her heart. She tried to be tender with me. She is awful. I said to her, 'Rita, have you sold your soul to the Devil?' and she shouted like a fiend: 'For happiness! Ha, ha, ha!' She threw herself backwards on that couch in your room and laughed and laughed and laughed as if I had been tickling her, and she drummed on the floor with the heels of her shoes. She is possessed. Oh, my dear innocent young Monsieur, you have never seen anything like that. That wicked girl who serves her rushed in with a tiny glass bottle and put it to her nose; but I had a mind to run out and fetch the priest from the church where I go to early mass. Such a nice, stout, severe man. But that false, cheating creature (I am sure she is robbing our Rita from morning to night), she talked to our Rita very low and quieted her down. I am sure I don't know what she said. She must be leagued with the Devil. And then she asked me if I would go down and make a cup of chocolate for her Madame. Madame—that's our Rita. Madame! It seems they were going off directly to Paris and her Madame had had nothing to eat since the morning of the day before. Fancy me being ordered to make chocolate for our Rita! However, the poor thing looked so exhausted

and white-faced that I went. Ah! the Devil can give
you an awful shake up if he likes."

Therese gave another deep sigh and raising her eyes
looked at me with great attention. I preserved an inscrutable expression, for I wanted to hear all she had to
tell me of Rita. I watched her with the greatest anxiety
composing her face into a cheerful expression.

"So Doña Rita is gone to Paris?" I asked negligently.

"Yes, my dear Monsieur. I believe she went straight
to the railway station from here. When she first got up
from the couch she could hardly stand. But before,
while she was drinking the chocolate which I made for
her, I tried to get her to sign a paper giving over the
house to me, but she only closed her eyes and begged
me to try and be a good sister and leave her alone for
half an hour. And she lying there looking as if she
wouldn't live a day. But she always hated me."

I said bitterly, "You needn't have worried her like
this. If she had not lived for another day you would
have had this house and everything else besides; a
bigger bit than even your wolfish throat can swallow,
Mademoiselle Therese."

I then said a few more things indicative of my disgust
with her rapacity, but they were quite inadequate, as I
wasn't able to find words strong enough to express my
real mind. But it didn't matter really because I don't
think Therese heard me at all. She seemed lost in rapt
amazement.

"What do you say, my dear Monsieur? What!
All for me without any sort of paper?"

She appeared distracted by my curt: "Yes." Therese
believed in my truthfulness. She believed me im-
plicitly, except when I was telling her the truth about
herself, mincing no words, when she used to stand
smilingly bashful as if I were overwhelming her with

compliments. I expected her to continue the horrible tale but apparently she had found something to think about which checked the flow. She fetched another sigh and muttered:

"Then the law can be just, if it does not require any paper. After all, I am her sister."

"It's very difficult to believe that—at sight," I said roughly.

"Ah, but that I could prove. There are papers for that."

After this declaration she began to clear the table, preserving a thoughtful silence.

I was not very surprised at the news of Doña Rita's departure for Paris. It was not necessary to ask myself why she had gone. I didn't even ask myself whether she had left the leased Villa on the Prado for ever. Later talking again with Therese, I learned that her sister had given it up for the use of the Carlist cause and that some sort of unofficial Consul, a Carlist agent of some sort, either was going to live there or had already taken possession. This, Rita herself had told her before her departure on that agitated morning spent in the house—in my rooms. A close investigation demonstrated to me that there was nothing missing from them. Even the wretched match-box which I really hoped was gone turned up in a drawer after I had, delightedly, given it up. It was a great blow. She might have taken that at least! She knew I used to carry it about with me constantly while ashore. She might have taken it! Apparently she meant that there should be no bond left even of that kind; and yet it was a long time before I gave up visiting and revisiting all the corners of all possible receptacles for something that she might have left behind on purpose. It was like the mania of those disordered minds who spend their days hunting for a treasure. I hoped for a forgotten hairpin, for some tiny piece of ribbon. Sometimes at night I reflected that such hopes were altogether insensate; but I remember once getting up at two in the morning to search for a little cardboard box in the bathroom, into which, I remembered, I had not looked before. Of course it was empty; and, anyway, Rita could not possibly have known of its existence. I got back to bed shivering violently, though the night was warm, and with a distinct impression that this thing would end by making me mad. It was no longer a question of "this sort of thing" killing me. The moral atmosphere of this torture was different. It would make me mad. And at that thought great shudders ran down my prone body, because, once, I had visited a famous lunatic asylum where they had shown me a poor wretch who was mad, apparently, because he thought he had been abominably fooled by a woman. They told me that his grievance was quite imaginary. He was a young man with a thin fair beard, huddled up on the edge of his bed, hugging himself forlornly; and his incessant and lamentable wailing filled the long bare corridor, striking a chill into one's heart long before one came to the door of his cell.

And there was no one from whom I could hear, to whom I could speak, with whom I could evoke the image of Rita. Of course I could utter that word of four letters to Therese; but Therese for some reason took it into her head to avoid all topics connected with her sister. I felt as if I could pull out great handfuls of her hair hidden modestly under the black handkerchief of which the ends were sometimes tied under her chin. But, really, I could not have given her any intelligible excuse for that outrage. Moreover, she was very busy from the very top to the very bottom of the house, which she persisted in running alone because she couldn't make up her mind to part with a few francs every month to a servant. It seemed to me that I was no longer such a favourite with her as I used to be. That, strange to say, was exasperating, too. It was as if some idea, some fruitful notion had killed in her all the softer and more humane emotions. She went about with brooms and dusters, wearing an air of sanctimonious thoughtfulness.

The man who to a certain extent took my place in Therese's favour was the old father of the dancing girls inhabiting the ground floor. In a tall hat and a well-to-do dark blue overcoat he allowed himself to be buttonholed in the hall by Therese who would talk to him interminably with downcast eyes. He smiled gravely at her, and meanwhile tried to edge towards the front door. I imagine he didn't put a great value on Therese's favour. Our stay in harbour was prolonged this time and I kept indoors like an invalid. One evening I asked that old man to come in and drink and smoke with me in the studio. He made no difficulties to accept, brought his wooden pipe with him, and was very entertaining in a pleasant voice. One couldn't tell whether he was an uncommon person or simply a ruffian, but in any case with his white beard he looked quite venerable. Naturally he couldn't give me much of his company as he had to look closely after his girls and their admirers; not that the girls were unduly frivolous, but of course being very young they had no experience. They were friendly creatures with pleasant, merry voices and he was very much devoted to them. He was a muscular man with a high colour and silvery locks curling round his bald pate and over his ears, like a *barocco* apostle. I had an idea that he had had a lurid past and had seen some fighting in

his youth. The admirers of the two girls stood in
great awe of him, from instinct no doubt, because his
behaviour to them was friendly and even somewhat
obsequious, yet always with a certain truculent glint in
his eye that made them pause in everything but their
generosity—which was encouraged. I sometimes wondered whether those two careless, merry, hard-working
creatures understood the secret moral beauty of the
situation.

My real company was the dummy in the studio and I
can't say it was exactly satisfying. After taking possession of the studio I had raised it tenderly, dusted its
mangled limbs and insensible, hard-wood bosom, and
then had propped it up in a corner where it seemed to
take on, of itself, a shy attitude. I knew its history.
It was not an ordinary dummy. One day, talking with
Doña Rita about her sister, I had told her that I thought
Therese used to knock it down on purpose with a broom,
and Doña Rita had laughed very much. This, she had
said, was an instance of dislike from mere instinct.
That dummy had been made to measure years before.
It had to wear for days and days the Imperial Byzantine
robes in which Doña Rita sat only once or twice herself;
but of course the folds and bends of the stuff had to be
preserved as in the first sketch. Doña Rita described
amusingly how she had to stand in the middle of her
room while Rose walked around her with a tape measure
noting the figures down on a small piece of paper which
was then sent to the maker, who presently returned it
with an angry letter stating that those proportions
were altogether impossible in any woman. Apparently
Rose had muddled them all up; and it was a long time
before the figure was finished and sent to the Pavilion
in a long basket to take on itself the robes and the
hieratic pose of the Empress. Later, it wore with the

same patience the marvellous hat of the "Girl in the Hat." But Doña Rita couldn't understand how the poor thing ever found its way to Marseilles minus its turnip head. Probably it came down with the robes and a quantity of precious brocades which she herself had sent down from Paris. The knowledge of its origin, the contempt of Captain Blunt's references to it, with Therese's shocked dislike of the dummy, invested that summary reproduction with a sort of charm, gave me a faint and miserable illusion of the original, less artificial than a photograph, less precise, too. . . . But it can't be explained. I felt positively friendly to it as if it had been Rita's trusted personal attendant. I even went so far as to discover that it had a sort of grace of its own. But I never went so far as to address set speeches to it where it lurked shyly in its corner, or drag it out from there for contemplation. I left it in peace. I wasn't mad. I was only convinced that I soon would be.

II

Notwithstanding my misanthropy I had to see a few people on account of all these Royalist affairs which I couldn't very well drop, and in truth did not wish to drop. They were my excuse for remaining in Europe, which somehow I had not the strength of mind to leave for the West Indies, or elsewhere. On the other hand, my adventurous pursuit kept me in contact with the sea where I found occupation, protection, consolation, the mental relief of grappling with concrete problems, the sanity one acquires from close contact with simple mankind, a little self-confidence born from the dealings with the elemental powers of nature. I couldn't give all that up. And besides all this was related to Doña Rita. I had, as it were, received it from her own hand, from that hand the clasp of which was as frank as a man's and yet conveyed a unique sensation. The very memory of it would go through me like a wave of heat. It was over that hand that we first got into the habit of quarrelling, with the irritability of sufferers from some obscure pain and yet half unconscious of their disease. Rita's own spirit hovered over the troubled waters of Legitimity. But as to the sound of the four magic letters of her name I was not very likely to hear it fall sweetly on my ear. For instance, the distinguished personality in the world of finance with whom I had to confer several times, alluded to the irresistible seduction of the power which reigned over my heart and my mind; which had a mysterious and unforgettable face, the brilliance of sunshine together with the unfathomable

splendour of the night as—Madame de Lastaola.
That's how that steel-grey man called the greatest
mystery of the universe. When uttering that assumed
name he would make for himself a guardedly solemn
and reserved face as though he were afraid lest I should
presume to smile, lest he himself should venture to
smile, and the sacred formality of our relations should
be outraged beyond mending.

He would refer in a studiously grave tone to Madame
de Lastaola's wishes, plans, activities, instructions,
movements; or picking up a letter from the usual litter
of paper found on such men's desks, glance at it to re-
fresh his memory; and, while the very sight of the handwriting would make my lips go dry, would ask me in a
bloodless voice whether perchance I had "a direct
communication from—er—Paris lately." And there
would be other maddening circumstances connected
with those visits. He would treat me as a serious
person having a clear view of certain eventualities,
while at the very moment my vision could see nothing
but streaming across the wall at his back, abundant
and misty, unearthly and adorable, a mass of tawny
hair that seemed to have hot sparks tangled in it.
Another nuisance was the atmosphere of Royalism,
of Legitimacy, that pervaded the room, thin as air,
intangible, as though no Legitimist of flesh and blood
had ever existed to the man's mind except perhaps myself. He, of course, was just simply a banker, a very
distinguished, a very influential, and a very impeccable
banker. He persisted also in deferring to my judgment and sense with an over-emphasis called out by
his perpetual surprise at my youth. Though he had
seen me many times (I even knew his wife) he could
never get over my immature age. He himself was
born about fifty years old, all complete, with his iron-

grey whiskers and his bilious eyes, which he had the
habit of frequently closing during a conversation. On
one occasion he said to me: "Bye-the-bye, the Marquis
of Villarel is here for a time. He inquired after you
the last time he called on me. May I let him know
that you are in town?"

I didn't say anything to that. The Marquis of
Villarel was the Don Rafael of Rita's own story.
What had I to do with Spanish grandees? And for that
matter what had she, the woman of all time, to do with
all the villainous or splendid disguises human dust takes
upon itself? All this was in the past, and I was acutely
aware that for me there was no present, no future,
nothing but a hollow pain, a vain passion of such
magnitude that being locked up within my breast it
gave me an illusion of lonely greatness with my miserable head uplifted amongst the stars. But when I
made up my mind (which I did quickly, to be done with
it) to call on the banker's wife, almost the first thing
she said to me was that the Marquis de Villarel was
"amongst us." She said it joyously. If in her husband's room at the bank legitimism was a mere unpop-
ulated principle, in her salon Legitimacy was nothing
but persons. "*Il m'a causé beaucoup de vous,*" she
said as if there had been a joke in it of which I ought
to be proud. I slunk away from her. I couldn't believe that the grandee had talked to her about me. I
had never felt myself part of the great Royalist enterprise. I confess that I was so indifferent to everything,
so profoundly demoralized, that having once got into
that drawing-room I hadn't the strength to get away;
though I could see perfectly well my volatile hostess
going from one to another of her acquaintances in
order to tell them with a little gesture, "Look! Over
there—in that corner. That's the notorious Monsieur

George." At last she herself drove me out by coming to sit by me vivaciously and going into ecstasies over "*ce cher* Monsieur Mills" and that magnificent Lord X; and ultimately, with a perfectly odious snap in the eyes and drop in the voice, dragging in the name of Madame de Lastaola and asking me whether I was really so much in the confidence of that astonishing person. "*Vous devez bien regretter son départ pour Paris,*" she cooed, looking with affected bashfulness at her fan. . . . How I got out of the room I really don't know. There was also a staircase. I did not fall down it head first—that much I am certain of; and I also remember that I wandered for a long time about the seashore and went home very late, by the way of the Prado, giving in passing a fearful glance at the Villa. It showed not a gleam of light through the thin foliage of its trees.

I spent the next day with Dominic on board the little craft, watching the shipwrights at work on her deck. From the way they went about their business those men must have been perfectly sane; and I felt greatly refreshed by my company during the day. Dominic, too, devoted himself to his business, but his taciturnity was sardonic. Then I dropped in at the café and Madame Léonore's loud "Eh, Signorino, here you are at last!" pleased me by its resonant friendliness. But I found the sparkle of her black eyes as she sat down for a moment opposite me while I was having my drink rather difficult to bear. That man and that woman seemed to know something. What did they know? At parting she pressed my hand significantly. What did she mean? But I didn't feel offended by these manifestations. The souls within these people's breasts were not volatile in the manner of slightly scented and inflated bladders. Neither had they the impervious skins which seem the rule in the fine world that wants only to get on. Somehow they had sensed that there was something wrong; and whatever impression they might have formed for themselves I had the certitude that it would not be for them a matter of grins at my expense.

That day on returning home I found Therese looking out for me, a very unusual occurrence of late. She handed me a card bearing the name of the Marquis de Villarel.

"How did you come by this?" I asked. She turned on at once the tap of her volubility and I was not surprised to learn that the grandee had not done such an extraordinary thing as to call upon me in person. A young gentleman had brought it. Such a nice young gentleman, she interjected with her piously ghoulish expression. He was not very tall. He had a very smooth complexion (that woman was incorrigible) and a nice, tiny black moustache. Therese was sure that he must have been an officer *en las filas legitimas*. With that notion in her head she had asked him about the welfare of that other model of charm and elegance, Captain Blunt. To her extreme surprise the charming young gentleman with beautiful eyes had apparently never heard of Blunt. But he seemed very much interested in his surroundings, looked all round the hall, noted the costly wood of the door panels, paid some attention to the silver statuette holding up the defective gas burner at the foot of the stairs, and, finally, asked whether this was in very truth the house of the most excellent Señora Doña Rita de Lastaola. The question staggered Therese, but with great presence of mind she answered the young gentleman that she didn't know what excellence there was about it, but that the house was her property, having been given to her by her own

sister. At this the young gentleman looked both
puzzled and angry, turned on his heel, and got back
into his fiacre. Why should people be angry with a poor
girl who had never done a single reprehensible thing in
her whole life?

"I suppose our Rita does tell people awful lies about
her poor sister." She sighed deeply (she had several
kinds of sighs and this was the hopeless kind) and added
reflectively, "Sin on sin, wickedness on wickedness!
And the longer she lives the worse it will be. It would
be better for our Rita to be dead."

I told "Mademoiselle Therese" that it was really impossible to tell whether she was more stupid or atrocious; but I wasn't really very much shocked. These
outbursts did not signify anything in Therese. One
got used to them. They were merely the expression
of her rapacity and her righteousness; so that our conversation ended by my asking her whether she had any
dinner ready for me that evening.

"What's the good of getting you anything to eat, my
dear young Monsieur?" she quizzed me tenderly. "You
just only peck like a little bird. Much better let me
save the money for you." It will show the super-
terrestrial nature of my misery when I say that I was
quite surprised at Therese's view of my appetite.
Perhaps she was right. I certainly did not know. I
stared hard at her and in the end she admitted that the
dinner was in fact ready that very moment.

The new young gentleman within Therese's horizon
didn't surprise me very much. Villarel would travel
with some sort of suite, a couple of secretaries at least.
I had heard enough of Carlist headquarters to know that
the man had been (very likely was still) Captain General of the Royal Bodyguard and was a person of great
political (and domestic) influence at Court. The card

was, under its social form, a mere command to present myself before the grandee. No Royalist devoted by conviction, as I must have appeared to him, could have mistaken the meaning. I put the card in my pocket and after dining or not dining—I really don't remember —spent the evening smoking in the studio, pursuing thoughts of tenderness and grief, visions, exalting and cruel. From time to time I looked at the dummy. I even got up once from the couch on which I had been writhing like a worm and walked towards it as if to touch it, but refrained, not from sudden shame but from sheer despair. By and by Therese drifted in. It was then late and, I imagine, she was on her way to bed. She looked the picture of cheerful, rustic innocence and started propounding to me a conundrum which began with the words:

"If our Rita were to die before long   .   .   ."

She didn't get any further because I had jumped up and frightened her by shouting: "Is she ill? What has happened? Have you had a letter?"

She had had a letter. I didn't ask her to show it to me, though I daresay she would have done so. I had an idea that there was no meaning in anything, at least no meaning that mattered. But the interruption had made Therese apparently forget her sinister conundrum. She observed me with her shrewd, unintelligent eyes for a bit, and then with the fatuous remark about the Law being just she left me to the horrors of the studio. I believe I went to sleep there from sheer exhaustion. Some time during the night I woke up chilled to the bone and in the dark. These were horrors and no mistake. I dragged myself upstairs to bed past the indefatigable statuette holding up the ever-miserable light. The black-and-white hall was like an ice-house.

The main consideration which induced me to call on the Marquis of Villarel was the fact that after all I was a discovery of Doña Rita's, her own recruit. My fidelity and steadfastness had been guaranteed by her and no one else. I couldn't bear the idea of her being criticized by every empty-headed chatterer belonging to the Cause. And as, apart from that, nothing mattered much, why, then—I would get this over.

But it appeared that I had not reflected sufficiently on all the consequences of that step. First of all the sight of the Villa looking shabbily cheerful in the sunshine (but not containing her any longer) was so perturbing that I very nearly went away from the gate. Then when I got in after much hesitation—being admitted by the man in the green baize apron who recognized me—the thought of entering that room, out of which she was gone as completely as if she had been dead, gave me such an emotion that I had to steady myself against the table till the faintness was past. Yet I was irritated as at a treason when the man in the baize apron instead of letting me into the Pompeiian dining-room crossed the hall to another door not at all in the Pompeiian style (more Louis XV rather—that Villa was like a *Salade Russe* of styles) and introduced me into a big, light room full of very modern furniture. The portrait *en pied* of an officer in a sky-blue uniform hung on the end wall. The officer had a small head, a black beard cut square, a robust body, and leaned with gauntleted hands on the simple hilt of a straight sword. That striking picture dominated a massive mahogany desk, and, in front of this desk, a very roomy, tall-backed armchair of dark green velvet. I thought I had been announced into an empty room till glancing along the extremely loud carpet I detected a pair of feet under the armchair.

I advanced towards it and discovered a little man, who had made no sound or movement till I came into his view, sunk deep in the green velvet. He altered his position slowly and rested his hollow, black, quietly burning eyes on my face in prolonged scrutiny. I detected something comminatory in his yellow, emaciated countenance, but I believe now he was simply startled by my youth. I bowed profoundly. He extended a meagre little hand.

"Take a chair, Don Jorge."

He was very small, frail, and thin, but his voice was not languid, though he spoke hardly above his breath. Such was the envelope and the voice of the fanatical soul belonging to the Grand-master of Ceremonies and Captain General of the Bodyguard at the Headquarters of the Legitimist Court, now detached on a special mission. He was all fidelity, inflexibility, and sombre conviction, but like some great saints he had very little body to keep all these merits in.

"You are very young," he remarked, to begin with. "The matters on which I desired to converse with you are very grave."

"I was under the impression that your Excellency wished to see me at once. But if your Excellency prefers it I will return in, say, seven years' time when I may perhaps be old enough to talk about grave matters."

He didn't stir hand or foot and not even the quiver of an eyelid proved that he had heard my shockingly unbecoming retort.

"You have been recommended to us by a noble and loyal lady, in whom His Majesty—whom God preserve —reposes an entire confidence. God will reward her as she deserves and you, too, Señor, according to the disposition you bring to this great work which has the blessing (here he crossed himself) of our Holy Mother the Church."

"I suppose your Excellency understands that in all this I am not looking for reward of any kind."

At this he made a faint, almost ethereal grimace.

"I was speaking of the spiritual blessing which rewards the service of religion and will be of benefit to your soul," he explained with a slight touch of acidity. "The other is perfectly understood and your fidelity is taken for granted. His Majesty—whom God preserve—has been already pleased to signify his satisfaction with your services to the most noble and loyal Doña Rita by a letter in his own hand."

Perhaps he expected me to acknowledge this announcement in some way, speech, or bow, or something, because before my immobility, he made a slight movement in his chair which smacked of impatience. "I am afraid, Señor, that you are affected by the spirit of scoffing and irreverence which pervades this unhappy country of France in which both you and I are strangers, I believe. Are you a young man of that sort?"

"I am a very good gun-runner, your Excellency," I answered quietly.

He bowed his head gravely. "We are aware. But I was looking for the motives which ought to have their pure source in religion."

"I must confess frankly that I have not reflected on my motives," I said. "It is enough for me to know that they are not dishonourable and that anybody can see they are not the motives of an adventurer seeking some sordid advantage."

He had listened patiently and when he saw that there was nothing more to come he ended the discussion.

"Señor, we should reflect upon our motives. It is salutary for our conscience and is recommended (he crossed himself) by our Holy Mother the Church. I have here certain letters from Paris on which I would consult your young sagacity which is accredited to us by the most loyal Doña Rita."

The sound of that name on his lips was simply odious. I was convinced that this man of forms and ceremonies and fanatical royalism was perfectly heartless. Perhaps he reflected on his motives; but it seemed to me that his conscience could be nothing else but a monstrous thing which very few actions could disturb appreciably. Yet for the credit of Doña Rita I did not withhold from him my young sagacity. What he thought of it I don't know. The matters we discussed were not of course of high policy, though from the point of view of the war in the South they were important enough. We agreed on certain things to be done, and finally, always out of regard for Doña Rita's credit, I put myself generally at his disposition or of any Carlist agent he would appoint in his place; for I did not suppose that he would remain very long in Marseilles. He got out of the chair laboriously, like a sick child might have done. The audience was over but he noticed my eyes wandering to the portrait and he said in his measured, breathed-out tones:

"I owe the pleasure of having this admirable work here to the gracious attention of Madame de Lastaola, who, knowing my attachment to the royal person of my Master, has sent it down from Paris to greet me in this house which has been given up for my occupation also through her generosity to the Royal Cause. Unfortunately she, too, is touched by the infection of this irreverent and unfaithful age. But she is young yet. She is young."

These last words were pronounced in a strange tone of menace as though he were supernaturally aware of some suspended disasters. With his burning eyes he was the image of an Inquisitor with an unconquerable soul in that frail body. But suddenly he dropped his eyelids and the conversation finished as characteristically as it had begun: with a slow, dismissing inclination of the head and an "Adios, Señor—may God guard you from sin."

III

I MUST say that for the next three months I threw myself into my unlawful trade with a sort of desperation, dogged and hopeless, like a fairly decent fellow who takes deliberately to drink. The business was getting dangerous. The bands in the South were not very well organized, worked with no very definite plan, and now were beginning to be pretty closely hunted. The arrangements for the transport of supplies were going to pieces; our friends ashore were getting scared; and it was no joke to find after a day of skilful dodging that there was no one at the landing place and have to go out again with our compromising cargo, to slink and lurk about the coast for another week or so, unable to trust anybody and looking at every vessel we met with suspicion. Once we were ambushed by a lot of "rascally Carabineers," as Dominic called them, who hid themselves among the rocks after disposing a train of mules well in view on the seashore. Luckily, on evidence which I could never understand, Dominic detected something suspicious. Perhaps it was by virtue of some sixth sense that men born for unlawful occupations may be gifted with. "There is a smell of treachery about this," he remarked suddenly, turning at his oar. (He and I were pulling alone in a little boat to reconnoitre.) I couldn't detect any smell and I regard to this day our escape on that occasion as, properly speaking, miraculous. Surely some supernatural power must have struck upwards the barrels of the Carabineers' rifles, for they missed us by yards.

And as the Carabineers have the reputation of shooting straight, Dominic, after swearing most horribly, ascribed our escape to the particular guardian angel that looks after crazy young gentlemen. Dominic believed in angels in a conventional way, but laid no claim to having one of his own. Soon afterwards, while sailing quietly at night, we found ourselves suddenly near a small coasting vessel, also without lights, which all at once treated us to a volley of rifle fire. Dominic's mighty and inspired yell: *"A plat ventre!"* and also an unexpected roll to windward saved all our lives. Nobody got a scratch. We were past in a moment and in a breeze then blowing we had the heels of anything likely to give us chase. But an hour afterwards, as we stood side by side peering into the darkness, Dominic was heard to mutter through his teeth: *"Le métier se gâte."* I, too, had the feeling that the trade, if not altogether spoiled, had seen its best days. But I did not care. In fact, for my purpose it was rather better, a more potent influence; like the stronger intoxication of raw spirit. A volley in the dark after all was not such a bad thing. Only a moment before we had received it, there, in that calm night of the sea full of freshness and soft whispers, I had been looking at an enchanting turn of a head in a faint light of its own, the tawny hair with snared red sparks brushed up from the nape of a white neck and held up on high by an arrow of gold feathered with brilliants and with ruby gleams all along its shaft. That jewelled ornament, which I remembered often telling Rita was of a very Philistinish conception (it was in some way connected with a tortoiseshell comb) occupied an undue place in my memory, tried to come into some sort of significance even in my sleep. Often I dreamed of her with white limbs shimmering in the gloom like a nymph haunting a riot of foliage and raising a perfect round arm to take an arrow of gold out of her hair to throw it at me by hand, like a dart. It came on, a whizzing trail of light, but I always woke up before it struck. Always. Invariably. It never had a chance. A volley of small arms was much more likely to do the business some day—or night.

At last came the day when everything slipped out of my grasp. The little vessel, broken and gone like the only toy of a lonely child, the sea itself, which had swallowed it, throwing me on shore after a shipwreck that instead of a fair fight left in me the memory of a suicide. It took away all that there was in me of independent life, but just failed to take me out of the world, which looked then indeed like Another World fit for no one else but unrepentant sinners. Even Dominic failed me, his moral entity destroyed by what to him was a most tragic ending of our common enterprise. The lurid swiftness of it all was like a stunning thunder-clap—and, one evening, I found myself weary, heartsore, my brain still dazed and with awe in my heart entering Marseilles by way of the railway station, after many adventures, one more disagreeable than another, involving privations, great exertions, a lot of difficulties with all sorts of people who looked upon me evidently more as a discreditable vagabond deserving the attentions of gendarmes than a respectable (if crazy) young gentleman attended by a guardian angel of his own. I must confess that I slunk out of the railway station shunning its many lights as if, invariably, failure made an outcast of a man. I hadn't any money in my pocket. I hadn't even the bundle and the stick of a destitute wayfarer. I was unshaven and unwashed, and my heart was faint within me. My attire was such that I daren't approach the rank of fiacres, where indeed I could perceive only two pairs of lamps, of which one suddenly drove away while I looked. The other I gave up to the fortunate of this earth. I didn't believe in my power of persuasion. I had no powers. I slunk on and on, shivering with cold, through the uproarious streets. Bedlam was loose in them. It was the time of Carnival.

Small objects of no value have the secret of sticking to a man in an astonishing way. I had nearly lost my liberty and even my life, I had lost my ship, a money-belt full of gold, I had lost my companions, had parted from my friend; my occupation, my only link with life, my touch with the sea, my cap and jacket were gone—but a small penknife and a latchkey had never parted company with me. With the latchkey I opened the door of refuge. The hall wore its deaf-and-dumb air, its black-and-white stillness.

The sickly gas-jet still struggled bravely with adversity at the end of the raised silver arm of the statuette which had kept to a hair's breadth its graceful pose on the toes of its left foot; and the staircase lost itself in the shadows above. Therese was parsimonious with the lights. To see all this was surprising. It seemed to me that all the things I had known ought to have come down with a crash at the moment of the final catastrophe on the Spanish coast. And there was Therese herself descending the stairs, frightened but plucky. Perhaps she thought that she would be murdered this time for certain. She had a strange, unemotional conviction that the house was particularly convenient for a crime. One could never get to the bottom of her wild notions which she held with the stolidity of a peasant allied to the outward serenity of a nun. She quaked all over as she came down to her doom, but when she recognized me she got such a shock that she sat down suddenly on the lowest step. She did not expect me for another week at least, and, besides, she explained, the state I was in made her blood take "one turn."

Indeed my plight seemed either to have called out or else repressed her true nature. But who had ever fathomed her nature! There was none of her treacly volubility. There were none of her "dear young gentlemans" and "poor little hearts" and references to sin. In breathless silence she ran about the house getting my room ready, lighting fires and gas-jets and even hauling at me to help me up the stairs. Yes, she did lay hands on me for that charitable purpose. They trembled. Her pale eyes hardly left my face. "What brought you here like this?" she whispered once.

"If I were to tell you, Mademoiselle Therese, you would see there the hand of God."

She dropped the extra pillow she was carrying and then nearly fell over it. "Oh, dear heart," she murmured, and ran off to the kitchen.

I sank into bed as into a cloud and Therese reappeared very misty and offering me something in a cup. I believe it was hot milk, and after I drank it she took the cup and stood looking at me fixedly. I managed to say with difficulty: "Go away," whereupon she vanished as if by magic before the words were fairly out of my mouth. Immediately afterwards the sunlight forced through the slats of the jalousies its diffused glow, and Therese was there again as if by magic, saying in a distant voice: "It's midday." . . . Youth will have its rights. I had slept like a stone for seventeen hours.

I suppose an honourable bankrupt would know such an awakening: the sense of catastrophe, the shrinking from the necessity of beginning life again, the faint

feeling that there are misfortunes which must be paid
for by a hanging. In the course of the morning
Therese informed me that the apartment usually
occupied by Mr. Blunt was vacant and added mysteriously that she intended to keep it vacant for a time,
because she had been instructed to do so. I couldn't
imagine why Blunt should wish to return to Marseilles.
She told me also that the house was empty except
for myself and the two dancing girls with their father.
Those people had been away for some time as the girls
had engagements in some Italian summer theatres,
but apparently they had secured a re-engagement for
winter and were now back. I let Therese talk because
it kept my imagination from going to work on subjects
which, I had made up my mind, were no concern of
mine. But I went out early to perform an unpleasant
task. It was only proper that I should let the Carlist
agent ensconced in the Prado Villa know of the sudden
ending of my activities. It would be grave enough news
for him, and I did not like to be its bearer for reasons
which were mainly personal. I resembled Dominic in
so far that I, too, disliked failure.

The Marquis of Villarel had of course gone long before. The man who was there was another type of
Carlist altogether, and his temperament was that of a
trader. He was the chief purveyor of the Legitimist
armies, an honest broker of stores, and enjoyed a great
reputation for cleverness. His important task kept
him, of course, in France, but his young wife, whose
beauty and devotion to her King were well known, represented him worthily at Headquarters, where his own
appearances were extremely rare. The dissimilar
but united loyalties of those two people had been re-
warded by the title of baron and the ribbon of some
order or other. The gossip of the Legitimist circles

appreciated those favours with smiling indulgence.
He was the man who had been so distressed and frightened by Doña Rita's first visit to Tolosa. He had an
extreme regard for his wife. And in that sphere of
clashing arms and unceasing intrigue nobody would
have smiled then at his agitation if the man himself
hadn't been somewhat grotesque.

He must have been startled when I sent in my name,
for he didn't of course expect to see me yet—nobody
expected me. He advanced soft-footed down the
room. With his jutting nose, flat-topped skull and
sable garments he recalled an obese raven, and when he
heard of the disaster he manifested his astonishment
and concern in a most plebeian manner by a low and
expressive whistle. I, of course, could not share his
consternation. My feelings in that connection were
of a different order; but I was annoyed at his unintelligent stare.

"I suppose," I said, "you will take it on yourself to
advise Doña Rita, who is greatly interested in this
affair."

"Yes, but I was given to understand that Madame
de Lastaola was to leave Paris either yesterday or this
morning."

It was my turn to stare dumbly before I could
manage to ask: "For Tolosa?" in a very knowing
tone.

Whether it was the droop of his head, play of light,
or some other subtle cause, his nose seemed to have
grown perceptibly longer.

"That, Señor, is the place where the news has got to
be conveyed without undue delay," he said in an agitated wheeze. "I could, of course, telegraph to our
agent in Bayonne who would find a messenger. But
I don't like, I don't like! The Alphonsists have agents.

too, who hang about the telegraph offices. It's no use letting the enemy get that news."

He was obviously very confused, unhappy, and trying to think of two different things at once.

"Sit down, Don George, sit down." He absolutely forced a cigar on me. "I am extremely distressed. That—I mean Doña Rita is undoubtedly on her way to Tolosa. This is very frightful."

I must say, however, that there was in the man some sense of duty. He mastered his private fears. After some cogitation he murmured: "There is another way of getting the news to Headquarters. Suppose you write me a formal letter just stating the facts, the unfortunate facts, which I will be able to forward. There is an agent of ours, a fellow I have been employing for purchasing supplies, a perfectly honest man. He is coming here from the north by the ten o'clock train with some papers for me of a confidential nature. I was rather embarrassed about it. It wouldn't do for him to get into any sort of trouble. He is not very intelligent. I wonder, Don George, whether you would consent to meet him at the station and take care of him generally till to-morrow. I don't like the idea of him going about alone. Then, to-morrow night, we would send him on to Tolosa by the west coast route, with the news; and then he can also call on Doña Rita who will no doubt be already there. . . ." He became again distracted all in a moment and actually went so far as to wring his fat hands. "Oh, yes, she will be there!" he exclaimed in most pathetic accents.

I was not in the humour to smile at anything, and he must have been satisfied with the gravity with which I beheld his extraordinary antics. My mind was very far away. I thought: Why not? Why shouldn't I also write a letter to Doña Rita, telling her that now nothing stood in the way of my leaving Europe, because, really, the enterprise couldn't be begun again; that things that come to an end can never be begun again. The idea—never again—had complete possession of my mind. I could think of nothing else. Yes, I would write. The worthy Commissary General of the Carlist forces was under the impression that I was looking at him; but what I had in my eye was a jumble of butterfly women and winged youths and the soft sheen of Argand lamps gleaming on an arrow of gold in the hair of a head that seemed to evade my outstretched hand.

"Oh, yes," I said, "I have nothing to do and even nothing to think of just now. I will meet your man as he gets off the train at ten o'clock to-night. What's he like?"

"Oh, he has a black moustache and whiskers, and his chin is shaved," said the newly fledged baron cordially. "A very honest fellow. I always found him very useful. His name is José Ortega."

He was perfectly self-possessed now, and walking soft-footed accompanied me to the door of the room. He shook hands with a melancholy smile. "This is a very frightful situation. My poor wife will be quite distracted. She is such a patriot. Many thanks, Don George. You relieve me greatly. The fellow is rather stupid and rather bad-tempered. Queer creature, but very honest! Oh, very honest!"

IV

I<small>T</small> W<small>AS</small> the last evening of Carnival. The same masks, the same yells, the same mad rushes, the same bedlam of disguised humanity blowing about the streets in the great gusts of mistral that seemed to make them dance like dead leaves on an earth where all joy is watched by death.

It was exactly twelve months since that other carnival evening when I had felt a little weary and a little lonely but at peace with all mankind. It must have been—to a day or two. But on this evening it wasn't merely loneliness that I felt. I felt bereaved with a sense of a complete and universal loss in which there was perhaps more resentment than mourning; as if the world had not been taken away from me by an august decree but filched from my innocence by an underhand fate at the very moment when it had disclosed to my passion its warm and generous beauty. This consciousness of universal loss had this advantage that it induced something resembing a state of philosophic indifference. I walked up to the railway station caring as little for the cold blasts of wind as though I had been going to the scaffold. The delay of the train did not irritate me in the least. I had finally made up my mind to write a letter to Doña Rita; and this "honest fellow" for whom I was waiting would take it to her. He would have no difficulty in Tolosa in finding Madame de Lastaola. The General Headquarters, which was also a Court, would be buzzing with comments on her presence. Most likely that "honest fellow" was already known to Doña Rita. For all I knew he might have been her discovery just as I was. Probably I, too, was regarded as an "honest fellow" enough; but stupid—since it was clear that my luck was not inexhaustible. I hoped that while carrying my letter the man would not let himself be caught by some Alphonsist guerilla who would, of course, shoot him. But why should he? I, for instance, had escaped with my life from a much more dangerous enterprise than merely passing through the frontier line in charge of some trustworthy guide. I pictured the fellow to myself trudging over the stony slopes and scrambling down wild ravines with my letter to Doña Rita in his pocket. It would be such a letter of farewell as no lover had ever written, no woman in the world had ever read, since the beginning of love on earth. It would be worthy of the woman. No experience, no memories, no dead traditions of passion or language would inspire it. She herself would be its sole inspiration. She would see her own image in it as in a mirror; and perhaps then she would understand what it was I was saying farewell to on the very threshold of my life. A breath of vanity passed through my brain. A letter as moving as her mere existence was moving would be something unique. I regretted I was not a poet.

I woke up to a great noise of feet, a sudden influx of people through the doors of the platform. I made out my man's whiskers at once—not that they were enormous, but because I had been warned beforehand of their existence by the excellent Commissary General. At first I saw nothing of him but his whiskers: they were black and cut somewhat in the shape of a shark's fin and so very fine that the least breath of air animated them into a sort of playful restlessness. The man's shoulders were hunched up and when he had made his way clear of the throng of passengers I perceived him as an unhappy and shivery being. Obviously he didn't expect to be met, because when I murmured an inquiring, "Señor Ortega?" into his ear he swerved away from me and nearly dropped a little handbag he was carrying. His complexion was uniformly pale, his mouth was red, but not engaging. His social status was not very definite. He was wearing a dark blue overcoat of no particular cut, his aspect had no relief; yet those restless side-whiskers flanking his red mouth and the suspicious expression of his black eyes made him noticeable. This I regretted the more because I caught sight of two skulking fellows, looking very much like policemen in plain clothes, watching us from a corner of the great hall. I hurried my man into a fiacre. He had been travelling from early morning on cross-country lines and after we got on terms a little confessed to being very hungry and cold. His red lips trembled and I noted an underhand, cynical curiosity when he had occasion to raise his eyes to my face. I was in some doubt how to dispose of him. but as we rolled on at a jog trot I came to the conclusion that the best thing to do would be to organize for him a shake-down in the studio. Obscure lodging houses are precisely the places most looked after by the police, and even the best hotels are bound to keep a register of arrivals. I was very anxious that nothing should stop his projected mission of courier to Headquarters. As we passed various street corners where the mistral blast struck at us fiercely I could feel him shivering by my side. However, Therese would have lighted the iron stove in the studio before retiring for the night, and, anyway, I would have to turn her out to make up a bed on the couch. Service of the King! I must say that she was amiable and didn't seem to mind anything one asked her to do. Thus while the fellow slumbered on the divan I would sit upstairs in my room setting down on paper those great words of passion and sorrow that seethed in my brain and even must have forced themselves in murmurs on to my lips, because the man by my side suddenly asked me: "What did you say?"—"Nothing," I answered, very much surprised. In the shifting light of the street lamps he looked the picture of bodily misery with his chattering teeth and his whiskers blown back flat over his ears. But somehow he didn't arouse my compassion. He was swearing to himself, in French and Spanish, and I tried to soothe him by the assurance that we had not much farther to go. "I am starving," he remarked acidly, and I felt a little compunction. Clearly, the first thing to do was to feed him. We were then entering the Cannebière and as I didn't care to show myself with him in the fashionable restaurant where a new face (and such a face, too) would be remarked, I pulled up the fiacre at the door of the Maison Dorée. That was more of a place of general resort where, in the multitude of casual patrons, he would pass unnoticed.

For this last night of Carnival the big house had decorated all its balconies with rows of coloured paper lanterns right up to the roof. I led the way to the grand salon, for as to private rooms they had been all retained days before. There was a great crowd of people in costume, but by a piece of good luck we managed to secure a little table in a corner. The revellers, intent on their pleasure, paid no attention to us. Señor Ortega trod on my heels and after sitting down opposite me threw an ill-natured glance at the festive scene. It might have been about half-past ten, then.

Two glasses of wine he drank one after another did

not improve his temper. He only ceased to shiver. After he had eaten something it must have occurred to him that he had no reason to bear me a grudge and he tried to assume a civil and even friendly manner. His mouth, however, betrayed an abiding bitterness. I mean when he smiled. In repose it was a very expressionless mouth, only it was too red to be altogether ordinary. The whole of him was like that: the whiskers too black, the hair too shiny, the forehead too white, the eyes too mobile; and he lent you his attention with an air of eagerness which made you uncomfortable. He seemed to expect you to give yourself away by some unconsidered word that he would snap up with delight. It was that peculiarity that somehow put me on my guard. I had no idea whom I was facing across the table and as a matter of fact I did not care. All my impressions were blurred; and even the promptings of my instinct were the haziest thing imaginable. Now and then I had acute hallucinations of a woman with an arrow of gold in her hair. This caused alternate moments of exaltation and depression from which I tried to take refuge in conversation; but Señor Ortega was not stimulating. He was preoccupied with personal matters. When suddenly he asked me whether I knew why he had been called away from his work (he had been buying supplies from peasants somewhere in Central France), I answered that I didn't know what the reason was originally, but I had an idea that the present intention was to make of him a courier, bearing certain messages from Baron H. to the Quartel Real in Tolosa.

He glared at me like a basilisk. "And why have I been met like this?" he enquired with an air of being prepared to hear a lie.

I explained that it was the Baron's wish, as a matter

of prudence and to avoid any possible trouble which might arise from enquiries by the police.

He took it badly. "What nonsense." He was—he said—an employé (for several years) of Hernandez Brothers in Paris, an importing firm, and he was travelling on their business—as he could prove. He dived into his side pocket and produced a handful of folded papers of all sorts which he plunged back again instantly.

And even then I didn't know whom I had there, opposite me, busy now devouring a slice of pâté de foie gras. Not in the least. It never entered my head. How could it? The Rita that haunted me had no history; she was but the principle of life charged with fatality. Her form was only a mirage of desire decoying one step by step into despair.

Señor Ortega gulped down some more wine and suggested I should tell him who I was. "It's only right I should know," he added.

This could not be gainsaid; and to a man connected with the Carlist organization the shortest way was to introduce myself as that "Monsieur George" of whom he had probably heard.

He leaned far over the table, till his very breast-bone was over the edge, as though his eyes had been stilettos and he wanted to drive them home into my brain. It was only much later that I understood how near death I had been at that moment. But the knives on the table-cloth were the usual restaurant knives with rounded ends and about as deadly as pieces of hoop-iron. Perhaps in the very gust of his fury he remembered what a French restaurant knife is like and something sane within him made him give up the sudden project of cutting my heart out where I sat. For it could have been nothing but a sudden impulse. His settled purpose was quite other. It was not my heart that he was after. His fingers indeed were groping amongst the knife handles by the side of his plate but what captivated my attention for a moment were his red lips which were formed into an odd, sly, insinuating smile. Heard! To be sure he had heard! The chief of the great arms smuggling organization!

"Oh!" I said, "that's giving me too much importance." The person responsible and whom I looked upon as chief of all the business was, as he might have heard, too, a certain noble and loyal lady.

"I am as noble as she is," he snapped peevishly, and I put him down at once as a very offensive beast. "And as to being loyal, what is that? It is being truthful! It is being faithful! I know all about her."

I managed to preserve an air of perfect unconcern. He wasn't a fellow to whom one could talk of Doña Rita. "You are a Basque," I said.

He admitted rather contemptuously that he was a Basque and even then the truth did not dawn upon me. I suppose that with the hidden egoism of a lover I was thinking of myself, of myself alone in relation to Doña Rita, not of Doña Rita herself. He, too, obviously. He said: "I am an educated man, but I know her people, all peasants. There is a sister, an uncle, a priest, a peasant, too, and perfectly unenlightened. One can't expect much from a priest (I am a free-thinker of course), but he is really too bad, more like a brute beast. As to all her people, mostly dead now, they never were of any account. There was a little land, but they were always working on other people's farms, a barefooted gang, a starved lot. I ought to know because we are distant relations. Twentieth cousins or something of the sort. Yes, I am related to that most loyal lady. And what is she, after all, but a Parisian woman with innumerable lovers, as I have been told."

"I don't think your information is very correct," I said, affecting to yawn slightly. "This is mere gossip of the gutter and I am surprised at you, who really know nothing about it——"

But the disgusting animal had fallen into a brown study. The hair of his very whiskers was perfectly still. I had now given up all idea of the letter to Rita. Suddenly he spoke again:

"Women are the origin of all evil. One should never trust them. They have no honour. No honour!" he repeated, striking his breast with his closed fist on which the knuckles stood out very white. "I left my village many years ago and of course I am perfectly satisfied with my position and I don't know why I should trouble my head about this loyal lady. I suppose that's the way women get on in the world."

I felt convinced that he was no proper person to be a messenger to Headquarters. He struck me as altogether untrustworthy and perhaps not quite sane. This was confirmed by him saying suddenly with no visible connection and as if it had been forced from him by some agonizing process: "I was a boy once," and then stopping dead short with a smile. He had a smile that frightened one by its association of malice and anguish.

"Will you have anything more to eat?" I asked.

He declined dully. He had had enough. But he drained the last of a bottle into his glass and accepted a cigar which I offered him. While he was lighting it I had a sort of confused impression that he wasn't such a stranger to me as I had assumed he was; and yet, on the other hand, I was perfectly certain I had never seen him before. Next moment I felt that I could have knocked him down if he hadn't looked so amazingly unhappy, while he came out with the astounding question:

"Señor, have you ever been a lover in your young days?"

"What do you mean?" I asked. "How old do you think I am?"

"That's true," he said, gazing at me in a way in which the damned gaze out of their cauldrons of boiling pitch at some soul walking scot free in the place of torment. "It's true, you don't seem to have anything on your mind." He assumed an air of ease, throwing an arm over the back of his chair and blowing the smoke through the gash of his twisted red mouth. "Tell me," he said, "between men, you know, has this wonderful celebrity—what does she call herself? How long has she been your mistress?"

I reflected rapidly that if I knocked him over, chair and all, by a sudden blow from the shoulder it would bring about infinite complications beginning with a visit to the Commissaire de Police on night-duty, and ending in God knows what scandal and disclosures of political kind; because there was no telling what, or how much, this outrageous brute might choose to say and how many people he might not involve in a most undesirable publicity. He was smoking his cigar with a poignantly mocking air and not even looking at me. One can't hit like that a man who isn't even looking at one; and then, just as I was looking at him swinging his leg with a caustic smile and stony eyes, I felt sorry for the creature. It was only his body that was there in that chair. It was manifest to me that his soul was absent in some hell of its own. At that moment I attained the knowledge of who it was I had before me. This was the man of whom both Doña Rita and Rose were so much afraid. It remained then for me to look after him for the night and then arrange with Baron H. that he should be sent away the very next day—and anywhere but to

Tolosa. Yes, evidently, I mustn't lose sight of him. I proposed in the calmest tone that we should go on where he could get his much-needed rest. He rose with alacrity, picked up his little hand-bag, and, walking out before me, no doubt looked a very ordinary person to all eyes but mine. It was then past eleven, not much, because we had not been in that restaurant quite an hour, but the routine of the town's night-life being upset during the Carnival the usual row of fiacres outside the Maison Dorée was not there; in fact, there were very few carriages about. Perhaps the coachmen had assumed Pierrot costumes and were rushing about the streets on foot yelling with the rest of the population. "We will have to walk," I said after a while.— "Oh, yes, let us walk," assented Señor Ortega, "or I will be frozen here." It was like a plaint of unutterable wretchedness. I had a fancy that all his natural heat had abandoned his limbs and gone to his brain. It was otherwise with me; my head was cool but I didn't find the night really so very cold. We stepped out briskly side by side. My lucid thinking was, as it were, enveloped by the wide shouting of the consecrated Carnival gaiety. I have heard many noises since, but nothing that gave me such an intimate impression of the savage instincts hidden in the breast of mankind; these yells of festivity suggested agonizing fear, rage of murder, ferocity of lust, and the irremediable joylessness of human condition: yet they were emitted by people who were convinced that they were amusing themselves supremely, traditionally, with the sanction of ages, with the approval of their conscience—and no mistake about it whatever! Our appearance, the soberness of our gait made us conspicuous. Once or twice, by common inspiration, masks rushed forward and forming a circle danced round us uttering discordant shouts of derision; for we were an outrage to the peculiar proprieties of the hour, and besides we were obviously lonely and defenceless. On these occasions there was nothing for it but to stand still till the flurry was over. My companion, however, would stamp his feet with rage, and I must admit that I myself regretted not having provided for our wearing a couple of false noses, which would have been enough to placate the just resentment of those people. We might have also joined in the dance, but for some reason or other it didn't occur to us; and I heard once a high, clear woman's voice stigmatizing us for a "species of swelled heads" (*espèce d'enflés*). We proceeded sedately, my companion muttered with rage, and I was able to resume my thinking. It was based on the deep persuasion that the man at my side was insane with quite another than Carnivalesque lunacy which comes on at one stated time of the year. He was fundamentally mad, though not perhaps completely; which of course made him all the greater, I won't say danger but, nuisance.

I remember once a young doctor expounding the theory that most catastrophes in family circles, surprising episodes in public affairs and disasters in private life, had their origin in the fact that the world was full of half-mad people. He asserted that they were the real majority. When asked whether he considered himself as belonging to the majority, he said frankly that he didn't think so; unless the folly of voicing this view in a company, so utterly unable to appreciate all its horror, could be regarded as the first symptom of his own fate. We shouted down him and his theory, but there is no doubt that it had thrown a chill on the gaiety of our gathering.

We had now entered a quieter quarter of the town and

Señor Ortega had ceased his muttering. For myself I had not the slightest doubt of my own sanity. It was proved to me by the way I could apply my intelligence to the problem of what was to be done with Señor Ortega. Generally, he was unfit to be trusted with any mission whatever. The instability of his temper was sure to get him into a scrape. Of course carrying a letter to Headquarters was not a very complicated matter; and as to that I would have trusted willingly a properly trained dog. My private letter to Doña Rita, the wonderful, the unique letter of farewell, I had given up for the present. Naturally I thought of the Ortega problem mainly in the terms of Doña Rita's safety. Her image presided at every council, at every conflict of my mind, and dominated every faculty of my senses. It floated before my eyes, it touched my elbow, it guarded my right side and my left side; my ears seemed to catch the sound of her footsteps behind me, she enveloped me with passing whiffs of warmth and perfume, with filmy touches of the hair on my face. She penetrated me, my head was full of her . . . And his head, too, I thought suddenly with a side glance at my companion. He walked quietly with hunched-up shoulders carrying his little hand-bag and he looked the most commonplace figure imaginable.

Yes. There was between us a most horrible fellowship; the association of his crazy torture with the sublime suffering of my passion. We hadn't been a quarter of an hour together when that woman had surged up fatally between us; between this miserable wretch and myself. We were haunted by the same image. But I was sane! I was sane! Not because I was certain that the fellow must not be allowed to go to Tolosa, but because I was perfectly alive to the difficulty of

stopping him from going there, since the decision was
absolutely in the hands of Baron H.

If I were to go early in the morning and tell that fat,
bilious man: "Look here, your Ortega's mad," he would
certainly think at once that I was, get very frightened,
and . . . one couldn't tell what course he would
take. He would eliminate me somehow out of the
affair. And yet I would not let the fellow proceed
to where Doña Rita was, because, obviously, he had
been molesting her, had filled her with uneasiness and
even alarm, was an unhappy element and a disturbing
influence in her life—incredible as the thing appeared!
I couldn't let him go on to make himself a worry and a
nuisance, drive her out from a town in which she wished
to be (for whatever reason) and perhaps start some ex-
plosive scandal. And that girl Rose seemed to fear
something graver even than a scandal. But if I were
to explain the matter fully to H. he would simply re-
joice in his heart. Nothing would please him more than
to have Doña Rita driven out of Tolosa. What a relief from his anxieties (and his wife's, too); and if I
were to go further, if I even went so far as to hint at
the fears which Rose had not been able to conceal from
me, why then—I went on thinking coldly with a stoical
rejection of the most elementary faith in mankind's
rectitude—why then, that accommodating husband
would simply let the ominous messenger have his
chance. He would see there only his natural anxieties
being laid to rest for ever. Horrible? Yes. But I
could not take the risk. In a twelvemonth I had
travelled a long way in my mistrust of mankind.

We paced on steadily. I thought: "How on earth am
I going to stop you?" Had this arisen only a month
before, when I had the means at hand and Dominic to
confide in, I would have simply kidnapped the fellow.

A little trip to sea would not have done Señor Ortega any harm; though no doubt it would have been abhorrent to his feelings. But now I had not the means. I couldn't even tell where my poor Dominic was hiding his diminished head.

Again I glanced at him sideways. I was the taller of the two and as it happened I met in the light of the street lamp his own stealthy glance directed up at me with an agonized expression, an expression that made me fancy I could see the man's very soul writhing in his body like an impaled worm. In spite of my utter inexperience I had some notion of the images that rushed into his mind at the sight of any man who had approached Doña Rita. It was enough to awaken in any human being a movement of horrified compassion; but my pity went out not to him but to Doña Rita. It was for her that I felt sorry; I pitied her for having that damned soul on her track. I pitied her with tenderness and indignation, as if this had been both a danger and a dishonour.

I don't mean to say that those thoughts passed through my head consciously. I had only the resultant, settled feeling. I had, however, a thought, too. It came on me suddenly, and I asked myself with rage and astonishment: "Must I then kill that brute?" There didn't seem to be any alternative. Between him and Doña Rita I couldn't hesitate. I believe I gave a slight laugh of desperation. The suddenness of this sinister conclusion had in it something comic and unbelievable. It loosened my grip on my mental processes. A Latin tag came into my head about the facile descent into the abyss. I marvelled at its aptness, and also that it should have come to me so pat. But I believe now that it was suggested simply by the actual declivity of the street of the Consuls which lies

on a gentle slope. We had just turned the corner.
All the houses were dark and in a perspective of complete solitude our two shadows dodged and wheeled
about our feet.

"Here we are," I said.

He was an extraordinarily chilly devil. When we
stopped I could hear his teeth chattering again. I
don't know what came over me, I had a sort of nervous
fit, was incapable of finding my pockets, let alone the
latchkey. I had the illusion of a narrow streak of light
on the wall of the house as if it had been cracked. "I
hope we will be able to get in," I murmured.

Señor Ortega stood waiting patiently with his hand-
bag, like a rescued wayfarer. "But you live in this
house, don't you?" he observed.

"No," I said, without hesitation. I didn't know how
that man would behave if he were aware that I was
staying under the same roof. He was half mad. He
might want to talk all night, try crazily to invade my
privacy. How could I tell? Moreover, I wasn't so
sure that I would remain in the house. I had some
notion of going out again and walking up and down the
street of the Consuls till daylight. "No, an absent
friend lets me use . . . I had that latchkey this
morning . . . Ah! here it is."

I let him go in first. The sickly gas flame was there
on duty, undaunted, waiting for the end of the world to
come and put it out. I think that the black-and-white
hall surprised Ortega. I had closed the front door without noise and stood for a moment listening, while he
glanced about furtively. There were only two other
doors in the hall, right and left. Their panels of ebony
were decorated with bronze applications in the centre.
The one on the left was of course Blunt's door. As the
passage leading beyond it was dark at the further end I

took Señor Ortega by the hand and led him along, unre-sisting, like a child. For some reason or other I moved on tiptoe and he followed my example. The light and the warmth of the studio impressed him favour-ably; he laid down his little bag, rubbed his hands to-gether, and produced a smile of satisfaction; but it was such a smile as a totally ruined man would perhaps force on his lips, or a man condemned to a short shrift by his doctor. I begged him to make himself at home and said that I would go at once and hunt up the woman of the house who would make him up a bed on the big couch there. He hardly listened to what I said. What were all those things to him! He knew that his destiny was to sleep on a bed of thorns, to feed on adders. But he tried to show a sort of polite interest. He asked: "What is this place?"

"It used to belong to a painter," I mumbled.

"Ah, your absent friend," he said, making a wry mouth. "I detest all those artists, and all those writers, and all politicos who are thieves; and I would go even farther and higher, laying a curse on all idle lovers of women. You think perhaps I am a Royalist? No. If there was anybody in heaven or hell to pray to I would pray for a revolution—a red revolution everywhere."

"You astonish me," I said, just to say something.

"No! But there are half a dozen people in the world with whom I would like to settle accounts. One could shoot them like partridges and no questions asked. That's what revolution would mean to me."

"It's a beautifully simple view," I said. "I imagine you are not the only one who holds it; but I really must look after your comforts. You mustn't forget that we have to see Baron H. early to-morrow morn-ing." And I went out quietly into the passage wonder-ing in what part of the house Therese had elected to

sleep that night.   But, lo and behold, when I got to the
foot of the stairs there was Therese coming down from
the upper regions in her nightgown, like a sleep-walker.
However, it wasn't that, because, before I could ex-
claim, she vanished off the first floor landing like a
streak of white mist and without the slightest sound.
Her attire made it perfectly clear that she could not
have heard us coming in.   In fact, she must have been
certain that the house was empty, because she was as
well aware as myself that the Italian girls after their
work at the opera were going to a masked ball to dance
for their own amusement, attended of course by their
conscientious father.   But what thought, need, or
sudden impulse had driven Therese out of bed like
this was something I couldn't conceive.

I didn't call out after her.   I felt sure that she would
return.   I went up slowly to the first floor and met her
coming down again, this time carrying a lighted candle.
She had managed to make herself presentable in an
extraordinarily short time.

"Oh, my dear young Monsieur, you have given me a
fright."

"Yes.   And I nearly fainted, too," I said.   "You
looked perfectly awful.   What's the matter with you?
Are you ill?"

She had lighted by then the gas on the landing and I
must say that I had never seen exactly that manner of
face on her before.   She wriggled, confused and shifty-
eyed, before me; but I ascribed this behaviour to her
shocked modesty and without troubling myself any
more about her feelings I informed her that there was a
Carlist downstairs who must be put up for the night.
Most unexpectedly she betrayed a ridiculous consternation, but only for a moment.   Then she assumed at
once that I would give him hospitality upstairs where

there was a camp-bedstead in my dressing-room. I
said:

"No. Give him a shake-down in the studio, where he
is now. It's warm in there. And remember! I
charge you strictly not to let him know that I sleep in
this house. In fact, I don't know myself that I will;
I have certain matters to attend to this very night.
You will also have to serve him his coffee in the morning.
I will take him away before ten o'clock."

All this seemed to impress her more than I had expected. As usual when she felt curious, or in some
other way excited, she assumed a saintly, detached
expression, and asked:

"The dear gentleman is your friend, I suppose?"

"I only know he is a Spaniard and a Carlist," I said,
"and that ought to be enough for you."

Instead of the usual effusive exclamations she murmured: "Dear me, dear me," and departed upstairs
with the candle to get together a few blankets and
pillows, I suppose. As for me I walked quietly downstairs on my way to the studio. I had a curious sensation that I was acting in a preordained manner, that
life was not at all what I had thought it to be, or else
that I had been altogether changed sometime during the
day, and that I was a different person from the man
whom I remembered getting out of my bed in the
morning.

Also feelings had altered all their values. The words,
too, had become strange. It was only the inanimate
surroundings that remained what they had always been.
For instance the studio. . . .

During my absence Señor Ortega had removed his
coat and I found him as it were in the air, sitting in his
shirt sleeves on a chair which he had taken pains to
place in the very middle of the floor. I repressed an

absurd impulse to walk round him as though he had
been some sort of exhibit. His hands were spread over
his knees and he looked perfectly insensible. I don't
mean strange, or ghastly, or wooden, but just insensible
—like an exhibit. And that effect persisted even after
he raised his black suspicious eyes to my face. He
lowered them almost at once. It was very mechanical.
I gave him up and became rather concerned about
myself. My thought was that I had better get out
of that before any more queer notions came into my
head. So I only remained long enough to tell him
that the woman of the house was bringing down some
bedding and that I hoped that he would have a good
night's rest. And directly I spoke it struck me that
this was the most extraordinary speech that ever was
addressed to a figure of that sort. He, however, did
not seem startled by it or moved in any way. He
simply said:

"Thank you."

In the darkest part of the long passage outside I met
Therese with her arms full of pillows and blankets.

COMING out of the bright light of the studio I didn't make out Therese very distinctly. She, however, having groped in dark cupboards, must have had her pupils sufficiently dilated to have seen that I had my hat on my head. This has its importance because after what I had said to her upstairs it must have convinced her that I was going out on some midnight business. I passed her without a word and heard behind me the door of the studio close with an unexpected crash. It strikes me now that under the circumstances I might have without shame gone back to listen at the keyhole. But truth to say the association of events was not so clear in my mind as it may be to the reader of this story. Neither were the exact connections of persons present to my mind. And, besides, one doesn't listen at a keyhole but in pursuance of some plan; unless one is afflicted by a vulgar and fatuous curiosity. But that vice is not in my character. As to plan, I had none. I moved along the passage between the dead wall and the black-and-white marble elevation of the staircase with hushed footsteps, as though there had been a mortally sick person somewhere in the house. And the only person that could have answered to that description was Señor Ortega. I moved on, stealthy, absorbed, undecided; asking myself earnestly: "What on earth am I going to do with him?" That exclusive preoccupation of my mind was as dangerous to Señor Ortega as typhoid fever would have been. It strikes me that this comparison is very exact. People recover from typhoid fever, but generally the chance is considered poor. This was precisely his case. His chance was poor; though I had no more animosity towards him than a virulent disease has against the victim it lays low. He really would have nothing to reproach me with; he had run up against me, unwittingly, as a man enters an infected place, and now he was very ill, very ill indeed. No, I had no plans against him. I had only the feeling that he was in mortal danger.

I believe that men of the most daring character (and I make no claim to it) often do shrink from the logical processes of thought. It is only the Devil, they say, that loves logic. But I was not a devil. I was not even a victim of the Devil. It was only that I had given up the direction of my intelligence before the problem; or rather that the problem had dispossessed my intelligence and reigned in its stead side by side with a superstitious awe. A dreadful order seemed to lurk in the darkest shadows of life. The madness of that Carlist with the soul of a Jacobin, the vile fears of Baron H., that excellent organizer of supplies, the contact of their two ferocious stupidities, and last, by a remote disaster at sea, my love brought into direct contact with the situation: all that was enough to make one shudder —not at the chance, but at the design.

For it was my love that was called upon to act here, and nothing else. And love which elevates us above all safeguards, above restraining principles, above all littlenesses of self-possession, yet keeps its feet always firmly on earth, remains marvellously practical in its suggestions.

I discovered that however much I had imagined I had given up Rita, that whatever agonies I had gone through, my hope of her had never been lost. Plucked out, stamped down, torn to shreds, it had remained with me secret, intact, invincible. Before the danger of the situation it sprang, full of life, up in arms—the undying child of immortal love. What incited me was independent of honour and compassion; it was the prompting of a love supreme, practical, remorseless in its aim; it was the practical thought that no woman need be counted as lost for ever, unless she be dead!

This excluded for the moment all considerations of ways and means and risks and difficulties. Its tremendous intensity robbed it of all direction and left me adrift in the big black-and-white hall as on a silent sea. It was not, properly speaking, irresolution. It was merely hesitation as to the next immediate step, and that step even of no great importance: hesitation merely as to the best way I could spend the rest of the night. I didn't think further forward for many reasons, more or less optimistic, but mainly because I have no homicidal vein in my composition. The disposition to gloat over homicide was in that miserable creature in the studio, the potential Jacobin; in that confounded buyer of agricultural produce, the punctual employé of Hernandez Brothers, the jealous wretch with an obscene tongue and an imagination of the same kind to drive him mad. I thought of him without pity but also without contempt. I reflected that there were no means of sending a warning to Doña Rita in Tolosa; for of course no postal communication existed with the Headquarters. And moreover what would a warning be worth in this particular case, supposing it would reach her, that she would believe it, and that she would know what to do? How could I communicate to another that certitude which was in my mind, the more absolute because without proofs that one could produce?

The last expression of Rose's distress rang again in my ears: "Madame has no friends. Not one!" and I saw Doña Rita's complete loneliness beset by all sorts of insincerities, surrounded by pitfalls; her greatest dangers within herself, in her generosity, in her fears, in her courage, too. What I had to do first of all was to stop that wretch at all costs. I became aware of a great mistrust of Therese. I didn't want her to find me in the hall, but I was reluctant to go upstairs to my rooms from an unreasonable feeling that there I would be too much out of the way; not sufficiently on the spot. There was the alternative of a live-long night of watching outside, before the dark front of the house. It was a most distasteful prospect. And then it occurred to me that Blunt's former room would be an extremely good place to keep a watch from. I knew that room. When Henry Allègre gave the house to Rita in the early days (long before he made his will) he had planned a complete renovation and this room had been meant for the drawing-room. Furniture had been made for it specially, upholstered in beautiful ribbed stuff, made to order, of dull gold colour with a pale blue tracery of arabesques and oval medallions enclosing Rita's monogram, repeated on the backs of chairs and sofas, and on the heavy curtains reaching from ceiling to floor. To the same time belonged the ebony and bronze doors, the silver statuette at the foot of the stairs, the forged iron balustrade reproducing right up the marble staircase Rita's decorative monogram in its complicated design. Afterwards the work was stopped and the house had fallen into disrepair. When Rita devoted it to the Carlist cause a bed was put into that drawing-room, just simply the bed. The room next to that yellow salon had been in Allègre's young days fitted as a fencing-room containing also a bath, and a complicated system of shower and jet arrangements, then quite up to date. That room was very large, lighted from the top, and one wall of it was covered by trophies of arms of all sorts, a choice collection of cold steel disposed on a background of Indian mats and rugs. Blunt used it as a dressing-room. It communicated by a small door with the studio.

I had only to extend my hand and make one step to reach the magnificent bronze handle of the ebony door, and if I didn't want to be caught by Therese there was no time to lose. I made the step and extended the hand thinking that it would be just like my luck to find the door locked. But the door came open to my push. In contrast to the dark hall the room was most unexpectedly dazzling to my eyes, as if illuminated *a giorno* for a reception. No voice came from it, but nothing could have stopped me now. As I turned round to shut the door behind me noiselessly I caught sight of a woman's dress on a chair, of other articles of apparel scattered about. The mahogany bed with a piece of light silk which Therese found somewhere and used for a counterpane was a magnificent combination of white and crimson between the gleaming surfaces of dark wood; and the whole room had an air of splendour with marble consoles, gilt carvings, long mirrors and a sumptuous Venetian lustre depending from the ceiling: a darkling mass of icy pendants catching a spark here and there from the candles of an eight-branched candelabra standing on a little table near the head of a sofa which had been dragged round to face the fireplace. The faintest possible whiff of a familiar perfume made my head swim with its suggestion.

I grabbed the back of the nearest piece of furniture and the splendour of marbles and mirrors, of cut crystals and carvings, swung before my eyes in the golden mist of walls and draperies round an extremely conspicuous pair of black stockings thrown over a music stool which remained motionless. The silence was profound. It was like being in an enchanted place. Suddenly a voice began to speak, clear, detached, infinitely touching in its calm weariness.

"Haven't you tormented me enough to-day?" it said. . . . My head was steady now but my heart began to beat violently. I listened to the end without moving. "Can't you make up your mind to leave me alone for to-night?" It pleaded with an accent of charitable scorn.

The penetrating quality of these tones which I had not heard for so many, many days made my eyes run full of tears. I guessed easily that the appeal was addressed to the atrocious Therese. The speaker was concealed from me by the high back of the sofa, but her apprehension was perfectly justified. For was it not I who had turned back Therese the pious, the insatiable, coming downstairs in her nightgown to torment her sister some more? Mere surprise at Doña Rita's presence in the house was enough to paralyze me; but I was also overcome by an enormous sense of relief, by the assurance of security for her and for myself. I didn't even ask myself how she came there. It was enough for me that she was not in Tolosa. I could have smiled at the thought that all I had to do now was to hasten the departure of that abominable lunatic—for Tolosa: an easy task, almost no task at all. Yes, I could have smiled, had not I felt outraged by the presence of Señor Ortega under the same roof with Doña Rita. The mere fact was repugnant to me, morally revolting; so that I should have liked to rush at him and throw him out into the street. But that was not to be done for various reasons. One of them, was pity. I was suddenly at peace with all mankind, with all nature. I felt as if I couldn't hurt a fly. The intensity of my emotion sealed my lips. With a fearful joy tugging at my heart I moved round the head of the couch without a word.

In the wide fireplace on a pile of white ashes the logs had a deep crimson glow; and turned towards them Doña Rita reclined on her side enveloped in the skins of wild beasts, like a charming and savage young chieftain before a camp fire. She never even raised her eyes, giving me the opportunity to contemplate mutely that adolescent, delicately masculine head, so mysteriously feminine in the power of instant seduction, so infinitely suave in its firm design, almost childlike in the freshness of detail: altogether ravishing in the inspired strength of the modelling. That precious head reposed in the palm of her hand; the face was slightly flushed (with anger perhaps). She kept her eyes obstinately fixed on the pages of a book which she was holding with her other hand. I had the time to lay my infinite adoration at her feet whose white insteps gleamed below the dark edge of the fur out of quilted blue silk bedroom slippers, embroidered with small pearls. I had never seen them before; I mean the slippers. The gleam of the insteps, too, for that matter. I lost myself in a feeling of deep content, something like a foretaste of a time of felicity which must be quiet or it couldn't be eternal. I had never tasted such perfect quietness before. It was not of this earth. I had gone far beyond. It was as if I had reached the ultimate wisdom beyond all dreams and all passions. She was that which is to be contemplated to all Infinity.

The perfect stillness and silence made her raise her eyes at last, reluctantly, with a hard, defensive expression which I had never seen in them before. And no wonder! The glance was meant for Therese and assumed in self-defence. For some time its character did not change and when it did it turned into a perfectly stony stare of a kind which I also had never seen before. She had never wished so much to be left in peace. She had never been so astonished in her life. She had arrived by the evening express only two hours before Señor Ortega, had driven to the house, and after having something to eat had become for the rest of the evening the helpless prey of her sister who had fawned and scolded and wheedled and threatened in a way that outraged all Rita's feelings. Seizing this unexpected occasion Therese had displayed a distracting versatility of sentiment: rapacity, virtue, piety, spite, and false tenderness—while, characteristically enough, she unpacked the dressing-bag, helped the sinner to get ready for bed, brushed her hair, and finally, as a climax, kissed her hands, partly by surprise and partly by violence. After that she had retired from the field of battle slowly, undefeated, still defiant, firing as a last shot the impudent question: "Tell me only, have you made your will, Rita?" To this poor Doña Rita with the spirit of opposition strung to the highest pitch answered: "No, and I don't mean to"—being under the impression that this was what her sister wanted her to do. There can be no doubt, however, that all Therese wanted was the information.

Rita, much too agitated to expect anything but a sleepless night, had not the courage to get into bed. She thought she would remain on the sofa before the fire and try to compose herself with a book. As she had no dressing-gown with her she put on her long fur coat over her nightgown, threw some logs on the fire, and lay down. She didn't hear the slightest noise of any sort till she heard me shut the door gently. Quietness of movement was one of Therese's accomplishments, and the harassed heir of the Allègre millions naturally thought it was her sister coming again to renew the scene. Her heart sank within her. In the end she became a little frightened at the long silence, and raised her eyes. She didn't believe them for a long time. She concluded that I was a vision. In fact, the first word which I heard her utter was a low, awed "No," which, though I understood its meaning, chilled my blood like an evil omen.

It was then that I spoke. "Yes," I said, "it's me that you see," and made a step forward. She didn't start; only her other hand flew to the edges of the fur coat, gripping them together over her breast. Observing this gesture I sat down in the nearest chair. The book she had been reading slipped with a thump on the floor.

"How is it possible that you should be here?" she said, still in a doubting voice.

"I am really here," I said. "Would you like to touch my hand?"

She didn't move at all; her fingers still clutched the fur coat.

"What has happened?"

"It's a long story, but you may take it from me that all is over. The tie between us is broken. I don't know that it was ever very close. It was an external thing. The true misfortune is that I have ever seen you."

This last phrase was provoked by an exclamation of sympathy on her part. She raised herself on her elbow and looked at me intently. "All over," she murmured.

"Yes, we had to wreck the little vessel. It was awful. I feel like a murderer. But she had to be killed."

"Why?"

"Because I loved her too much. Don't you know that love and death go very close together?"

"I could feel almost happy that it is all over, if you hadn't had to lose your love. Oh, *amigo* George, it was a safe love for you."

"Yes," I said. "It was a faithful little vessel. She would have saved us all from any plain danger. But this was a betrayal. It was—never mind. All that's past. The question is, what will the next one be?"

"Why should it be that?"

"I don't know. Life seems but a series of betrayals. There are so many kinds of them. This was a betrayed plan, but one can betray confidence, and hope and— desire, and the most sacred . . ."

"But what are you doing here?" she interrupted.

"Oh, yes! The eternal why. Till a few hours ago I didn't know what I was here for. And what are you here for?" I asked point blank and with a bitterness she disregarded. She even answered my question quite readily with many words out of which I could make very little. I only learned that for at least five mixed reasons, none of which impressed me profoundly, Doña Rita had started at a moment's notice from Paris with nothing but a dressing-bag, and permitting Rose to go and visit her aged parents for two days, and then follow her mistress. That girl of late had looked so perturbed and worried that the sensitive Rita, fearing that she was tired of her place, proposed to settle a sum of money on her which would have enabled her to devote herself entirely to her aged parents. And did I know what that extraordinary girl said? She had said: "Don't let Madame think that I would be too proud to accept anything whatever from her; but I can't even dream of leaving Madame. I believe Madame has no friends. Not one." So instead of a large sum of money Doña Rita gave the girl a kiss and as she had been worried by several people who wanted her to go to Tolosa she bolted down this way just to get clear of all those busybodies. "Hide from them," she went on with ardour. "Yes, I came here to hide," she repeated twice as if delighted at last to have hit on that reason among so many others. "How could I tell that you would be here?" Then with sudden fire which only added to the delight with which I had been watching the play of her physiognomy she added: "Why did you come into this room?"

She enchanted me. The ardent modulations of the sound, the slight play of the beautiful lips, the still, deep sapphire gleam in those long eyes inherited from the dawn of ages and that seemed always to watch unimaginable things, that underlying faint ripple of gaiety that played under all her moods as though it had been a gift from the high gods moved to pity for this lonely mortal, all this within the four walls and displayed for me alone gave me the sense of almost intolerable joy. The words didn't matter. They had to be answered, of course.

"I came in for several reasons. One of them is that I didn't know you were here."

"Therese didn't tell you?"

"No."

"Never talked to you about me?"

I hesitated only for a moment. "Never," I said. Then I asked in my turn, "Did she tell you I was here?"

"No," she said.

"It's very clear she did not mean us to come together again."

"Neither did I, my dear."

"What do you mean by speaking like this, in this tone, in these words? You seem to use them as if they were a sort of formula. Am I a dear to you? Or is anybody? . . . or everybody? . . ."

She had been for some time raised on her elbow, but then as if something had happened to her vitality she sank down till her head rested again on the sofa cushion.

"Why do you try to hurt my feelings?" she asked.

"For the same reason for which you call me dear at the end of a sentence like that: for want of something more amusing to do. You don't pretend to make me believe that you do it for any sort of reason that a decent person would confess to."

The colour had gone from her face; but a fit of wickedness was on me and I pursued, "What are the motives of your speeches? What prompts your actions? On your own showing your life seems to be a continuous running away. You have just run away from Paris. Where will you run to-morrow? What are you everlastingly running from—or is it that you are running after something? What is it? A man, a phantom—or some sensation that you don't like to own to?"

Truth to say, I was abashed by the silence which was her only answer to this sally. I said to myself that I would not let my natural anger, my just fury be disarmed by any assumption of pathos or dignity. I suppose I was really out of my mind and what in the middle ages would have been called "possessed" by an evil spirit. I went on enjoying my own villainy.

"Why aren't you in Tolosa? You ought to be in Tolosa. Isn't Tolosa the proper field for your abilities, for your sympathies, for your profusions, for your generosities—the king without a crown, the man without a fortune? But here there is nothing worthy of your talents. No, there is no longer anything worth any sort of trouble here. There isn't even that ridiculous Monsieur George. I understand that the talk of the coast from here to Cette is that Monsieur George is drowned. Upon my word I believe he is. And serve him right, too. There's Therese, but I don't suppose that your love for your sister . . ."

"For goodness' sake don't let her come in and find you here."

Those words recalled me to myself, exorcised the evil spirit by the mere enchanting power of the voice. They were also impressive by their suggestion of something practical, utilitarian, and remote from sentiment. The evil spirit left me and I remained taken aback slightly.

"Well," I said, "if you mean that you want me to leave the room I will confess to you that I can't very well do it yet. But I could lock both doors if you don't mind that."

"Do what you like as long as you keep her out. You two together would be too much for me to-night. Why don't you go and lock those doors? I have a feeling she is on the prowl."

I got up at once saying, "I imagine she has gone to bed by this time." I felt absolutely calm and responsible. I turned the keys one after another so gently that I couldn't hear the click of the locks myself. This done I recrossed the room with measured steps, with downcast eyes, and approaching the couch without raising them from the carpet I sank down on my knees and leaned my forehead on its edge. That penitential attitude had but little remorse in it. I detected no movement and heard no sound from her. In one place a bit of the fur coat touched my cheek softly, but no forgiving hand came to rest on my bowed head. I only breathed deeply the faint scent of violets, her own particular fragrance enveloping my body, penetrating my very heart with an inconceivable intimacy, bringing me closer to her than the closest embrace, and yet so subtle that I sensed her existence in me only as a great, glowing, indeterminate tenderness, something like the evening light disclosing after the white passion of the day infinite depths in the colours of the sky and an unsuspected soul of peace in the protean forms of life. I had not known such quietness for months; and I detected in myself an immense fatigue, a longing to remain where I was without changing my position to the end of time. Indeed to remain seemed to me a complete solution for all the problems that life presents —even as to the very death itself.

Only the unwelcome reflection that this was impossible made me get up at last with a sigh of deep grief at the end of the dream. But I got up without despair. She didn't murmur, she didn't stir. There was something august in the stillness of the room. It was a strange peace which she shared with me in this unexpected shelter full of disorder in its neglected splendour. What troubled me was the sudden, as it were material, consciousness of time passing as water flows. It seemed to me that it was only the tenacity of my sentiment that held that woman's body, extended and tranquil above the flood. But when I ventured at last to look at her face I saw her flushed, her teeth clenched—it was visible —her nostrils dilated, and in her narrow, level-glancing eyes a look of inward and frightened ecstasy. The edges of the fur coat had fallen open and I was moved to turn away. I had the same impression as on the evening we parted that something had happened which I did not understand; only this time I had not touched her at all. I really didn't understand. At the slightest whisper I would now have gone out without a murmur, as though that emotion had given her the right to be obeyed. But there was no whisper; and for a long time I stood leaning on my arm, looking into the fire and feeling distinctly between the four walls of that locked room the unchecked time flow past our two stranded personalities.

And suddenly she spoke. She spoke in that voice that was so profoundly moving without ever being sad, a little wistful perhaps and always the supreme expression of her grace. She asked as if nothing had happened:

"What are you thinking of, *amigo?*"

I turned about. She was lying on her side, tranquil above the smooth flow of time, again closely wrapped up in her fur, her head resting on the old-gold sofa cushion bearing like everything else in that room the decoratively enlaced letters of her monogram; her face a little pale now, with the crimson lobe of her ear under the tawny mist of her loose hair, the lips a little parted, and her glance of melted sapphire level and motionless, darkened by fatigue.

"Can I think of anything but you?" I murmured, taking a seat near the foot of the couch. "Or rather it isn't thinking, it is more like the consciousness of you always being present in me, complete to the last hair, to the faintest shade of expression, and that not only when we are apart but when we are together, alone, as close as this. I see you now lying on this couch but that is only the insensible phantom of the real you that is in me. And it is the easier for me to feel this because that image which others see and call by your name— how am I to know that it is anything else but an enchanting mist? You have always eluded me except in one or two moments which seem still more dream-like than the rest. Since I came into this room you have done nothing to destroy my conviction of your unreality

apart from myself.   You haven't offered me your hand,
to touch.   Is it because you suspect that apart from
me you are but a mere phantom, and that you fear
to put it to the test?"

One of her hands was under the fur and the other
under her cheek.   She made no sound.   She didn't offer
to stir.   She didn't move her eyes, not even when I had
added after waiting for a while:

"Just what I expected.   You are a cold illusion."

She smiled mysteriously, right away from me, straight
at the fire, and that was all.

VI

I HAD a momentary suspicion that I had said something stupid. Her smile amongst many other things seemed to have meant that, too. And I answered it with a certain resignation:

"Well, I don't know that you are so much mist. I remember once hanging on to you like a drowning man . . . But perhaps I had better not speak of this. It wasn't so very long ago, and you may . . ."

"I don't mind. Well . . ."

"Well, I have kept an impression of great solidity. I'll admit that. A woman of granite."

"A doctor once told me that I was made to last for ever," she said.

"But essentially it's the same thing," I went on. "Granite, too, is insensible."

I watched her profile against the pillow and there came on her face an expression I knew well when with an indignation full of suppressed laughter she used to throw at me the word "Imbecile." I expected it to come, but it didn't come. I must say, though, that I was swimmy in my head and now and then had a noise as of the sea in my ears, so I might not have heard it. The woman of granite, built to last for ever, continued to look at the glowing logs which made a sort of fiery ruin on the white pile of ashes. "I will tell you how it is," I said. "When I have you before my eyes there is such a projection of my whole being towards you that I fail to see you distinctly. It was like that from the beginning. I may say that I never saw you distinctly

till after we had parted and I thought you had gone
from my sight for ever. It was then that you took
body in my imagination and that my mind seized on a
definite form of you for all its adorations—for its profa-
nation, too. Don't imagine me grovelling in spiritual
abasement before a mere image. I got a grip on you
that nothing can shake now."

"Don't speak like this," she said. "It's too much
for me. And there is a whole long night before us."

"You don't think that I dealt with you sentimentally
enough perhaps? But the sentiment was there; as clear
a flame as ever burned on earth from the most remote
ages before that eternal thing which is in you, which is
your heirloom. And is it my fault that what I had to
give was real flame, and not a mystic's incense? It is
neither your fault nor mine. And now whatever we say
to each other at night or in daylight, that sentiment
must be taken for granted. It will be there on the day
I die—when you won't be there."

She continued to look fixedly at the red embers; and
from her lips that hardly moved came the quietest possible whisper: "Nothing would be easier than to die for
you."

"Really," I cried. "And you expect me perhaps
after this to kiss your feet in a transport of gratitude
while I hug the pride of your words to my breast. But
as it happens there is nothing in me but contempt for
this sublime declaration. How dare you offer me this
charlatanism of passion? What has it got to do between you and me who are the only two beings in the
world that may safely say that we have no need cf
shams between ourselves? Is it possible that you are a
charlatan at heart? Not from egoism, I admit, but
from some sort of fear. Yet, should you be sincere,
then—listen well to me—I would never forgive you. I

would visit your grave every day to curse you for an
evil thing."

"Evil thing," she echoed softly.

"Would you prefer to be a sham—that one could forget?"

"You will never forget me," she said in the same
tone at the glowing embers. "Evil or good. But, my
dear, I feel neither an evil nor a sham. I have got to
be what I am, and that, *amigo*, is not so easy; because
I may be simple, but like all those on whom there is
no peace I am not One. No, I am not One!"

"You are all the women in the world," I whispered
bending over her. She didn't seem to be aware of anything and only spoke—always to the glow.

"If I were that I would say: God help them then.
But that would be more appropriate for Therese. For
me, I can only give them my infinite compassion. I
have too much reverence in me to invoke the name of a
God of whom clever men have robbed me a long time
ago. How could I help it? For the talk was clever and
—and I had a mind. And I am also, as Therese says,
naturally sinful. Yes, my dear, I may be naturally
wicked but I am not evil and I could die for you."

"You!" I said. "You are afraid to die."

"Yes. But not for you."

The whole structure of glowing logs fell down, raising
a small turmoil of white ashes and sparks. The tiny
crash seemed to wake her up thoroughly. She turned
her head upon the cushion to look at me.

"It's a very extraordinary thing, we two coming together like this," she said with conviction. "You
coming in without knowing I was here and then telling
me that you can't very well go out of the room. That
sounds funny. I wouldn't have been angry if you had
said that you wouldn't. It would have hurt me. But

nobody ever paid much attention to my feelings. Why do you smile like this?"

"At a thought. Without any charlatanism of passion I am able to tell you of something to match your devotion. I was not afraid for your sake to come within a hair's breadth of what to all the world would have been a squalid crime. Note that you and I are persons of honour. And there might have been a criminal trial at the end of it for me. Perhaps the scaffold."

"Do you say these horrors to make me tremble?"

"Oh, you needn't tremble. There shall be no crime. I need not risk the scaffold, since now you are safe. But I entered this room meditating resolutely on the ways of murder, calculating possibilities and chances without the slightest compunction. It's all over now. It was all over directly I saw you here, but it had been so near that I shudder yet."

She must have been very startled because for a time she couldn't speak. Then in a faint voice:

"For me! For me!" she faltered out twice.

"For you—or for myself? Yet it couldn't have been selfish. What would it have been to me that you remained in the world? I never expected to see you again. I even composed a most beautiful letter of farewell. Such a letter as no woman had ever received."

Instantly she shot out a hand towards me. The edges of the fur cloak fell apart. A wave of the faintest possible scent floated into my nostrils.

"Let me have it," she said imperiously.

"You can't have it. It's all in my head. No woman will read it. I suspect it was something that could never have been written. But what a farewell! And now I suppose we shall say good-bye without even a handshake. But you are safe! Only I must ask you not to come out of this room till I tell you you may."

I was extremely anxious that Señor Ortega should never even catch a glimpse of Doña Rita, never guess how near he had been to her. I was extremely anxious the fellow should depart for Tolosa and get shot in a ravine; or go to the Devil in his own way, as long as he lost the track of Doña Rita completely. He then, probably would get mad and get shut up, or else get cured, forget all about it, and devote himself to his vocation, whatever it was—keep a shop and grow fat. All this flashed through my mind in an instant and while I was still dazzled by those comforting images, the voice of Doña Rita pulled me up with a jerk.

"You mean not out of the house?"

"No, I mean not out of this room," I said with some embarrassment.

"What do you mean? Is there something in the house then? This is most extraordinary! Stay in this room? And you, too, it seems? Are you also afraid for yourself?"

"I can't even give you an idea how afraid I was. I am not so much now. But you know very well, Doña Rita, that I never carry any sort of weapon in my pocket."

"Why don't you, then?" she asked in a flash of scorn which bewitched me so completely for an instant that I couldn't even smile at it.

"Because if I am unconventionalized I am an old European," I murmured gently. "No, *Excellentissima*, I shall go through life without as much as a switch in my hand. It's no use you being angry. Adapting to this great moment some words you've heard before: I am like that. Such is my character!"

Doña Rita frankly stared at me—a most unusual expression for her to have. Suddenly she sat up.

"Don George," she said with lovely animation, "I insist upon knowing who is in my house."

"You insist! . . . But Therese says it is *her* house."

Had there been anything handy, such as a cigarette box, for instance, it would have gone sailing through the air spouting cigarettes as it went. Rosy all over, cheeks, neck, shoulders, she seemed lighted up softly from inside like a beautiful transparency. But she didn't raise her voice.

"You and Therese have sworn my ruin. If you don't tell me what you mean I will go outside and shout up the stairs to make her come down. I know there is no one but the three of us in the house."

"Yes, three; but not counting my Jacobin. There is a Jacobin in the house."

"A Jac . . . ! Oh, George, is this the time to jest?" she began in persuasive tones when a faint but peculiar noise stilled her lips as though they had been suddenly frozen. She became quiet all over instantly. I, on the contrary, made an involuntary movement before I, too, became as still as death. We strained our ears; but that peculiar metallic rattle had been so slight and the silence now was so perfect that it was very difficult to believe one's senses. Doña Rita looked inquisitively at me. I gave her a slight nod. We remained looking into each other's eyes while we listened and listened till the silence became unbearable. Doña Rita whispered composedly: "Did you hear?"

"I am asking myself . . . I almost think I didn't."

"Don't shuffle with me. It was a scraping noise."

"Something fell."

"Something! What thing? What are the things that fall by themselves? Who is that man of whom you spoke? Is there a man?"

"No doubt about it whatever. I brought him here myself."

"What for?"

"Why shouldn't I have a Jacobin of my own? Haven't you one, too? But mine is a different problem from that white-haired humbug of yours. He is a genuine article. There must be plenty like him about. He has scores to settle with half a dozen people, he says, and he clamours for revolutions to give him a chance."

"But why did you bring him here?"

"I don't know—from sudden affection . . ."

All this passed in such low tones that we seemed to make out the words more by watching each other's lips than through our sense of hearing. Man is a strange animal. I didn't care what I said. All I wanted was to keep her in her pose, excited and still, sitting up with her hair loose, softly glowing, the dark brown fur making a wonderful contrast with the white lace on her breast. All I was thinking of was that she was adorable and too lovely for words! I cared for nothing but that sublimely æsthetic impression. It summed up all life, all joy, all poetry! It had a divine strain. I am certain that I was not in my right mind. I suppose I was not quite sane. I am convinced that at that moment of the four people in the house it was Doña Rita who upon the whole was the most sane. She observed my face and I am sure she read there something of my inward exaltation. She knew what to do. In the softest possible tone and hardly above her breath she commanded: "George, come to yourself."

Her gentleness had the effect of evening light. I was soothed. Her confidence in her own power touched me profoundly. I suppose my love was too great for madness to get hold of me. I can't say that I passed to a complete calm, but I became slightly ashamed of myself. I whispered:

"No, it was not from affection, it was for the love of you that I brought him here. That imbecile H. was going to send him to Tolosa."

"That Jacobin!" Doña Rita was immensely surprised, as she might well have been. Then resigned to the incomprehensible: "Yes," she breathed out, "what did you do with him?"

"I put him to bed in the studio."

How lovely she was with the effort of close attention depicted in the turn of her head and in her whole face honestly trying to approve. "And then?" she enquired.

"Then I came in here to face calmly the necessity of doing away with a human life. I didn't shirk it for a moment. That's what a short twelvemonth has brought me to. Don't think I am reproaching you, O blind force! You are justified because you *are*. What-ever had to happen you would not even have heard of it."

Horror darkened her marvellous radiance. Then her face became utterly blank with the tremendous effort to understand. Absolute silence reigned in the house. It seemed to me that everything had been said now that mattered in the world; and that the world itself had reached its ultimate stage, had reached its appointed end of an eternal, phantom-like silence. Suddenly Doña Rita raised a warning finger. I had heard nothing and shook my head; but she nodded hers and murmured excitedly, "Yes, yes, in the fencing-room, as before."

In the same way I answered her: "Impossible! The door is locked and Therese has the key." She asked then in the most cautious manner:

"Have you seen Therese to-night?"

"Yes," I confessed without misgiving. "I left her making up the fellow's bed when I came in here."

"The bed of the Jacobin?" she said in a peculiar tone as if she were humouring a lunatic.

"I think I had better tell you he is a Spaniard—that he seems to know you from early days. . . ." I glanced at her face, it was extremely tense, apprehensive. For myself I had no longer any doubt as to the man and I hoped she would reach the correct conclusion herself. But I believe she was too distracted and worried to think consecutively. She only seemed to feel some terror in the air. In very pity I bent down and whispered carefully near her ear, "His name is Ortega."

I expected some effect from that name but I never expected what happened. With the sudden, free, spontaneous agility of a young animal she leaped off the sofa, leaving her slippers behind, and in one bound reached almost the middle of the room. The vigour, the instinctive precision of that spring, were something amazing. I just escaped being knocked over. She landed lightly on her bare feet with a perfect balance, without the slightest suspicion of swaying in her instant immobility. It lasted less than a second, then she spun round distractedly and darted at the first door she could see. My own agility was just enough to enable me to grip the back of the fur coat and then catch her round the body before she could wriggle herself out of the sleeves. She was muttering all the time, "No, no, no." She abandoned herself to me just for an instant during which I got her back to the middle of the room. There she attempted to free herself and I let her go at once. With her face very close to mine, but apparently not knowing what she was looking at she repeated again twice, "No—No," with an intonation which might well have brought dampness to my eyes but which only made me regret that I didn't kill the honest Ortega at sight. Suddenly Doña Rita swung round and seizing her loose hair with both hands started twisting it up before one of the sumptuous mirrors. The wide fur sleeves slipped down her white arms. In a brusque movement like a downward stab she transfixed the whole mass of tawny glints and sparks with the arrow of gold which she perceived lying there, before her, on the marble console. Then she sprang away from the glass muttering feverishly, "Out —out—out of this house," and trying with an awful, senseless stare to dodge past me who had put myself in her way with open arms. At last I managed to seize her by the shoulders and in the extremity of my distress I shook her roughly. If she hadn't quieted down then I believe my heart would have broken. I spluttered right into her face: "I won't let you. Here you stay." She seemed to recognize me at last, and suddenly still, perfectly firm on her white feet, she let her arms fall and, from an abyss of desolation, whispered, "O! George! No! No! Not Ortega."

There was a passion of mature grief in this tone of appeal. And yet she remained as touching and helpless as a distressed child. It had all the simplicity and depth of a child's emotion. It tugged at one's heartstrings in the same direct way. But what could one do? How could one soothe her? It was impossible to pat her on the head, take her on the knee, give her a chocolate or show her a picture-book. I found myself absolutely without resource. Completely at a loss.

"Yes, Ortega. Well, what of it?" I whispered with immense assurance.

VII

My brain was in a whirl. I am safe to say that at this precise moment there was nobody completely sane in the house. Setting apart Therese and Ortega, both in the grip of unspeakable passions, all the moral economy of Doña Rita had gone to pieces. Everything was gone except her strong sense of life with all its implied menaces. The woman was a mere chaos of sensations and vitality. I, too, suffered most from inability to get hold of some fundamental thought. The one on which I could best build some hopes was the thought that, of course, Ortega did not know anything. I whispered this into the ear of Doña Rita, into her precious, her beautifully shaped ear.

But she shook her head, very much like an inconsolable child and very much with a child's complete pessimism she murmured, "Therese has told him."

The words, "Oh, nonsense," never passed my lips, because I could not cheat myself into denying that there had been a noise; and that the noise was in the fencing-room. I knew that room. There was nothing there that by the wildest stretch of imagination could be conceived as falling with that particular sound. There was a table with a tall strip of looking-glass above it at one end; but since Blunt took away his campaigning kit there was no small object of any sort on the console or anywhere else that could have been jarred off in some mysterious manner. Along one of the walls there was the whole complicated apparatus of solid brass pipes, and quite close to it an enormous bath sunk into the floor. The greatest part of the room along its whole length was covered with matting and had nothing else but a long, narrow leather-upholstered bench fixed to the wall. And that was all. And the door leading to the studio was locked. And Therese had the key. And it flashed on my mind, independently of Doña Rita's pessimism, by the force of personal conviction, that, of course, Therese would tell him. I beheld the whole succession of events perfectly connected and tending to that particular conclusion. Therese would tell him! I could see the contrasted heads of those two formidable lunatics close together in a dark mist of whispers compounded of greed, piety, and jealousy, plotting in a sense of perfect security as if under the very wing of Providence. So at least Therese would think. She could not be but under the impression that (providentially) I had been called out for the rest of the night.

And now there was one sane person in the house, for I had regained complete command of my thoughts. Working in a logical succession of images they showed me at last as clearly as a picture on a wall, Therese pressing with fervour the key into the fevered palm of the rich, prestigious, virtuous cousin, so that he should go and urge his self-sacrificing offer to Rita, and gain merit before Him whose Eye sees all the actions of men. And this image of those two with the key in the studio seemed to me a most monstrous conception of fanaticism, of a perfectly horrible aberration. For who could mistake the state that made José Ortega the figure he was, inspiring both pity and fear? I could not deny that I understood, not the full extent but the exact nature of his suffering. Young as I was I had solved for myself that grotesque and sombre personality. His contact with me, the personal con-

tact with (as he thought) one of the actual lovers of
that woman who brought to him as a boy the curse of
the gods, had tipped over the trembling scales. No
doubt I was very near death in the "grand salon"
of the Maison Dorée, only that his torture had gone too
far. It seemed to me that I ought to have heard his
very soul scream while we were seated at supper.
But in a moment he had ceased to care for me. I was
nothing. To the crazy exaggeration of his jealousy I
was but one amongst a hundred thousand. What was
my death? Nothing. All mankind had possessed
that woman. I knew what his wooing of her would
be: Mine—or Dead.

All this ought to have had the clearness of noon-day,
even to the veriest idiot that ever lived; and Therese
was, properly speaking, exactly that. An idiot. A
one-ideaed creature. Only the idea was complex; therefore it was impossible really to say what she wasn't
capable of. This was what made her obscure processes so awful. She had at times the most amazing
perceptions. Who could tell where her simplicity
ended and her cunning began? She had also the faculty
of never forgetting any fact bearing upon her one idea;
and I remembered now that the conversation with me
about the will had produced on her an indelible impression of the Law's surprising justice. Recalling
her naïve admiration of the "just" law that required
no "paper" from a sister, I saw her casting loose the
raging fate with a sanctimonious air. And Therese
would naturally give the key of the fencing-room to
her dear, virtuous, grateful, disinterested cousin, to
that damned soul with delicate whiskers, because she
would think it just possible that Rita might have locked
the door leading from her room into the hall; whereas
there was no earthly reason, not the slightest likelihood,

that she would bother about the other. Righteousness demanded that the erring sister should be taken unawares.

All the above is the analysis of one short moment. Images are to words like light to sound—incomparably swifter. And all this was really one flash of light through my mind. A comforting thought succeeded it: that both doors were locked and that really there was no danger.

However, there had been that noise—the why and the how of it? Of course in the dark he might have fallen into the bath, but that wouldn't have been a faint noise. It wouldn't have been a rattle. There was absolutely nothing he could knock over. He might have dropped a candlestick if Therese had left him her own. That was possible, but then those thick mats— and then, anyway, why should he drop it? and, hang it all, why shouldn't he have gone straight on and tried the door? I had suddenly a sickening vision of the fellow crouching at the key-hole, listening, listening, listening, for some movement or sigh of the sleeper he was ready to tear away from the world, alive or dead. I had a conviction that he was still listening. Why? Goodness knows! He may have been only gloating over the assurance that the night was long and that he had all these hours to himself.

I was pretty certain that he could have heard nothing of our whispers, the room was too big for that and the door too solid. I hadn't the same confidence in the efficiency of the lock. Still! . . . Guarding my lips with my hand I urged Doña Rita to go back to the sofa. She wouldn't answer me and when I got hold of her arm I discovered that she wouldn't move. She had taken root in that thick-pile Aubusson carpet; and she was so rigidly still all over that the brilliant stones in the shaft of the arrow of gold, with the six candles at the head of the sofa blazing full on them, emitted no sparkle.

I was extremely anxious that she shouldn't betray herself. I reasoned, save the mark, as a psychologist. I had no doubt that the man knew of her being there; but he only knew it by hearsay. And that was bad enough. I could not help feeling that if he obtained some evidence for his senses by any sort of noise, voice, or movement, his madness would gain strength enough to burst the lock. I was rather ridiculously worried about the locks. A horrid mistrust of the whole house possessed me. I saw it in the light of a deadly trap. I had no weapon, I couldn't say whether he had one or not. I wasn't afraid of a struggle as far as I, myself, was concerned, but I was afraid of it for Doña Rita. To be rolling at her feet, locked in a literally tooth-and-nail struggle with Ortega, would have been odious. I wanted to spare her feelings, just as I would have been anxious to save from any contact with mud the feet of that goatherd of the mountains with a symbolic face. I looked at her face. For immobility it might have been a carving. I wished I knew how to deal with that embodied mystery, to influence it, to manage it. Oh, how I longed for the gift of authority! In addition, since I had become completely sane, all my scruples against laying hold of her had returned. I felt shy and embarrassed. My eyes were fixed on the bronze handle of the fencing-room door as if it were something alive. I braced myself up against the moment when it would move. This was what was going to happen next. It would move very gently. My heart began to thump. But I was prepared to keep myself as still as death and I hoped Doña Rita would have sense enough to do the same. I stole another glance at her face and at that moment I heard the word: "Beloved!" form itself in the still air of the room, weak, distinct, piteous, like the last request of the dying.

With great presence of mind I whispered into Doña Rita's ear: "Perfect silence!" and was overjoyed to discover that she had heard me, understood me; that she even had command over her rigid lips. She answered me in a breath (our cheeks were nearly touching): "Take me out of this house."

I glanced at all her clothing scattered about the room and hissed forcibly the warning "Perfect immobility"; noticing with relief that she didn't offer to move, though animation was returning to her and her lips had remained parted in an awful, unintended effect of a smile. And I don't know whether I was pleased when she, who was not to be touched, gripped my wrist suddenly. It had the air of being done on purpose because almost instantly another: "Beloved!" louder, more agonized if possible, got into the room and, yes, went home to my heart. It was followed without any transition, preparation, or warning, by a positively bellowed: "Speak, perjured beast!" which I felt pass in a thrill right through Doña Rita like an electric shock, leaving her as motionless as before.

Till he shook the door handle, which he did immedi-ately afterwards, I wasn't certain through which door he had spoken. The two doors (in different walls) were rather near each other. It was as I expected. He was in the fencing-room, thoroughly aroused, his senses on the alert to catch the slightest sound. A situation not to be trifled with. Leaving the room was for us out of the question. It was quite possible for him to dash round into the hall before we could get clear of the front door. As to making a bolt of it upstairs there was the same objection; and to allow ourselves to be chased all over the empty house by this maniac would have been mere folly. There was no advantage in locking ourselves up anywhere upstairs where the original doors and locks were much lighter. No, true safety was in absolute stillness and silence, so that even his rage should be brought to doubt at last and die expended, or choke him before it died; I didn't care which.

For me to go out and meet him would have been stupid. Now I was certain that he was armed. I had remembered the wall in the fencing-room decorated with trophies of cold steel in all the civilized and savage forms; sheaves of assegais, in the guise of columns and grouped between them stars and suns of choppers, swords, knives; from Italy, from Damascus, from Abyssinia, from the ends of the world. Ortega had only to make his barbarous choice. I suppose he had got up on the bench, and fumbling about amongst them must have brought one down, which, falling, had produced that rattling noise. But in any case to go to meet him would have been folly, because, after all, I might have been overpowered (even with bare hands) and then Doña Rita would have been left utterly defenceless.

"He will speak," came to me the ghostly, terrified murmur of her voice. "Take me out of the house before he begins to speak."

"Keep still," I whispered. "He will soon get tired of this."

"You don't know him."

"Oh, yes, I do. Been with him two hours."

At this she let go my wrist and covered her face with her hands passionately. When she dropped them she had the look of one morally crushed.

"What did he say to you?"

"He raved."

"Listen to me. It was all true!"

"I daresay, but what of that?"

These ghostly words passed between us hardly louder than thoughts; but after my last answer she ceased and gave me a searching stare, then drew in a long breath. The voice on the other side of the door burst out with an impassioned request for a little pity, just a little, and went on begging for a few words, for two words, for one word—one poor little word. Then it gave up, then repeated once more, "Say you are there, Rita. Say one word, just one word. Say 'yes.' Come! Just one little yes."

"You see," I said. She only lowered her eyelids over the anxious glance she had turned on me.

For a minute we could have had the illusion that he had stolen away, unheard, on the thick mats. But I don't think that either of us was deceived. The voice returned, stammering words without connection, pausing and faltering, till suddenly steadied it soared into impassioned entreaty, sank to low, harsh tones, voluble, lofty sometimes and sometimes abject. When it paused it left us looking profoundly at each other.

"It's almost comic," I whispered.

"Yes. One could laugh," she assented, with a sort of sinister conviction. Never had I seen her look exactly like that, for an instant another, an incredible Rita! "Haven't I laughed at him innumerable times?" she added in a sombre whisper.

He was muttering to himself out there, and unexpectedly shouted: "What?" as though he had fancied he had heard something. He waited a while before he started up again with a loud: "Speak up, Queen of the goats, with your goat tricks. . . ." All was still for a time, then came a most awful bang on the door. He must have stepped back a pace to hurl himself bodily against the panels. The whole house seemed to shake. He repeated that performance once more, and then varied it by a prolonged drumming with his fists. It *was* comic. But I felt myself struggling mentally with an invading gloom as though I were no longer sure of myself.

"Take me out," whispered Doña Rita feverishly, "take me out of this house before it is too late."

"You will have to stand it," I answered.

"So be it; but then you must go away yourself. Go now, before it is too late."

I didn't condescend to answer this. The drumming on the panels stopped and the absurd thunder of it died out in the house. I don't know why precisely then I had the acute vision of the red mouth of José Ortega wriggling with rage between his funny whiskers. He began afresh but in a tired tone:

"Do you expect a fellow to forget your tricks, you wicked little devil? Haven't you ever seen me dodging about to get a sight of you amongst those pretty gentlemen, on horseback, like a princess, with pure cheeks like a carved saint? I wonder I didn't throw stones at you. I wonder I didn't run after you shouting the tale —curse my timidity! But I daresay they knew as much as I did. More. All the new tricks—if that were possible."

While he was making this uproar, Doña Rita put her fingers in her ears and then suddenly changed her mind and clapped her hands over my ears. Instinctively I disengaged my head, but she persisted. We had a short tussle without moving from the spot, and suddenly I had my head free, and there was complete silence. He had screamed himself out of breath, but Doña Rita muttering: "Too late, too late," got her hands away from my grip and slipping altogether out of her fur coat seized some garment lying on a chair near by (I think it was her skirt), with the intention of dressing herself, I imagine, and rushing out of the house. Determined to prevent this, but indeed without thinking very much what I was doing, I got hold of her arm. That struggle was silent, too; but I used the least force possible and she managed to give me an unexpected push. Stepping back to save myself from falling I overturned the little table, bearing the six-branched candlestick. It hit the floor, rebounded with a dull ring on the carpet, and by the time it came to a rest every single candle was out. He on the other side of the door naturally heard the noise and greeted it with a triumphant screech: "Aha! I've managed to wake you up," the very savagery of which had a laughable effect. I felt the weight of Doña Rita grow on my arm and thought it best to let her sink on the floor, wishing to be free in my movements and really afraid that now he had actually heard a noise he would infallibly burst the door. But he didn't even thump it. He seemed to have exhausted himself in that scream. There was no other light in the room but the darkened glow of the embers and I could hardly make out amongst the shadows of furniture Doña Rita sunk on her knees in a penitential and despairing attitude. Before this collapse I, who had been wrestling desperately with her a moment before, felt that I dare not touch her. This emotion, too, I could not understand; this abandonment of herself, this conscience-stricken humility. A humbly imploring request to open the door came from the other side. Ortega kept on repeating: "Open the door, open the door," in such an amazing variety of intonations, imperative, whining, persuasive, insinuating, and even unexpectedly jocose, that I really stood there smiling to myself, yet with a gloomy and uneasy heart. Then he remarked, parenthetically as it were, "Oh, you know how to torment a man, you brown-skinned, lean, grinning, dishevelled imp, you. And mark," he expounded further, in a curiously doctoral tone— "you are in all your limbs hateful: your eyes are hateful and your mouth is hateful, and your hair is hateful, and your body is cold and vicious like a snake—and altogether you are perdition."

This statement was astonishingly deliberate. He drew a moaning breath after it and uttered in a heart-rending tone, "You know, Rita, that I cannot live without you. I haven't lived. I am not living now. This isn't life. Come, Rita, you can't take a boy's soul away and then let him grow up and go about the world, poor devil, while you go amongst the rich from one pair of arms to another, showing all your best tricks. But I will forgive you if you only open the door," he ended in an inflated tone: "You remember how you swore time after time to be my wife. You are more fit to be Satan's wife but I don't mind. You shall be *my* wife!"

A sound near the floor made me bend down hastily with a stern: "Don't laugh," for in his grotesque, almost burlesque discourses there seemed to me to be truth, passion, and horror enough to move a mountain.

Suddenly suspicion seized him out there. With perfectly farcical unexpectedness he yelled shrilly: "Oh, you deceitful wretch! You won't escape me! I will have you. . . ."

And in a manner of speaking he vanished. Of course I couldn't see him but somehow that was the impression. I had hardly time to receive it when crash! . . . he was already at the other door. I suppose he thought that his prey was escaping him. His swiftness was amazing, almost inconceivable, more like the effect of a trick or of a mechanism. The thump on the door was awful as if he had not been able to stop himself in time. The shock seemed enough to stun an elephant. It was really funny. And after the crash there was a moment of silence as if he were recovering himself. The next thing was a low grunt, and at once he picked up the thread of his fixed idea.

"You will have to be my wife. I have no shame. You swore you would be and so you will have to be." Stifled low sounds made me bend down again to the kneeling form, white in the flush of the dark red glow. "For goodness' sake don't," I whispered down. She was struggling with an appalling fit of merriment, repeating to herself, "Yes, every day, for two months. Sixty times at least, sixty times at least." Her voice was rising high. She was struggling against laughter, but when I tried to put my hand over her lips I felt her face wet with tears. She turned it this way and that, eluding my hand with repressed low, little moans. I lost my caution and said, "Be quiet," so sharply as to startle myself (and her, too) into expectant stillness.

Ortega's voice in the hall asked distinctly: "Eh? What's this?" and then he kept still on his side listening, but he must have thought that his ears had deceived him. He was getting tired, too. He was keeping quiet out there—resting. Presently he sighed deeply; then in a harsh melancholy tone he started again.

"My love, my soul, my life, do speak to me. What am I that you should take so much trouble to pretend that you aren't there? Do speak to me," he repeated tremulously, following this mechanical appeal with a string of extravagantly endearing names, some of them quite childish, which all of a sudden stopped dead; and then after a pause there came a distinct, unutterably weary: "What shall I do now?" as though he were speaking to himself.

I shuddered to hear rising from the floor, by my side, a vibrating, scornful: "Do! Why, slink off home looking over your shoulder as you used to years ago when I had done with you—all but the laughter."

"Rita," I murmured, appalled. He must have been struck dumb for a moment. Then, goodness only knows why, in his dismay or rage he was moved to speak in French with a most ridiculous accent.

"So you have found your tongue at last—*Catin!* You were that from the cradle. Don't you remember how . . ."

Doña Rita sprang to her feet at my side with a loud cry, "No, George, no," which bewildered me completely. The suddenness, the loudness of it made the ensuing silence on both sides of the door perfectly awful. It seemed to me that if I didn't resist with all my might something in me would die on the instant. In the straight, falling folds of the nightdress she looked cold like a block of marble; while I, too, was turned into stone by the terrific clamour in the hall.

"Therese, Therese," yelled Ortega. "She has got a man in there." He ran to the foot of the stairs and screamed again, "Therese, Therese! There is a man with her. A man! Come down, you miserable starved peasant, come down and see."

I don't know where Therese was but I am sure that this voice reached her, terrible, as if clamouring to heaven, and with a shrill over-note which made me certain that if she was in bed the only thing she would think of doing would be to put her head under the bedclothes. With a final yell: "Come down and see," he flew back at the door of the room and started shaking it violently.

It was a double door, very tall, and there must have been a lot of things loose about its fittings, bolts, latches, and all those brass applications with broken screws, because it rattled, it clattered, it jingled; and produced also the sound as of thunder rolling in the big, empty hall. It was deafening, distressing, and vaguely alarming as if it could bring the house down. At the same time the futility of it had, it cannot be denied, a comic effect. The very magnitude of the racket he raised was funny. But he couldn't keep up that violent exertion continuously, and when he stopped to rest we could hear him shouting to himself in vengeful tones. He saw it all! He had been decoyed there! (Rattle, rattle, rattle.) He had been decoyed into that town, he screamed, getting more and more excited by the noise he made himself, in order to be exposed to this! (Rattle, rattle.) By this shameless "*Catin! Catin! Catin!*"

He started at the door again with superhuman vigour.

Behind me I heard Doña Rita laughing softly, statuesque, turned all dark in the fading glow. I called out to her quite openly, "Do keep your self-control." And she called back to me in a clear voice: "Oh, my dear, will you ever consent to speak to me after all this? But don't ask for the impossible. He was born to be laughed at."

"Yes," I cried. "But don't let yourself go."

I don't know whether Ortega heard us. He was exerting then his utmost strength of lung against the infamous plot to expose him to the derision of the fiendish associates of that obscene woman! . . . Then he began another interlude upon the door, so sustained and strong that I had the thought that this was growing absurdly impossible, that either the plaster would begin to fall off the ceiling or he would drop dead next moment, out there.

He stopped, uttered a few curses at the door, and seemed calmer from sheer exhaustion.

"This story will be all over the world," we heard him begin. "Deceived, decoyed, inveigled, in order to be made a laughing-stock before the most debased of all mankind, that woman and her associates." This was really a meditation. And then he screamed: "I will kill you all." Once more he started worrying the door but it was a startlingly feeble effort which he abandoned almost at once. He must have been at the end of his strength. Doña Rita from the middle of the room asked me recklessly loud: "Tell me! Wasn't he born to be laughed at?" I didn't answer her. I was so near the door that I thought I ought to hear him panting there. He was terrifying, but he was not serious. He was at the end of his strength, of his breath, of every kind of endurance, but I did not know it. He was done up, finished; but perhaps he did not know it himself. How still he was! Just as I began to wonder at it, I heard him distinctly give a slap to his forehead. "I see it all!" he cried. "That miserable, canting peasant-woman upstairs has arranged it all. No doubt she consulted her priests. I must regain my self-respect. Let her die first." I heard him make a dash for the foot of the stairs. I was appalled; yet to think of Therese being hoisted with her own petard was like a turn of affairs in a farce. A very ferocious farce. Instinctively I unlocked the door. Doña Rita's contralto laugh rang out loud, bitter, and contemptuous; and I heard Ortega's distracted screaming as if under torture. "It hurts! It hurts! It hurts!" I hesitated just an instant, half a second, no more, but before I could open the door wide there was in the hall a short groan and the sound of a heavy fall.

The sight of Ortega lying on his back at the foot of

the stairs arrested me in the doorway.   One of his legs
was drawn up, the other extended fully, his foot very
near the pedestal of the silver statuette holding the
feeble and tenacious gleam which made the shadows so
heavy in that hall.   One of his arms lay across his
breast.   The other arm was extended full length on
the white-and-black pavement with the hand palm
upwards and the fingers rigidly spread out.   The
shadow of the lowest step slanted across his face but one
whisker and part of his chin could be made out.   He
appeared strangely flattened.   He didn't move at all.
He was in his shirt-sleeves.   I felt an extreme distaste
for that sight.   The characteristic sound of a key
worrying in the lock stole into my ears.   I couldn't
locate it but I didn't attend much to that at first.   I
was engaged in watching Señor Ortega.   But for his
raised leg he clung so flat to the floor and had taken on
himself such a distorted shape that he might have
been the mere shadow of Señor Ortega.   It was rather
fascinating to see him so quiet at the end of all that
fury, clamour, passion, and uproar.   Surely there was
never anything so still in the world as this Ortega.   I
had a bizarre notion that he was not to be disturbed.

A noise like the rattling of chain links, a small grind
and click exploded in the stillness of the hall and a voice
began to swear in Italian.   These surprising sounds
were quite welcome, they recalled me to myself, and I
perceived they came from the front door which seemed
pushed a little ajar.   Was somebody trying to get in?
I had no objection, I went to the door and said: "Wait a
moment, it's on the chain."   The deep voice on the
other side said: "What an extraordinary thing," and I
assented mentally.   It was extraordinary.   The chain
was never put up, but Therese was a thorough sort
of person, and on this night she had put it up to keep

no one out except myself. It was the old Italian and his daughters returning from the ball who were trying to get in.

Suddenly I became intensely alive to the whole situation. I bounded back, closed the door of Blunt's room, and the next moment was speaking to the Italian. "A little patience." My hands trembled but I managed to take down the chain and as I allowed the door to swing open a little more I put myself in his way. He was burly, venerable, a little indignant, and full of thanks. Behind him his two girls, in short-skirted costumes, white stockings, and low shoes, their heads powdered and earrings sparkling in their ears, huddled together behind their father, wrapped up in their light mantles. One had kept her little black mask on her face, the other held hers in her hand.

The Italian was surprised at my blocking the way and remarked pleasantly, "It's cold outside, Signor." I said, "Yes," and added in a hurried whisper: "There is a dead man in the hall." He didn't say a single word but put me aside a little, projected his body in for one searching glance. "Your daughters," I murmured. He said kindly, "*Va bene, va bene.*" And then to them, "Come in, girls."

There is nothing like dealing with a man who has had a long past of out-of-the-way experiences. The skill with which he rounded up and drove the girls across the hall, paternal and irresistible, venerable and reassuring, was a sight to see. They had no time for more than one scared look over the shoulder. He hustled them in and locked them up safely in their part of the house, then crossed the hall with a quick, practical stride. When near Señor Ortega he trod short just in time and said: "In truth, blood"; then selecting the place, knelt down by the body in his tall hat and respectable overcoat, his white beard giving him immense authority somehow. "But—this man is not dead," he exclaimed, looking up at me. With profound sagacity, inherent as it were in his great beard, he never took the trouble to put any questions to me and seemed certain that I had nothing to do with the ghastly sight. "He managed to give himself an enormous gash in his side," was his calm remark. "And what a weapon!" he exclaimed, getting it out from under the body. It was an Abyssinian or Nubian production of a bizarre shape; the clumsiest thing imaginable, partaking of a sickle and a chopper with a sharp edge and a pointed end. A mere cruel-looking curio of inconceivable clumsiness to European eyes.

The old man let it drop with amused disdain. "You had better take hold of his legs," he decided without appeal. I certainly had no inclination to argue. When we lifted him up the head of Señor Ortega fell back desolately, making an awful, defenceless display of his large, white throat.

We found the lamp burning in the studio and the bed made up on the couch on which we deposited our burden. My venerable friend jerked the upper sheet away at once and started tearing it into strips.

"You may leave him to me," said that efficient sage, "but the doctor is your affair. If you don't want this business to make a noise you will have to find a discreet man."

He was most benevolently interested in all the proceedings. He remarked with a patriarchal smile as he tore the sheet noisily: "You had better not lose any time." I didn't lose any time. I crammed into the next hour an astonishing amount of bodily activity. Without more words I flew out bare-headed into the last night of Carnival. Luckily I was certain of the right sort of doctor. He was an iron-grey man of forty and of a stout habit of body, but who was able to put on a spurt. In the cold, dark, and deserted by-streets, he ran with earnest and ponderous footsteps, which echoed loudly in the cold night air, while I skimmed along the ground a pace or two in front of him. It was only on arriving at the house that I perceived that I had left the front door wide open. All the town, every evil in the world could have entered the black-and-white hall. But I had no time to meditate upon my imprudence. The doctor and I worked in silence for nearly an hour and it was only then while he was washing his hands in the fencing-room that he asked:

"What was he up to, that imbecile?"

"Oh, he was examining this curiosity," I said.

"Oh, yes, and it accidentally went off," said the doctor, looking contemptuously at the Nubian knife I had thrown on the table. Then while wiping his hands: "I would bet there is a woman somewhere under this; but that of course does not affect the nature of the wound. I hope this blood-letting will do him good."

"Nothing will do him any good," I said.

"Curious house this," went on the doctor. "It belongs to a curious sort of woman, too. I happened to see her once or twice. I shouldn't wonder if she were to raise considerable trouble in the track of her pretty feet as she goes along. I believe you know her well."

"Yes."

"Curious people in the house, too. There was a Carlist officer here, a lean, tall, dark man, who couldn't sleep. He consulted me once. Do you know what became of him?"

"No."

The doctor had finished wiping his hands and flung the towel far away.

"Considerable nervous over-strain. Seemed to have a restless brain. Not a good thing, that. For the rest a perfect gentleman. And this Spaniard here, do you know him?"

"Enough not to care what happens to him," I said, "except for the trouble he might cause to the Carlist sympathizers here, should the police get hold of this affair."

"Well, then, he must take his chance in the seclusion of that conservatory sort of place where you have put him. I'll try to find somebody we can trust to look after him. Meantime, I will leave the case to you."

VIII

Directly I had shut the door after the doctor I started shouting for Therese. "Come down at once, you wretched hypocrite," I yelled at the foot of the stairs in a sort of frenzy as though I had been a second Ortega. Not even an echo answered me; but all of a sudden a small flame flickered descending from the upper darkness and Therese appeared on the first floor landing carrying a lighted candle in front of a livid, hard face, closed against remorse, compassion, or mercy by the meanness of her righteousness and of her rapacious instincts. She was fully dressed in that abominable brown stuff with motionless folds, and as I watched her coming down step by step she might have been made of wood. I stepped back and pointed my finger at the darkness of the passage leading to the studio. She passed within a foot of me, her pale eyes staring straight ahead, her face still with disappointment and fury. Yet it is only my surmise. She might have been made thus inhuman by the force of an invisible purpose. I waited a moment, then, stealthily, with extreme caution, I opened the door of the so-called Captain Blunt's room.

The glow of embers was all but out. It was cold and dark in there; but before I closed the door behind me the dim light from the hall showed me Doña Rita standing on the very same spot where I had left her, statuesque in her nightdress. Even after I shut the door she loomed up enormous, indistinctly rigid and inanimate. I picked up the candelabra, groped for a candle all over the carpet, found one, and lighted it. All that time Doña Rita didn't stir. When I turned towards her she seemed to be slowly awakening from a trance. She was deathly pale and by contrast the melted, sapphire-blue of her eyes looked black as coal. They moved a little in my direction, incurious, recognizing me slowly. But when they had recognized me completely she raised her hands and hid her face in them. A whole minute or more passed. Then I said in a low tone: "Look at me," and she let them fall slowly as if accepting the inevitable.

"Shall I make up the fire?" . . . I waited. "Do you hear me?" She made no sound and with the tip of my finger I touched her bare shoulder. But for its elasticity it might have been frozen. At once I looked round for the fur coat; it seemed to me that there was not a moment to lose if she was to be saved, as though we had been lost on an Arctic plain. I had to put her arms into the sleeves, myself, one after another. They were cold, lifeless, but flexible. Then I moved in front of her and buttoned the thing close round her throat. To do that I had actually to raise her chin with my finger, and it sank slowly down again. I buttoned all the other buttons right down to the ground. It was a very long and splendid fur. Before rising from my kneeling position I felt her feet. Mere ice. The intimacy of this sort of attendance helped the growth of my authority. "Lie down," I murmured, "I shall pile on you every blanket I can find here," but she only shook her head.

Not even in the days when she ran "shrill as a cicada and thin as a match" through the chill mists of her native mountains could she ever have felt so cold, so wretched, and so desolate. Her very soul, her grave, indignant, and fantastic soul, seemed to drowse like an exhausted traveller surrendering himself to the sleep of death. But when I asked her again to lie down she managed to answer me, "Not in this room." The dumb spell was broken. She turned her head from side to side, but oh! how cold she was! It seemed to come out of her, numbing me, too; and the very diamonds on the arrow of gold sparkled like hoar frost in the light of the one candle.

"Not in this room; not here," she protested, with that peculiar suavity of tone which made her voice unforgettable, irresistible, no matter what she said. "Not after all this! I couldn't close my eyes in this place. It's full of corruption and ugliness all round, in me, too, everywhere except in your heart, which has nothing to do where I breathe. And here you may leave me. But wherever you go remember that I am not evil, I am not evil."

I said: "I don't intend to leave you here. There is my room upstairs. You have been in it before."

"Oh, you have heard of that," she whispered. The beginning of a wan smile vanished from her lips.

"I also think you can't stay in this room; and, surely, you needn't hesitate . . ."

"No. It doesn't matter now. He has killed me. Rita is dead."

While we exchanged these words I had retrieved the quilted, blue slippers and had put them on her feet. She was very tractable. Then taking her by the arm I led her towards the door.

"He has killed me," she repeated in a sigh. "The little joy that was in me."

"He has tried to kill himself out there in the hall," I said. She put back like a frightened child but she couldn't be dragged on as a child can be.

I assured her that the man was no longer there but

she only repeated, "I can't get through the hall. I can't walk. I can't . . ."

"Well," I said, flinging the door open and seizing her suddenly in my arms, "if you can't walk then you shall be carried," and I lifted her from the ground so abruptly that she could not help catching me round the neck as any child almost will do instinctively when you pick it up.

I ought really to have put those blue slippers in my pocket. One dropped off at the bottom of the stairs as I was stepping over an unpleasant-looking mess on the marble pavement, and the other was lost a little way up the flight when, for some reason (perhaps from a sense of insecurity), she began to struggle. Though I had an odd sense of being engaged in a sort of nursery adventure she was no child to carry. I could just do it. But not if she chose to struggle. I set her down hastily and only supported her round the waist for the rest of the way. My room, of course, was perfectly dark but I led her straight to the sofa at once and let her fall on it. Then as if I had in sober truth rescued her from an Alpine height or an Arctic floe, I busied myself with nothing but lighting the gas and starting the fire. I didn't even pause to lock my door. All the time I was aware of her presence behind me, nay, of something deeper and more my own—of her existence itself—of a small blue flame, blue like her eyes, flickering and clear within her frozen body. When I turned to her she was sitting very stiff and upright, with her feet posed hieratically on the carpet and her head emerging out of the ample fur collar, as a gem-like flower above the rim of a dark vase. I tore the blankets and the pillows off my bed and piled them up in readiness in a great heap on the floor near the couch. My reason for this was that the room was large, too large for the fireplace, and the couch was nearest to the fire. She gave no sign but one of her wistful attempts at a smile. In a most business-like way I took the arrow out of her hair and laid it on the centre table. The tawny mass fell loose at once about her shoulders and made her look even more desolate than before. But there was an invincible need of gaiety in her heart. She said funnily, looking at the arrow sparkling in the gas light:

"Ah! That poor philistinish ornament!"

An echo of our early days, not more innocent but so much more youthful, was in her tone; and we both, as if touched with poignant regret, looked at each other with enlightened eyes.

"Yes," I said, "how far away all this is. And you wouldn't leave even that object behind when you came last in here. Perhaps it is for that reason it haunted me —mostly at night. I dreamed of you sometimes as a huntress nymph gleaming white through the foliage and throwing this arrow like a dart straight at my heart. But it never reached it. It always fell at my feet as I woke up. The huntress never meant to strike down that particular quarry."

"The huntress was wild but she was not evil. And she was no nymph, but only a goatherd girl. Dream of her no more, my dear."

I had the strength of mind to make a sign of assent and busied myself arranging a couple of pillows at one end of the sofa. "Upon my soul, goatherd, you are not responsible," I said. "You are not! Lay down that uneasy head," I continued, forcing a half-playful note into my immense sadness, "that has even dreamed of a crown—but not for itself."

She lay down quietly. I covered her up, looked once into her eyes and felt the restlessness of fatigue over-power me so that I wanted to stagger out, walk straight

before me, stagger on and on till I dropped.   In the end
I lost myself in thought.   I woke with a start to her
voice saying positively:

"No.   Not even in this room.   I can't close my eyes.
Impossible.   I have a horror of myself.   That voice in
my ears.   All true.   All true."

She was sitting up, two masses of tawny hair fell on
each side of her tense face.   I threw away the pillows
from which she had risen and sat down behind her on
the couch.   "Perhaps like this," I suggested, drawing
her head gently on my breast.   She didn't resist, she
didn't even sigh, she didn't look at me or attempt to
settle herself in any way.   It was I who settled her
after taking up a position which I thought I should be
able to keep for hours—for ages.   After a time I grew
composed enough to become aware of the ticking of the
clock, even to take pleasure in it.   The beat recorded
the moments of her rest, while I sat, keeping as still
as if my life depended upon it with my eyes fixed idly
on the arrow of gold gleaming and glittering dimly on
the table under the lowered gas-jet.   And presently
my breathing fell into the quiet rhythm of the sleep
which descended on her at last.   My thought was that
now nothing mattered in the world because I had the
world safe resting in my arms—or was it in my heart?

Suddenly my heart seemed torn in two within my
breast and half of my breath knocked out of me.   It
was a tumultuous awakening.   The day had come.
Doña Rita had opened her eyes, found herself in my
arms, and instantly had flung herself out of them with
one sudden effort.   I saw her already standing in the
filtered sunshine of the closed shutters, with all the
childlike horror and shame of that night vibrating
afresh in the awakened body of the woman.

"Daylight," she whispered in an appalled voice.

'"Don't look at me, George. I can't face daylight. No —not with you. Before we set eyes on each other all that past was like nothing. I had crushed it all in my new pride. Nothing could touch the Rita whose hand was kissed by you. But now! Never in daylight."

I sat there stupid with surprise and grief. This was no longer the adventure of venturesome children in a nursery-book. A grown man's bitterness, informed, suspicious, resembling hatred, welled out of my heart.

"All this means that you are going to desert me again?" I said with contempt. "All right. I won't throw stones after you . . . Are you going, then?"

She lowered her head slowly with a backward gesture of her arm as if to keep me off, for I had sprung to my feet all at once as if mad.

"Then go quickly," I said. "You are afraid of living flesh and blood. What are you running after? Honesty, as you say, or some distinguished carcass to feed your vanity on? I know how cold you can be—and yet live. What have I done to you? You go to sleep in my arms, wake up and go away. Is it to impress me? Charlatanism of character, my dear."

She stepped forward on her bare feet as firm on that floor which seemed to heave up and down before my eyes as she had ever been—goatherd child leaping on the rocks of her native hills which she was never to see again. I snatched the arrow of gold from the table and threw it after her.

"Don't forget this thing," I cried, "you would never forgive yourself for leaving it behind."

It struck the back of the fur coat and fell on the floor behind her. She never looked round. She walked to the door, opened it without haste, and on the landing in the diffused light from the ground-glass skylight there appeared, rigid, like an implacable and obscure fate, the awful Therese—waiting for her sister. The heavy ends of a big black shawl thrown over her head hung massively in biblical folds. With a faint cry of dismay Doña Rita stopped just within my room.

The two women faced each other for a few moments silently. Therese spoke first. There was no austerity in her tone. Her voice was as usual, pertinacious, unfeeling, with a slight plaint in it; terrible in its unchanged purpose.

"I have been standing here before this door all night," she said. "I don't know how I lived through it. I thought I would die a hundred times for shame. So that's how you are spending your time? You are worse than shameless. But God may still forgive you. You have a soul. You are my sister. I will never abandon you—till you die."

"What is it?" Doña Rita was heard wistfully, "my soul or this house that you won't abandon."

"Come out and bow your head in humiliation. I am your sister and I shall help you to pray to God and all the Saints. Come away from that poor young gentleman who like all the others can have nothing but contempt and disgust for you in his heart. Come and hide your head where no one will reproach you—but I, your sister. Come out and beat your breast: come, poor Sinner, and let me kiss you, for you are my sister!"

While Therese was speaking Doña Rita stepped back a pace and as the other moved forward still extending the hand of sisterly love, she slammed the door in Therese's face. "You abominable girl!" she cried fiercely. Then she turned about and walked towards me who had not moved. I felt hardly alive but for the cruel pain that possessed my whole being. On the way she stooped to pick up the arrow of gold and then moved on quicker, holding it out to me in her open palm.

"You thought I wouldn't give it to you. *Amigo*, I wanted nothing so much as to give it to you. And now, perhaps—you will take it."

"Not without the woman," I said sombrely.

"Take it," she said. "I haven't the courage to deliver myself up to Therese. No. Not even for your sake. Don't you think I have been miserable enough yet?"

I snatched the arrow out of her hand then and ridiculously pressed it to my breast; but as I opened my lips she who knew what was struggling for utterance in my heart cried in a ringing tone:

"Speak no words of love, George! Not yet. Not in this house of ill-luck and falsehood. Not within a hundred miles of this house, where they came clinging to me all profaned from the mouth of that man. Haven't you heard them—the horrible things? And what can words have to do between you and me?"

Her hands were stretched out imploringly. I said, childishly disconcerted:

"But, Rita, how can I help using words of love to you? They come of themselves on my lips!"

"They come! Ah! But I shall seal your lips with the thing itself," she said. "Like this. . . ."

SECOND NOTE

THE narrative of our man goes on for some six months more, from this, the last night of the Carnival season up to and beyond the season of roses. The tone of it is much less of exultation than might have been expected. Love as is well known having nothing to do with reason, being insensible to forebodings and even blind to evidence, the surrender of those two beings to a precarious bliss has nothing very astonishing in itself; and its portrayal, as he attempts it, lacks dramatic interest. The sentimental interest could only have a fascination for readers themselves actually in love. The response of a reader depends on the mood of the moment, so much so that a book may seem extremely interesting when read late at night, but might appear merely a lot of vapid verbiage in the morning. My conviction is that the mood in which the continuation of his story would appear sympathetic is very rare. This consideration has induced me to suppress it—all but the actual facts which round up the previous events and satisfy such curiosity as might have been aroused by the foregoing narrative.

It is to be remarked that this period is characterized more by a deep and joyous tenderness than by sheer passion. All fierceness of spirit seems to have burnt itself out in their preliminary hesitations and struggles against each other and themselves. Whether love in its entirety has, speaking generally, the same elementary meaning for women as for men, is very doubtful. Civilization has been at work there. But the fact is that those two display, in every phase of discovery and response, an exact accord. Both show themselves amazingly ingenuous in the practice of sentiment. I believe that those who know women won't be surprised to hear me say that she was as new to love as he was. During their retreat in the region of the Maritime Alps, in a small house built of dry stones and embowered with roses, they appear all through to be less like released lovers than as companions who had found out each other's fitness in a specially intense way. Upon the whole, I think that there must be some truth in his insistence of there having always been something childlike in their relation. In the unreserved and instant sharing of all thoughts, all impressions, all sensations, we see the naïveness of a children's foolhardy adventure. This unreserve expressed for him the whole truth of the situation. With her it may have been different. It might have been assumed; yet nobody is altogether a comedian; and even comedians themselves have got to believe in the part they play. Of the two she appears much the more assured and confident. But if in this she was a comedienne then it was but a great achievement of her ineradicable honesty. Having once renounced her honourable scruples she took good care that he should taste no flavour of misgivings in the cup. Being older it was she who imparted its character to the situation. As to the man if he had any superiority of his own it was simply the superiority of him who loves with the greater self-surrender.

This is what appears from the pages I have discreetly suppressed—partly out of regard for the pages themselves. In every, even terrestrial, mystery there is as it were a sacred core. A sustained commentary on love is not fit for every eye. A universal experience is exactly the sort of thing which is most difficult to appraise justly in a particular instance.

How this particular instance affected Rose, who was the only companion of the two hermits in their rose-embowered hut of stones, I regret not to be able to report; but I will venture to say that for reasons on which I need not enlarge, the girl could not have been very reassured by what she saw. It seems to me that her devotion could never be appeased; for the conviction must have been growing on her that, no matter what happened, Madame could never have any friends. It may be that Doña Rita had given her a glimpse of the unavoidable end, and that the girl's tarnished eyes masked a certain amount of apprehensive, helpless desolation.

What meantime was becoming of the fortune of Henry Allègre is another curious question. We have been told that it was too big to be tied up in a sack and thrown into the sea. That part of it represented by the fabulous collections was still being protected by the police. But for the rest, it may be assumed that its power and significance were lost to an interested world for something like six months. What is certain is that the late Henry Allègre's man of affairs found himself comparatively idle. The holiday must have done much good to his harassed brain. He had received a note from Doña Rita saying that she had gone into retreat and that she did not mean to send him her address, not being in the humour to be worried with letters on any subject whatever. "It's enough for you"—she wrote—"to know that I am alive." Later, at irregular intervals, he received scraps of paper bearing the stamps of various post offices and containing the simple statement: "I am still alive," signed with an enormous, flourished, exuberant R. I imagine Rose

had to travel some distances by rail to post those
messages. A thick veil of secrecy had been lowered
between the world and the lovers; yet even this veil
turned out not altogether impenetrable.

He—it would be convenient to call him Monsieur
George to the end—shared with Doña Rita her perfect
detachment from all mundane affairs; but he had to
make two short visits to Marseilles. The first was
prompted by his loyal affection for Dominic. He
wanted to discover what had happened or was happen-
ing to Dominic and to find out whether he could do
something for that man. But Dominic was not the
sort of person for whom one can do much. Monsieur
George did not even see him. It looked uncommonly
as if Dominic's heart were broken. Monsieur George
remained concealed for twenty-four hours in the very
house in which Madame Léonore had her café. He
spent most of that time in conversing with Madame
Léonore about Dominic. She was distressed, but her
mind was made up. That bright-eyed, nonchalant,
and passionate woman, was making arrangements to
dispose of her café before departing to join Dominic.
She would not say where. Having ascertained that
his assistance was not required Monsieur George,
in his own words, "managed to sneak out of the town
without being seen by a single soul that mattered."

The second occasion was very prosaic and shockingly
incongruous with the super-mundane colouring of these
days. He had neither the fortune of Henry Allègre
nor a man of affairs of his own. But some rent had to
be paid to somebody for the stone hut and Rose could
not go marketing in the tiny hamlet at the foot of the
hill without a little money. There came a time when
Monsieur George had to descend from the heights of
his love in order, in his own words, "to get a supply

of cash." As he had disappeared very suddenly and completely for a time from the eyes of mankind it was necessary that he should show himself and sign some papers. That business was transacted in the office of the banker mentioned in the story. Monsieur George wished to avoid seeing the man himself but in this he did not succeed. The interview was short. The banker naturally asked no questions, made no allusions to persons and events, and didn't even mention the great Legitimist Principle which presented to him now no interest whatever. But for the moment all the world was talking of the Carlist enterprise. It had collapsed utterly, leaving behind, as usual, a large crop of recriminations, charges of incompetency and treachery, and a certain amount of scandalous gossip. The banker (his wife's salon had been very Carlist indeed) declared that he had never believed in the success of the cause. "You are well out of it," he remarked with a chilly smile to Monsieur George. The latter merely observed that he had been very little "in it" as a matter of fact, and that he was quite indifferent to the whole affair.

"You left a few of your feathers in it, nevertheless," the banker concluded with a wooden face and with the curtness of a man who knows.

Monsieur George ought to have taken the very next train out of the town but he yielded to the temptation to discover what had happened to the house in the street of the Consuls after he and Doña Rita had stolen out of it like two scared yet jubilant children. All he discovered was a strange, fat woman, a sort of virago, who had, apparently, been put in as a caretaker by the man of affairs. She made some difficulties to admit that she had been in charge for the last four months; ever since the person who was there before had eloped with some Spaniard who had been lying in the house ill with fever for more than six weeks. No, she never saw the person. Neither had she seen the Spaniard. She had only heard the talk of the street. Of course she didn't know where these people had gone. She manifested some impatience to get rid of Monsieur George and even attempted to push him towards the door. It was, he says, a very funny experience. He noticed the feeble flame of the gas-jet in the hall still waiting for extinction in the general collapse of the world.

Then he decided to have a bit of dinner at the Restaurant de la Gare where he felt pretty certain he would not meet any of his friends. He could not have asked Madame Léonore for hospitality because Madame Léonore had gone away already. His acquaintances were not the sort of people likely to happen casually into a restaurant of that kind and moreover he took the precaution to seat himself at a small table so as to face the wall. Yet before long he felt a hand laid gently on his shoulder, and, looking up, saw one of his acquaintances, a member of the Royalist club, a young man of a very cheerful disposition but whose face looked down at him with a grave and anxious expression.

Monsieur George was far from delighted. His surprise was extreme when in the course of the first phrases exchanged with him he learned that this acquaintance had come to the station with the hope or finding him there.

"You haven't been seen for some time," he said. "You were perhaps somewhere where the news from the world couldn't reach you? There have been many changes amongst our friends and amongst people one used to hear of so much. There is Madame de Lastaola for instance, who seems to have vanished from the world which was so much interested in her. You have no idea where she may be now?"

Monsieur George remarked grumpily that he couldn't say.

The other tried to appear at ease. Tongues were wagging about it in Paris. There was a sort of international financier, a fellow with an Italian name, a shady personality, who had been looking for her all over Europe and talked in clubs—astonishing how such fellows get into the best clubs—oh! Azzolati was his name. But perhaps what a fellow like that said did not matter. The funniest thing was that there was no man of any position in the world who had disappeared at the same time. A friend in Paris wrote to him that a certain well-known journalist had rushed South to investigate the mystery but had returned no wiser than he went.

Monsieur George remarked more unamiably than before that he really could not help all that.

"No," said the other with extreme gentleness, "only of all the people more or less connected with the Carlist affair you are the only one that had also disappeared before the final collapse."

"What!" cried Monsieur George.

"Just so," said the other meaningly. "You know that all my people like you very much, though they hold various opinions as to your discretion. Only the other day Jane, you know my married sister, and I were talking about you. She was extremely distressed. I assured her that you must be very far away or very deeply buried somewhere not to have given a sign of life under this provocation."

Naturally Monsieur George wanted to know what it was all about; and the other appeared greatly relieved.

"I was sure you couldn't have heard. I don't want

to be indiscreet, I don't want to ask you where you were. It came to my ears that you had been seen at the bank to-day and I made a special effort to lay hold of you before you vanished again; for, after all, we have been always good friends and all our lot here liked you very much. Listen. You know a certain Captain Blunt, don't you?"

Monsieur George owned to knowing Captain Blunt but only very slightly. His friend then informed him that this Captain Blunt was apparently well acquainted with Madame de Lastaola, or, at any rate, pretended to be. He was an honourable man, a member of a good club, he was very Parisian in a way, and all this, he continued, made all the worse that of which he was under the painful necessity of warning Monsieur George. This Blunt on three distinct occasions when the name of Madame de Lastaola came up in conversation in a mixed company of men had expressed his regret that she should have become the prey of a young adventurer who was exploiting her shamelessly. He talked like a man certain of his facts and as he mentioned names . . .

"In fact," the young man burst out excitedly, "it is *your* name that he mentions. And in order to fix the exact personality he always takes care to add that you are that young fellow who was known as Monsieur George all over the South amongst the initiated Carlists."

How Blunt had got enough information to base that atrocious calumny upon, Monsieur George couldn't imagine. But there it was. He kept silent in his indignation till his friend murmured, "I expect you will want him to know that you are here."

"Yes," said Monsieur George, "and I hope you will consent to act for me altogether. First of all, pray, let him know by wire that I am waiting for him. This will be enough to fetch him down here, I can assure you. You may ask him also to bring two friends with him. I don't intend this to be an affair for Parisian journalists to write paragraphs about."

"Yes. That sort of thing must be stopped at once," the other admitted. He assented to Monsieur George's request that the meeting should be arranged for at his elder brother's country place where the family stayed very seldom. There was a most convenient walled garden there. And then Monsieur George caught his train promising to be back on the fourth day and leaving all further arrangements to his friend. He prided himself on his impenetrability before Doña Rita; on the happiness without a shadow of those four days. However, Doña Rita must have had the intuition of there being something in the wind, because on the evening of the very same day on which he left her again on some pretence or other, she was already ensconced in the house in the street of the Consuls, with the trustworthy Rose scouting all over the town to gain information.

Of the proceedings in the walled garden there is no need to speak in detail. They were conventionally correct, but an earnestness of purpose which could be felt in the very air lifted the business above the common run of affairs of honour. One bit of byplay unnoticed by the seconds, very busy for the moment with their arrangements, must be mentioned. Disregarding the severe rules of conduct in such cases Monsieur George approached his adversary and addressed him directly.

"Captain Blunt," he said, "the result of this meeting may go against me. In that case you will recognize publicly that you were wrong. For you are wrong and you know it. May I trust your honour?"

In answer to that appeal Captain Blunt, always cor-

rect, didn't open his lips but only made a little bow.
For the rest he was perfectly ruthless. If he was utterly
incapable of being carried away by love there was nothing equivocal about his jealousy. Such psychology
is not very rare and really from the point of view
of the combat itself one cannot very well blame him.
What happened was this. Monsieur George fired on
the word and, whether luck or skill, managed to hit
Captain Blunt in the upper part of the arm which was
holding the pistol. That gentleman's arm dropped
powerless by his side. But he did not drop his weapon.
There was nothing equivocal about his determination.
With the greatest deliberation he reached with his left
hand for his pistol and taking careful aim shot Monsieur George through the left side of his breast. One
may imagine the consternation of the four seconds and
the activity of the two surgeons in the confined, drowsy
heat of that walled garden. It was within an easy
drive of the town and as Monsieur George was being
conveyed there at a walking pace a little brougham
coming from the opposite direction pulled up at the
side of the road. A thickly veiled woman's head looked
out of the window, took in the state of affairs at a glance,
and called out in a firm voice: "Follow my carriage."
The brougham turning round took the lead. Long
before this convoy reached the town another carriage
containing four gentlemen (of whom one was leaning
back languidly with his arm in a sling) whisked past
and vanished ahead in a cloud of white, Provençal
dust. And this is the last appearance of Captain
Blunt in Monsieur George's narrative. Of course he
was only told of it later. At the time he was not in a
condition to notice things. His interest in his surroundings remained of a hazy and nightmarish kind for
many days together. From time to time he had the

impression that he was in a room strangely familiar to him, that he had unsatisfactory visions of Doña Rita, to whom he tried to speak as if nothing had happened, but that she always put her hand on his mouth to prevent him and then spoke to him herself in a very strange voice which sometimes resembled the voice of Rose. The face, too, sometimes resembled the face of Rose. There were also one or two men's faces which he seemed to know well enough though he didn't recall their names. He could have done so with a slight effort, but it would have been too much trouble. Then came a time when the hallucinations of Doña Rita and the faithful Rose left him altogether. Next came a period, perhaps a year, or perhaps an hour, during which he seemed to dream all through his past life. He felt no apprehension, he didn't try to speculate as to the future. He felt that all possible conclusions were out of his power, and therefore he was indifferent to everything. He was like that dream's disinterested spectator who doesn't know what is going to happen next. Suddenly for the first time in his life he had the soul-satisfying consciousness of floating off into deep slumber.

When he woke up after an hour, or a day, or a month, there was dusk in the room; but he recognized it perfectly. It was his apartment in Doña Rita's house; those were the familiar surroundings in which he had so often told himself that he must either die or go mad. But now he felt perfectly clear-headed and the full sensation of being alive came all over him, languidly delicious. The greatest beauty of it was that there was no need to move. This gave him a sort of moral satisfaction. Then the first thought independent of personal sensations came into his head. He wondered when Therese would come in and begin talking. He saw vaguely a human figure in the room but that was a man. He was speaking in a deadened voice which had yet a preternatural distinctness.

"This is the second case I have had in this house, and I am sure that directly or indirectly it was connected with that woman. She will go on like this leaving a track behind her and then some day there will be really a corpse. This young fellow might have been it."

"In this case, Doctor," said another voice, "one can't blame the woman very much. I assure you she made a very determined fight."

"What do you mean? That she didn't want to . . ."

"Yes. A very good fight. I heard all about it. It is easy to blame her, but, as she asked me despairingly, could she go through life veiled from head to foot or go out of it altogether into a convent? No, she isn't guilty. She is simply—what she is."

"And what's that?"

"Very much of a woman. Perhaps a little more at the mercy of contradictory impulses than other women. But that's not her fault. I really think she has been very honest."

The voices sank suddenly to a still lower murmur and presently the shape of the man went out of the room. Monsieur George heard distinctly the door open and shut. Then he spoke for the first time, discovering, with a particular pleasure, that it was quite easy to speak. He was even under the impression that he had shouted:

"Who is here?"

From the shadow of the room (he recognized at once the characteristic outlines of the bulky shape) Mills advanced to the side of the bed. Doña Rita had telegraphed to him on the day of the duel and the man of books, leaving his retreat, had come as fast as boats and trains could carry him South. For, as he said

later to Monsieur George, he had become fully awake
to his part of responsibility. And he added: "It was
not of you alone that I was thinking." But the very
first question that Monsieur George put to him was:

"How long is it since I saw you last?"

"Something like ten months," answered Mills'
kindly voice.

"Ah! Is Therese outside the door? She stood there
all night, you know."

"Yes, I heard of it. She is hundreds of miles away
now."

"Well, then, ask Rita to come in."

"I can't do that, my dear boy," said Mills with affec-
tionate gentleness. He hesitated a moment. "Doña
Rita went away yesterday," he said softly.

"Went away? Why?" asked Monsieur George.

"Because, I am thankful to say, your life is no longer
in danger. And I have told you that she is gone because, strange as it may seem, I believe you can stand
this news better now than later when you get stronger."

It must be believed that Mills was right. Monsieur
George fell asleep before he could feel any pang at that
intelligence. A sort of confused surprise was in his
mind but nothing else, and then his eyes closed. The
awakening was another matter. But that, too, Mills
had foreseen. For days he attended the bedside patiently, letting the man in the bed talk to him of Doña
Rita but saying little himself; till one day he was asked
pointedly whether she had ever talked to him openly.
And then he said that she had, on more than one occasion. "She told me amongst other things," Mills
said, "if this is any satisfaction to you to know, that
till she met you she knew nothing of love. That you
were to her in more senses than one a complete revelation."

"And then she went away. Ran away from the revelation," said the man in the bed bitterly.

"What's the good of being angry?" remonstrated Mills, gently. "You know that this world is not a world for lovers, not even for such lovers as you two who have nothing to do with the world as it is. No, a world of lovers would be impossible. It would be a mere ruin of lives which seem to be meant for something else. What this something is, I don't know; and I am certain," he said with playful compassion, "that she and you will never find out."

A few days later they were again talking of Doña Rita. Mills said:

"Before she left the house she gave me that arrow she used to wear in her hair to hand over to you as a keepsake and also to prevent you, she said, from dreaming of her. This message sounds rather cryptic."

"Oh, I understand perfectly," said Monsieur George. "Don't give me the thing now. Leave it somewhere where I can find it some day when I am alone. But when you write to her you may tell her that now at last—surer than Mr. Blunt's bullet—the arrow has found its mark. There will be no more dreaming. Tell her. She will understand."

"I don't even know where she is," murmured Mills.

"No, but her man of affairs knows. . . . Tell me, Mills, what will become of her?"

"She will be wasted," said Mills sadly. "She is a most unfortunate creature. Not even poverty could save her now. She cannot go back to her goats. Yet who can tell? She may find something in life. She may! It won't be love. She has sacrificed that chance to the integrity of your life—heroically. Do you remember telling her once that you meant to live your life integrally—oh, you lawless young pedant! Well, she is gone; but you may be sure that whatever she finds now in life it will not be peace. You understand me? Not even in a convent."

"She was supremely lovable," said the wounded man, speaking of her as if she were lying dead already on his oppressed heart.

"And elusive," struck in Mills in a low voice. "Some of them are like that. She will never change. Amid all the shames and shadows of that life there will always lie the ray of her perfect honesty. I don't know about your honesty, but yours will be the easier lot. You will always have your . . . other love—you pig-headed enthusiast of the sea."

"Then let me go to it," cried the enthusiast. "Let me go to it."

He went to it as soon as he had strength enough to feel the crushing weight of his loss (or his gain) fully, and discovered that he could bear it without flinching. After this discovery he was fit to face anything. He tells his correspondent that if he had been more romantic he would never have looked at any other woman. But on the contrary. No face worthy of attention escaped him. He looked at them all; and each reminded him of Doña Rita, either by some profound resemblance or by the startling force of contrast.

The faithful austerity of the sea protected him from the rumours that fly on the tongues of men. He never heard of her. Even the echoes of the sale of the great Allègre collection failed to reach him. And that event must have made a noise enough in the world. But he never heard. He does not know. Then, years later, he was deprived even of the arrow. It was lost to him in a stormy catastrophe; and he confesses that next day he stood on a rocky, wind-assaulted shore, looking at the seas raging over the very spot of his loss and thought that it was well. It was not a thing that one could leave behind one for strange hands—for the cold eyes of ignorance. Like the old King of Thule with the gold goblet of his mistress he would have had to cast it into the sea, before he died. He says he smiled at the romantic notion. But what else could he have done with it?

THE END